SECOND TIME AROUND

After a freak accident and eight weeks in a coma, Suzie Connors' family are elated when their adored mother regains consciousness — and is absolutely fine. Except she's not. Blissfully unaware of her children's shock at having to deal with the changes in their mum, Suzie has had a wake-up call and intends to live life to the full, with or without their approval. As her older children battle with the ensuing emotional burden, university exams and the blurred lines between work life and love life, Suzie's youngest daughter Sharon is faced with some major issues of her own, and the one person she would have turned to — her mother — is no longer there for her. An emotional story about family, second chances and what happens when, in the blink of an eye, life changes forever. . .

SECOND TIME AROUND

COLETTE CADDLE

LARGE
PRINT

First published in Ireland 2016
by
Simon & Schuster UK Ltd

First Isis Edition
published 2020
by arrangement with
Simon & Schuster UK Ltd

A catalogue record for this book is available
from the British Library.

ISBN 978–1–78541–887–7

CHAPTER
ONE

What was that incessant noise? Beeps, buzzing, and some other sound, something more rhythmic, but so bloody loud that it was doing Suzie's head in. It was moving, too, and, after a moment, she realised that she was moving with it. A wave of fear washed over her. What the hell was going on? This wasn't funny any more.

Suzie opened her mouth to call for help but no sound came out. Cold fingers of terror gripped her as she realised that she was pinned down. Panicking, Suzie struggled to free herself but it was useless: she couldn't move. She tried to open her eyes but that didn't work either, yet Suzie was pretty sure that she wasn't blindfolded. She tried again but her lids refused to budge.

What was happening to her? Suzie had never felt so trapped and frightened. The beeping sped up, adding to her hysteria, and another, higher-pitched, alarm, louder than the others, joined the cacophony. And then she heard voices and she called out, begging them to help her, to make it all stop. But they didn't seem to even hear her, so she screamed as loud as she could, and then there was finally a voice, low and reassuring.

"It's okay, Suzie, relax, I've got you."

The voice was soothing, assured and calm, and so she let go, trusting it, and allowing herself to drift into oblivion.

Jess Connors stroked her mother's cool hand, humming the melody Suzie had always sung to her as a child when she was ill or couldn't sleep. It was a simple song, something about a seesaw, but it had always dried Jess's tears and made her feel safe. She looked around the room — bare but for two chairs, the equipment around the bed and cautionary notices on the wall — and wished herself anywhere else. A piece of red-and-gold foil fluttered forlornly above the window, presumably the remnants of a Christmas decoration. The festive colours seemed disgustingly inappropriate and she itched to climb up onto a chair and take it down.

The window itself was annoying. Most of the wards Jess passed every day had small windows, high up in the wall, offering no glimpse of trees or sky to cheer an ailing body. Yet this small cell, whose residents were rarely conscious, had a large, south-facing window. A shaft of sunlight streamed in now, casting a golden glow over her mum's pale cheeks. She looked so small and fragile. Jess blinked back her tears.

"Come on, Mum, enough's enough. Don't you want to get out of this place? I know I do. Please wake up."

There was a cursory knock on the door and a nurse hurried in. "Hi, Jess. How are you today?"

"Grand, thanks, Ann." Jess moved out of her way, surreptitiously wiping her eyes. Grand. What a stupid word. Her mother had been in a coma for weeks and there was no sign of her coming out of it, but Jess was "grand". She leaned against the wall and watched the nurse go through the routine checks. At this stage, Jess could easily step in and take over the nurse's duties, if she fancied a break.

"Giving her a manicure today?" Ann asked, nodding towards the bedside table.

Jess forced a smile and nodded. "She always said that my granny's hands were as rough as a labourer's and was determined to keep hers soft. She used coconut oil." She grimaced, realising she'd spoken in the past tense.

"She'll be delighted when she wakes up to see that you kept them so nice for her." The nurse shone a torch into her mum's eyes. "Aren't you lucky, Suzie, to have Jess to pamper you?"

"Do you think that she will?" Jess traced a crack in the floor tile with the toe of her boot. "Wake up, I mean."

"Of course she will," the nurse said.

Jess's head snapped up to stare at her. The other staff never answered that question, yet there was a quiet confidence about Ann that made Jess wonder. The woman was probably in her fifties and had worked in this unit for years. Maybe being around comatose patients so long had given her an instinct her superiors didn't possess. Jess could almost see her brother shake his head, incredulous that she could still be optimistic after nearly eight weeks.

"Can she hear us?" She searched the nurse's face, her bullshit radar on.

Ann shrugged. "Lots of patients who've woken from a coma told me they were conscious of voices, music and smells." She chuckled. "One man gave out hell about one of the doctors' overpowering aftershave. He was determined to wake up just to tell him to switch to a different brand or he'd never get a woman." She stepped back, made a note on the clipboard and put it back on the end of the bed. "I'm all done now. You can get on with your beauty treatment. Enjoy, Suzie."

Jess pulled up a chair and poured lotion into her palm and massaged it into her mother's right hand. "Did you hear that? Is it true, Mum? Can you hear me? Can you smell this nice cream? I wish you'd give me a sign. Just a blink or a twitch wouldn't kill you, would it? If this was a Hollywood movie, you'd wake up now and make some stupid joke, you know that, right?" Jess's eyes drifted from her mother's soft hand to her own bitten nails. "I could do with a manicure myself, and a haircut. Still, there'll be plenty of time for that when you wake up. I just want you to get better, Mum, we all do. Even Mandy phones to see how you're doing."

She chuckled, amused by her aunt's uncharacteristic concern.

"I wonder what she's after. You haven't got some family jewels stashed away, have you?" Jess thought of her layabout grandfather and long-suffering granny who'd struggled to make ends meet. "Probably not. She

4

wanted to come see you, but don't worry: I told her there wasn't much point at the moment."

Jess started to file her mother's nails. "Sorry your son hasn't been in much. It's not because he doesn't care. Noel just can't handle seeing you like this. Sharon says all men are useless when it comes to health issues. She told me that my dear brother-in-law keeled over in the labour ward. Did you know that?" Jess grinned. "They had to drag Keith outside and, after bringing in that fancy camera of his, the only photos they have are the ones the midwife took with her phone.

"Sharon will be in tomorrow after she's dropped Bobby to school. He's drawn another picture for you. Try not to get too excited." Jess glanced up at her nephew's previous efforts over the bed. Still, he was only four. "Nora was on again." Jess smiled as she thought of how supportive her mother's old friend had been. "She's fed up that she lives so far away, but she'll be up to see you on Wednesday. I didn't realise how close you two still were until this happened. Aileen sends her love, too. She's a great neighbour, making sure the bins are emptied and keeping an eye on Noel, slipping him pies and scones. Just as well, as he's worse than useless. You really spoil him, you know that?"

Jess went round the bed to do the other hand. "Sorry, no polish. They need to be able to see the colour of your nails for some reason." As she started to massage the cream into her mother's other hand, she froze, convinced she'd felt Suzie's fingers move. She stared at her mother's hand, but it lay perfectly still in hers. Jess sighed. Her imagination was working

5

overtime. She'd really have to stop getting her hopes up. She knew everyone thought so. They didn't understand why she came in twice a day.

"She doesn't even know you're there," her aunt had said, rather cruelly, Jess thought.

"You don't know that, Mandy," she'd snapped. "Anyway, I want to be there."

Jess glanced at the clock, realising she should make a move. She had a deadline to meet. Working as a freelance journalist was a dream job. Writing articles for three different papers and a travel piece for a monthly magazine meant lots of variety. Today her copy about Ireland's Wild Atlantic Way was due in. She was quite pleased with it but wanted to run through it one last time before emailing it to Marilyn, the editor. The photos that would go with it would look wonderful in the quality, glossy magazine pages, although the one taken of her wasn't the best. Even she could see that, despite her smile, she looked drawn and anxious.

"All done." Jess kissed her mother's cheek and stood up to go. She stared hard at her for a moment, searching for any sign of change, willing her mum to move — but nothing. She sighed. "See you later."

In the tiny loo down the corridor, Jess splashed her face with water and dragged a brush through her hair. She looked at her reflection, noting that she was as pale as her mother and almost as skinny. Spending most of your time in a hospital and living in fear did that to you. After applying a layer of balm to her dry, cracked lips, she straightened her sweatshirt and, shoulders back, went out to the car park.

$\star$ $\star$ $\star$

"How're you doing?" Katie asked later that evening as they settled in a corner of a city centre bar with two glasses of lager.

"I'm grand," Jess said, seeing the worry in her friend's eyes. She cracked a smile. "I should have that tattooed across my forehead."

"Tell me honestly."

"Honestly? I'm broken-hearted, Katie."

Katie squeezed her hand. "It sucks, Jess. It seems so wrong, your lovely, bubbly mum just lying there."

"It doesn't even look like her," Jess said. "I don't want to be there, but I don't want to leave her, either. Does that make sense?"

"Yeah, but maybe you shouldn't go in quite as often," Katie said gently.

"If *I* don't go, who will? Sharon's always running round after her precious son, and Noel finds it too upsetting. As if *I'm* having a bundle of laughs." She was fed up with her brother and sister but she couldn't say that. They needed each other right now. She put down the glass with a shaky hand and splashed beer across the table.

"Hey, calm down," Katie urged. "I'm sorry, I didn't mean to upset you."

"You didn't, I'm sorry." Jess pulled her lank hair back and massaged her temples. She could feel a headache building. "It's just that Mum may as well be dead the way Noel talks, and sometimes I think that he and Sharon would prefer that. It would be easier and tidier if she died and we could have a funeral and move on."

7

Katie's eyes widened, shocked. "That's not true, Jess. Of course they care. We all deal with stuff differently and you and your mum were very close."

"Are," Jess snapped.

"Sorry?"

"You used the past tense."

"Aw, Jess, I didn't mean —"

"I know," Jess said, feeling weary. Why was she having a go at Katie when she'd only ever been kind and supportive? "Sorry. Truth is, I keep doing it too. Maybe they're right. Maybe I should give up on her, but I just can't accept that she's gone, Katie."

"Of course you can't and you shouldn't."

"Really?" Jess looked up at her to check her friend wasn't placating her.

"No way." Katie was adamant. "The doctors haven't given up, have they?"

Jess thought about that. "They don't commit themselves one way or the other. It's all 'wait and see' and 'still early days'."

"There you go, then, and they don't even know your mum. She's a fighter, Jess, and you can bet she'll fight bloody hard to find her way back to you."

Jess had to smile at that. If Mum was even the slightest bit aware of what was going on, then she *would* fight. "You're right. Thanks, Katie."

Jess's phone vibrated and she grabbed it, as always hoping for good news and dreading bad. She smiled when she saw that it was a text from Louis.

How are you doing? I'm free at 6 if you want to talk. L.

Katie's eyes widened. "I know that smile. That's from a man. Have you been holding out on me?" she smirked.

Jess shook her head but couldn't prevent the tell-tale blush. "The editor at the *Gazette* who's been really sweet and supportive since Mum's accident."

"I sense romance in the air. Is he hot? When do I get to meet him?"

"No romance," Jess said emphatically. "Mum's my priority, you know that."

"Fair enough, but you need some downtime too. Keep the faith, yeah?" Katie was looking at her with worried eyes.

Jess gave a weak smile and nodded. "Yeah."

CHAPTER
TWO

Suzie became conscious of a soft tapping, fingers on a keyboard, she realised. Jess! Always working, she thought affectionately. Suzie tried to reach out to her daughter and call her name but nothing came out. After a few minutes, the effort of trying to attract attention proved too much for her and, weary and frustrated, Suzie slipped back into unconsciousness. Hang on, Jess. Don't give up on me yet.

The next time she became conscious of her surroundings, her eldest daughter was there again. You shouldn't be here all the time, Suzie wanted to say, but, when she tried to speak, her voice still wouldn't obey her brain. Yet she was conscious now of people and smells and sounds. That had to be a good sign, didn't it? She must be getting better. This time she let herself drift off, wearing a smile that no one could see.

Suzie was woken by a crash and then giggling out in the corridor. There was only one light on over the bed. It hurt her eyes. She blinked. Was she dreaming? No, surely you didn't dream of long narrow clinical lights that highlighted a rather bad paint job. She gasped as she took in her surroundings, her eyes settling on her daughter's head, resting on the edge of the bed, her dark hair fanned out across the cover.

"Jess," Suzie said but nothing came out. She tried again, concentrating as hard as she could. "Jess." The sound that emerged was a cross between a hiss and a croak. She wondered if she could do anything else and tried flexing her fingers and toes. Holy shit! They were working! It was hard work but they were working. "Jess," she said again and this time she was able to move her hand so it brushed off her daughter's head.

Jess jerked up, rubbing her eyes and yawning.

Suzie smiled, her heart ready to burst with happiness.

Her daughter looked up and met her eyes, gasping, her eyes wide in disbelief. "Mum? Mum, oh, Mum." Jess hugged her, before jumping up and running out into the corridor and calling for the nurses. "She's awake! My mum's awake!"

Suzie lost track of time, drifting in and out of consciousness. She often woke during the night, when there was no one around to talk to or answer her questions. When she opened her eyes, she sighed when she saw that the only light came from the corridor. "Feck it!" she muttered, disappointed yet again.

"Mum?"

She looked over to see her daughter in the chair. "You should be at home in bed," she croaked although she was delighted to see Jess.

Jess's face lit up. "You can speak!"

"Of course I can," Suzie retorted, although her words were little more than a whisper.

"Who am I?" Jess demanded, her eyes begging for recognition.

"You're Jess, my eldest daughter." Suzie smiled.

"How many children do you have?"

Suzie blinked. Why was Jess asking such stupid questions? "Three. You, Sharon, Noel." She glanced around the room, taking in for the first time the machines by the bed and the drips going into her arm. "What happened?"

"You had an accident and you're in the hospital, have been for weeks."

Suzie tried to process this but her head hurt and she felt tired. She closed her eyes, weary. Thinking was a fierce, tiring business altogether.

Suzie had no idea how much time had passed before she opened her eyes to daylight and the sight of her family gathered around the bed. As usual, Jess was at her side. Sharon sat in one of the chairs, Sharon's husband, Keith, perched on the arm, reading a newspaper, and Suzie's son, Noel, was sitting on the window ledge messing with his phone.

"Mum?" Jess was the first one to spot she was awake.

Suzie tried to smile. "Water?" she whispered.

Jess gave a regretful shrug. "Sorry, not yet, but I can moisten your lips." She dipped a swab into a jug of water and ran it across her mother's mouth. Suzie caught it in between her teeth and sucked for all she was worth.

12

"The doctors said to wait, Mum." Jess tugged the swab out and tossed it into the bin.

Suzie scowled. "Fuck them."

"Mum!" Sharon raised her eyebrows.

There was a deep chuckle. "Hey, sis. How are you feeling?"

Suzie glanced down to see Mandy, draped across the end of the bed, showing an ample amount of toned, tanned thigh. "Oh, Christ. I haven't seen a get-together like this since Uncle Bill's funeral," she croaked. "I'm dying, right?"

"Nah. Pity, though," Noel said, grinning. "I'd planned to buy a round-the-world ticket out of the life assurance."

Sharon glared at her brother and came to hug Suzie. "Welcome back, Mum. You scared the hell out of us." She perched on the edge of the bed. "How are you feeling?"

"Shite. Tell me about this accident." Suzie had a feeling she'd already had this conversation with her family but she couldn't remember the answer. She couldn't seem to retain anything in her head for more than a few hours. It scared her but the consultant said these things took time. "Rome wasn't built in a day" were his exact words, although what Rome had to do with anything Suzie had no idea.

"We went along to the opening of the leisure centre in the hotel in Howth and, after a few glasses of bubbly, you climbed onto the treadmill, fell off and banged your head on the way down," Mandy said, sounding bored.

"Bollocks! What would I be doing in a health club?"

Her daughters exchanged a look and then Sharon scowled at her aunt. "Mandy dragged you along because they were doling out free drink."

"The equipment shouldn't have been switched on," Keith said.

"They were about to give us a demo," Mandy protested, "but your mother put paid to that."

"Still. I'll get some legal advice on the matter."

Suzie nodded in approval at her son-in-law, "Yeah, let's sue the bastards."

"You don't understand, Doctor," Sharon told the consultant. "My mother never swears. And as for blasphemy . . ." She trailed off, shaking her head. "It's completely out of character. Even in her sleep she's cursing."

Jess bit her lip and avoided her little brother's eyes.

"Ms Connors —"

"It's Mulvey. Sharon Mulvey."

The consultant looked weary. "It's not uncommon for people who suffer traumatic brain injury to change."

Jess frowned. "In what way, exactly?"

"In any number of ways, but largely temperament. That said, it's been known for some to even speak with a different accent or in another language. Or others, like your mum, forget what's expected of them in normal, social situations and can sometimes be insensitive. But I'm quite pleased with her progress. She's awake, cognisant and, physically, as good as new."

"Will she get better?" Sharon asked, ignoring the positives.

He shrugged. "I'm afraid I can't answer that. Some people revert to the way they were before the injury but it may take weeks, even months. Others don't but, with help, can learn how to fit in again."

Jess looked at her sister in exasperation. "So, she swears. Does it matter? When will you discharge her, Doctor?"

"In a few days."

Jess beamed. "That's wonderful, Doctor, thank you."

"Go home."

"That's a lovely way to talk to your daughter." Jess pretended to look offended.

"You've spent far too much time in that bloody chair. It's a wonder you can still walk. What about your job?"

Jess pointed at her laptop. "Where I go, it goes. I can write anywhere, even in this place." Jess yawned and glanced at her watch. "But I will head off. I'm giving your house a spring clean in the morning. God only knows what's growing under Noel's bed."

Suzie chuckled. "I thought he might have become self-sufficient these last few weeks."

"Nah. Sharon did his ironing and kept the freezer stocked and I nipped in to clean and load the washing machine. If any woman is ever crazy enough to take him on, she won't thank us." She paused. "It's great to be able to talk to you again, Mum. I've missed you."

"Likewise," Suzie said.

"Sharon's bringing Bobby in to see you tomorrow. He can't wait to see his granny."

Suzie snorted in disbelief. "Ha, pull the other one. Sharon's probably had to promise him a fiver to come along. I wish she'd get him to call me something else. It's not very flattering being called a granny when you're in your forties."

Jess looked surprised and then shook her head, her smile sad.

"What?" Suzie frowned.

"Nothing. Have a good night's sleep, Mum. See you tomorrow." Jess hugged her once more and left.

Alone, Suzie found her thoughts turning to her luck in surviving this brush with death. She still had no memory of the accident and only vaguely knew the hotel where it had taken place. It wasn't the sort of place she hung out in. What on earth had made her go? And what was she doing climbing onto a treadmill? Suzie figured she must have been plastered, not that she drank much; at least she didn't think so.

She was glad she'd survived. It would have been such a humiliating way to die — she could imagine the sniggers at the funeral. But, she had, and here she was, eight weeks later, and she seemed to be fine. What were the chances? It was like a sign, a warning, even. From what she could remember, she was an ordinary woman who'd lived an ordinary life, taking pleasure in simple things, her life revolving round her family. Apart from the occasional outing to the cinema or dinner with her old mate, Nora, Suzie rarely went anywhere. How had she ended up in such a rut?

When she'd married John Connors and moved to Limerick, Suzie had left behind her friends and her job and become a stay-at-home mum. Mind you, once Sharon and Noel came along, she'd had her hands full. Moving to such a rural location was one hell of a shock for a Dublin girl who'd lived her life in a busy suburb just minutes from the city centre. Having been brought up in a noisy, crowded house, nothing could have prepared Suzie for the silence and isolation of her new home.

Once Noel started school, she'd made noises about finding a part-time job, but John hadn't been that keen. He worked for a meat-processing company and had reached the dizzy heights of purchasing director. They didn't need the money, he told her, and he didn't like the idea of his family turning into latchkey kids. If she was honest, she hadn't either but she had often missed the camaraderie she'd enjoyed when she'd worked in CML.

She smiled as she thought of her one and only job. It had been the perfect position for her. Designing screen presentations had come as naturally to her as breathing. Chrissie, her tutor, had urged her to go for this job in the large conference-management company, despite the fact that she'd no work experience and was pregnant. Suzie still remembered how nervous she'd felt when she walked into the sumptuous offices of CML for the first time. She knew that Gina, her interviewer, had loved the mock presentation that she'd been asked to prepare prior to their meeting. But she'd also seen her worried frown when Suzie had told her about her condition. And so it was a pleasant shock when she was called for a second interview and subsequently got the job. It had taken her a while to settle into CML. The small staff seemed so close and she'd felt like an outsider. She had nothing in common with them and, as the days passed, she became more and more self-conscious about her accent, education and background. What a chip on her shoulder she'd had, thinking her colleagues were judging her. The truth was that she'd been the one guilty of that. They'd been great and become true friends, getting her through one of the most difficult points in her life. She'd lost touch with them, as people do when their lives move in different directions. Sad, really. She should do something about that, maybe call Gina and meet up for coffee.

Her thoughts returned to Limerick and the frosty reception she'd got from John's family and friends. His parents were quiet, stern people with little to say and Maurice, John's only brother, wasn't much better. Where John had got his outgoing personality and sense of humour, Suzie couldn't imagine. On arriving in the small community, she had been a curiosity but after a few weeks, she was accepted as the Dubliner that John Connors had married and left to her own devices.

Her isolation ended the day she was coming back from the shop with Jess snuggled up warm in her buggy, oblivious of the bumpy ride down the narrow lane, and came across Nora Browne bent over the engine of her car and muttering to herself.

"Oh, come on, you can't break down on me again. You've only just had a feckin' service. What is it? Are you allergic to the bloody cold?"

Suzie burst out laughing and winced when the woman lifted her head and bashed it on the bonnet. "Ow!"

"Oh, sorry."

Nora grinned and rubbed her head. "I don't suppose you know anything about cars?"

"No, but I can make you a cuppa while you phone someone who does."

The woman considered her for a moment and then slammed the bonnet shut and stuck her hand out. "That's the best offer I'm likely to get. Nora Browne."

"Suzie Connors."

"Ah, John's wife. You're my neighbour!"

Suzie had frowned, glancing around at the acres of fields around them. "Neighbour?"

Nora laughed. "Absolutely. I'm only a ten-minute drive up the road."

And they'd been best friends since.

Fuck! Suzie sprang up in the bed. Had anyone told Nora she was awake? With a sigh, she sank back into the pillows, remembering that she'd been awake a couple of weeks now and Jess had assured her that she'd told the world and its mother that Suzie Connors was alive and kicking. No doubt Nora had been at the top of the list.

You could always rely on Jess. Suzie would have gone nuts in those first few weeks in Limerick if it hadn't been for her elder daughter. She had been a sweet-natured three-year-old and as good company as an adult, maybe better. When Suzie looked at her daughter she often wondered how she'd managed to produce a beauty like Jess. Although she had the Clarke blue eyes, that was where the resemblance to her mother ended. Jess was petite with a luxurious mane of dark hair and sallow skin that tanned easily unlike the Connors or Clarke complexions that freckled and burned.

Sharon was a honeymoon baby, and rather than feel threatened by this new addition to the family, Jess had been delighted with her little sister. Almost four years later Noel had completed their little family and with her good friend, Nora, nearby to laugh and cry with, she had been quite content with her life in Limerick. Until John had to go and spoil it.

Suzie frowned. Where had that come from? She was pretty sure he'd done something to upset her, something serious, but she couldn't for the life of her remember what. She shook her head, exasperated. How come some moments in her life were as clear as crystal and others so vague or completely absent?

For example, she had few memories of Sharon's and Noel's early days, and yet she remembered so much more about her eldest. Should she really still have these gaps in her memory? It was bloody frustrating and a bit scary. Not that she planned to tell anyone. It would only mean more fucking tests, and Suzie wasn't staying in this room a moment longer than she had to.

CHAPTER
THREE

Katie carried two beers over, oblivious of the admiring looks from the guys who parted to let her through. "It's like a scrum trying to get a drink in this place," she said, squeezing into the seat next to Jess. "To your mum!"

"To Mum." Jess smiled.

"Remind me why we're here again." Katie looked round with distaste.

The stuffy pub was packed and the noise level had risen as more alcohol was consumed.

"One of the guys is leaving the *Gazette* and the boss asked me to drop by. One drink and we can go."

"It's a small paper. Do you really care that much about them? They're lucky you write for them, if you ask me."

Jess smiled. "It's small but Louis lets me cover current affairs and politics and I want to build on that and move away from the lighter, fluffier pieces the bigger papers ask me to do." She pulled a face. "It's hard to get taken seriously as a journalist if you're commenting on the fashion at an awards ceremony."

Katie looked round the dingy bar, her eyes narrowing as they settled on Jess's colleagues from the newspaper.

"Not the friendliest bunch, are they? A couple of women over there are staring at you, and not in a good way; and that guy you introduced me to looked straight at my boobs."

"Don't feel special. Tim's like that with all women and he's the religious correspondent." Jess smirked. She didn't comment on her female co-workers. She knew they resented her and she didn't like to dwell on the reason why.

"Is the editor nice, at least?"

"He is." Jess smiled, remembering the day she'd stumbled from the hospital after the doctors had explained they didn't know if Mum would ever wake up, and gone straight to the monthly meeting at the *Gazette*. She'd sat through it, unable to take anything in. When it was over Louis Healy had taken her aside and asked if everything was okay, and she'd broken down, sobbing. It was embarrassing, crying on your boss's shoulder just a few weeks into a job, but she was beyond caring. Louis had led her into the privacy of his office and given her a large brandy in a paper cup from a bottle stashed in his filing cabinet.

"For emergencies," he'd said with a grin.

Jess was numb in those first dreadful weeks, going through the motions on automatic pilot, and she'd never forget how kind Louis had been. When she wasn't by her mother's bedside, he'd urged her to write, pouring her sadness and loss into her work. It was a welcome distraction and she'd written some of her best pieces during that difficult time.

They started to meet for coffee or a drink outside the office, as Louis was concerned that the other staff would accuse him of giving Jess special treatment. At first, she had thought she'd imagined the lingering looks, the light pressing of cheeks, later accompanied by a kiss to the side of her mouth. Then his hand on her back as he bent over her, studying her copy, so close she could feel the warmth of his breath on her cheek. He was a lot older than she was and not really her type, but, when he finally took her in his arms, it was easier to go along with it than to push him away. She was flattered and comforted by the attention.

"Can we get out of here now?" Katie asked, breaking in on her thoughts. "You've done your duty and I'm starving. Pizza?"

"Sounds good." Jess smiled.

When she finally left Katie, Jess decided to call in on her mum before going home. She had some research to do for a piece she was writing on the price and availability of childcare for a tabloid newspaper, but she wanted to check her mum was doing okay first. Noel was in his final term of university studying engineering and spending most of his time either at lectures or in the library so Suzie was alone much of the time. Jess wondered how long it would be before she stopped worrying about her mum.

"In here," her mother called when Jess let herself in and tossed her coat and bag on the hall table. She followed the sound of the radio and found her mother sitting at the kitchen table, brochures spread out in front of her.

"Hey." Jess kissed her forehead and dropped into a chair. "I was out with Katie and just dropped in to say hello on my way home."

"Dropped in to check up on me, more like."

Jess smiled. "Someone has to. Shouldn't you be heading to bed?"

"I've spent enough feckin' time in bed," her mother retorted.

"What's all this?" Jess looked at the flyers and leaflets covering the kitchen table.

"I've decided that I need some hobbies."

Jess picked up the nearest flyer and looked at her in alarm. "Ice-skating? You're kidding."

"It's okay, I've decided against that one. It's a bit tame."

"Tame? You could break your leg or hip."

"Christ, I'm forty-eight not eighty-eight," her mother growled. "Still, I was never the sporty type. This is more my kind of thing." She jabbed a finger at another leaflet. "I walked miles when I lived in Limerick, mainly to try and get Noel to sleep and because there was feck all else to do."

"Hill walking. I suppose it would get you out in the fresh air," Jess said, although she'd sleep easier if her mother would just get back into her old routine of knitting and reading.

"I quite fancy meditation, too."

Jess's lips twitched as she took the brochure Suzie handed her. "Buddhism?"

"I always thought it was mumbo-jumbo but I've been reading up on it and it sounds fascinating. There are several classes, from meditation to mindfulness to loving kindness. I thought that Sharon might like to come along. Lord knows, she could do with loosening up a bit. It's as if she's a poker stuck up her arse."

Jess grinned. Mum's tactlessness could be embarrassing, but funny, too. "You might want to word it a bit more diplomatically when you speak to Shaz," she advised.

"If I can't talk straight to my own daughter what's the world coming to?" she retorted. "All I'm saying is that, if she relaxed a little, she might be able to control her son."

"I think that might take a lot of classes," Jess mumbled, although she still found her mother's change in attitude towards her beloved grandchild alarming. She had always doted on Bobby and turned a blind eye to his bad behaviour, much the way Sharon did.

Jess had found out in their teenage years that she had little in common with her sister, who was interested only in clothes, makeup and boys. She couldn't wait to leave school, just wanting to party and get a boyfriend. The older they became, the more they clashed, Jess yelling at her sister to turn down the music when she was trying to study and Sharon ignoring her. It had been a relief when Sharon left home and, with some space between them, they got on better — not that they sought out each other's company.

The devastation of Mum's accident had probably brought them closer than they'd been since they were children, and her mum was right about one thing: Sharon really did need to learn to relax. The fun-loving teenager had become an anxious young mother who was ruled by her son's moods.

"I thought that you might like to do this with me," Suzie said.

Jess took the leaflet and laughed. "Salsa? I don't think so."

"You were the one who said I should get out more," Suzie pointed out with a sulky expression.

Jess rolled her eyes and grinned. "I should have known that would come back to haunt me. Yes, you should get out more, but you don't need *me* with you. Go with women your own age."

"Like who?" her mother demanded.

Jess cast around for a name and smiled, triumphant. "I'm sure Aileen would be interested." Her mother's neighbour was a good mate and always up for a laugh.

"Aileen has two left feet and not a note in her head. Anyway, she's coming to the book club with me."

"Mum, I'm delighted that you plan to live a fuller life but you don't have to try everything at once. It's only a little over two weeks since you left hospital."

"I'm bored out of my mind at home all day, twiddling my feckin' thumbs," Suzie complained.

"Well, what did you do before you hit your head?"

Her mother scowled. "Boring crap like weeding, shopping and I knitted a sweater for that ungrateful little bugger who, after a month's work, said the colour was wrong and the wool made him itchy."

Jess sighed. She wasn't close to her nephew and she agreed that he could be a little terror, but it took some getting used to hearing Mum call him such terrible names. She'd always adored her grandson and defended him whenever he was in trouble.

"I suppose I could redecorate," Suzie mused, glancing around. "The place is looking a bit tired."

"Don't even think about it!" Just the thought of her mother up a ladder made Jess's head ache. She sighed. "Fine. I'll go to one dance class with you but, if it's full of desperate women and perverts, I'm out of there."

Her mother gave a triumphant grin. "Great. It's on Friday nights at eight. I'll check when it starts."

"Oh." Jess's heart sank. That was the one evening of the week that Louis usually spent at her flat. After he'd signed off on the paper, he would pick up a takeaway and a bottle of wine and come over.

"Is there a problem?" Suzie's eyes narrowed.

Jess shook her head. Louis would understand. "No. Friday's fine."

There was a commotion in the hall and Sharon's wheedling voice. "No, Bobby, I told you, it's too late for sweets, it's almost bedtime. Maybe Granny will give you a breadstick."

Suzie rolled her eyes. "What on earth are they doing here at this hour?"

The door opened and Sharon walked in, her son trailing behind her.

"Hi, Shaz, hi, Bobby, it's good to see you." Jess tousled the child's hair but he jerked his head away. Okay. "Everything all right, Shaz?" she asked. Sharon was wearing that tense, pinched look that so often marred her pretty face these days.

"Fine," she said, sounding stressed. "We were in town and just dropped in on the way home because we bought Granny a present, didn't we, Bobby?"

The child said nothing and Sharon set down a large bag from an expensive shop on Grafton Street.

Suzie eyed it, frowning. "You shouldn't be spending your money on me."

"Why not? You deserve a treat after all you've been through. Go on, open it!" Sharon looked at her expectantly.

Jess clamped a hand firmly over her mouth as her mother pulled out a heavy woollen dress and stared at it in horror.

"What do you think?" Sharon prompted, searching her mother's face.

"It looks . . . warm," Jess said, smiling, praying her mother would be nice. It was a dreadful dress. What had Sharon been thinking?

"Try it on and let's see how it looks," Sharon urged.

"Aw, Shaz, are you kidding me?"

"What?"

"It's like something my mother would have worn. No, actually, it's more like something she'd have taken to the charity shop."

Jess winced. So much for prayers.

"I told you she'd hate it," Bobby said.

Suzie looked at him in surprise. "You were right."

"Mum, there's no need to be rude," Jess protested, embarrassed by her mother's candour.

"It's fine," Sharon said with a grim smile. "I'd offer to exchange it but obviously I have terrible taste. I'll give you the receipt and you can change it yourself."

"Sharon, she doesn't mean it," Jess murmured.

"I told her to get blue," Bobby said. "That colour is yuck."

"It is," Suzie agreed, examining the shapeless moss-green garment.

"I need the loo." Sharon left the room, slamming the door behind her.

"Oh, Mum. Could you not have just said it was lovely?"

Bobby raised his head, frowning. "But that's a lie."

"Quite right," Suzie agreed.

"Not really, just a little fib." Jess smiled at the child. "Sometimes it's okay to tell fibs to make someone feel good."

"It's still a lie. Mum says we should never tell lies."

"Well, I don't know many who keep to that rule," Suzie muttered.

"But wasn't it kind of them to get you a present, Mum?" Jess said, with a pointed nod at her nephew.

"I suppose."

"I told her to get the blue one," Bobby repeated.

"Right." Jess gave him a bright smile. "How about a biscuit?"

When Sharon returned, Suzie mumbled a lame apology but her daughter waved it away, her eyes narrowing as they homed in on her son. "Bobby, what are you eating?"

Mum rolled her eyes at Jess. "I gave him a biscuit."

"But it's chocolate. You know that he's lactose-intolerant. Spit it out, Bobby, and go and rinse your mouth."

"Oh, for fuck's sake, Sharon, will you lighten up and let the child eat?"

"And will you stop swearing in front of my son?"

Jess looked from one angry face to the other and put her hands up. "Can you both calm down? There was only a tiny bit of chocolate on the biscuit, Shaz, and he's almost finished it now."

"Huh. You won't be the one holding his head over the loo in the middle of the night. Come on, Bobby, we're going."

"God, give me patience," Suzie muttered.

"Don't go, Shaz. Have a cuppa," Jess said, but Sharon was already marching down the hall, dragging her son behind her.

Jess looked over at her mother and sighed. What were they going to do with her?

"What?" Suzie scowled, her mouth set in a stubborn line.

"Sharon never did have great taste," Mandy smirked when Suzie told her the story. She glanced around the gloomy lounge. "Why on earth are we here, Suzie? I thought you said there was going to be some craic."

"It's supposed to be karaoke night." Suzie took a sip of chilled wine. She was limited to two glasses for the moment, so she relished every drop and made it last. "Maybe it's in a different room. I'll go to Reception and find out." She left the lounge and walked up to the desk, tapping on the counter, waiting for the girl to finish a call. After being ignored for a few seconds, Suzie realised it was a personal call and, leaning on the desk, said, "Excuse me," loudly.

The receptionist gave an exaggerated sigh. "I'm on a call, madam."

"A personal one. So, unless you want me to complain to your manager, you'll end it and help the customer. I believe that's your job."

"I've got to go, Shelly." She hung up and scowled at Suzie. "Yes?"

"Where is the karaoke on?" Suzie snapped.

"In the lounge."

Suzie checked her watch. "But it was supposed to start at eight and it's almost half past now."

"On Fridays," the girl added with a smug smile.

Bitch, Suzie thought and turning on her heel went back in to her sister. "Sorry, I got it wrong. It's on Fridays, not Thursdays."

"Thank God for that." Mandy smiled at the businessmen sitting at the bar and crossed her legs, giving them a flash of thigh.

"You're such a slut, Mandy," Suzie said in disgust. "Is sex all you ever think of? What about love? Someone must have made your heart race at least once." As the words left her mouth, Suzie had a moment of déjà vu and shivered.

Mandy watched her curiously. "What?"

"Nothing." She shook off the uneasy feeling. "Seriously, though, wouldn't you like to share your life with one special person? You must get lonely."

"At least I have a sex life. What about you?" Mandy retorted. "You've been a widow for eleven years now and you've lived like a nun. Aren't you frustrated?"

"No." John had died at thirty-eight, got caught between two pieces of farm machinery on a visit to one of his suppliers. With three devastated children to look after, Suzie hadn't had time to dwell on her own shock and pain. She'd taken her family back to Dublin, the place that was still home to her, and away from reminders of how they had lost their dad. Noel had just turned nine and went through months of nightmares and bedwetting. Even if Suzie had been interested in dating and met someone, she would never have introduced a strange man into their lives. As time went on and the sad memories faded, Suzie had felt quite content with her life. But her family were grown now and Suzie's brush with death was making her re-evaluate her life. Time was flying by while she sat on the sidelines, watching. It wasn't too late to travel or take up new hobbies, but, as far as men were concerned, she figured she'd missed the boat.

"What man would be interested in a middle-aged granny with stretch marks, flabby arms and wrinkles?" she said to her sister.

"Have you looked in the mirror lately?" Mandy said, eyebrows raised.

Suzie pulled self-consciously on her ponytail, liberally sprinkled with grey. "I try not to."

"Granted, your hair is a disgrace and you dress like a granny —"

"Feck off! I do not," Suzie scowled at her.

Mandy carried on regardless. "But you've lost a lot of weight since the accident and you could look years younger if you wanted to. I bet I could have you set up with a guy in six months, maybe less."

Suzie roared laughing at the idea. Although, now that Mandy mentioned it, she realised that she'd had to wear a belt on her jeans since she came home and her old dresses were like tents.

"I'll take you shopping and, trust me, you won't recognise yourself."

"I suppose a couple of new outfits would be nice," Suzie admitted.

"You need a lot more than a couple."

"I'm not spending a fortune on designer clothes," Suzie warned her sister, "not with Bobby around. They'd be destroyed in no time."

Mandy raised her eyebrows in surprise. "Your little angel?"

"Little devil, more like. Although, I think the problem is the mother, not the child. Sharon's blind to his faults and doesn't discipline him, and Keith doesn't seem to have the guts to stand up to her. I think I'll have to step in and sort them out."

"Good luck with that." Mandy smirked, raising her hand to attract the waiter's attention.

"What would you say to a parachute jump?" Suzie's mind had wandered, as it tended to these days.

"I'd say no, thank you. Have you lost your mind? Can't you stick to boring stuff like going to strip clubs and seeing the world?"

"We can do that too." Suzie laughed.

34

"Are you interested in travelling?" Mandy's eyes lit up.

"Absolutely." Suzie hadn't actually given it much thought but now that Mandy mentioned it, there were so many places she'd love to visit. And why not? She was a free agent. What was to stop her going where she wanted, whenever the mood took her? A rebellious thrill ran through her. Yes, travel was definitely going on her to-do list.

CHAPTER
FOUR

The following evening, Suzie dragged Mandy along to the karaoke night. She wasn't keen but, as soon as Suzie mentioned she was seriously considering a holiday, her sister had changed her tune. Suzie chuckled. Mandy would do anything if it meant a free trip.

Because John had died in an accident at work, Suzie had been awarded a handsome settlement and had no money worries. There was more than enough to see her to her grave and leave the children a small inheritance. It drove Mandy nuts that her sister still lived in the same little estate, and bought her clothes from chain stores, but Suzie remembered all too well what it was like growing up in the Clarke household, even if Mandy didn't. It had made her naturally cautious and careful with money and people, while her sister had grown up greedy and exploitative.

Suzie was reminded of something Aileen had said one night shortly after she came out of hospital. She'd nipped in with a couple of bottles of wine to celebrate Suzie's homecoming and they'd got talking about families. Aileen and Mandy never got along and, after her neighbour had a few drinks, her tongue was well and truly loosened.

"I wouldn't trust that one as far as I'd throw her," she'd said.

"She's family, and, besides," Suzie had laughed, "haven't you heard the saying: keep your friends close, and your enemies closer?"

"You see her as the enemy?" Aileen had said, her eyes round.

"It's just an expression," Suzie had replied, but wondered at her own words, which she'd said without thinking.

Her family didn't seem that fond of their aunt, either, but, when Suzie wanted a companion, she could rely on Mandy to come running. She didn't feel remotely guilty for using her sister. She always footed the bill and she wasn't sure why, but she felt Mandy owed her.

The karaoke proved a good laugh and, after a few drinks, even Mandy was up on stage, singing her heart out if slightly off-key. When Suzie went out to the loo she left Mandy and another woman, arm in arm and belting out "I Will Survive". She was hurrying back to her seat, not wishing to miss the fun, when she saw a couple waiting for the lift. The man looked vaguely familiar and Suzie suppressed a snort when she saw him fondle his companion's arse. Oh shit, it was Louis Healy and the pretty girl with him definitely wasn't his wife. She looked young enough to be his daughter. Dirty old bastard! The girl turned her head to smile up at him and Suzie nearly had a heart attack. "Jess?"

Her daughter swung round, her eyes wide in shocked surprise. "Mum, hi."

"Hi? Hi? Is that all you've got to say?"

"Fuck," the man muttered.

Suzie glowered at him. "I'm guessing that was the plan."

"Mum!" Jess's face burned with embarrassment at the attention they were attracting.

Suzie ignored her and as the door to the lift opened she kept her eyes on Healy. "I suggest you go on up to your room," she said, "and that way I won't have to tell your wife what I thought you were about to do to my daughter."

"Mum, stop it, please. You've got it all wrong."

"Have I? This man is Louis Healy, right?"

"Yes, but —"

"The same Louis Healy who's happily married with three children?"

Louis looked from Suzie to her daughter and, with a grim smile, stepped into the lift, jabbing the button for his floor.

Sick to her stomach, Suzie turned to go back into the bar. "Wait for me in Reception," she muttered over her shoulder, trembling with rage.

"Mum, it's not what you think —"

"Reception!" Suzie barked, clenching her hands by her side, alarmed by how much she wanted to slap her daughter.

Mandy glanced from mother to daughter as they went home in a taxi. She squeezed Jess's hand and the girl gave a small nod. She could almost feel the fury coming off her sister.

"Calm down, Suzie, it's not the end of the world," she murmured once they were inside the house.

Suzie shot her a scathing look. "Well, you would say that."

"Hey, don't start on me," Mandy retorted.

Suzie closed her eyes. "Sorry. I'm just upset to find that my daughter's a tart."

"He said they were separated." An ashen-faced Jess repeated, tearfully, from the sofa.

Rather than winning her sympathy, the tears seemed to infuriate Suzie. "Let's get this straight. Louis Healy is the editor of the *Gazette*. You've worked with him since a few weeks before my accident — that's over four months ago now — and it never came up in conversation that he was married with kids?"

"Of course it did, but I told you, he said they were separated."

"They didn't look separated when I saw them having lunch in Howth the other day. In fact, they looked very cosy. You know his wife, don't you? Maeve, the woman who did the flowers for Sharon's wedding?"

Mandy saw the shock on Jess's face. This was obviously news to her.

"You will stop seeing him now," Suzie said.

"I can't stop seeing him, Mum. I write for him."

"And since when did that involve hotel rooms?"

Her daughter hung her head and said nothing.

Suzie glowered at her. "So, you *are* sleeping with him. Where is your self-respect? Why would you give yourself to a man like that? He's not giving you work because you're talented. All he wants is your body and the rampant sex that he doesn't get at home."

"Christ. Don't hold back, Suzie," Mandy said as Jess shrank further into the sofa.

"It's true." Suzie stood over her daughter, anger radiating from her. "How many other women journalists do you think he's fucked in hotel rooms? Do you really want to debase yourself by being another notch on his belt? You're a fool and I'm ashamed of you."

"I told you, I didn't know."

"Stop lying to me. You're not a child, Jess. You're a smart twenty-seven-year-old woman and you knew exactly what you were doing. I swear to God, if you keep seeing him I will tell his wife myself."

Jess's eyes widened. "You wouldn't, you can't."

"Try me. Now, get the hell out of here. I can't stand the sight of you."

Jess stood, staring at her for a moment and then ran from the room. They heard the front door close moments later.

Mandy went through to the kitchen and brought back two glasses of wine. "You were a bit hard on her."

"She deserved it. All that education and she honestly believes Louis when he says that he's footloose and fancy-free? She could have destroyed not only his marriage but his relationship with his children, too."

"It takes two to tango."

Suzie sank into a chair, frowning.

"What is it?" Mandy studied her sister's expression.

But Suzie just shook her head. "Nothing. I'm just upset."

"You're not really going to shop her, are you?"

"I wish I had the guts to carry out my threats, but I can't do that to her."

"No, not if you want your relationship to survive this."

"I don't know why she can't find a nice lad and settle down. I mean, she's so beautiful."

"Guys often feel threatened by beautiful women and don't have the courage to approach them," Mandy assured her, speaking from experience. "It takes the brazen ones to try it on and, let's face it, Jess has always been a bit needy."

"What do you mean by that?" Suzie looked at her.

"She's old-fashioned and naïve, looking for her prince, the perfect man who'll love her and look after her."

"And she thought that man was Louis Healy? Then she's not as smart as I thought." Suzie shook her head in disbelief, sighing. "At least we'll be starting salsa classes on Friday nights soon. Perhaps she'll get lucky."

Mandy burst out laughing. "You won't find any real men at dance classes, just weirdos hoping to get their paws on a woman, *any* woman."

"At least while she's with me I know that she's not with that bastard." Suzie sniffed.

"If you're planning to go dancing and travelling, you definitely need a new wardrobe." Mandy changed the subject, tired of examining her niece's love life. "As my esteemed boss is out of town, why don't I pick you up first thing?"

Suzie brightened. "Yeah, why not? I'll make an appointment with Veronica to get my roots done, too."

"Are you mad? That woman is the reason you look old. I'll book you in with Adrian."

"Feck off. I'm not paying those prices."

"Don't you think you deserve it?" Mandy asked.

Suzie was silent for a moment and then looked at her, a glint in her eye. "You know, maybe I do."

Mandy looked at her, astonished. "Seriously?"

"Yeah, why not?"

"You won't regret it." Mandy promised, looking forward to the challenge of knocking ten years off her sister. Well, maybe five.

The hairdresser walked round Suzie, tugging her hair this way and that. "I think a short cut, but we'll keep the thickness and go ash-blonde."

Mandy nodded enthusiastically. "Oh, yes. That should look quite striking."

"Should?" Adrian pouted at her.

"Will," Mandy said. "Sorry, Adrian."

"I don't know." Suzie hesitated, not liking his attitude and the way the two of them were trying to push her into this.

Adrian squeezed her shoulder and smiled for the first time. "Trust me, darling. You will love it."

Suzie sat up straighter and nodded. "Go for it. After all, you only live once."

When later she looked at her reflection, Suzie could have cried. What had she done? She looked like an old woman, completely washed out. Adrian saw her shocked expression and patted her shoulder. "Don't worry. The black gown is draining you of colour and you're wearing no eye makeup."

That was true, Suzie had to admit, but she still felt she'd made a huge mistake. Why had she trusted this guy? Then one of the other stylists took a turquoise scarf from around her shoulders and tossed it over to him. "Try that."

"Perfect." Adrian beamed and draped the material round Suzie's neck and shoulders.

"Oh," Suzie breathed when she saw the way the scarf brought out the blue in her eyes and the healthy pink of her cheeks and lips. "That's amazing."

"From now on, wear strong colours. Blues, reds, purples," he advised. "No beige and definitely no prints and stripes."

"You should come shopping with us," Mandy told him. "She needs a new wardrobe as she's dropped two dress sizes."

"How fantastic!" The hairdresser beamed again. "Just remember: plain colours, and go for figure-hugging clothes to show off that fab figure. Then steer clear of chocolate, girl."

"Fuck that," Suzie said. "I'll just buy everything in two sizes." She looked up to see the stylist's jaw drop. "Oops, sorry. I got a bang on the head and I never really know what's going to come out when I open my mouth."

"None of us do," her sister told him. Suzie paid for her new style and Mandy's trim and blow-dry, ignoring the three-figure amount, and walked out into the street feeling like a new woman.

"Ready?" Mandy asked.

Suzie grinned. "Ready."

CHAPTER
FIVE

Four department stores and six shopping bags later, Suzie led her sister into a fancy French restaurant for a late lunch.

"I wish you'd hit your head years ago if this is the effect it has on you," Mandy said, clinking her wine glass against Suzie's.

"Do you mean lunch or shopping?"

"Both. You've always been so careful with your money, and unadventurous too. You didn't trust foreign or fancy foods and now you're sitting here eating oysters and swilling wine."

Suzie chuckled. "Meet the new Suzie Connors who's planning to live life to the full."

"You certainly look like a new woman. Fair play to Adrian, that hairstyle has taken years off you."

It was true. In Brown Thomas, Suzie had agreed to let a beauty consultant do her makeup and couldn't believe it when she looked in the mirror. Now, dressed in a turquoise dress and the shoes Mandy had persuaded her to buy, despite their ridiculous price, Suzie felt a million dollars. She looked round at the other diners — friends lunching, business types and a couple of TV personalities — and felt that she fitted in quite well. "I could get used to this."

"No reason why you shouldn't," Mandy said. You're a wealthy woman and, if your solicitor can prove that the hotel's gym staff were negligent, you could be a lot richer."

Spending money still didn't come easily to Suzie. Days like today would always be the exception not the rule. But her sister was right. She could afford to do whatever she wanted, within reason. It was a liberating thought.

The mind was a strange thing, she mused. She had no trouble recalling her family and friends or the basics of her life history, but there were gaps that she discovered only when the family talked about times that she had no memory of. That upset her a little. Then there were silly things such as her likes and dislikes. Mandy had almost passed out when she'd ordered the oysters and then pronounced them delicious. Apparently, the only fish she'd eaten in the past had been the battered sort from the chippy. While it was all a bit scary, it was exciting, too. From what she'd been told, Suzie wasn't that impressed with the woman she'd been before the accident. She sounded dull and a pushover. But not anymore. She caught sight of her image in the mirrored wall across the way and smiled. Mandy had always been the prettiest Clarke girl and now, despite the ten-year age difference, Suzie felt she could hold her own. Not that stuff like that mattered but it was nice to feel more confident. She looked over at Mandy.

"So where should we go on holiday?"

Mandy put down her cutlery, her face lighting up. "For noise, excitement and fun? There's only one place to go. New York, baby."

Suzie hadn't been away in years, and then only on package deals where John had snored happily in the sun while she kept an eye on the kids. The thought of going somewhere just for *her* was exciting. "I'll need to renew my passport."

"And clear it with the consultant," her sister said.

"I don't need to clear anything with anyone," Suzie retorted. Between doctors and family she was fed up being told what to do. She was better now and well able to make her own decisions.

"You need medical clearance or you won't be able to get travel insurance," Mandy pointed out.

"Fine. I'm due back for a check-up in a few weeks. I'll sort it out then."

Mandy drained her glass. "Come on. If we're going to New York, we'd better get back to the shops. By the time I've kitted you out, you'll be able to give Samantha a run for her money."

"Samantha?" Suzie looked at her.

"The character from *Sex and the City*?" Suzie still hadn't a clue who she was talking about and Mandy's eyes widened. "It was one of your favourite shows."

Suzie felt a wave of panic. "I don't remember."

"Don't worry about it, you have the box set. Now, let's go."

Several hours later, Suzie dropped her bags in the hall, kicked off her shoes and went into the kitchen to make a much-needed coffee. Noel was at the table, working. She was surprised to see him. He was usually holed up in his room or out with his mates. She smiled affectionately at the ink on his fingers, his mop of sandy hair and the wispy excuse of a beard. He was so like Sharon, although not as uptight. Still, he didn't have a crazy kid to deal with. "Hello, love. How's the studying going?" He closed the book he'd been reading and shoved it into his backpack. "Fine," he said and took out a pad.

Suzie frowned at the shadows under his bloodshot eyes. "You look knackered. Why don't you get an early night and you'll feel fresher in the morning?"

He gave a wide yawn and dragged his hand through his hair. "I can't sleep. I conk out as soon as I hit the pillow but then I wake up a couple of hours later and lie there, thinking."

"You've been working too hard," Suzie said, wishing there was something she could do to help. Then she remembered the pills the doctor had prescribed for her a while back for anxiety. She grinned. "Wait here." Upstairs she rummaged in the locker by her bed until she found an almost full blister pack of white pills. She returned to the kitchen and put them on the table in front of him. "Here, these should do the trick."

Noel stared at the pack. "Where did you get these, a dealer?"

She chuckled. "The doc gave me them when I was leaving the hospital. They're supposed to help you relax."

"I thought that you didn't approve of pill popping."

She wrinkled her nose trying to remember whether she did or not. "I suppose that's true but, you're under a lot of pressure, and, if these help and get you through the exams, then what's the harm?"

"Cheers, Mum." Noel grinned and took a pill, glugging it down with a glass of water.

"Hungry?" she asked.

"Always."

"Why don't you phone for pizza? I'm not in the mood for cooking and I had a huge lunch with Mandy. We've spent the day shopping."

"You two are very pally these days. You never used to do girly stuff together. In fact, you've never really got on at all."

"Really?" Suzie shrugged. "Maybe it takes something serious to bring people closer."

"Maybe." Noel cocked his head on one side, looking at her properly for the first time. "Your hair's different."

"Finally, he notices." Suzie grinned and did a twirl. "What do you think?"

"Suits ya. You'll be bringing home an oul' fella next," he teased.

"Feck off. If I'm going to get a fella, he'll be a toy boy."

He closed his eyes and groaned. "Too much information, Mum. Mind you, in that getup, you just might pull."

She threw back her head and laughed. "Open a bottle of wine for me, would you, love? I'm going to have an early night and read my book."

"I thought the doc said to go easy on the booze for a while."

"Ah, fuck that. A little of what you fancy does you good, that's what my da used to say. In fact that's probably the only bit of good advice the oul' bastard gave me."

He burst out laughing. "Ah, Mum"

She smiled. "What?"

He shook his head. "It's good to have you home."

She smiled and hugged him. "It's good to be here."

Noel was watching a movie online when he heard his sister letting herself in.

"Hey, lazy, how come you're not studying?"

He didn't bother looking up. "I'm on a break, Jess. What's your excuse?"

"I wanted to check on Mum. I tried to call a few times and there was no answer."

"She was out shopping with Mandy all day so she's exhausted and having an early night."

"She went shopping with Mandy?" Jess stared at him.

He chuckled. "I know, right? They seem to be best buddies all of a sudden. She got a new hairstyle, too."

Jess's eyes widened as she sank into a chair. "Is it bad?"

"No, she looks great. By the way, she's talking about going to New York for a few days."

"What?" Jess looked horrified.

He sighed when he saw her worried frown. "I only said she was *thinking* about it, Jess."

"She's so hyper at the moment. She wants to do everything, go everywhere. It's exhausting."

Noel shrugged. "It's probably just the euphoria of being alive. Hardly surprising. Who cares what she does as long as she's happy?"

"True, although I wish she'd learn to be more tactful. If she keeps saying exactly what she thinks, someone's going to thump her. She told Keith the other day that he was putting on a lot of weight and Sharon that there was a parenting programme on TV that she should watch."

Noel sniggered. "It is quite entertaining, though."

"Easy for you to be smug," Jess scoffed. "She hasn't had a go at you yet."

"That's because I'm perfect." He shot her a knowing look. "I don't mess around with married women."

"She told you." Jess looked shocked and embarrassed.

"Oh, yeah, and in very colourful language, too. What were you thinking? How could you mess around with a married guy?"

"I thought he was separated, not that it's any of your business. Mum had no right to tell you."

"In case you hadn't noticed, Mum doesn't worry about minor things like confidentiality. I hope you've dropped him, or she's liable to drag you up to their house and let his wife deal with you."

Jess bit her lip, blanching. "She wouldn't."

Noel stared at her and shook his head. "You haven't finished with him, have you?"

"I haven't had a chance," she protested. "He's out of the country at the moment."

"Huh, on business with another lady reporter, eh?" He shook his head. He didn't know why he felt so pissed off with Jess. Maybe it was because she was the eldest of the family and — he'd always thought — the smartest of the three of them.

Jess stood up, glaring. "Fuck off, Noel, and stay out of my business."

"Gladly." He listened to her march down the hall. "Don't wake Mum," he called after her, and then flinched as the front door slammed. "Thanks."

CHAPTER
SIX

"Bobby! No, darling, please don't do that." Sharon tried to keep her voice even, but she was fast losing patience. Her son had refused to eat his shepherd's pie and was instead lining up his peas beside his plate. They kept rolling out of order and he finally lost patience and shoved the plate off the table. It landed with a plop at his father's feet, the gravy splashing Keith's leather shoes.

"Right, young man, that's it." Keith grabbed Bobby by the arm and dragged him from the table.

"Keith, stop. He's only a child, he doesn't know any better," she said as her son started to kick and scream.

"For God's sake, Sharon, he's almost five. He needs to learn that we won't tolerate this sort of behaviour."

Sharon pulled Bobby away from her husband and into the protective circle of her arms. She could feel his heart pounding in his chest but slowly, as she held him tight, he started to calm down. "Good boy."

Keith looked at them in disgust. "What's the bloody point? How is Bobby ever going to learn right from wrong with you fawning all over him?"

He left the room and, moments later, Sharon heard the TV blaring. She cuddled her son closer. "It's okay, sweetie. Daddy isn't cross with you."

"He is."

"Well, he doesn't mean to be. He works very hard and loses his temper when he gets tired."

"Only with me," Bobby said.

Sharon was thrown by the perceptive comment. "How about some ice cream?" He nodded and sat back at the table while she went to the freezer. She put a dish of vanilla-and-chocolate ice-cream in front of him. "Now, what do you say?"

"Thank you," he mumbled.

"Good boy." Sharon wondered how many mothers felt as victorious as she did when she managed to prise a polite response from her child.

The phone rang and Sharon tensed when she heard her mother's voice.

"Hi, love. All set for our first meditation class?"

Sharon groaned. "Is that tonight?"

"Yes, and don't try to worm your way out of it — I'm looking forward to it."

"It's just that Bobby isn't in great form and he gets unsettled when I go out before bedtime."

Suzie tutted. "Won't his dad be there? If you don't come, I can't go either. It's not on a bus route and you know that I'm not allowed to drive yet."

Sharon buckled under the emotional blackmail. "Fine. I'll pick you up at six thirty."

"Great. I know you'll enjoy it. It's supposed to be very calming."

Sharon bristled. "And why do I need calming?"

"Don't be so bloody touchy," her mother groaned. "I'm simply saying that you're a busy mum and it's important to take some time out for yourself. The healthier and happier you are, the better you can handle things."

"You've been reading those brochures again."

Suzie chuckled. "I have but, you have to admit, it makes sense."

"It does," Sharon conceded. "See you later, Mum." She sat staring at the phone. She hadn't been coping well lately and even her mother had noticed.

Sharon felt like such a failure. She'd longed to be a mother and was devastated to find that she wasn't a very good one. Not that she neglected Bobby, quite the reverse, as Keith was fond of pointing out. But she had expected to have a strong bond with her child. She'd assumed that she would know what he wanted, what he needed and that she would always be able to comfort and protect him. But Sharon had tried everything to get through to Bobby and failed. She had told him he must play nicely with other children and share his toys, and had encouraged him to talk, but all without success. As for the tantrums, she couldn't even figure what triggered them, never mind how to manage them. The only thing she could do was hold Bobby and let him know she was there, and wait until the tirades passed.

She knew her friends and family didn't agree with her methods. Only Mum had stood by her, never once criticising or interfering and, when even Sharon lost patience, had taken over and tried to cajole Bobby to be good. But that was Mum before the accident.

Since she'd woken up, Sharon had seen a very different side of her mother. Not only did Suzie speak her mind, she was cutting and unkind when she did. Sharon had shed many a tear over some of the things she'd said and done lately. It hurt and felt as though she'd lost her only supporter.

Why couldn't Mum go back to the way she was before the accident? Sharon knew she should be grateful that she was alive at all, but it was hard to pretend that everything was the same as before. Suzie hardly spent any time with them now. In the past she had always been on hand to babysit or simply join her daughter and grandchild when they went to the park or playground. But, these days, she made excuses not to see them or said straight out that she was too tired to put up with Bobby's moods. Sometimes Sharon thought her mother didn't even *like* her grandson, let alone love him.

She wished she could talk to Keith about it, but they couldn't seem to talk about anything these days without it ending in a row. Though he hadn't actually said it, Sharon knew that her husband was disappointed in his son and although it hurt, she could understand it.

Keith had seen himself doing all the dad stuff with his son like kicking a football around and teaching him to ride a bike. But Bobby wasn't interested and lacked the coordination to be any good at either. Sharon suggested that Keith do things with his son that *he* enjoyed and not the other way round, but that hadn't worked, either. When Keith tried to play with Bobby and his trains or cars, his son got agitated. All he wanted to do was line them up and, even then, it had to be a specific order, which neither of his parents had managed to decipher. Keith had given up. These days he hardly talked to his son, which broke Sharon's heart and she was finding it harder and harder to hide her resentment.

When they talked it was about the trivia of life. What bills needed paying, were the bins out, and whether they should convert the playroom into an office. It was full of unused toys. There were only a few precious things that Bobby bothered with and they fitted into a small box that he kept by his bed. Once he was asleep, Sharon watched television while Keith messed about on his laptop and there was little or no conversation.

As for their sex life, it was almost non-existent, unless they'd had a couple of glasses of wine and Keith was in the mood. Sharon never was. She found it hard to give herself to the man who was so cold towards her son. But she let him make love to her because it was easier than making an issue of it. She sometimes wondered how much more she could take. Meditation might not help, but Mum was right: she did need time away from her family. She wasn't keen on spending it with her mother but at least it would mean escaping this claustrophobic atmosphere for a while.

Suzie emerged from her house in maroon leggings and a matching top, making Sharon feel dowdy in her old tracksuit.

"How do I look?" Suzie asked, climbing into the passenger seat.

"Fine. You do realise that we're probably going to be lying on a filthy floor?"

Her mum shrugged. "I don't own any sporty type of clothes and the brochure said to dress for comfort."

"Your hair's nice. What made you change the colour?" Sharon asked. Suzie's hair had originally been a slightly darker shade of Sharon's honey-blonde bob.

"Mandy's hairdresser talked me into it. He said it would suit my colouring. It's all part of the new me."

"Are you after a man?" Sharon joked, waiting for the usual rebuke. She and Jess had been trying to fix Mum up for years but Suzie would have none of it.

"I'm after several," her mother retorted. "If I am going to put myself out there, then I intend to have fun."

"Are you pulling my leg?" Sharon asked with a nervous giggle.

Suzie frowned. "No. Why?"

"It's just that you've never dated before. You met dad and married him."

"I dated a couple of boys before him," Suzie assured her.

"But none since. So, why now?"

"This feels like a fresh start. There are lots of things I want to do."

"I thought you were happy," Sharon said, feeling upset for some reason.

"I was. I am. My life's been fine but boring. Now I want more."

"More what?"

Suzie shrugged. "I'd like to try new things, visit new places and make new friends. I want to live my life to the full." She grinned over at Sharon. "I may even get a tattoo."

"Great." Sharon shuddered, imagining her mother turning into a Madonna or Cher lookalike.

It was quite dark inside the hall and Sharon wondered how often this floor was cleaned. The teacher called for quiet, told them to remove their shoes and find a comfortable position. Sharon began to twist and turn and fidget, making her mother roll her eyes and sigh. She continued to strive to get comfortable but she couldn't help wondering who had last used the mat she was sitting on. The teacher had told them to close their eyes and concentrate on her voice or the soothing music and breathe deeply. Sharon seemed to be the only one having a problem complying. Her mother sat cross-legged beside her, perfectly serene.

"Relax."

Sharon looked up to see the teacher looking down at her, smiling. "I can't find a comfortable position and, the more I try to concentrate, the faster my breathing is and the less relaxed I am. Sorry." She gave a nervous titter. "I don't think I'm cut out for this."

The woman's eyes flickered to Suzie. "It comes easier to some than to others. There's no right or wrong way. If concentrating on your breathing doesn't work for you, try closing your eyes and let your mind wander and enjoy the feeling of doing nothing, of simply being."

Sharon let out a long sigh. It was true she didn't get much time to just "be". When she wasn't looking after Bobby she was cleaning or cooking or shopping, all the time worrying about her son. Was it any wonder she was exhausted?

"Clench and unclench your toes and fingers a few times. Tense your entire body for ten seconds, then release. That will help you to relax."

Sharon did as she was told, and then let out a long sigh.

"Good, very good." The teacher smiled her approval. "There's no time limit on this and no exam to pass. Just enjoy the peace." She moved on to advise someone else leaving Sharon clenching and unclenching.

"Wasn't that brilliant?" Suzie said on the way home. "I feel so rested."

"I'm not surprised. You fell asleep."

"I did not. I was just concentrating on my breathing."

"You were snoring, Mum." Sharon grinned.

"I wasn't . . . was I?" Her mother laughed. "Ah, feck it! I'm sure I wasn't the first and I won't be the last. Are you glad you came along? I know that I bullied you into it but I thought the break would do you good."

"It did," Sharon had to admit. Although she hadn't managed to relax quite as much as her mother, she did feel calmer.

"You should practise those exercises in bed at night and dump those sleeping tablets," Suzie said.

"Maybe," Sharon said, although she couldn't imagine sleeping a wink without her little white pills, which brought at least five precious hours of oblivion.

"Coming in for a cuppa?" Suzie asked as Sharon stopped outside her house.

"No, thanks. I'm bushed."

Suzie grinned. "Don't forget, clench and release."

Sharon laughed. "I won't. Night, Mum."

"Bye, love, safe home."

Sharon pulled away, thinking how, whenever they used to part, Mum would always say, "Hugs and kisses to my little angel." Now she rarely mentioned Bobby unless it was to give out about him. Sharon swallowed the lump in her throat. There was no use in crying. Her mother was a different person now and she just had to accept that.

Before Sharon got the front door open, she could hear Keith yelling and Bobby's wails. She closed her eyes and took a moment before letting herself in and hurrying upstairs.

"Bobby, for the last time, put on these pyjamas or you can sleep outside." This was greeted with a terrified wail.

"Keith? What's going on?" Her husband was on their bed, Bobby pinned between his thighs. He was so busy shouting that he was oblivious of her. "Keith, stop." With an effort Sharon kept her voice calm, but her grip on his arm as she pulled him off her son would leave him in no doubt that she was furious. "What the hell are you doing?" she hissed, determined not to enter a shouting match that would further upset Bobby.

Keith stiffened. "He won't get ready for bed."

Sharon looked at the pyjamas in his hand. "They're the wrong ones. He only wears the blue pair."

"But they're the same except for the colour."

"You can either let him put on the blue ones or spend the rest of the night arguing. Which would you prefer?"

Keith climbed off his son and shoved the pyjamas into her hands in disgust. "You do it. This is fucking madness. I've had enough."

He stormed downstairs while she gathered a trembling Bobby into her arms. "It's okay, darling. Daddy's had a bad day."

Bobby sobbed, as she led him to the bathroom. She smothered a sigh as she realised he'd wet himself. Keith must have really scared him. She'd need to do lots of deep breathing to stop herself from throttling her husband. She helped Bobby wash and change into the blue pyjamas before putting him to bed, all the while murmuring soothing endearments.

It was nearly an hour before he finally drifted off and she slipped out of his room. She leaned against the banister, exhausted and trembling, debating whether to confront her husband or just go to bed. The latter would be more sensible, easier, but she remembered the sight of Keith trembling with rage over her cowering son and knew that she couldn't ignore this. If she had arrived home a few minutes later, would Keith have hit him? Was he capable of it? She'd never thought so but seeing him so out of control tonight had scared her. Sharon did a few clenches and unclenches and went downstairs. If she was to get through to her husband she'd have to keep her temper in check.

Keith was slouched on the sofa watching a football match, can of beer in hand, pretending to be absorbed in the game. He might appear calm, but Sharon could tell from the tension in his jaw that he was still fuming. With Bobby or her? Probably both. She felt suddenly weary of the constant war she was waging and not just with Keith. Sometimes it felt as if it were she and Bobby against the entire world. Well, it was time to change all that. Keith was her husband and Bobby's father and they deserved his support and loyalty and love. She wondered about the last word. Did Keith love them? It hadn't felt that way in a long time. He seemed to be drifting further away every day.

Sharon sat down opposite him, finally ready to confront something she'd been trying so hard to ignore. "Keith, I think that we should take Bobby to see a doctor."

"There's nothing wrong with him other than he's a spoiled brat," he retorted.

"I think there's more to it than that."

"I don't." He turned down the volume and sat forward, his eyes beseeching hers. "Let's try it my way for a while, Sharon. He needs strong parenting, that's all."

"Strong parenting? Is that what I just witnessed? Sitting on top of our son, terrifying him?"

Keith sat back, sulking. "I didn't touch him. I was restraining him so that he couldn't hurt himself."

"You frightened the living daylights out of him. He wet himself, Keith. Is that the way you're going to get him to behave? By making him scared of you?"

Keith remained implacable. "He needs toughening up and to learn some manners. We should send him to a boarding school. He wouldn't get away with this crap in one of those places."

Sharon sat staring at him for a long moment and then stood up, realising she was wasting her breath when he was in this mood. Without another word, she went upstairs and got ready for bed. She was pulling the duvet cover back when she froze. No, she couldn't sleep with Keith. Not tonight. Going out to the linen cupboard, Sharon took a quilt and pillow and, going into Bobby's room, curled up on the twin bed next to him. "I'll look after you, sweetheart," she whispered. "I'll never let anything or anyone hurt you. Promise."

CHAPTER
SEVEN

Nora Browne put down the phone after she got Suzie's answering machine yet again. Of course she was glad that her friend was well enough to be out and about so much, but disappointed that, any time she suggested getting together, Suzie had blown her off. After a few weeks of this, Nora decided to call Jess and make sure that everything was okay.

It wasn't. Suzie had changed and the girls weren't handling it too well. Jess tried to explain the sort of behaviour and comments and Nora settled in her chair by the window and let the girl pour her heart out.

"She's changed so much, Nora, and we're all treading on eggshells, pretending everything is the same and trying to hide our feelings when she says something nasty or cruel," Jess finished with a heavy sigh.

"Perhaps it's time that you stopped pretending," Nora suggested. "The three of you should sit her down and tell her how her behaviour is affecting you. Maybe you should go with her when she goes for her next check-up and tell them what's going on. I'm sure there must be some way they can help her."

"I wish I shared your confidence, Nora, but I've been reading up on this and I don't think there's a pill or even an operation that can change the way things are. The consultant as much as said so at the time. We just weren't listening."

Nora's heart went out to her as she heard the sadness in Jess's voice. "Don't give up on her, sweetheart. Doctors don't know everything. If nothing else she can get some sort of therapy. If they can help people with anger-management issues, then they must be able to teach your mum to be more tactful."

"True. It's hardest for Sharon. Mum is, at best, indifferent to Bobby and sometimes she's really horrible to him."

"Oh, Lord." Nora said, shocked to hear this. Suzie had always been besotted with her grandchild. "Probably best not to leave them alone together for the moment," she suggested.

"Sharon keeps him away from Mum as much as possible, and at least, Bobby being Bobby, he doesn't seem bothered."

"I wish there was something I could do to help. I've told her I'll come to Dublin any time to see her — Limerick's only a couple of hours on the motorway — but she doesn't seem interested in meeting up."

"She's spending a lot of time with Mandy."

"Mandy?" Nora exclaimed and then cursed herself for reacting in such a horrified way. She forced a laugh, hoping Jess hadn't noticed. "That's odd, they never seemed that close."

"They weren't."

Jess sounded unimpressed, making Nora wonder what exactly she knew about her infamous aunt.

"Mandy took her shopping the other day and bought clothes that, well, really don't suit her."

Nora felt anger bubble up inside. "Be more specific."

"Er, well, I wouldn't have the nerve to wear some of them."

That evil cow, Nora seethed. There was no doubt that Suzie needed a new wardrobe but she'd expected her to go shopping with the girls or even ask for her help. It was a real slap in the face to think she'd turned to her sister. Nora's eyes filled with tears. It seemed their friendship was another casualty of Suzie's accident.

"She's thrilled with her new look, so I don't have the heart to say anything. I honestly think Mandy did it just for a laugh. She has a warped sense of humour."

"Bitch," Nora muttered.

"What was that?"

"Nothing."

"I should get some work done," Jess said. "Sorry for crying on your shoulder."

"Don't be. I'm always here for you, Jess, you know that."

Jess thanked her and rang off.

Feeling a little lost and sad, Nora sat down with her laptop in her sunny kitchen to work. She designed greeting cards for a US Internet company and also supplied a few local artisan shops. Nora stared at the screen in front of her and waited for the inspiration to come, but she found it hard to concentrate, images of Mandy sniggering at her newfound friendship with her big sister filling her head. What to do? Hop in the car and drive to Dublin and remind Suzie what Mandy was really like? Even if she did, would Suzie believe her? Despite her being out of hospital nearly a month, the ripple effects from Suzie's accident continued relentlessly. Nora settled down to work on a Get Well card and prayed that Suzie would get better too.

Jess wandered around her small flat, too preoccupied to focus on the eight-hundred-word article she should be writing on the issue of vending machines in schools. She had been giving her mother a wide birth, not that it seemed Suzie wanted anything to do with her, either. Jess felt relieved. Mum was so hard to be around right now and she knew her sister felt the same. Her phone gave a toot and she groaned when she read the message from Louis.

See you at six in Vaughans?

So he was back. She sighed at the thought of confronting him but what choice did she have? Jess typed a reply.

Fine

Louis had never been one for long or elaborate texts and now she knew why. If his wife happened to read this she would probably believe him if he said he was meeting a colleague.

Jess had gone over and over in her head what she would say. Sometimes she felt like punching Louis for leading her on. Others, she was overcome with sadness that this man she'd thought she was falling for turned out to be a lying rat. She seemed to have a knack for collecting bad guys. Ed, her last boyfriend, had actually come on to Katie one night when Jess was away. Her friend had told him in no uncertain terms where to go, before telling Jess about her cheating boyfriend. Jess sometimes felt there was a neon sign over her head saying GULLIBLE FOOL.

The pub Louis had suggested was off the beaten track, where, hopefully, they wouldn't meet anyone they knew. Despite her threats, Jess knew that her mother wouldn't tell Louis's wife, no matter how much she disapproved. She hadn't been completely honest with her mother. She'd found out quite soon that Louis was married but he'd assured her that he was only still with his wife for the sake of the kids. If it all came out, perhaps it would force Louis's hand. Maybe he'd leave his wife. Oh, who was she kidding? They'd only known each other a few months and he'd made no declarations of love or talked about a future together. But when he'd held her in his arms, murmuring how he couldn't get enough of her, she'd allowed herself to believe they had a future and it was more than just a fling.

Jess sat in the corner of the bar, keeping an eye on the door and glancing at her watch. He was an hour late — an hour, and not a word. She'd tried to call him but it went straight to voicemail and she was afraid to leave a message. Something must have happened. Perhaps one of the kids was sick; maybe he'd been in a car accident. And then, just as she was really starting to worry, he walked in.

"Hey, babe." He slid in beside her and kissed her neck.

"Where were you?"

"The boss invited us for drinks."

"Drinks?" She blinked. "And you couldn't call?"

"Don't be mad, darling." He put his hand on her thigh and nuzzled her neck.

Jess steeled herself to resist him and moved away, fixing him with a glare. "Where do you tell Maeve you are when you're with me?"

His smile disappeared. "Let me worry about Maeve. I have it all under control."

"Exactly what have you got under control? Are you going to separate?"

"No, I told you. We agreed to stay together until the children were older. Surely you can understand that?"

Jess toughened herself against his reproachful look. "So you have separate lives, sleep in separate beds?"

"We have an understanding."

"What kind of understanding?"

"It's you that I'm interested in, Jess, that's all you need to know." He smiled, stroking her arm.

Jess pulled away, grabbed her bag and stood up. "And what you need to know, Louis, is that it's over." She walked away, not giving him a chance to reply, and was surprised and, admittedly, disappointed when he didn't follow her.

As she drove home, Jess fought back tears, telling herself she was doing the right thing. What kind of a man behaved like that? How could he make love to her and then go home to his wife and maybe even make love to her too? She felt a wave of nausea at the thought and wondered, What now? Would Louis move on or would he try to woo her back? And, if he did, would she be strong enough to say no?

Jess wasn't the only one having man trouble. Mandy opened one eye and glared at Jeff, whose snores were becoming progressively louder. He had turned out to be yet another disappointment. So suave, sexy and rich, he had told her all about his high-powered job that took him all over the world, dropping names of the politicians and famous people he hung out with and describing the Porsche he had on order; the Ford he'd driven her home in was just a rental. Once he was asleep and she'd had a chance to glance through his wallet, she found that, rather than being VP of the company, he was a salesman, and a tiny photo tucked in the back showed a smiling woman and two surly-looking teenagers, confirming she'd been taken for a ride. Granted, the sex had been good, but not *that* good. Mandy, unlike her niece, was not interested in a man with ties. She wanted one who was free to spend his money on her and her alone.

She was starting to doubt that she would ever find him. Her thoughts, inevitably, turned to the only man who had ever held her attention completely for the duration of their relationship, and he hadn't even been rich. He had talked about them building a new life together and she believed he'd meant it. Certainly, no one had made her feel the way he had, not that she really gave them a chance. He had ruined her for anyone else. She didn't need or want love now. She just needed a relatively affluent, single or widowed lover who would take care of her. That wasn't much to ask for, was it? She was willing to play the part of the adoring girlfriend. Nothing in life was free, after all.

An even louder snore prompted her to give the man beside her a sharp prod. "Time to go, lover boy. I have an appointment."

"Can I see you again, darling?" he said as he was leaving.

She gave him a wide smile. "I'll call you."

After he'd gone, Mandy flopped back on to the bed and retrieved her laptop from underneath it to check her emails. There was one from her boss.

Flying in at 3.45. Pick me up in the usual spot. D.

"You could say please," she muttered. Still, it would be nice to have Douglas back. She missed the banter. When she applied for the job as personal assistant to a travel writer she'd imagined herself seeing the world, staying in glamorous hotels and mixing with clever, witty people. But, except for his trips to London to meet with his publisher, Douglas Thornton rarely went anywhere. As for her accompanying him, two years in the job and she'd never got further than Dublin airport. Nor did he entertain. His infrequent visitors were taken

72

for a pub lunch and he'd return home alone. He had a cool, indifferent manner that Mandy figured was a deliberate ploy to keep people at a distance. She'd had a good look around for signs of a wife and kids but had come up with zilch. She was reasonably sure he was straight but there was no woman on the scene and he showed no interest in Mandy, which was an entirely new experience for her. Any man with a pulse usually gave her the eye.

Despite Douglas's peculiarities, though, he had a dry humour she enjoyed and it was actually relaxing not having to fend off male attention for a change.

In the past, Mandy had tired of most jobs within six months or had to leave because she'd got involved with a colleague and it became awkward once she tired of them, as she always did.

Douglas was different, though. He fascinated and frustrated her in equal measures and, in doing so, managed to achieve what only one man had before: he held her interest. They'd fallen into an easy relationship and rubbed along quite well together, their conversation peppered with teasing and sparring.

"How can you write travel books if you don't travel?" she'd asked one day over lunch in the kitchen.

"I assure you, I've visited all these places."

"Yeah, years ago, but places change. You need to keep up."

Douglas had shaken his head and given her a patronising smile. "They're not holiday brochures, Amanda. They're a description of a country, its culture and its people, and those things rarely change." He'd

73

tapped the manuscript between them. "Don't you ever read what you type?"

"I try not to," she quipped. "I'm sorry but it all sounds a bit pretentious to me. It's like people who rant on about a painting of a triangle that costs millions, arguing about what it's trying to 'say' to us. I'll tell you what it's saying. The so-called artist is laughing all the way to the bank."

He'd laughed, really laughed, at that, and she'd caught a glimpse of the man he could be, perhaps once was.

"I won't argue with you. I've had to listen to my fair share of so-called authorities on art over the years and wanted to punch them for being so damn pompous and boring."

She'd nodded in agreement. "And don't you just hate people who go on about wine and the different scents and flavours and which year was best? I bet most of them wouldn't be able to tell the difference between a bottle that cost a thousand and a tenner."

Douglas had pulled a face at that. "I was probably among them at one stage in my life," he'd admitted.

Mandy sensed that her boss was going to open up about his past and sat forward, eager to learn more. "Tell me more."

He'd glanced at his watch and stood up. "Some other time. I've got work to do."

And she had got no further information about him.

Mandy knew Douglas was in his late sixties but he didn't look or behave like a man of that age, despite the

74

baggy cords and ancient check shirts. He had probably been quite a catch twenty years ago. He had lovely blue eyes, a deep laugh and good teeth, too. There was definitely life in the old dog yet. She wondered what or who had turned him into a hermit.

Maybe she should take him in hand. She'd given Suzie a makeover; there was no reason why she couldn't do the same for Douglas. She'd be a little more restrained, though. Mandy chuckled as she thought of some of the outfits she'd persuaded her sister to buy. She would need to be much more circumspect with Douglas. Yes, organising her boss's wardrobe would be a hell of a lot more exciting than typing his manuscripts, and she'd welcome the challenge. Mandy complained about how boring her job was, but she was well aware that she had a very cushy number. Once she got the work done, Douglas didn't mind her reading or shopping online as long as she answered the phone, checked his email and kept the coffee pot full. The only downside, although she secretly enjoyed it, was that she had to tolerate his scathing commentary on her active love life.

"What age group do you target, eighteen to eighty?" he'd ask.

"Why, are you applying?" she'd retort.

After she'd blown off one guy, he'd texted incessantly, begging her to give them another chance, proclaiming he loved her. Finally, Douglas had snatched up the vibrating phone and read the texts.

"Sounds like he's desperate to see you." He raised an eyebrow at one particular text. "*All* of you."

She'd grabbed it back. "He's a pest who can't take the hint that we're done." With that her phone started to ring and she groaned. "Not again."

Douglas took it from her. "Hello? No, I'm afraid she's in the shower. This is her husband, can I help? Hello? Hello?" He grinned at her. "That's odd. He hung up."

After that he'd quizzed her regularly, seemingly fascinated as to why she was so fickle and couldn't settle with one guy. Mandy deflected the questions with flippant remarks. "I'm set it my ways and I've no interest in becoming the good little wife at home, ironing shirts and cooking. I want to live, not exist."

"So, basically, you just want a wallet on legs."

"Legs aren't mandatory," she'd shot back and walked out of the room, his chuckles following her.

Mandy pulled into the drop zone outside Dublin airport, pretending she didn't see the parking attendant's gestures, and watched Douglas stride through the doors and climb in next to her. Giving the approaching attendant a cheeky wave, Mandy pulled out.

"You're pushing your luck, Amanda," Douglas warned. "That guy will be waiting for you next time. He's probably given your registration to all his mates."

"No worries. I'll wear a low-cut top in future, job done."

"You have no shame."

He actually sounded critical and, when she glanced at him, she saw a weary resignation. She was surprised to find that his obvious disappointment in her hurt.

"How's your sister?"

"Suzie? She's doing really well. We're planning a trip to New York."

He glanced over, eyebrows raised. "I didn't think you were close."

"Why do you say that?" She frowned. This man was far too perceptive. She needed to be more careful.

"Oh, comments like 'she's more like my mother than my sister', 'old before her time' and 'too good to be true' spring to mind."

"All true, believe me. We're very different," she said, forcing a laugh. "But she's more chilled since she woke up, and we've become quite close."

"Hmm."

She glared across at him. He was really beginning to piss her off. "What does that mean?"

"Nothing."

She fumed inwardly, knowing that he had made some kind of judgement call and she had come out wanting, yet again. It was infuriating but she knew from experience that there was no point in badgering him. He had a habit of making cryptic comments but would never be drawn into further discussion or argument. She went to overtake the car in front, crashing the gears.

"Everything okay, Amanda?" he asked calmly.

"Everything's just hunky-dory, thanks, Douglas," she said through gritted teeth, tightening her grip on the wheel and imagining it was his neck.

CHAPTER
EIGHT

Suzie studied her to-do list with a critical eye. Salsa classes, choir, meditation, book club, travel. It was pathetic and she'd accomplished only two. Jess hadn't asked any more about the dancing and Suzie had left it at that. Despite the fact that her daughter protested her innocence over the Louis affair, Suzie was still furious. Even if she believed the man was separated, why would her beautiful girl put so little value on herself that she'd settle for the likes of him? How could she care for a man who said he would walk away from his wife and kiddies? It was just as well she was doing meditation, Suzie thought. She needed something to keep her from throttling Jess.

The first book club session that she and Aileen attended had been a good laugh. Well, except for the feckin' snobs who only wanted to read highbrow fiction. As if that was going to happen! It really annoyed her that the romantic, comic and mystery novels that she adored were looked down on. There were some sniffs of disapproval and a few eye rolls when she said her piece but, most of the others had sighed with relief or nodded in agreement and she and Aileen had enjoyed a laugh and made some new friends.

Suzie had also sent off her passport for renewal and called the consultant about getting a note saying she was fit to travel. Out of the question, his secretary told her. The consultant wouldn't do that without seeing her first. Bloody red tape.

Mandy had told her about a couple of hotels in New York that would be perfect bases for sightseeing and shopping, telling her to have a look at them online. Suzie had nearly passed out when she saw the price of the rooms. Still, this was a special trip to celebrate her return to the land of the living, so why not push the boat out? Lord knows she'd spent precious little on herself over the years.

"Cooee! Anybody home?"

"Come on over, Aileen," she called.

The woman climbed over Suzie's hydrangeas and walked into the kitchen, smiling. "All set?"

"Yes." Suzie stood up and reached for her jacket. "I can't wait."

"Now, don't get carried away," Aileen warned. "This is a huge decision. You want to make very sure that you're doing the right thing. Would you not get young Noel to come along?"

"No, he's still asleep. The poor lad is worn out with all this bloody studying."

Aileen frowned, obviously not happy. "What about Jess?"

Suzie snorted. Jess was the last person whose opinion she wanted at the moment. "What's it to do with her? It will be my dog, I'll be the one feeding, walking and cleaning up the shite."

"Ah, you're an awful woman," Aileen chuckled. "Come on then, let's go."

The dog rescue centre was on the far side of Dublin, and Aileen told her the procedure as she drove. "If you find a dog you like, then you talk to an adoption consultant to find about their background and temperament and whether you're a good match or not. If you still want to go ahead, the dog should really meet the rest of the family —"

"What? Why?" Suzie looked at her, baffled.

"They want to make sure that it's going to be happy and well treated. And, if that goes well, they'll arrange to visit to make sure that you have the space he or she needs."

"Crikey, you would think it was a child, not a feckin' dog!"

"They have to be careful, Suzie. So many people buy or adopt a dog or puppy and then realise they can't cope with them or simply get fed up with the hassle and mess."

Suzie hadn't really thought about any of this. Perhaps she was taking on too much. "But you haven't had problems with Hector, have you? He's a good little dog."

Aileen laughed. "He was murder for the first few weeks. He howled all the time. I couldn't leave him alone and, when I'd get up in the morning, there would be poo and wee all over the place. It's like having a new

80

baby, Suzie, and they're nearly a year old before they really start to behave."

Suzie's heart sank. She wasn't sure that she could handle that. She had lots of plans and spending a year cleaning up after a mutt wasn't among them. "Perhaps this isn't such a good idea after all."

Aileen pulled into a parking spot and switched off the engine. "Well, we're here now. Still want to go in and have a look or will we go for a coffee?"

"Ah, sure, I suppose there's no harm in looking."

Minutes later she was drooling over one puppy after the next, her worries forgotten when she looked at the cute little bundles of fluff. As luck would have it, there weren't many people visiting and an adoption consultant soon approached them.

"I'm Mary. Can I help you?"

"I'm not sure what I want," Suzie confessed.

"No problem. Why don't we have a walkabout and you can meet the gang?"

"That would be great, thanks." She and Aileen followed the girl around and when Suzie pointed to any she liked, Mary told her about the dog's background, how big it was likely to grow and the exercise and care it would need. "Oh, look!" Suzie fell to her knees in front of a cage with greyhound puppies.

"Oh, please, Suzie." Aileen rolled her eyes. "They may be small and cute now but once they grow to full size it would be a full-time job exercising one. And you need to look after yourself. You're still recovering, remember?"

"Recovering?" Mary frowned.

Suzie pulled a face. "I had a little accident."

Aileen snorted. "She had a head injury and was in a coma for two months," she said, ignoring Suzie's glower. "She's only been home a few weeks."

"Nearly two months and I'm fine, and will you please stop telling everyone my business?" Suzie snapped.

"Sorry," Aileen said, but didn't look it.

"It is an important factor," the girl said with a kind smile.

"But I'm right as rain," Suzie protested.

Aileen's eyes widened expressively and Mary looked from one to the other. Suzie sighed. "Honestly, I'm grand."

"Good, but your friend was right to tell me," Mary said calmly. "It will help us find you the perfect match. But I have to tell you that having a boisterous puppy around tests most people's temper and they're a lot of work if you still tire easily."

"She does," Aileen said, jumping in again. "She needs at least one nap every day."

"Will you shut up, Aileen. I can speak for myself."

But Aileen wasn't cowed by Suzie's rebuke at all. "I told you, if you want the right pet, you have to be honest, with yourself as much as everyone else."

Mary nodded in agreement. "Will there be anyone to help you with the dog?"

"My son lives with me."

"But he's studying for his finals and has a part-time job," Aileen interrupted again, ignoring the daggers Suzie was shooting at her.

82

"I have two daughters who are always in and out."

"Any grandchildren?"

Suzie groaned at the thought of Bobby. "Yes, one. I'd probably have to lock up the dog when he visits."

The girl tickled the greyhound's tummy and then straightened, frowning. "I don't think a puppy is such a good idea."

"But I want a dog," Suzie wailed, even though she'd walked into the centre full of doubt.

"Come with me." Mary led them down to an office at the back of the kennels. "Forgive the mess," she said, gesturing to the papers covering her desk and chairs. A large golden retriever stood up and wagged his tail. "I thought you should meet Percy."

"Oh, isn't he lovely?" Aileen gushed, bending over the beautiful dog to pat him.

Suzie smiled. "Aw, he's gorgeous. Is he yours?"

"No. Percy is an assistance dog. He belongs to a lovely lady who's in hospital at the moment so he's spending some time with us."

Suzie looked at her, frowning. "An assistance dog?"

"Yes. He's been trained especially to aid people with disabilities, physical and mental," Mary explained. "He's incredibly gentle and obedient and wonderful with children, even the difficult ones."

"Really?" Suzie's ears pricked up.

Mary nodded. "Oh, yes. Dogs have a very calming effect and it's great to watch a relationship develop between a child and his dog."

Suzie crouched down and scratched behind his ear. "Hey, Percy."

Wagging his tail, he nuzzled her hand in acknowledgement.

"Want to see some of his tricks?" Mary grinned. "Percy? Door."

The dog went over and closed the door with his snout.

Aileen clapped her hands, laughing. "Aw, isn't he clever?"

Suzie watched in delight as the dog did anything Mary asked, before, on her gentle command, returning to his bed by her chair. "He is special, isn't he?"

"I think so." Mary smiled.

"But why are you showing him to me?"

"Everyone always wants a cute little puppy," Mary explained, "but sometimes an adult, well-trained dog can be a much better option."

"Mary has a point," Aileen said. "And, if you're heading off to New York for a fortnight, where would you leave a puppy?"

Suzie sighed. "I hadn't even thought of that."

Mary gave her a kind smile. "Why don't you take some time and have a think about it? We're not going anywhere and, sadly, there are always plenty of dogs who need a good home."

Suzie patted Percy one last time. "Thanks, Mary, I'll do that."

"Disappointed?" Aileen asked as they drove home.

"A little, but relieved, too. And," she added grudgingly, "thanks for reining me in. Taking a puppy would have been a huge mistake, no matter how cute. I'd have taken Percy on the spot, though."

"He was gorgeous, wasn't he?" Aileen sighed. "You'd certainly feel safe with him in the house."

Suzie nodded. "And there was something very solid and peaceful about him, wasn't there? I'll read up on golden retrievers and have a think."

"And you should discuss it with the family."

Suzie's phone buzzed. It was a text from Sharon.

Hey, Mum. Sorry to ask but can you look after Bobby for a couple of hours?

"Ah, for Christ's sake!" she said crossly.

Aileen looked over at her. "What?"

"I have to mind Bobby."

"When?"

"Now."

Aileen tutted her disapproval. "Will I drop you over there?"

"Oh, no, Sharon's dropping him over to me. That way her house stays nice and tidy and the brat wrecks my place instead," Suzie said bitterly.

"If you're not up to having him, say so," Aileen said, looking cross. "It's a bit of a liberty when you're only just getting back on your feet."

"I've refused a couple of times already," Suzie admitted, "and Sharon's been driving me anywhere I need to go, so I owe her one." Still, Suzie was annoyed that she would have to spend the afternoon dealing with the child. "I wouldn't mind only Sharon lets him get away with murder and she's so bloody touchy, I'm afraid to say a word against the little fecker."

Aileen laughed. "Now that I don't believe."

"I'm telling you, you'd need the patience of a saint to put up with him." Suzie saw Aileen looking at her in surprise. "Yes, I know. I've been told how I used to dote on him but, I've changed."

"Don't I know it!"

"Be honest with me, Aileen. How much?"

Aileen gave a long sigh before responding. "You were a pain in the arse, Suzie. You were a great mother with endless patience and you made me feel like a lousy one."

Suzie absorbed this in silence. It explained why her family were always whispering in corners and looking at her as if she were from another planet. They must be in shock.

"Then Bobby came along," Aileen continued, "and you were besotted, regularly taking him for the weekend so that Sharon and Keith could get a break."

"I never did!" Suzie was stunned. She could barely tolerate the child for an hour these days. How had she coped with him for an entire weekend?

Aileen nodded. "You did. And it wasn't easy. Even I could hear his carry on morning and night, and you trying to calm him down. You used to promise him surprises and treats if he behaved."

"Jesus! I was as bad as Sharon."

"Worse." Aileen glanced over at her, looking guilty. "Sorry, but you did ask."

Suzie wasn't sure that she wanted to hear more, but she knew she had to. "And the rest of the family?"

"What?"

"Was I different with them too?"

Aileen sighed. "You couldn't do enough for them. When Jess moved out, you cooked and froze dinners for her to take home for the week."

Suzie groaned. Instead of empowering her children, she'd made them completely dependent on her. "Go on," she whispered.

"Suzie —"

"Please, Aileen."

"You gave her the money to buy her car and paid her college fees."

That didn't surprise Suzie. She wasn't short of money and she'd spent her life trying to make up for how John had treated her elder daughter. She frowned. Now where had that come from?

Aileen smiled. "In fairness, she's a good daughter and was distraught when you had the accident. She never missed a day visiting you and she'd always call or drop in to me, to let me know how you were doing."

"I sensed her presence at times," Suzie said, feeling guilty at how tough she'd been on Jess since seeing her with Louis.

"I've been a bit too honest, haven't I?" Aileen said, looking upset.

"No at all. I needed to hear that. I knew my memory was dodgy but I didn't realise how much."

"It will probably come back in time." Aileen patted her hand.

Suzie wasn't so sure. "I'm going to have lots more questions, Aileen, but they can wait for another day. I'm tired now."

Aileen pulled into her driveway and turned in her seat. "I'm not going anywhere and I'll tell you anything you want to know."

"Truly?"

"Promise. I thank God for the day you moved in next door. You got me through my divorce; now it's my turn to help you."

Suzie hugged her. "Thank you."

"Sorry we didn't find your puppy."

"Ah, but we got to meet Percy!"

"True enough." Aileen laughed. "Go and rest, Suzie, before Bobby comes over."

Once in the front door, Suzie paused to listen for sounds of her son, but all was quiet. Stretching out on her bed, she mulled over what Aileen had said. She was particularly upset about Sharon. She had been criticising her daughter for ruining Bobby when it seemed she was equally responsible. And Aileen said she was a great mother? She snorted in disgust. It sounded as if she had continued to treat her family like children, mollycoddling them like some unpaid housekeeper and childminder. Had Jess become a doormat for that swine, Louis Healy, because that was the example Suzie had set? She hadn't got around to discussing Noel, although she doubted her neighbour would have anything to say about her only son. He was a good lad who'd never given her a day's trouble and was growing into a fine young man.

Suzie wondered who, other than Aileen, would be totally honest with her. There was her sister, of course, she was a straight talker, but something held Suzie back from confiding in her. Then she remembered Nora.

"Jesus!" Suzie shook her head, incredulous. She'd been so busy reinventing herself and working on her bloody list, she hadn't returned her old friend's calls. She'd phone her first thing tomorrow and arrange to meet, she decided. Perhaps Nora could come and stay for a couple of days. They used to do that, at least Suzie thought they had. She knew for a fact that she hadn't gone to Limerick. She hadn't set foot in the county since the day she'd moved back to Dublin and didn't plan to. Nora had come to her. She was a kind woman and a good friend and Suzie realised that she had practically abandoned her. She had some fences to mend but, despite her lousy memory, Suzie's gut told her that Nora would forgive her.

CHAPTER
NINE

Nora lit up when her phone rang and Suzie's voice filled the car.

"Nora? It's Suzie."

"Hey, you, this is a nice surprise."

"Really?" Suzie sounded doubtful. "Sorry I haven't been in touch. I wouldn't blame you if you hung up."

"I am going to hang up," Nora said, smiling as she overtook the lorry in front.

"You are?" Suzie sounded like a lost child and Nora was delighted that she'd obeyed her instincts.

"Yes, because you need to get ready."

"For?"

"I'm about an hour from Dublin so get your gladrags on. I'm taking you to lunch."

When Nora pulled up outside Suzie's house, the door was flung open and Suzie came out with open arms and a wide smile. "It's so good to see you."

Nora clung to her, feeling quite emotional. "You too." She stepped back and smiled. "How are you feeling?"

Suzie frowned. "Not great."

Nora studied her and was frightened when she saw the anxiety in Suzie's eyes. "What is it? Are you getting headaches, dizzy spells?" The doctors had given them a list of symptoms to watch out for.

"No, nothing like that. I'll tell you when I've a glass in my hand."

"Fair enough. Shall we just wander down to the Italian on the seafront or do you fancy going further afield?"

Suzie shook her head. "No, it's a nice day. Let's make the most of it and walk."

Nora raved about Suzie's hair and told her she looked well but decided it was best not to comment on the tight, low-cut dress she was wearing. Obviously Mandy's choice, she thought grimly. When they reached the restaurant she continued to make small talk until they'd ordered and the wine had arrived before pursuing the conversation.

"So, tell me what's on your mind."

Suzie took a long drink. "I had a frank conversation with Aileen, yesterday. She was telling me what I used to be like before the accident."

"Oh?" Nora decided to listen to exactly what had been said before commenting. Aileen was a good sort and had been kind to Suzie but she wasn't one to pull her punches.

"I've made a right fucking mess of things." Suzie looked miserable.

"I don't follow."

"She told me how I always used to fuss over Bobby, spoiling him. That I'm partly responsible for turning him into the little demon I'm now complaining about."

"I'm not sure I'd go that far," Nora said, although it was true that, before the accident, Bobby had been the apple of Suzie's eye.

"I would," Suzie retorted, annoyed. "Then there's Jess. I've made her totally dependent on me. It's probably my fault that she ended up having an affair with a married man."

Nora stared at her. "Jess is having an affair?"

"Not any more, she isn't. I warned her to end it. Screwing one of her editors and, of course, it had to be the one from the local paper. I know him, and his wife. They have three little kids. Jess claims she thought that he was separated."

"I'm sure that's true, Suzie. Jess would never knowingly get involved with a married man."

Doubt clouded Suzie's eyes. "Maybe. Sometimes I want to scream at her and others I want to hold her and say I'm sorry. The thing is, I don't remember much of what happened before the accident. I can't believe that I wouldn't have known if she was involved with someone. We were always so close. Sometimes I'm not sure if I'm remembering or imagining things."

"That must be scary." Nora's heart went out to her. For all Suzie's assertiveness, underneath she was obviously uneasy.

"There are so many gaps in my memory, Nora. I only remembered yesterday that you stayed over at least once a month. How could I forget that? We had some great nights."

"We did." Nora smiled.

"Can we do that again?"

"Of course," Nora said, delighted, while wondering exactly how much invisible damage had been done to Suzie in the accident. "You should talk to Jess, Suzie, clear the air. Don't be cross with her, give her the benefit of the doubt. I imagine she's gutted that you've fallen out. She adores you and nearly went out of her mind with worry when you were ill."

"I know that. I suppose I'm more cross with myself than I am with her. I should have seen what was going on. I thought she could talk to me about anything. Why didn't she tell me about him?"

"Perhaps it started after the accident."

"Maybe," Suzie said but didn't look convinced.

"As for your grandson, you raised three great kids and I'm sure that Bobby will grow into one, too. Wasn't Noel a bit of a handful around the same age?"

Suzie brightened and she nodded. "Yes. He was a right little terror for a year or so. I'd forgotten that."

"You see? Bobby didn't lick it off a stone." Nora laughed and sat back as their food arrived.

She wondered how best to handle this woman, who, one minute, was blaming herself for everything and, the next, was spoiling for a row. "He's the first grandchild and you're the only grandparent he has. It would be weird if you hadn't spoiled him."

Suzie seemed to consider this as she reached for her glass. "That's true, but he's not a baby anymore. It's time he learned some manners."

"He's not your problem," Nora told her. "Imagine if your mother had muscled in on disciplining your three. You'd have been furious."

Suzie sighed, obviously frustrated. "Then I'll just have to be more honest with Sharon and I won't put up with any nonsense when he's in my house."

Nora suppressed a sigh. The changes in Suzie's personality were complex. She seemed to be beyond not only listening to reason but understanding it. "I think that you might be better trying to work with Sharon on this one. The more you criticise her, the more defensive she'll become and, frankly, Suzie, she may just stop coming round at all."

"Good! I plan to live my own life now. They can all do what they want."

Oh, Lord. This wasn't going well at all. Nora looked longingly at her wine but raised a hand and asked the waiter for some water.

"Stay over," Suzie said. "Please?"

Nora smiled and nodded. She took a sip of wine as she searched for inspiration on how to get through to her friend. Finally she looked Suzie straight in the eye. "Let me play devil's advocate for a minute. Come on, hear me out," she said as Suzie rolled her eyes. "You listened to Aileen."

"Go on, then," Suzie muttered, tucking into her lasagne.

94

"Look at this from the kids' point of view, bearing in mind what Aileen already told you. She said, and I agree, you lived for the family, always putting them before yourself. That may not always have been a good thing but, nevertheless, that's what they were used to — your fault, not theirs."

"More fool me." Suzie scowled.

Nora carried on regardless. "Then, wham, you have an accident. Those first couple of days, it didn't look like you were going to make it. Imagine how they must have felt, Suzie. Not only were they bracing themselves to become orphans, they were losing a fantastic, loving mother. Imagine their grief."

Suzie put down her fork and reached for her wine but said nothing.

Nora prayed that she was getting through and not making matters worse. She ploughed on.

"It was almost worse when you didn't die. Forgive me, I don't mean we wished you dead but, every moment of every day that your kids weren't by your bedside, they were waiting for that call. And they lived like that for two months, Suzie. Two months! Can you imagine what that must have been like?"

Suzie said nothing, just stared into her drink.

"I can't begin to describe their joy and excitement when you woke up. I drove straight up from Limerick when Jess phoned, and went directly to the hospital. Her expression." Nora shook her head, smiling. "It was like a child's on Christmas morning. Sharon was weeping one moment and laughing the next. And

Noel." Nora sighed, drawing Suzie's eyes to hers. "He cried in my arms like a baby."

Tears filled Suzie's eyes, but Nora wasn't finished. "As far as everyone was concerned it was party time. But they were anxious, too, treating you like a piece of delicate china and watching you like hawks when you fell asleep, checking that you were still breathing. When you came home they were nervous wrecks, especially Noel, as he was living with you."

"Noel doesn't let anything rattle him," Suzie assured her.

"He may play the clown, but, trust me, he worries about you just as much as the girls do. As the days rolled by, they began to notice more and more, the changes in you. The girls were a bit shocked and embarrassed by your colourful language but Noel thought it was funny. He didn't really take on board that the changes in your personality ran deeper than simply swearing."

"They don't." Suzie finally found her voice, her face flushed and angry. "I'm fine and getting better every day."

Nora felt dreadful doing this to her friend but, now that she'd started, she had to finish it, even if Suzie wanted no more to do with her afterwards. "Physically, maybe, but emotionally you're totally unpredictable. You're making hasty decisions and constantly lashing out at the girls without any thought of the hurt you're causing. Once they had a loving mother and best friend; now they're trying to deal with an angry woman who criticises them and blows a fuse at the slightest thing. I'm sorry, but there's no nice way of saying it, Suzie: you're hard to live with. But — and it's very important that you hear this — it's not your fault." Nora felt herself begin to tear up now and she reached for Suzie's hand. "It's all down to that bloody fall. The thing is, that doesn't make it any easier for your kids. You may have been the one to take the fall, Suzie, but they're victims of that dreadful accident as much as you are."

At this stage, Nora expected Suzie to tell her to fuck off and walk out, but instead she sat there in silence, which was almost more alarming. "Suzie?" The pain in her friend's eyes when they met Nora's tore at her heart. "I'm sorry. I've probably said too much. But it's hard standing on the side-line and watching your family go through this."

"There must be something I can do," Suzie said looking shell-shocked.

"I'm not sure that there is right now but, with time, you'll probably make a complete recovery."

"Don't." Suzie put up her hand and Nora fell silent, realising that it was too late to try to cheer her up after all that she'd said. God, what had she done?

"They'd have been better off if I'd died."

"Don't say that."

Suzie carried on, staring into space. "It's true. They'd have been able to mourn and then move on. Instead I'm making them hate me. I'm going to drive them away and there's not a damn thing that I can do about it."

Feeling sick, Nora decided to try giving Suzie a taste of her own medicine. She topped up their glasses. "That's a very melodramatic and pessimistic attitude. Cop on and have a drink. I'm sure there's plenty you can do. There must be support groups for people with TBIs — traumatic brain injuries," she added when Suzie looked blank.

"Jess mentioned one a couple of weeks ago. I thought that she was suggesting it to make me feel better, but she wasn't thinking of me at all, was she?"

"She's your eldest, Suzie; she knows you well and was the first to pick up on how your personality had changed. I'm sure that she thinks that talking to other people in your situation would be as beneficial to you as the family."

"I have these dreams," Suzie declared.

Nora frowned at the sudden change of subject. "Oh?"

"Nightmares, really. At least I think they are. I'm never sure if that's all they are or if they're memories of bad times."

Feeling on decidedly dodgy ground, Nora shrugged. "I think we all have them." At least Suzie was having this conversation with her and not the dreaded Mandy. It occurred to her that Suzie's little sister might be planting ideas in her head. Nora would put nothing past that manipulative bitch. She considered warning Suzie about her sister, then decided against it. She'd let Suzie come to her own conclusions as time went on. Hopefully it wouldn't take long for her to remember what Mandy was really like.

"So, am I still welcome to stay the night or do you want me to feck off back to Limerick?" She said it with a smile but watched Suzie, anxious that she'd lost a friend.

"Stay." Suzie took her hand, her grip so firm it hurt. "And, as I said to Aileen, please never stop giving it to me straight. Promise?"

Nora swallowed the lump in her throat and nodded. "Promise. So, what now?"

Suzie thought about that for a second. "I suppose I should check out these groups, maybe go along and talk to other weirdos."

Nora smiled. "You're not a weirdo, you're injured; the walking wounded, I suppose. Ask Jess, I think you'll find that she has the name and number of every organisation in the country."

"I was horrible to her about seeing that man, Nora, but the thing is, I can't guarantee I'll be any nicer to her the next time I see her. I get so angry, and afterwards I feel exhausted. Then I spend the night either lying awake replaying the row, or fall asleep and have these fucking nightmares."

"So, explain that to her, to the three of them. The more that they understand what's going on in your head, the less chance there is of them feeling hurt when you lash out."

"The priority has to be Bobby. I need to help Sharon sort that child out."

Nora sighed, feeling as if her long, heartfelt speech had been a waste of time. Would Suzie even remember what she'd said tomorrow? "No, Suzie, that's his parents' job. Your priority is to get better for the sake of all the family."

"I don't fancy sitting in a circle and sharing." Suzie stuck her lip out like a stubborn child.

"Wouldn't it be worth it if it meant giving your kids back their mum?"

Suzie gave a heavy sigh. "I suppose, given that I survived, I owe it to them to try."

"So, you'll do it?" Nora persisted.

"Fine. Yes, I'll do it," Suzie said, scowling.

"Good for you." Nora smiled and crossed her fingers.

CHAPTER
TEN

Suzie was just putting on a wash when her mobile phone rang. She scanned the kitchen, trying to figure out where the ringing was coming from. "For fuck's sake!" she muttered, finally locating it in the pocket of the jacket she'd left on the back of a chair. "Hello?"

"Mrs Connors?"

"Yes?"

"Hi. My name is Mary. I'm calling from the DSPCA, the rescue centre."

"Oh, hello, Mary." Suzie smiled as she recalled her morning meeting all the lovely doggies. "How's Percy?"

Mary laughed. "Well, funny you should ask, he's the reason that I'm calling."

"Oh?" Suzie settled herself at the kitchen table to listen. Twenty minutes later she was banging on Aileen's back door. "Aileen? Aileen, are you there?" she shouted.

"I'm coming, I'm coming!" Her neighbour thumped down the stairs and threw it open, breathing heavily. "What is it, Suzie? What's wrong? Your feckin' house better be on fire after the fright you gave me."

"No, everything's grand. In fact, it's better than grand."

"Get in here and put on that kettle while I catch my breath. This better be good."

Suzie did as she was told and, as they were waiting for the kettle to boil, she turned to look at her friend, sitting at the table, chest heaving. "I just got a call from Mary at the rescue centre. Remember Percy, the assistance dog?"

Aileen smiled. "Aw, sure, who could forget that oul' pet? He was almost human. What about him?" Her eyes widened. "Ah, don't tell me he's died."

"Now how would that be good news? Of course he's not dead, but his owner is." Suzie carried two mugs of tea to the table.

"And that's good news? That bloody head injury has knocked every ounce of compassion out of you, do you know that? May she rest in peace."

"Amen." Suzie crossed herself. "But don't you see? It means Percy needs a new home. Mary remembered how fond I was of him and thought we would make a good match."

Aileen's eyes widened. "Are you going to take him? Really, Suzie?"

"I don't know, maybe. Mary's bringing him over tomorrow. We agreed that he could stay with me for a couple of weeks' trial and then I could decide whether I want to adopt him or not."

"That's a good idea but where will you put him?"

Suzie frowned. "I'm not sure. He's used to being indoors."

"You could put his bed in the porch by the back door, and, as he's so obedient, you'll probably be able to let him come and go the rest of the time. I'd keep him away from Bobby in case he's afraid of dogs."

Suzie grinned. "Ah, Aileen, who could be afraid of Percy? There's more chance of the poor dog being scared of that little demon. I need to make a list of stuff to buy. A bed and some toys. Oh, and food." She frowned at Mary. "Feck! I never asked what he eats."

"Why don't you put a list of questions together and phone Mary back? There's no point in spending a fortune if you decide you can't keep him," Aileen warned.

"Yes, that's a good idea, I'll do that." Suzie hopped up and headed for the door.

"What about your tea?"

"I don't have time for tea. I have to get ready!"

"I hope it works out for you," Aileen called after her, laughing.

Mandy dropped the phone with a curse. This was the fourth time her sister had blown her off when she tried to discuss their New York trip, this time muttering something about dog food. Mandy wasn't impressed. She'd been on Douglas's laptop all week checking out clubs and restaurants in New York that she wanted to try, and the shops that she wanted to take Suzie and her credit card to, but her sister had been quite abrupt and wouldn't even let her book the flights, muttering something about family and responsibilities. Perhaps her memory was returning, which would be really bloody annoying. And it had looked as if things were going Mandy's way. She sighed as she looked longingly at the image of the four-star hotel on the screen before her. She'd been meant for greater things, she deserved better. She'd lost out in love, so she felt entitled to make up for it with material comforts, and Suzie could easily afford it.

"Very nice."

Mandy jumped at Douglas's voice behind her. "Isn't it?"

He nodded at the screen. "Is that where you're staying?"

"We haven't decided yet," she demurred. He would just love it if she told him the holiday was in doubt. It would give him a great laugh altogether. "We're not sure of our dates yet. Suzie has to get the all-clear from her doctor."

"But it is definitely happening?"

"Of course, why wouldn't it?"

He shrugged, his expression all innocence. "No reason, other than you've been mooning and sighing over that website all morning."

She glared at him. "I'm going, Douglas. Nothing's going to stop me."

His eyes widened at her vehemence and she flashed him a smile to hide her anger. He was still her employer — well, for the moment. "Sorry, it's just that it's been so long since I visited the States and I adore New York."

"Really?" He blinked as if that made no sense to him at all. "Why?"

"Because it's exciting, it's happening and there are opportunities around every corner."

"And muggers."

"You are such a cynic. Surely you've written about New York, about Greenwich Village, the Chelsea Hotel, Brooklyn, Central Park?"

He laughed. "Oh, please. Did you even visit any of those landmarks? I bet you confined yourself to the shops, bars and the clubs."

Shit, he knew her too damn well. "And what's wrong with enjoying the good things in life?"

"You're missing out on so much, Amanda. Art, music, history." He reached for his jacket. "I'm going out. Lock up when you're leaving, would you?"

Mandy opened her mouth to ask where he was going but he was already halfway out of the door. Good riddance. If he could take the afternoon off, then she didn't see why she couldn't do the same. She'd check his email, set the answering service and go into town. To hell with Douglas Thornton and his smart mouth. She quickly scanned the emails and then pulled up short when she saw the last one from the Department of Tourism in Croatia. What the hell?

"Amanda? What are you still doing here?"

She jerked up from the sofa. She'd been reading her novel and dozed off. Not because of the story, but more to do with the amount of Douglas's wine she'd consumed. "You're back!"

He picked up the empty glass and raised an eyebrow. "And you're pissed."

"No! Well . . ." She blinked, trying to focus on one of him. "A little tipsy, maybe. But I was celebrating."

"Celebrating what, exactly?"

"You got an email from Croatia's Department of Tourism. They want to honour you for the piece that you wrote about them. Apparently, you've contributed hugely to their country being tipped as a top cultural and historical destination."

Douglas wrinkled his brow. "Which publication was that in?"

She shrugged. "No idea. Who cares? They're inviting you over to a special reception, all expenses paid."

He tossed his jacket in a chair. "Draft a letter of refusal for me to sign, would you?" He wandered into the kitchen and poured himself a glass from the second bottle of wine she'd opened.

"I don't think so." Sobered by his reaction, Amanda swung her feet off the sofa and followed him, glaring. "You're going."

His eyes widened, incredulous. "Excuse me?"

"No, actually, I don't excuse you. This is a great honour and if you refuse it you are being insulting and condescending."

"It isn't the big deal you think it is," he assured her. "I've been invited to awards ceremonies in several countries over the years, but there's no such thing as a free lunch or holiday. They'll take me to visit all the sights they want to promote and expect me to write about them."

"And what's wrong with that?" she demanded, feeling really cross now.

"Why are you so angry?" He looked bemused.

"Because you have so much and you don't appreciate it." She flung her hands out and spun

106

around, suddenly furious. "This gorgeous house, no money worries, the freedom to go anywhere you want, whenever you want to. You spend your life cooped up inside like a geriatric. Why don't you just move into a nursing home and have done with it?"

"Not a bad idea. I'll think about it," he said, his eyes crinkling up in amusement, but, when she continued to glare at him, he sank into a chair and looked at her. "Can't you just accept that I don't enjoy the same things in life that you do?"

"Sure I can, but sticking two fingers up at a country for appreciating you isn't very polite and, if nothing else, I thought that you had manners."

He stared at her, scratched his head and then gave a sigh of resignation. "Fine. I'll go."

She stared, unable to believe her ears. "Really?"

"Yeah. Why not?"

"Great." She jumped to her feet. "There's a lot to do and we don't have much time."

"Why, when is it?"

"Six weeks."

He laughed. "Trust me, Amanda, I can be ready for a trip in six hours."

Seriously? She stared at him and then shook her head. How could someone so intelligent be this dense? "May I be frank, Douglas?"

He laughed. "Have you ever been anything else? Go ahead. Say your piece."

"If I saw you on the street I'd think you were a homeless person." The laughter left his eyes and he opened his mouth, but she hurried on before he could say anything. "If I met you at night, I'd cross the road. Sure, if you spoke I'd know immediately that you're an educated man and, on close inspection, you're clean and don't smell. But the thing is, Douglas, I don't think many people would want to get close enough to find out. I'm not trying to be hurtful, by the way. I'm just giving it to you straight. I think that you've become so immersed in your writing, you've forgotten that, well, appearances matter."

He sat silent for a moment, seemingly lost in thought. She couldn't tell whether he was hurt or angry, but there was despondency in his eyes. Damn it, maybe she'd gone too far. She really wanted him to go to Croatia, not slip into depression. He had to because she was determined that she was going with him. She hadn't told him that the invitation extended to a companion; time enough for that. Best to take this one slowly, although, as the silence lengthened, she figured she'd blown it. She was on the point of backtracking when he started to speak, his voice low. He didn't look up at her, but stared out into the gardens. "You're right. Appearances do matter."

She couldn't believe her ears and clapped her hands in delight. "I'm glad you agree. It won't take much for me to bring you up to date." She saw scepticism in his eyes and scowled. Still, she already knew what he thought of her; she wouldn't dwell on it. With a bit of luck he'd look like a different man in a few days and they'd be on their way to a five-star hotel in Zagreb. She gave him what she hoped looked like a sincere smile. "Don't worry, I won't try to turn you into a male model. A cool, college-professor image is what we're after. No suits, just a couple of tailored jackets, good jeans, and some nice shirts. Oh, and —" she looked down with distaste at his ancient, scuffed boots — "shoes. You need some proper shoes."

"Fair enough," he said, looking like a sulky schoolboy.

"And a haircut and a shave, obviously."

"Obviously. I'm not spending days trekking round shops, Amanda," he warned.

"We can take care of it all in a couple of days," she said, giving him her sunniest smile, which made him look even more suspicious. "In fact we can get started first thing."

"Tomorrow?"

"Why not?"

"I have work to do," he protested.

"That's your best excuse? You forget I'm your assistant and happen to know that you are ahead of schedule." She stood up, slung her bag over her shoulder and gave him a triumphant smile. "See you in the morning, showered and wearing a white shirt and your black jeans — the ones that don't have a hole in them — and we'll get started."

The next morning she expected to have to pull him out of bed, but was surprised to find him showered, dressed and waiting for her, dressed in accordance with her instructions. Feeling triumphant, Mandy drove them into town in her little Mini, refusing point blank to get into his scruffy old Volvo, even though Douglas had to almost fold himself in two to fit into her car. She found a parking spot on Stephen's Green and tugged him towards Grafton Street. "First stop, the barber's."

"But I always go to the guy in the village," he protested.

"This time we need someone who doesn't use a rusty blade." She steered him into the opulent barbershop and, while he was looking around warily, she whispered instructions to the sharp-eyed proprietor. With an innocent smile, Mandy left him, saying she'd wait for him in the coffee shop across the road.

When he walked into the café forty minutes later, Mandy did a double-take. Gone was the matted fuzz from his face, revealing a surprisingly strong jaw. With his hair shorter and tidied up and eyebrows trimmed, Douglas looked years younger and quite attractive, in an aristocratic, elder-statesman sort of way. Blue shirts were definitely in order to make the most of those eyes, she thought, and began to feel quite excited about her new project. By the time she'd reinvented Douglas Thornton, she'd be quite proud to be seen out with him.

CHAPTER
ELEVEN

Aileen tapped on the back door. "Only me," she said, and walked in carrying a batch of scones fresh from the oven.

"Ooh, lovely, thanks." Suzie smiled at her neighbour's thoughtfulness and produced butter and jam.

"What time will he be here?" Aileen asked as she plastered butter on a scone and took a bite.

Suzie glanced at the clock. "Any minute. I'm a bit nervous now, to be honest."

"It will be grand. Remember, you can send him back if he's too much for you."

"I suppose." The doorbell rang and Suzie stared at Aileen. "That must be them!"

Aileen chuckled. "Well, don't just sit there, woman. Go and let them in."

Suzie threw open the front door. "Hi, Mary, good to see you. Where's Percy?"

The girl smiled. "Don't worry, he's in the van. I just wanted to make sure I was at the right house before I took him out."

Suzie followed her outside and her heart lifted when she caught sight of the handsome golden retriever. "Hello, Percy."

He panted and wagged his tail. Mary laughed and released him from his crate. "I think he remembers you."

Suzie crouched down to pet him. "He's so gorgeous. How old is he, Mary?"

"Almost five."

"The same age as my grandson."

"I'm sure they'll be great friends."

Maybe, but Suzie wasn't taking any chances. She wouldn't leave Bobby alone with Percy. God only knew what the kid would do to the poor animal. "Come on, Percy. There's someone else here who's looking forward to seeing you again." She took the lead from Mary, who followed with Percy's few belongings. In her little kitchen the dog looked enormous and she could only begin to imagine how her family would react when they saw him. Aileen immediately dropped to her knees and started to make a fuss of him.

"Hello, Percy."

"Mary, you remember Aileen?" Suzie said.

The two women said hello and Mary went to look out on the small garden.

"Have I enough space for him?" Suzie asked, watching her anxiously.

"Plenty, once you take him for a good, long walk every day."

"Oh, I will, don't worry." Suzie filled Percy's water bowl and set it down on the floor.

"Where will he sleep?" Mary asked.

"In here." Suzie nervously showed her the small area by the back door.

"That's fine. Keep his bowls here, too, so that he knows this is his spot. He's a good dog and well trained, but don't be tempted to spoil him. Feeding him from the table is a really bad idea. The occasional treat is okay but best given to him in his own space."

Mary joined them for a cuppa and told them all about the dog's likes and habits and taught Suzie some key words and actions that Percy would understand.

"Down," Suzie told the dog and immediately he slumped at her feet, panting and looking up at her. "Good boy," she said, delighted with herself.

"I'd better get going." Mary stood up to leave. "Any problems, Suzie, just give me a call."

"Will do." She walked Mary to the door and the dog went to follow. "Stay," she told him and was chuffed when he did exactly that.

"You're a natural." Mary grinned.

"Isn't he gorgeous?" Aileen was sitting on the floor, scratching Percy's tummy when Suzie came back into the kitchen.

"He is." Suzie sank down beside them and stroked the dog's head. He looked up at her with his beautiful brown eyes that seemed so clever and loving. "Do you think he wonders where his last owner went? If he misses her?"

"Probably. You'll need to give him lots of cuddles to comfort him." Aileen sighed. "Don't leave him out in the garden too much or I'll spend all my day looking in at him."

"You can come and see him whenever you want, especially if you bring scones," Suzie grinned.

"Done. Seriously, though, any time you want me to take him for a walk, just say the word. I know how tired you get and the kids will be pushing you to send him back if they think he's too much for you."

Suzie nodded, realising she was right. "Cheers, Aileen. I may take you up on that."

Aileen fondled and scratched behind the dog's ear before getting to her feet. "I'll be off, so. Bye-bye, doggy. See ya, Suzie. Best of luck."

Alone in the kitchen, Suzie looked into Percy's sad eyes. "I need you to be at your most adorable today, Percy. You're going to be meeting the rest of my family and we want them to fall in love with you, got it?" He licked her hand, his eyes on her face. "Ah, you're adorable. How could anyone not love you?"

Suzie was dozing on the sofa when she heard the bang of the hall door. "Who's that?"

"Only me, Mum," Noel called. "I'm starving. Is there anything to eat?"

Percy stood up and looked at the door, growling, and, when Noel walked in, immediately placed himself between Suzie and Noel. She laughed. "Well, look at that: he's protecting me! It's okay, Percy. This is Noel. Hold your hand out to him so he can get your scent," she told her son.

"He looks like he wants a lot more than my scent," Noel retorted but did as he was told.

Percy trotted over, had a good sniff round him before going back and lying down at Suzie's feet. Feeling

114

pleased as Punch, she patted his head and gave Noel a smug grin. "Isn't he great?"

"He's big." Noel squatted down and scratched the dog's head. "I thought you were going for a small breed."

"That was the idea, but Percy is special. He's been trained to help people with disabilities. His owner died and the shelter figured he had earned an early retirement. He's mine if I want him."

"So you can take him back?"

The look of relief on his face pissed Suzie off. "Yes, he's on a fortnight's trial. Why?"

Noel chuckled as the dog licked his hand. "He's great, Mum, but do you really think that this is a good time to get a pet? You're only just getting back on your feet."

"It's perfect timing. He'll aid my recovery."

"Maybe but he'll also moult, shit and a dog his size will cost a fortune to feed. Then there's vet's bills and insurance."

Suzie's confidence wavered but she scowled at her son. "I think there's just enough in the bank to cover it. I want this dog, Noel. Can't you just be happy for me?"

"I am, but look at the size of him and the size of this place." Noel waved a hand round their small lounge. "It doesn't seem fair to the animal."

"Mary said it was fine," Suzie said, feeling defensive.

"Well, she would. She's trying to offload the thing," he said sarcastically.

"It's not like that at all," Suzie retorted, getting annoyed. "They are very particular who they place dogs with. The animal's welfare is their first priority."

"And you're my first priority, Mum," he said, his eyes full of concern. "Why not just let me take him back now? If you hang on to him for the two weeks and decide you can't cope with him, he'll have become attached to you and he's already lost one owner."

She fixed her son with a steely glare. "You can cut out the emotional blackmail. He's staying. Come on, Percy, let's go for a walk." She put the dog on the lead and opened the back door.

"Mum —"

"See you later," Suzie called over her shoulder as she led the dog down the side passage. She headed down onto the coast road and turned right, frowning, her eyes on the city skyline. If that was Noel's reaction she could just imagine the hard time her daughters would give her. She shivered in the breeze rolling in off the coast, wishing she'd stopped to put on a jacket. Quickening her pace, she turned into St Anne's park. She cheered up as she walked, marvelling at the nods and smiles from other dog walkers. This was an entirely new social life that she hadn't known existed. Maybe she should get Jess to walk Percy; she might meet a decent fella. She figured you had to be decent if you loved dogs.

The thought made her grin and she glanced down at the dog trotting calmly by her side. She saw a bench ahead and decided to take a rest. She hadn't walked so far or so fast since she came out of hospital. She'd have to learn to pace herself if she wanted to keep Percy. Her

116

family would, no doubt, be looking for any excuse to get rid of him. The dog had a sniff around, relieved himself against an oak tree and then settled at her feet. "How could they not love you?" she said with an affectionate smile, patting him. She checked her watch and decided to head for home at a more leisurely pace. Sharon and Bobby were dropping in on their way home from school and she didn't want to look exhausted. "Come on, Percy, time to go back and face the music. You need to be a good boy, got it?" He looked up at her and licked her hand, making her laugh.

At home, she quickly filled Percy's bowl with fresh water and, when he'd lapped up half of it, she pointed to the dog's basket. "Bed." She watched, open-mouthed as Percy stepped into it and then settled down, dropping his head onto his paws. "Well I'll be damned. You're going to be no trouble at all, are you?" She went into the kitchen, closing the door behind her, and made some ham sandwiches and heated spaghetti hoops, knowing from experience that Bobby would probably just shred the sandwiches and tread them into her carpets. Still, she chuckled, Percy could clean up after him, although she wasn't sure Mary would approve.

"Hey, Mum, where are you?" Sharon called out in a singsong voice.

Suzie heard the front door close and bags and coats being dropped in the hall. "In the kitchen!" she called back and prayed that Percy behaved, although she had more faith in the dog than in her grandson.

She let Sharon prattle on and fuss over Bobby and waited until they'd started eating before mentioning the dog. "I have a surprise, Bobby."

Sharon looked astonished and pleased. "A surprise? Oh, Bobby, I wonder what it is?"

"What is it, Granny?" Bobby looked up at her.

"There's someone I want you both to meet." Suzie went into the passageway, put the dog on his lead, just in case, and led him into the kitchen, taking care to sit down as far away from both of them as possible. "Sit," she said and Percy did, looking with interest at their two visitors, his tail wagging.

"Doggy!" Bobby's eyes widened and he smiled.

"Who's this, then?" Sharon asked, looking less than happy.

Suzie bristled at her tone. What was wrong with everyone? Percy was not only a handsome, friendly animal, he was well behaved too, which was more than could be said for Sharon's son.

Bobby climbed down and moved slowly towards them.

"Don't touch him, Bobby, he might bite."

Suzie glared at her. "He won't bite. Come and sit beside me, Bobby." She shifted over to make room for him. "Percy will want to sniff you but don't be afraid. That's just how dogs get to know you." Bobby did as she told him and Percy looked up at the little boy. "Stay, Percy," Suzie murmured, praying that he wouldn't choose now to disobey her, but Percy did as he was told. Bobby sat quietly as the dog sniffed him and nudged his arm. The child laughed and reached

118

out a hand to touch his coat. Susie smiled. "He's wagging his tail. That means he likes you."

"Mum, I'm not sure —"

Suzie silenced her daughter with a look and turned her attention back to the dog. "Good dog, Percy. This is Bobby."

The dog wagged his tail again and settled at Bobby's feet.

"He likes me." Bobby smiled.

Suzie beamed at her daughter. "See?"

"Great." Sharon said and then frowned. "He doesn't have fleas, does he?"

CHAPTER
TWELVE

Jess decided to drop in on her mother on the way to a meeting in the city centre. It was a good excuse not to stay long. It had been a while since she'd visited and she felt guilty, but she found it tough being around her mother. She'd stay twenty minutes and bail. Her phone buzzed, making her jump. No, Louis, not again. She glanced at it and saw that it was just Sharon. She'd call her later. She read Louis's last text again.

Meet me, let's talk.

Whatever reaction she'd been expecting, this wasn't it. He'd left lots of messages, pleading with her to see him; he'd even sent roses. Jess was afraid to meet him, afraid he'd talk her round. It was one thing sleeping with him when she swallowed his lies but, if she went back to him now, she'd deserve all of the names her mum had called her. She'd officially be "the other woman". A mistress. The term made her cringe with shame. She had to stay strong.

Jess let herself into her mother's house. All was quiet and she wondered if her mum was sleeping in. She tiptoed into the kitchen and saw Suzie through the window, hanging out washing. She made to go out and join her but jumped back when she pushed open the door and was confronted by a large dog, who barked at her. Jess yelped in surprise and backed into the kitchen, her heart thumping in her chest.

"What is it, Percy?" Suzie hurried in and then smiled when she saw her daughter. "Hi, Jess —" She stopped when she saw her face. "What is it? What's wrong?"

Jess pressed herself against the far wall, keeping her eyes on the dog. "You know I'm terrified of dogs. What's it doing here? Whose is it?"

"Mine."

Jess's eyes widened and she dragged her eyes from the dog to stare, horrified, at her mum. "How could you get a dog without even talking to me first? Is this because of Louis? Did you get that bloody animal just to punish me?"

Suzie shook her head, looking confused. "What are you talking about? Of course I didn't. I adopted him because I wanted a dog. While I admit it was a whim, when I met Percy it just felt right. He's a very special dog and wouldn't hurt a fly." She gave a heavy sigh. "I didn't know you were afraid of dogs."

Jess stared at her and realised it was true. Would this bloody head injury never stop hurting them? "You don't remember."

Suzie's eyes narrowed and she settled the dog in his basket then closed the door on him before coming to sit at the table. "Tell me."

Jess checked that the door was closed properly and then sat down opposite her. "When I was a toddler, I

121

was attacked by a dog. You told me that your friend, Pamela, came to my rescue but she couldn't get to me in time." Jess turned her head and drew back her hair, revealing a pale scar that ran from her right ear lobe to just above her right eyebrow.

Suzie gasped, her eyes widening in shock. "I didn't remember, I swear. Even now, when you say it" — she shrugged, looking upset — "nothing. I'm so sorry, Jess."

"It's not your fault," Jess said, wondering how many times she'd said that in the last few weeks. It was true, but she was finding it harder and harder to cope with her mother's behaviour and attitude.

"This is your chance to overcome your fear, love," Mum was saying now, her eyes excited. "Percy's a wonderful dog, trained to protect people, not injure them. Since he was a puppy, that's all he's known. That other dog hurt you and I can understand your fear. It was stupid of me not to have dealt with it years ago."

Jess shrugged. "It's okay. Lots of people are afraid of dogs. Just keep him away from me, please?"

"You'll come to love him," Suzie assured her, "but, if you don't want him around, that's fine."

"You mean you'll get rid of him?" Jess smiled, grateful.

Suzie blinked. "Well, no, but I'll keep him outside when you're here."

"Gee, thanks." Jess stared at her and, standing up, went to the door. "Now I know where I come on your list of priorities," she said and left, tears filling her eyes as she got into her car and drove away.

Jess was trying her damnedest to write a funny piece on dating when her phone buzzed. Her heart sank when she saw it was a text from Louis. She'd noticed that they were getting less loving and more demanding. When would he give up? The only ones she'd responded to were work-related and, as a result, he'd criticised the last two pieces she'd sent in and used them as an excuse to drag her into the office to "discuss" them. On both occasions it had been late in the evenings when there were few staff around and he'd sat too close, brushing against her at every opportunity.

"You know you want me as much as I want you, Jess," he'd said the last time. She couldn't believe the risks he was taking. Anyone who saw them would know damn well what was going on or what wasn't. Either way, she'd be labelled. She'd have to stop it, stop him, but she had no idea how to without jeopardising her position. The obvious answer was to stop writing for the *Gazette* but as Louis was the only one giving her the chance to write articles on politics and current affairs she was loathe to do that. Why should she lose everything just because he wanted her? And was it her imagination, or did he want her more since they'd been found out? Did he get some kick out of the dangerous position he was in? She sighed, knowing that if he didn't back off she'd have no other choice but to walk away.

In the old days she'd have gone to her mother for advice. Yes, Mum would have been upset and disappointed at Jess having got herself into this mess but she would have counselled and advised her. Now, Jess could just imagine the tongue-lashing she'd get — you made your bed, et cetera. While her mother was telling everyone exactly what she thought of them, they were all pussyfooting around her, pretending that everything was fine. But it wasn't. Nora was right. Maybe they should tell her that.

Jess had tried to talk to Noel about it, but he seemed to be in a world of his own at the moment and waved away her concerns. He didn't see the changes that she and Sharon did. Her little sister had been reduced to tears a few times lately but, then, it was worse for her. Not only had she lost her mother and friend, but Bobby had lost his doting granny too. Not that the child seemed bothered. Like so many at that age, he seemed to be in a world of his own half the time and, once engrossed in one of his toys, he wouldn't even react when he was called. But Suzie had gone from fussing over the child and excusing his behaviour to being positively nasty and Sharon was distraught.

Jess found herself in an increasingly pivotal position in the family dynamic, comforting Sharon, showering Bobby with more love than she ever had before, and keeping tabs on Noel. She'd gone from being daughter to carer and now to mother.

Most of the time Jess had been able to keep on Mum's good side although it was hard work. But, since Mum had seen her with Louis, things had gone steadily downhill. Though she'd forgiven Jess, her mother still seemed angry and would attack her, out of the blue, for no apparent reason.

124

Tears welled up in Jess's eyes, blurring the words on the screen. Her phone rang and with a tired sigh, she sniffed back her tears and answered it. "Hello, Jess Connors?" she said, trying to sound upbeat and professional. She hadn't looked at the display and there was a good chance it was Amelia, Beth or Jordan, her other editors.

"Hi, hon."

She smiled, relieved to hear Katie's bubbly voice. "Hey, Katie, how are you?"

"Busy. Are you going to Jen's party?"

"I don't think so. I've a lot on." Jess did not feel in a party mood.

"Is it your mum? I thought she was better now."

Jess was filled with guilt at the sympathy in her friend's voice. She hadn't told Katie anything about Louis, letting her believe the reason she wasn't available much was all down to her mum but now she needed to confide in her. Maybe Katie would have some suggestions as to how Jess could extricate herself from this mess with the minimum amount of disruption to her career or income. "She's fine but we need to keep an eye on her, you know? And Noel's exams start next week, so he's got too much on his plate to be much help."

"Yeah, well, you've a lot on your plate, too," Katie argued. "Don't put everyone else first, Jess, not all the time."

Jess's guilt mounted. "Should you be going partying, miss? Don't you have exams to prepare for?" Katie worked as a receptionist in an accountancy firm but had found she liked working with numbers and had gone back to study accountancy at night.

"Excuse me, I am completely organised. I have a strict schedule. If I get four hours' revision done this evening and six tomorrow, I'll have earned a night out. I've also scheduled in coffee to sober me up on Sunday. Meet me then, at least, usual place?"

"Yeah, I'd like that," Jess said.

"You sure you're okay?"

Jess smiled at the concern in her voice. "Yes, I'm tired, that's all."

They said their goodbyes and Jess turned her attention back to the blank screen. Her guilty feelings at lying to her friend were interrupted by the buzz of her phone. She picked it up again and froze when she saw the caller. He never phoned unless it was about work, so, taking a deep breath, she answered.

"Louis, hi."

"Hey, sweetheart. A client just cancelled, I thought we could get together."

Jess sank back in her chair feeling weary. "Louis, I've told you, it's over."

"I need to talk to you, it's important, Jess. I could be there in thirty minutes. Do you want the job or not?"

Job? She frowned, hesitating. His tone was very brisk and professional. Was this really a business call?

"Look, forget it, I'll give it to someone else. It's just you're always saying that you want to write pieces on politics —"

"No, it's fine," she said hurriedly. "I can drop in to you if you want."

"I'm not in the office. I'll see you soon." Louis said, a smile in his voice, and hung up, leaving her wondering if she'd been out-manoeuvred.

Jess paced nervously as she waited for him, pausing at the window from time to time. She jumped when the doorbell rang, and taking a deep breath, she smoothed back her hair and hurried down to let him in. She opened her mouth to say hello only to find herself slammed against the wall, Louis's hand closing round her throat.

"You haven't been answering my texts, Jess."

"Louis!" she gasped, shocked by the attack and the crazed look in his eyes. "Stop, you're hurting me." She thought of banging on the wall for her landlady and then remembered that she was away.

"Why aren't you answering my texts?" he repeated, his voice low and intense.

She mustn't panic, she must calm Louis down and convince him that she would play along, at least until he loosened his grip. Then she'd . . . Well, she didn't know what she'd do. Despite the fact that she could barely breathe, she forced herself to answer. "You lied to me, Louis. I thought that I meant more to you."

The pressure eased off on her neck and his expression softened.

"Sweetheart, you know it's you that I want." His hands moved down over her body. "I can't get enough of you." He leaned in to kiss her, pulling her against the length of his body.

127

"Let's go upstairs." She reached around him to supposedly close the front door, intending to make a run for it but his arm shot out, barring her way.

"Let me, darling."

"Hi, Jess. Am I too early?"

Jess looked up in surprise and relief when she saw who was standing on her doorstep, his steely gaze on Louis. It was Cal, Noel's friend, happily a rather tall, broad-shouldered and intimidating figure who easily moved Louis's hand and placed himself between the two of them. Jess thought quickly. "Cal, hey, how's it going? Sorry, I'd completely forgotten you were coming. This is Louis Healy, editor at the *Gazette*." She met Louis's eyes and gave an apologetic shrug.

"Am I interrupting? Only you said you were interested in writing that article for me and I'm a bit short on time."

"No, please come in, Cal," she said, aware of the tremor in her voice. "You don't mind, do you, Louis? This was a prior engagement that I forgot." She forced herself to meet his eyes.

Louis gave a grim smile and nodded. "Business is business. Give me a shout if you want to talk about the political piece. I want it by this Friday so time's ticking."

What piece? she wondered, hesitating then realising it was probably just a line. "I really appreciate it," she gushed and put a gentle hand on his arm.

Slightly mollified, he nodded, glared at Cal and left. She immediately closed the door and almost collapsed against it, breathing heavily.

"Are you okay?"

"Yeah, thanks. What are you doing here?" Not that she was complaining: his timing couldn't have been better. Cal McLoughlin was the first friend Noel had made when they'd moved up to Dublin. He'd lived round the corner and, although he was six years older, he had taken pity on the obviously devastated young boy and befriended Noel and they'd remained firm friends ever since. Jess used to have quite a crush on the boy with the floppy, dirty-blond hair and hazel eyes but, sadly, he'd always treated her like a sister.

"I'll explain that in a moment but first let's get you a cuppa. You look like you could do with it. Then you can tell me what the story is with that asshole."

And, as they sat in her tiny kitchen with mugs of tea, Jess surprised herself by doing exactly that. Cal didn't interrupt or advise but just nodded encouragement when she faltered, his eyes soft with kindness and concern. If only her own family were as easy to talk to.

"I know I was stupid," she said, when she'd finished her rather sordid little story. "I should have realised he was only after one thing. We never went on a proper date. He said that he was protecting me, that his staff wouldn't take me seriously if they knew I was dating the editor."

"You weren't stupid: you were trusting and there are plenty of middle-aged men these days who are, genuinely, separated or divorced."

"I wish Mum saw it that way," Jess said, still smarting from her mother's reaction. "She hardly talks to me these days and, when she does, it's usually to make cheap shots. Even Noel's annoyed with me. I'm surprised you're visiting the pariah of the family," she joked.

"I doubt Noel's mood has anything to do with you."

"What do you mean?"

"I'm worried about him, Jess."

"Why?" Jess was immediately on alert. Cal wasn't an alarmist and he'd never approached her about her brother before. "Is he in some kind of trouble?"

"I'm not sure but I've never seen him so withdrawn. I could understand that when your mum was in hospital, but not now."

"The pressure of the exams coming up must be getting to him."

"Maybe," Cal said, but he didn't seem convinced.

"Did you talk to him?"

He gave a lopsided grin. "I tried but he blew me off. When you graduate in psychology, friends start to get a little nervous round you, wondering if you're analysing them all the time."

"I can imagine." She smiled, immediately wondering what he thought of *her*.

He met her eyes. "Just like you're doing right now."

She laughed. "Guilty. So, what do you want me to do?"

"Have a chat. He might open up to you."

"If he doesn't talk to you, he'll hardly talk to me, especially now that I'm a fallen woman."

"Tell him it was a mistake and that you're upset about falling out with your mum and need his help to patch things up."

130

Noel was soft and Jess knew that he would help her if she asked, but she still didn't think it would mean he'd unburden himself to her. "You know him well, Cal. What do you think is wrong?"

He shrugged and shook his head. "I'm not sure but I think it's related in some way to your mum. If you ask the right questions, you might get to the bottom of what's bothering him."

She looked at him. He was a good friend to them all and his request couldn't be taken lightly. "I'll talk to him."

"Thanks, Jess." he smiled.

"He's lucky to have such a good friend."

"He's been a good friend to me too," he assured her. "You all have."

"That's not the way I remember it." She smiled at him. "Instead of being out having a good time with kids your own age, you were always in our house and you brought Noel out of himself."

Cal looked at her. "Your house was my refuge. I came over to escape my folks' rows."

Jess stared at him. "I didn't know."

"But your mum did. She knew that they were using me as a pawn and it was tearing me apart. They didn't like me spending so much time at your place but Suzie told them how much it was helping Noel to get over the death of his father so, what could they say? I owe her a lot."

Jess felt sad as she too remembered how strong and kind her mum had been during those dark, difficult day when Sharon and Noel were so upset. Jess had been almost sixteen and, never having been particularly close to her dad, had adjusted more easily to their change in circumstances.

Cal stood up. "I'll leave you to it. Promise me you won't put yourself in a position where you're alone with that man again."

Jess sighed. "I'll do my best, but he's holding my job over my head."

"You write for plenty of publications, Jess."

"I do, but not the sort of articles I want. Louis gives me topics I can really get my teeth into."

"But at a price," he pointed out.

"True," Jess said and walked down with him to the door. "I'll give you a call when I've talked to Noel."

"Great, thanks. And remember: any problems with that guy, call me."

"I will," Jess promised and smiled as he gave her a quick hug and strode off down the road.

CHAPTER
THIRTEEN

Sharon tensed when she heard the door and, after checking that Bobby was engrossed in his movie, went into the kitchen to take Keith's dinner out of the oven. She was leaving it on the table and going back to rejoin her son when Keith walked into the room.

"Please, Sharon, stop this."

"Stop what?" she asked. He looked sad and tired and she wanted to go to him but she also wanted him to reach out to his son and, until he did, she couldn't forgive him.

"The silent treatment."

She met his eyes. "I don't know what to say. Between you and Mum, I feel as if Bobby and I are always under attack."

"Don't lump me in with your mother," he protested.

"True, she can't help the way she speaks to me," Sharon snapped, "but *you* can."

"I do try but I get so frustrated that I can't get through to Bobby."

"You won't get anywhere by shouting at him or sitting on top of him," she retorted.

"I'm sorry about that. Please, Sharon. I can't stand this atmosphere any more."

"Me neither," she admitted, tears welling up. Immediately his arms went round her and she snuggled into him. "Sometimes I wish Mum had died. Can you believe that, Keith? Isn't that a terrible thing to say?" The tears spilled out onto her cheeks and his shirt. "I feel so guilty about feeling that way but I can't help it. That injury seems to have knocked all the love out of her. Sometimes I think she hates me and she definitely hates Bobby."

Keith's arms tightened round her. "Of course she doesn't. We have to make allowances for her. There are some things she simply doesn't seem to understand anymore."

Sharon couldn't stop crying. It was as if the floodgates had opened.

"It will be okay, darling, I promise you." He stroked her hair and rocked her as if she were a small child.

"How?" she sobbed. There was a roar from the next room and, with a tired sigh, Sharon pulled away.

"Wait." Keith held her firmly and looked into her eyes. "We will sort this but we can't talk here. We need to get away from the house for a few hours and have a proper chat about Bobby. I'm sure there are options open to us."

Sharon wasn't sure she liked the sound of that. Options? What options? She thought of what the teacher had said, what she had withheld from Keith, and shivered.

"Your mum says she'll babysit any time we need a break."

134

Sharon stared at him, incredulous. "My mum? You think I'd leave him with her?"

"Oh, come on, Sharon, she's looked after him lots of times and he's been fine."

"I don't trust her with him, that's the honest truth."

"She would never hurt him." Keith's jaw clenched and he looked at her, his eyes determined. "We're going out and your mother is going to babysit and that's an end to it."

Sharon remained stiff as a board in his arms, her eyes stubborn. "Only after Bobby's asleep."

He sighed, nodding. "Fine, once he's asleep."

Sharon couldn't bring herself to phone her mother to ask for the favour, so Keith did it. Suzie agreed but she still wasn't happy. After she'd taken Bobby to school the next morning, she called her sister. Jess picked up straightaway and answered, sounding bright and breezy.

"Hey, Shaz, how are you feeling?"

"Fine, thanks. You're sounding very chirpy this morning."

"Yeah, I feel it. I was up at seven working on an article and I'm actually ahead of all my deadlines this week which makes a pleasant change."

Sharon hadn't even loaded the washing machine yet and her sister's cheerful voice made her feel inadequate. "Good for you," she said, trying to inject some enthusiasm into her voice. "Does that mean you could come over for a coffee and a chat?" Sharon realised that she was holding her breath.

"Is everything okay?"

"Not really," Sharon admitted.

"Put the kettle on. I'm on my way."

"Thanks, Jess," Sharon said, never more grateful that she had a big sister to turn to. She filled the kettle and set out mugs and biscuits. She was just looking critically at her tired, anxious face in the mirror when the doorbell rang.

Jess stood there, grinning, holding up a bag. "I brought doughnuts."

Sharon groaned and patted her stomach. "I really shouldn't. I seem to be piling on the weight lately."

"Rubbish."

"You haven't seen me trying to get into my jeans."

Jess followed her into the sunny kitchen and pulled up a chair. "So, what's up?"

Sharon made the tea and sat down. She selected a doughnut and licked some of the sticky sugar coating off before replying. "Do you really need to ask?"

"Mum." Jess said.

"Mum," Sharon agreed. "She's getting to you too?"

"I can't bear to be around her, to be honest. I always seem to end up angry or upset. And now there's a bloody dog, too. She says she didn't remember I was scared of them, but I wonder."

"I don't visit much either," Sharon admitted, relieved that it wasn't just her. "She's getting more and more critical and the way she talks to Bobby, the things she says to him, honestly, sometimes I want to slap her."

Jess nodded in sympathy. "Sensitive she isn't. I time my visits for when she's not there and leave a message or send a text saying, 'Sorry I missed you.' I do check to

136

see if anything needs doing around the house, but she seems to be coping fine."

"She gets tired easily," Sharon said.

"Yes, I've noticed that."

"What does Noel think?" Sharon swallowed the last of the doughnut and found herself eyeing another. Where was this appetite coming from?

"We haven't really had the chance to discuss it."

"So I know what Mum fights with me about, but what's she doing to upset you? You've always been close, I don't remember you ever rowing."

Jess gave her a look that was both embarrassed and defensive. "Okay, I'll tell you but don't give me a hard time."

Sharon looked at her curiously. "Of course I won't. Why would I?"

"Mum saw me with a guy —"

"You're dating? That's great, Jess, I'm delighted for you." Secretly, Sharon hoped he was an improvement on the others. Jess seemed to go for men who didn't treat her very well. Sharon could never understand it. She'd always been a bit jealous of her big sister's good looks but while Sharon was out having a good time, Jess was studying. Sharon's partying had come to a stop, though, when she met Keith and, within weeks had fallen hook, line and sinker for him. Thankfully, he felt the same way. When she'd told him, anxiously, she was pregnant, he'd been thrilled and immediately asked her to marry him. Bobby had just turned one and she was twenty when they tied the knot. So much for her dream of being free and having lots of fun! Not that she had any regrets. But it would be nice occasionally to forget that she was a wife and mother and just be Sharon again.

She looked back at her sister, wondering what Jess was so reluctant to talk about. "Come on, tell me all about him, and don't worry if he doesn't get Mum's thumbs-up. As long as you're happy, to hell with her."

"It's a bit more complicated than that," Jess said in a small voice. "He's married."

Sharon looked at her in dismay. "Oh, Jess."

Jess put up a hand. "Don't."

"I'm not going to give you a sermon, I promise. I'm the one who got herself pregnant at eighteen, so I'm hardly in a position to throw stones."

"At least Keith was single. I told Mum that I thought Louis was separated, but I don't think she believes me."

"Are you still seeing him?" Sharon asked, feeling sorry for her sister.

Jess shook her head. "No."

"Good for you. Did you love him?"

Jess ran her finger through the crumbs on her plate. "I'm beginning to wonder," she admitted. "I thought he cared about me but now I'm not so sure. I may have been one in a long line of affairs."

"Shithead," Sharon pronounced. "You're better off without him."

"Yeah. The only problem is that it's Louis Healy, the editor of the *Gazette* and he gives me the meatiest subjects to write about. Still, that will probably change now. He didn't take it very well when I finished with him. I've discovered that he has a rather nasty side."

"Oh, well, fuck that, Jess." She put a hand to her mouth and groaned. "Listen to me. I'm turning into Mum."

Jess giggled. "Not a chance."

"But, seriously, if he's going to play dirty then you can too. I'm sure that he'd leave you alone if you threatened to shop him to his wife."

"I don't have the stomach for that kind of thing, Shaz, and, anyway, what's she done to deserve that sort of grief?"

Sharon sighed. "Look, just concentrate on your other jobs, don't talk to him and, whatever you do, don't meet up with him."

Jess smiled at her. "I won't. Thanks, Shaz."

"Don't thank me yet, sweetie, I'm buttering you up because I need a favour."

Jess gave a dramatic roll of her eyes. "I should have known there'd be a catch. Go on, then, spit it out."

"Keith wants to take me out one night next week. We have some things we need to talk — or argue — about and he thought we should do it on neutral territory."

"Makes sense. So you want me to babysit? No problem."

"It's a little more complicated than that. Mum is babysitting, only . . ." Sharon couldn't bring herself to say it.

"Only . . . ?" Jess prompted and then her eyes widened in understanding. "You don't trust her."

Sharon swallowed the lump in her throat. "I don't think she'd harm Bobby, not deliberately but, given how she behaves with him in front of us, well, how do I know what she's capable of if she's left alone with him?"

Jess stared at her for a moment and then finally shook her head, her eyes bright with tears. "Every time I think I've got my head round what's happened to Mum, something new comes along to knock the wind out of me. I'm beginning to wonder if we'll ever have the same relationship again."

"I've been reading up online. There are support groups."

Jess gave a wry smile. "I've been reading, too. The nurse gave me leaflets and contact numbers when they were discharging Mum, and I never thought that we would need anything like that. But they knew this was probably on the cards, didn't they?"

Sharon shrugged. "To be honest, I'm not sure they have a clue what lies ahead. From what I've read, nearly all sufferers of traumatic brain injury react differently, improve at various rates or not at all, and have completely different problems afterwards."

"I suppose it's down to what part of the brain is injured."

"I assume so. On the bright side, Mum seems to be at the healthier end of the scale. I remind myself of that every night before I go to sleep."

Jess reached out and squeezed her hand. "I'm glad we at least have each other. I think I'd crack up if I was going through this alone."

"Likewise. Have you still got those leaflets?"

"They're somewhere in the flat. Do you think we should persuade her to get some help?"

"We've got to do something." Sharon gave a weary sigh. She always seemed to feel tired these days. "Right now, though, I can't think further ahead than leaving Bobby alone with Mum."

"You want me to be here as well?" Jess looked less than comfortable at the idea.

"Please. If you dropped by supposedly to see me and stayed, that would be great."

Jess looked at her. "Babysit the babysitter? I'll try, Shaz but she'll probably tell me to get lost."

"Please, Jess? Yes, you'll be doing me a favour but you'll have her cornered and she'll have to listen to your side of the story. I'm sure she'll mellow when she knows you've finished with the man. You know Mum adores you."

"Mellow? Ha! You didn't see the state of her that night. I thought she was going to have a heart attack. As for finishing with Louis" — Jess sighed — "I'm a sorry, pathetic fool. If he turns on the charm I'm not convinced I'll be able to resist him, sad bitch that I am."

Sharon looked at her, shocked at the disgust and self-loathing in her sister's voice. "Hang on a sec. The woman I talked to on the phone a little while ago was telling me how she was on top of things. She was focused, confident and knew exactly what she wanted."

Jess raised tortured eyes to her. "Yeah, but that woman has a habit of disappearing whenever he's around."

"You're so much stronger than you realise, Jess," Sharon told her. "You're the one who got me and Noel through these last few months. You can easily walk away from this guy. Writing's your thing, Jess, and you're good at it. In fact, why don't you write down all the nasty things he's said, the times he's let you down and made you downright miserable, and read it every time you feel yourself weaken?"

"That's not a bad idea," Jess said with a reluctant smile.

"Good. Now will you come and keep an eye on Mum or not?"

Jess relented. "Yeah, okay. I suppose we have to thrash things out sooner or later."

Sharon hugged her. "Thank you! I'm sure that Bobby will be asleep and I promise we won't stay out long."

"Perhaps there'll be some protection for me too. Mum can hardly yell at me with Bobby upstairs asleep."

Sharon gave her a wary look. "I wouldn't count on it but I'll keep my fingers crossed for you."

CHAPTER
FOURTEEN

Suzie was up and dressed and feeling much better when Nora texted to say that she was in Dublin and suggested meeting for a late lunch. It was exactly what Suzie needed and she agreed immediately. Aileen would be happy to keep an eye on Percy, not that he seemed to need it, she thought fondly. Suzie hoped that Nora wasn't planning on telling her any more home truths. She needed a laugh and a chat and then maybe she'd tell her friend about the group that she'd contacted and was going to meet next week. She felt very nervous about it and wouldn't mind some moral support, but the lady she'd talked to had made it clear that it was a group of TBI survivors only. The purpose was that they could vent their frustrations to each other without hurting their loved ones, which, she supposed, made sense. She still wasn't looking forward to it.

Suzie studied the menu, disappointed in Nora's choice of restaurant. It looked very fancy, but the food was weird and everything seemed to involve salad. Still, it was in the heart of Dublin and she was enjoying people-watching from their table by the large picture window.

"So, how's the list coming along?" Nora asked once they had ordered.

"It's not." Suzie took a sip of her chilled wine that Nora had chosen and nodded her approval. "Apart from the meditation and the book club, I haven't organised anything else."

"Perhaps it's just as well now that you've a dog to mind." Nora smiled.

"Ha, true. I can't wait for you to meet him, Nora. He's a pet, gentle and loving. I'm thrilled I got him."

"So, you're definitely keeping him?"

"Absolutely, although in Jess's eyes that will make me public enemy number one. Did you know that she'd been attacked by a dog when she was little?"

Nora nodded slowly. "It happened before you came to Limerick. I remember you showing me the scar. You'd changed her hair to cover it so other children wouldn't be asking her about it and reminding her."

"Did I?" Suzie was frightened that she'd forgotten something like that. "I'd better talk to her. I pretty much dismissed her fear but, still, this dog wouldn't hurt a fly."

"I'm sure that she'll get used to him. How's Sharon doing?"

Suzie rolled her eyes. "Rowing with Keith about Bobby, from what I can gather. He's taking her out some night next week to have a heart-to-heart while I babysit. I'm hoping he'll be able to talk some sense into her."

"It's good of you to babysit, I'm sure —"

Nora was interrupted by a knock on the window. Suzie laughed and waved. "It's Mandy." She beckoned her sister to join them. "You don't mind, do you, Nora?"

"Do I have a choice?" Nora sighed, clearly unimpressed.

"Oh, don't be like that. I know she's a bit much but she means well." Suzie saw Nora's eyes widen in disbelief but Mandy had already breezed in and Suzie stood up to hug her sister. Nora didn't stir, her cool smile making it clear that Mandy wasn't welcome. Annoyed, Suzie snatched a glass from the next table and poured a liberal amount of wine into it. Nora's mouth settled into a thin line but Suzie ignored her.

"On another shopping spree?" she asked Mandy.

"No, hanging around waiting for Douglas. He's in the library."

"Do you drive him everywhere?" Nora asked.

"God forbid. No, his rust-bucket wouldn't start, so he asked me to give him a lift. Why the man won't buy a new car is beyond me. Lord knows he can well afford it. The only thing keeping that wreck together is dirt." Mandy took a sip of wine and glanced at her watch. "I suppose I should let him know where I am."

"We've already ordered," Suzie said. "Do you want something to eat?"

"No, I'm fine." Mandy tapped a text into her phone and took another sip.

Nora, rather pointedly, poured her a glass of water and gave an innocent shrug when Suzie glared at her.

"How are your plans for Croatia coming along?" Suzie asked.

"Slowly, very slowly. Douglas is not a man to be rushed."

"Mandy's trying to wangle an all-expenses-paid holiday in Zagreb," Suzie explained.

"Nice," Nora said.

Mandy gave a dreamy sigh. "It will be. I've been checking out the hotel online and it's very luxurious."

"He 'and companion' have been invited," Suzie explained, "but he doesn't know that she plans to be the companion yet."

"Why not just ask him outright?" Nora asked, looking bored.

"I need to pick my moment. He's a grumpy bugger and I'm not flavour of the month right now, as I dumped some of his old clothes."

Nora raised her eyebrows. "That was a bit presumptuous."

"It was only a couple of jackets and jeans and they were ancient. We'd bought him replacements and I didn't think he'd miss the stuff."

"If you did that to me you'd get a kick up the arse and be out of a job," Suzie told her.

Their salads were served and Mandy stole a prawn from her sister's plate. "Douglas is lucky to have me. Not many would put up with him."

"Are you kidding me?" Suzie scoffed. "You have it easy! If you decide to move on, tell Douglas that I'm more than happy to replace you."

146

"Seriously?" Nora asked, sitting forward. "Would you be interested in getting back into the workplace?"

Suzie felt a spark of excitement at the thought of being back in an office again. "Do you know, I really think I would? Being idle is bad for the old grey matter. I need stimulation."

"You were doing quite well before you got married," Mandy remembered. "Mam was always going on about your high-powered job and telling me I'd have to study if I wanted to get on as well as you." She flashed a smile. "I proved her wrong, though. There are easier ways."

Suzie saw Nora's expression and figured she'd have to keep these two women apart. Had her friend always had a low opinion of her sister? Yet another thing that she couldn't remember. She pushed the rabbit food round her plate wondering if she could order a side of chips.

Mandy groaned as her phone rang. "Typical. As soon as I get a glass in my hand, Douglas is ready to go."

"Ask him to join us," Suzie suggested on impulse. "I'm curious to meet him."

Mandy answered the phone and gave Douglas directions to the restaurant. "He's just going to say a quick hi," she said after he'd rung off. "The man is so antisocial, it's unbelievable."

"It's hard to imagine the two of you getting on. Why on earth would you want to go to Croatia with him?" Nora said.

"It will be fine. He can wander around old ruins while I'm in the spa or sunbathing." She winked and then, glancing at the door, lowered her voice. "Here he is now, not another word, ladies."

Following Mandy's gaze, Suzie blinked and blinked again. It couldn't be. He hesitated a moment and she saw that he was just as surprised to see her, but then his face broke into a broad smile as he made his way over to them.

Mandy made the introductions. "Suzie, this is Douglas Thornton. Douglas, this is my sister and her friend, Nora."

Thornton? Suzie frowned, confused. Why was he calling himself that? He took her hand and held it between his, blue eyes twinkling.

"It's wonderful to meet you, Suzie. I've heard a lot about you. I hope you're recovering well from your accident."

"I am, thanks," she said, wondering why he was pretending they didn't know each other, but deciding to play along. He must have his reasons. "It's lovely to finally meet you. Mandy talks a lot about you too."

He glanced at her sister and raised an eyebrow. "Mandy?"

She scowled. "Childhood nickname. Don't use it if you expect me to answer."

"I'll try to remember that." Douglas chuckled, shook hands with Nora and then pulled up a chair next to Suzie. She couldn't believe that after all this time he was sitting here beside her. He looked older and greyer but still handsome, although more subdued, and there was sadness and weariness in his eyes. "You're not what I was expecting," she said, mischievously.

148

He smirked. "Likewise."

"That just goes to prove neither of you ever listen to me," Mandy complained, although they were both oblivious of her.

"I loved your book on Malta," Suzie said and saw his surprise and pleasure at the praise.

"You read it?"

"Only because she picked it up at my place," Mandy butted in, earning a glare from Nora for her bitchiness.

"That's true," Suzie admitted, not bothered. "I've never bought a travel book. We've only ever gone to the usual touristy places, but your book made me want to be more adventurous."

"Thank you," said Douglas. "That's a wonderful compliment."

"Perhaps you should add that to your list," Nora suggested with an affectionate smile.

"Oh, come on, sis. If you went on a sun holiday you would spend it by the pool like the rest of us," Mandy scoffed.

Suzie thought about it. "That was true in the past but not now. Life's too precious to just sit around doing nothing all day."

"I've always hated beach holidays," Nora agreed. "I like to explore."

Douglas laughed. "That's not Amanda's idea of fun."

"I like to explore, too." She grinned. "The bars, the clubs and definitely the shops."

Douglas smiled at Suzie. "All this time working for me and I haven't managed to convert her. It's really not good for my ego."

"I don't think you need her approval. She was telling me that you've won an award."

"It's really not that big a deal, more of an appreciation for writing about their country. The less well known East European locations are grateful for promotion, especially of a cultural nature."

"Yet Mandy says that you don't travel much," Suzie remarked.

He held her gaze, his eyes misting over. "I did all my travelling years ago. Now it's time to stay put and do the hard work and write about it."

Of course. That made sense. Suzie gave a brief nod of understanding and sympathy. There was so much that she wanted to ask him, but she understood why he wouldn't want to have that conversation now. It was clear that Mandy knew nothing about his past. She wished the two women anywhere in the world except at this table right now.

Mandy scowled and tapped her watch. "I hate to break this up but, if we don't move, I'm going to get a parking ticket."

Douglas stood up and took Suzie's hand. "It's been a real pleasure."

Suzie sighed in frustration. "It's a pity you have to go. There's so much I'd like to ask . . . about your work." She was aware that it must sound like a come-on to her sister and friend but didn't care.

He looked pleased. "Next time," he promised.

Mandy forced herself between them and gave Suzie a brief hug, clearly unimpressed by the rapport between her boss and sister. Suzie didn't give a damn. She watched Douglas as he said goodbye to Nora and followed Mandy outside, pausing in the doorway to raise his hand.

She waved back and sighed.

"Good Lord, what was all that about?" Nora asked, staring at her, smiling.

"He seems nice."

"Nice?" Nora raised her eyebrows. "I have never seen any man affect you the way that he did."

"What are you talking about? We were just chatting."

"Oh, please. It was as if you were the only two people in the room."

Suzie was sorely tempted to confide in Nora, but the fact that Doug had said nothing made her hold back. There must be a reason he was going by a different name and had pretended they didn't know each other. She smiled at her curious friend. "I liked him, what's the big deal?"

"Don't you think that he's a little bit old for you?"

"Is he?" Suzie suppressed a chuckle.

"I can't believe Mandy's setting her cap at him. Does she honestly believe that he'll take her to Zagreb? They're like chalk and cheese."

The idea of Douglas going anywhere with Mandy worried Suzie. The two might well be opposites, but Douglas had always been a sucker for a pretty face. And Mandy wouldn't care about his age, just the weight of his wallet. Would he be able to resist her if they were thrown together in a luxurious suite? Would he want to? Mandy certainly wouldn't turn him down. To her, sex was a commodity, and she wouldn't let the minor fact that he was a pensioner get in the way of a potential meal ticket. As the saying went: better to be an old man's darling than a young man's slave.

"Suzie, stop looking so fierce. He isn't in the least interested in Mandy. There was only one woman the esteemed Mr Thornton saw today and that was you."

Suzie was amused. "You think he fancies me? Don't be silly."

Nora grinned. "I'd put money on it and I think you made it clear that the feeling was mutual."

"Was I that obvious? I need to learn to hide my feelings better." Suzie chuckled. If only Nora knew.

"There's nothing to be embarrassed about. I'm just, well, surprised."

"I doubt it will come to anything."

"Don't be so negative," Nora said, nudging her. "He was hardly going to make a move in front of me and your sister — his employee."

That was a good point. Maybe Doug would get in touch and, if he didn't, she could always call him. She'd just have to nab her sister's phone and check the contacts list. She felt cheered by the thought.

"I bet you'll have heard from him before the end of the week and, if you don't, it's his loss," Nora said as they got up to leave.

"Thanks." Suzie smiled. Nora was probably right, although it wouldn't be the romantic encounter that she envisaged.

CHAPTER
FIFTEEN

Mandy shot a sideways glance at her boss. He'd been silent since they'd got in the car but there was a slight, almost bemused, smile playing round his lips. Suzie, really? It wasn't as if Mandy cared, but it was still a shock to the system for a man to be attracted to Suzie rather than her. She'd never seen him like this before. Douglas was lost in thought as she drove them home, oblivious of her breaking the speed limit and overtaking on the inside. He hadn't even noticed her cutting off another driver on a roundabout and the furious driver giving her the finger. She opened her mouth to question him but closed it again. There was no point in shooting her mouth off. It would be much better to be cool and wait.

"Amanda?"

"Yeah?"

"Can I have Suzie's number?"

Really? She couldn't believe her ears but, after a moment, managed to give a careless shrug. "Sure."

He looked over at her. "I meant now."

She glanced over and saw his finger poised to enter it into his phone. "Oh." She called it out. "Douglas?"

"Yeah?"

"I should warn you, Suzie's not really on the market."

"She has a partner?"

"No. She's only ever loved one man and, despite the fact that he's been gone eleven years, she hasn't dated since."

He seemed to ponder that for a moment, and then continued typing. "Noted."

She looked over at him. "Noted? What does that mean?"

"It means I appreciate the information."

"But you're still going to contact her?"

"Correct."

The tapping recommenced and, though Mandy longed to know what he was typing, she wouldn't give him the satisfaction of asking. He sent the text and fidgeted in his seat as he waited for an answer. Moments later his phone buzzed and the delighted grin that spread across his face told Mandy that her sister was most definitely interested.

"Don't you want to know what she said?" Douglas teased.

"I think I can guess. Just don't go getting your hopes up. To say Suzie's behaviour has been unpredictable since her accident is putting it mildly."

"If I didn't know better I'd think that you were jealous."

Mandy raised her eyebrows. "It's a good thing you know better. Go on, then, tell me, are you going on a date?"

"We are. I think I'll take her to a photo exhibition."

"Wow, you really know how to show a girl a good time."

He tutted. "You're such a philistine."

"Trust me, it's not Suzie's thing either. I doubt she's ever been in a gallery."

With that his phone buzzed and he laughed. "You're right, but she said she'd love to go."

Mandy rolled her eyes. "She's lying. What's going on, Douglas? You haven't dated since I came to work for you —"

"I didn't know I was under surveillance," he retorted.

"You stuck your oar into my love life so you can't object to me asking a few questions."

"Go on, then."

She pulled up outside his house and turned to look at him. "Why Suzie?"

He got a dreamy look on his face and shrugged. "She makes me smile."

"Great," she said, but for some reason his words were like a slap in the face.

"Yes!"

Nora turned away from the buskers she'd been enjoying and turned to Suzie. "What?"

"Douglas. He's taking me out."

Nora shook her head, bemused. "We've only just left him and he's asked you out on a date?"

Suzie chuckled. "I know, weird, huh?"

"I told you that you made an impression."

"It looks like it."

"Are you excited?"

"I am," Suzie answered honestly. It would be nice to catch up and talk about old times.

Nora hugged her. "I'm delighted. He seems like a nice man and it will be good for you to have some male company for a change."

Suzie smiled. It would be great. She and Doug had always been close despite the fact that there was twenty years between them, and she was sure that hadn't changed.

Her phone rang, the Cher ringtone making her jump. Thinking it was Doug again, she grinned as she pulled it from her pocket. "Hello?"

"Mum?"

Suzie frowned. "Jess?"

"Yeah. I can barely hear you, it's really noisy here."

"Where are you?" Suzie shouted, putting a finger in her other ear and shrugging when Nora shot her a questioning look.

"I'm at the hospital with Sharon."

Suzie gasped and clenched the phone tighter. "Why, what's happened?"

"Sorry, Mum, I can't hear you. Mum?" Jess shouted back. "I'm on my way over to pick you up. Bye."

"Jess? Jess?" Suzie stood, dazed for a moment.

"Suzie?"

"I need to get home right away. Sharon's in hospital."

"Oh my God, why?"

"No idea, Jess just said that she was on her way to pick me up."

156

Nora walked to the corner and stuck her hand out. Immediately a taxi screeched out of the rank and pulled up in front of them. "Come on. Keep calm. I'm sure everything will be fine."

Suzie sat in silence, Nora clutching her hand. Just as the car turned into her road, Jess was pulling into the driveway.

"Will I come with you?" Nora asked.

"No, thanks, Nora. I'll call you." Suzie handed over her keys and jumped out of the cab as Jess was stepping from her car. "What's happened? Is Sharon okay?"

"I honestly don't know, Mum. Apparently she fainted in a supermarket and was carted off in an ambulance. My number was the last one dialled on her mobile phone so they contacted me. I called Keith and waited at the hospital until he arrived before coming to get you. There was no news when I left. They were running tests. That's all I know."

"She just fainted and they took her to the hospital? Why would they do that?"

Jess shrugged, as she crawled through city traffic. "No idea. Perhaps it was just a precaution."

"The supermarket's afraid of being sued, more like," Suzie retorted. "By the time we get there she'll probably be ready to come home."

"Well, that would be good news, then, wouldn't it?" Jess said, her voice sharp.

"Yes, of course it would." Suzie scowled at her eldest.

"Phone Keith and see if he knows any more," Jess instructed.

Feeling like a naughty child, Suzie bit her lip and did as she was told, but it went straight to his voicemail. "No answer."

Suzie paced in front of the hospital's reception desk, her eyes on the large double door where people were coming and going. Occasionally she caught sight of patients on trolleys and her anxiety began to increase. She was about to push past the queue and demand to see her daughter when a young woman in a white coat came through the double door, talked to the receptionist and then approached her.

"Mrs Connors?"

"Yes, is my daughter okay?"

"She's being admitted."

"What? But why?"

"I'm afraid I don't have that information, but I can take you to her husband. I'm sure that he'll be able to fill you in."

Suzie followed her down the long and all-too-familiar corridors. She hadn't expected to be back here so soon. The young woman stopped outside a door and opened it and Suzie saw Keith sitting at a table, filling out forms. "What's going on, Keith? Is Sharon okay?"

He gave a weak smile and nodded. "Yes."

"Why are they admitting her, then?" Suzie demanded.

"Sit down," Keith said. "Sharon is fourteen weeks pregnant."

"Oh!" Suzie found herself smiling. "That's great news."

"I'm still trying to get my head round it," he admitted. "I'm happy but worried, too."

Suzie was mystified. "Why?"

"You don't remember," Keith grimaced.

"Remember what?"

"Sharon had a really tough pregnancy with Bobby."

Suzie searched her memory but could find nothing.

"Her blood pressure's sky high, apparently, so she's going to have to take it easy."

A nurse poked her head round the door. "Mr Mulvey? I can take you up to your wife's ward now."

Sharon was sitting in bed, hooked up to a drip and looking upset when they walked in.

"Keith, what are you doing here? You have to go and pick up Bobby."

Keith perched on the edge of the bed and took her hand. "Calm down. I called Zach's mum and she's taking him back to their place."

"He's not that friendly with Zach." Sharon frowned.

"He'll be fine for a couple of hours. Stop worrying and tell me what the doctor said."

Sharon ran a tired hand through her hair. "I'm not sure. I haven't taken much in since they told me I'm pregnant."

Suzie hugged her. "Congratulations, love."

Sharon gave a half-hearted smile. "Thanks, Mum."

"When are they going to let you out of here?" Suzie looked around with distaste.

"I'm not sure. They're waiting for some test results."

"I'll go and see what I can find out." Keith kissed her cheek and left them.

"You'll be fine, love." Suzie smiled. "I'm sure they're just being overcautious."

"Yeah."

"Here you are!" Jess came in and plonked down on the end of the bed. "I've been all over the place looking for you. How are you doing, sis? Have they figured out why you fainted?"

"My blood pressure's very high and, oh yeah" — she gave her sister a lame grin — "I'm pregnant."

"Really?" Jess smiled and then Suzie saw her face change as she obviously remembered what she hadn't. "Is the baby okay?"

"Yes, that much I do know."

"That's good news at least. When are you due?"

Sharon frowned. "December, I think."

"Any problems?"

"Hypertension." Sharon sighed.

"What?" Suzie asked.

"High blood pressure," Jess translated, looking in concern at her sister. "Surely they can give you something to bring it down?"

"Yes, maybe, oh, I'm not sure," Sharon said, looking slightly weepy. "I'm tired."

"Hey, don't worry, it'll be fine," Jess assured her. "You look so much better than you did."

"You're a bit peaky," Suzie said, "but that's the beige top. Never wear beige, Sharon. It's really not your colour."

Sharon sighed. "Jeez, thanks, Mum."

"What? I'm just saying," Suzie said, wondering why such simple comments annoyed her daughters. Noel wasn't so touchy.

160

"I hope they're going to let me go home or Bobby will be really upset."

"Forget about Bobby for the moment," Jess said, gently. "Lying here worrying won't help bring your blood pressure down. If anything, it might delay them letting you go home."

"Will you help with Bobby, Jess? If I'm kept in longer, I mean?"

Sharon stared at her sister, something passing between them that Suzie didn't understand.

"Of course I will," Jess promised.

"And haven't you got me?" Suzie said, trying to sound more positive than she felt.

"Thanks, Mum, but Jess has the car," Sharon said, "and I'm not happy with you taking on too much too soon."

"I suppose," Suzie said, feeling relieved if a little guilty, "but Jess's right: you must stop worrying."

There was a buzz and Suzie watched Jess dig out her phone and redden.

"Everything all right?" Sharon asked.

"Yeah, just work."

Suzie stared at her and, when Jess wouldn't meet her eyes, she just knew that the message was from that bastard, Louis Healy. "How is work going, Jess?" she asked.

"Busy," Jess mumbled.

Suzie tried to quash the bubble of hot anger building inside. "You do too much. I think you should drop one of the papers. The *Gazette*, for example."

"I get to write the articles I want to write for the *Gazette*, Mum. It's good experience and could lead to bigger things."

Suzie lost it. "What? You screwing more editors?"

"Mum!" Sharon looked horrified.

"Sorry, Sharon, but I'm not stupid. Your sister's getting that work because of her body not her talent."

"Mum!" Sharon hissed again. "Stop it — now."

Jess stood up and faced her. "Yes, Mum, stop it. You're not doing Sharon any good. If you have anything to say to me, at least have the decency to leave her out of it, instead of attacking me in a hospital ward."

Suzie was suddenly conscious of the silence from the other patients in the room and Sharon's face, crimson with embarrassment. Suzie looked back at Jess, who was glaring at her from cold, hard eyes, her mouth set in a grim line. Lovely Jess, who was always smiling and kind, who'd sat by her hospital bed every day.

"Go home, Mum," Sharon said.

Suzie met her eyes and saw the same coldness there.

"Go on, I'll call you later," Sharon added, her voice softer.

Suzie looked round the room and watched the occupants hastily avert their eyes. She looked back at Jess, but she'd turned her back on her mother and now sat on the bed by her little sister, who took her hand and squeezed it. Suzie felt like the outsider and realised she'd overstepped some mark. Yet again. She didn't understand how; she'd only spoken her mind. "You know where I am if you need me." Suzie's smile faltered when neither of them replied. "Take care, then," she said, with forced cheerfulness and, ignoring the curious stares, walked the length of the ward and out of the door, shaken by the joint dismissal by her daughters. Why would they turn on her like that? Maybe she'd been hard on Jess, but it was only because she loved her and didn't want to see her waste herself on a scumbag and get a bad reputation. Then, no matter how talented she was or how hard she worked, people would always think she'd risen through the ranks on her back rather than her own two feet. Was it wrong that she cared about that? Wasn't it her duty as a mother to try to do the best for her child?

Suzie felt confused and cross but was surprised, on the bus home, to find her cheeks wet with tears.

CHAPTER
SIXTEEN

Four days later, the obstetrician smiled at Sharon and Keith and disappeared through the split in the curtains. Sharon put her head in her hands and groaned. She felt the bed give as her husband sat down beside her and stroked her hair.

"Hey, this is good news, you're coming home."

"Yeah, to go to bed."

"Stop exaggerating. You just have to take it easy."

"How am I supposed to do that?" She heard her own voice rising and took a deep breath. The doctors and nurses had made it clear that her stress and anxiety would hurt her and the baby and, though the news of her pregnancy had come as a shock, once she got used to the idea, she was quite excited about it. She stroked her still-flat stomach. "Sorry, Baby. Mummy's sorry."

Keith lifted her chin and smiled at her. "We'll figure it out. Hey, we've a new baby on the way."

His eyes shone with happiness and Sharon gave a grudging smile. "Yeah."

He leaned forward and brushed his mouth against hers in the softest of kisses. "Everything will be perfect."

164

"But how will we manage? I'm not allowed to drive or carry anything heavy. I have to rest for a couple of hours during the day." Panic threatened and she kept rubbing her tummy, willing herself to stay calm.

"I told you, we'll work it out. I can drop Bobby to school and we could arrange for him to go to the after-school club at the crèche next door until I'm finished work."

"No. That would be a disaster. Not only would we be changing his whole routine, he'd have to deal with lots of different adults and children, all strangers. You know he couldn't cope with that." She could see Keith fighting to hold in his frustration but she wouldn't give in on this. She knew that it was wrong for Bobby and would be a huge setback in their son's development.

"We don't have many options, sweetheart. My mother has her hands full looking after Dad, or you know that she'd be happy to help."

"I know that," Sharon assured him. Neither of Keith's parents were in good health and certainly wouldn't be able to cope with Bobby.

Keith looked at her, his eyes beseeching. "We need your Mum, Sharon. We need to get past whatever is going on between her and Jess and do what's best for *our* family."

She knew that he was right, but the thought of entrusting Bobby to her mother's care still scared the hell out of her. She needed to have some control, some way to keep a tight rein on her mother. She'd been a great mum to them, so surely, somewhere beneath this new, hard shell, the softer woman was still in there.

Sharon finally met her husband's eyes. "If she does it, she does it in our house, where I can keep an eye on her."

"Absolutely not. You would never relax. Every time you heard her raise her voice you'd be running down to check up on her. He goes to your mum's house. I know it's not an ideal solution but it's all we've got."

Sharon closed her eyes and racked her brain for a better one, but she felt so incredibly tired, and it would be a relief to let someone else take control for a while. She nodded in resignation. "Okay, but we need to put some controls in place."

"Controls?"

"We need to explain the situation to Bobby's teacher so that she can watch out for any change in his behaviour."

He nodded. "Makes sense."

"And I'll ask Jess to drop in from time to time to keep an eye on Mum."

"Remember, Noel lives there too," he pointed out.

Sharon brightened. She was pretty sure that Noel's exams ended next week and he'd be free for the summer. "That's true. We could give him a few quid to hang around and keep an eye on Mum. He'd be glad of the cash."

Keith laughed. "I'd be happy to line his pockets rather than a stranger's, and, remember, love, it's only for four to five hours, five days a week. The rest of the time Bobby will be with us. It will all be fine, you'll see."

And Sharon felt herself relax for the first time. Maybe this could actually work. It might even mean that Keith would develop a better relationship with their son.

"Get your stuff together and let's go home, Shaz. Then I'll go and see your mum."

"Shouldn't I do it?" Sharon asked although she had no real wish to. She hadn't seen her mother since that dreadful scene when she'd been so awful to Jess.

"No. You look after junior and leave your mum to me. I'll handle it, I promise."

Tears filled her eyes, as they did so often these days. At least now she knew the reason for them and her huge appetite. She fondled her tummy and smiled at her husband. "I love you."

He hugged her. "I love you too."

Suzie tutted irritably as Keith stood at the window, jangling his keys. She banged down the kettle and glared at him. "For fuck's sake, will you stop fidgeting, Keith? You're worse than Bobby."

"Sorry." He pocketed the keys and sat down at the table. "It's been a difficult few days."

Suzie put the coffee in front of him and sat down. "Is Sharon's condition worse than you're letting on?"

"It's probably more serious than even she realises," he admitted. "It's not really the baby's life they're worried about."

Suzie gasped. "What do we do?"

"Sharon needs to be stress-free and have total rest for the remainder of the pregnancy. I wanted Bobby to go to a childminder after school and then I'd pick him up on my way home from work, but Sharon won't hear of it. She says changing his routine and sending him to a stranger would be even worse."

"I suppose that's true," Suzie admitted.

"Which is why I was hoping you would take him."

Suzie stared at him, realising she'd completely snookered herself. She tried to come up with an excuse, but how could she say no? Her daughter's life was at stake. If anything happened to Sharon, she'd never be able to forgive herself. It would be damn near impossible to keep her temper with the little brat, and she knew that minding him would exhaust her, but she'd just have to get on with it. There was no other option. She took a deep breath and looked Keith in the eye. "Of course I will."

"I'm really grateful, Suzie — only there's something else. Sharon will only agree to this if you treat Bobby . . . well, the way she does." He held up his hand as she opened her mouth to tell him where to go. "I know that you, like me, think that she's far too soft on him. But the fact is, Suzie, if you're hard on him and he comes home upset, then it defeats the purpose. We have to keep Sharon calm so that her blood pressure stays under control. If that means both of us biting our tongues for a few months and letting Bobby get away with murder, it's a small price to pay for a healthy wife and baby. It would only be for a few hours, five days a week. Think you can manage that?"

Suzie thought of how she lashed out, lost her temper and swore, and felt real fear for a moment. *Could* she control herself? She looked up at his anxious expression as he waited for her answer. "I'll do my very best, Keith. That's all I can promise."

"That's good enough for me. Thanks, Suzie. I can't tell you what a weight you've taken off my shoulders."

She looked at him, surprised to see that his eyes were bright with tears.

"You're a good lad, and Sharon is lucky to have you," she said, grudgingly when he was leaving.

"And I'm lucky to have her and the best mother-in-law in the world."

"Ah, now, less of that bullshit," she said, flapping her hands at him. "When do I start?"

"Wednesday?"

So soon? Suzie felt panicky but she managed a grim smile. "Grand. And you don't need to collect Bobby from school, Keith. I'll do it. I'm supposed to be taking exercise."

He frowned. "Let me run that by the boss and I'll get back to you. But thanks. Oh, there was one other thing. I'm pushing my luck now but can you babysit tomorrow night?"

Suzie felt herself blushing. "Oh, no, sorry, Keith. I'm going out."

"No worries, I'll ask Jess. Bye, Suzie."

"Bye, love."

Jess checked her ringing phone and let it go to voicemail. She wasn't ready to talk to her mother yet. She was fed up of the barbs and insults and making allowances for her bad behaviour because of that brain injury. There was no reason why she had to pretend she liked the woman her mother had become. She didn't. Mum had become an insensitive, hard bitch and that was an end to it. Jess wasn't going to let her hurt her any more. And as Suzie was so keen on straight-talking, Jess decided, the gloves were off.

The phone rang again and, when she saw it was her sister, she answered. "Hi, Sharon? How are you feeling?"

"Better, thanks. I'm home but with strict instructions to rest."

"I'm glad you're home but exactly how do you get to rest when you have a child?" Specifically Bobby. Ten minutes in his company when he was in one of his moods was exhausting.

"I can't, not alone," Sharon agreed and proceeded to tell Jess the plan. Which was all very well and Jess had offered to help, but spending time with both her nephew and Mum was asking a hell of a lot. She realised that Sharon had stopped talking and was waiting for an answer.

"I know that you probably don't want to see Mum at the moment, but I would feel so much better if you could drop in and out and play spy. Please?"

Jess closed her eyes and let her head fall back against the cushions. "Of course."

"Really?"

"Yeah, but don't blame me if your son is scarred for life when he sees his aunty throttle his granny."

Sharon laughed. "Thanks, Jess. Thanks so much."

She went on to tell Jess about asking Noel to help, which made sense. If they were all involved in Bobby's care, it shortened the amount of time each of them had to spend with the child, which would make it less likely any of them would blow a fuse. She felt bad thinking that way about her nephew but it was a fact. How would Sharon cope with him when she had a baby to look after, too? Jess shuddered.

She stared at the phone in her hand and debated whether to call her mother or just drop in. They had to talk and they couldn't do it in front of Sharon. She decided to go round there. It would be harder to say what needed saying face to face, but Jess had found out that there was more chance of getting through to Suzie if you were looking her in the eye. Not bothering with makeup, she threw on jogging pants and a hoody and tied her long hair back into a ponytail before setting off for her mother's house. Though it was May, it was a chilly morning and she took the shortest route along the busy main road. She'd come home along the coast when it was warmer. She'd probably need the longer walk to blow off steam after this conversation.

The small house sat in a sprawling estate in Kilbarrack and, as she approached her family home, Jess noticed that the wall could do with a coat of paint, and the grass and flowerbeds were overgrown. She'd have to nag Noel to do something about it. She pulled out her keys, then hesitated. Given how strained things were at the moment, it seemed inappropriate to let herself in, so she rang the doorbell. Suzie came to the door, her face lighting up when she saw her. For an instant, Jess thought that she looked like she used to, always greeting her with a welcoming smile. Instead of the fancy tops and tight trousers she'd taken to wearing, Suzie was dressed in a warm top and comfortable jeans and, like Jess, she wore no makeup.

"Jess, what a nice surprise. I've been calling you." There was no reproach in her voice but a wariness in her eyes. "Have you lost your key?"

"No."

Suzie frowned when she offered no explanation but didn't comment. "Come on in. I'll put on the kettle."

Jess didn't want tea but she went along with the ritual, perching on the edge of the chair. "Where's Noel?"

"He has his last exam today and then a few of them are going out on the town tonight. I'm so glad it's finally over. He could do with a rest."

"He'll have plenty of time to rest," Jess scoffed, irritated that, while her mother's personality had changed and she was lashing out at everyone, Noel was still the blue-eyed boy. Suzie brought the tea to the table and opened a packet of chocolate biscuits. "You said you've been calling me. What was it you wanted to say?" Jess prompted.

"I wanted to say sorry for talking to you like that in the hospital."

Jess shook her head. What kind of an apology was that? "So, you're not sorry for what you said, just where you said it?"

172

Suzie looked cross. "Why are you trying to trip me up? You know how I feel about your relationship with Louis Healy."

"Now you call it a 'relationship'? In the hospital I was fucking my way to the top."

"I never said that."

Jess shrugged. "The words may have been different but your meaning was clear. It was certainly obvious to all the patients and staff on the ward."

"Well, I'm sorry, but I get angry every time I think of you letting that man maul you. You're worth ten of him — no, twenty. You're not still seeing him, are you?"

"Frankly, it's none of your business. I'm an adult, Mum, and I'll do what I want, I don't need your permission and I have no interest in your opinion."

Suzie looked gobsmacked. She sat in silence for a long moment. "No, you don't," she said finally, "but, if you have an ounce of the self-respect or integrity I believe you to, then you will stay away from him."

Jess gave a small nod. She was not going to admit she'd broken up with Louis. Maybe it was childish but she wanted her mother to realise that she wouldn't tolerate her interference.

"The reason I came over is to tell you that you can't lash out like that any more. That behaviour is completely unacceptable and it's not good for Sharon." She saw her mother's eyes widen but forced herself to continue. "I understand that you are thoughtless and insensitive because of your brain injury, but you have to understand how hurtful it is for us. In a way, we've lost our mum. Well, Sharon and I have. It seems Noel can do no wrong."

"That's not true!" her mother protested.

"It is, but that's fine. We all spoiled him. What's not fine is the way you talk to Sharon about Bobby and the way you talk to him too."

Suzie's expression was stubborn. "I speak my mind."

"No one wants to hear your opinion," Jess said bluntly. "This isn't about you, Mum. It's not even about Bobby. Sharon's life and the health of her baby are all that matters now. We need to work together to keep her calm and" — she glared at her mother — "if that means not speaking your mind, then that's the way it's going to be, okay?"

Suzie stared at her, looking stunned, and finally nodded.

"Good." She stood up to leave.

"Jess?" She paused in the doorway and looked back at her mother.

"I'll do my best."

Jess gave her a grudging smile. "That's all I ask."

Strolling back along Dollymount beach, Jess felt optimistic. That had gone much better than she'd expected. To get an apology was one thing but seeing some understanding in her mother's expression of the harm she was doing was worth so much more.

Jess thought of what lay ahead of them and sighed. How she was going to juggle her workload and help look after a child was beyond her. She often boasted that she could work from anywhere but it was impossible around Bobby. She hadn't been the best aunt so far. She never knew what to say to the child. Her attempts to engage him were usually blanked and she'd end up putting on a kid's movie and watching it with him, although she seemed to enjoy them more than he did.

Noel was the one who seemed best able to reach the child. Perhaps it was because he was still a big kid himself and a bit of a nerd. He didn't try to charm or impress Bobby. He just hung out with him. Jess's thoughts turned to Cal and the promise she'd made to check on Noel. It had gone completely out of her head since Sharon had been rushed to hospital, but she'd arrange to see him soon. Apart from sussing out if he was worried about anything, she needed to impress on him how important it was that they keep their mother under control. Jess had played down Sharon's scare as Noel was in the middle of his exams, but, now that he was done, she could tell him the full story.

Keith had called her after the obstetrician had taken him aside for a private word, leaving him in no doubt of the seriousness of Sharon's condition. When he'd told Jess she'd promised faithfully that he had their support and they'd do everything they could to help. She hoped they could rely on Suzie to step up to the plate. She felt more confident now that they'd talked — or, rather, *she'd* talked and her mother had seemed to listen. They'd cope. It might not be the easiest thing they'd ever done but, one way or another, they'd cope.

CHAPTER
SEVENTEEN

Jess's phone vibrated in the pocket of her hoody and she tugged it out, groaning when she saw that it was from Louis. She stared at it for a moment, then shoving it back into her pocket, carried on walking. She didn't really want to read it. She could always say that she hadn't received it if it was work-related, and he'd be forced to email her. On the other hand, he might decide to pay her another visit. Jess left the beach, clambered back up onto the boardwalk and, crossing to her favourite café, ordered a coffee. She took it to a table overlooking the bay and set the phone on the table in front of her. After a couple of sips, she read Louis's text.

Business trip to Cork tomorrow, overnight. Come with me.

Her heart skipped a beat at the request and she remembered the early days of their romance when Louis had been sweet and loving. As she sat pondering how best to respond, another message came through, this time from Keith, asking her if she'd babysit tomorrow night. Relieved that the decision had been taken out of her hands, Jess fired off a text to Keith saying yes and then one to Louis saying that she couldn't go to Cork as she had family commitments. Of course, she should have just said no but, if Keith hadn't asked her to babysit, she knew that she might have been tempted to go with him. There was no hope for her.

The phone vibrated again: a message from Keith, thanking her; but there was no response from Louis. She shivered, wondering if Louis would make her pay for this. She had managed to avoid him since the day that Cal had interrupted them but she knew he was annoyed. She shook her head. There was no point in worrying about that now. She checked her emails. There was one from Beth and another from Dermot, both looking for pieces by Friday. Good. If she was kept busy, she'd have no time to worry about Louis. Jess finished her coffee and headed home to work.

Suzie was getting ready for her "date" when her sister rang.

"What are you going to wear?"

Remembering that Mandy thought that this was a *real* date, Suzie grinned and pretended to be nervous and excited. The second was true, but not for the reason Mandy thought. Still, maybe if her sister thought they were dating, she'd back off and let Doug go to Zagreb alone. "I haven't a clue, Mandy. Any ideas?"

"Something casual and comfortable," her sister advised. "Douglas will be dragging you round for hours and he certainly won't bother dressing up."

Suzie had to smile at that. If Mandy had seen him in his heyday she'd have been flabbergasted by the man's style. It also occurred to her that her sister didn't want her to look her best.

"He looked smart enough the other day," she said to Mandy.

"Only because I put on a wash and left those clothes out for him."

Suzie frowned. She didn't like the idea of Mandy having access to Douglas's bedroom, let alone his closets. Surely a personal assistant shouldn't be quite *that* personal. She decided it was time for straight talking. "Mandy, do you have a problem with me going out with Douglas?"

There was a short silence on the other end of the line and then a splutter of laughter. "Of course not. Once you stick with visiting galleries and leave the four-star hotels to me, it's cool."

Suzie scowled. The one thing worse than Mandy being able to have almost any man, was the fact that she knew it. Suzie hoped Doug wouldn't take the bait. She didn't know why she felt so protective of him. Sure, it would be wonderful to see him happy again but with a nice woman who would be a companion and a friend, not someone who wanted him for his money. Still, remembering the clever businessman she'd worked for, she knew that she should have more faith in him.

"I'm on my way out too," Mandy was saying. "Have a good evening and don't do anything I'd do."

There was no chance of that. "Bye, Mandy."

178

Suzie continued to dither over what to wear, finally narrowing it down to two outfits, which she left out on the bed. Nora was in Dublin and had offered to come round and do her hair, so Suzie decided to let her choose.

When Nora walked into the bedroom, she raised her eyebrows when she saw her selections.

"Let me guess. You bought these when you were on your shopping spree with Mandy."

"Yeah, why? What's wrong with them?"

"Honestly?"

"Of course, honestly," Suzie snapped. What bloody use was an opinion if it wasn't an honest one?

"Okay, here goes. You look great, Suzie and you know I love your new hairstyle, but these clothes just don't suit you. They're for a young woman, although I'm not even sure either of your daughters would wear them."

Suzie looked at the clothes and mentally went through the girls' wardrobes and realised Nora was right. Jess wore rich but muted colours that suited her colouring, and, though she didn't have much money, she always looked classy. Sharon was much more adventurous and adored fashion and pretty colours, but she never wore the short skirts or skimpy tops that Mandy had persuaded her to buy.

Suzie frowned, trying to figure out what was wrong with the two outfits. One was a simple, above-the-knee black dress and she had to hold her breath in order to zip it up. The effects were that her breasts were pushed up, giving her an ample cleavage. The other outfit was tight blue jeans teamed with a blue halter neck that again flattered her breasts and made her look and feel young and sexy. Maybe Nora was just jealous that she was able to wear clothes like this now, but no. She immediately dismissed the thought. Nora was an attractive, confident woman with her own unique style.

"Remember what you were wearing the day we met Douglas?"

Suzie frowned as she tried to recall. "My blue top and trousers?" It was the only outfit she'd selected herself and Mandy had dismissed it as frumpy.

"It brought out the lovely blue of your eyes and you looked relaxed and comfortable. That's the Suzie Douglas fell for."

Suzie had to grin at the thought of Doug Hamilton falling for Suzie Clarke!

Luckily, Nora's attention was still focused on the clothes. "Do you think you're going to look or feel comfortable in either of these outfits?"

She glanced at her new wardrobe and sighed. Few of them were made with comfort in mind but Mandy said you had to suffer to be beautiful.

"Honestly, Suzie? Dressed like that you just look like an older version of Mandy. But Douglas didn't ask your sister out: he asked *you*."

"I look pathetic trying to pretend I'm younger than I am, don't I?"

Nora gave a tactful shrug. "You're gorgeous and sexy and look younger than your years. You have nothing to prove, sweetheart. Just be you."

180

Suzie wondered about Mandy's motives. Had she deliberately set her up to look like a silly old fool? Yet, she wore this sort of stuff all the time and could carry it off. But then she was ten years younger. "I spent a fortune on this lot, Nora," she said in disgust. "I can hardly dump it all."

Nora smiled. "Don't be daft. You don't have to dump it. All you need to do is mix things up a little. For example, wear the skimpier tops with a cardigan or wrap and longer skirt or trousers. And flat shoes and opaque tights will make the short skirts look a lot classier."

"And my little black dress? I suppose you want me to put that in the giveaway bag."

"No way, it's good fabric and well made. Wear it with flat shoes and a chunky necklace or a colourful scarf and you'll look great."

Suzie looked at her in admiration and smiled. "That's clever. You should go into the styling business."

"And compete with Mandy?" Nora said in mock horror. "As if I'd dare!"

"Mandy wasn't thinking about what suited me at all, was she? She was just dressing me in the way she dresses and I went along with it because she always looks so bloody sexy. I've always envied her and, once I finally had a figure, I couldn't wait to show it off."

Nora hugged her. "That's understandable, Suzie. And, whatever else she might have got wrong, she made up for it with the hair."

Suzie grinned. "True."

An hour later, her hair and makeup done, Suzie stood in front of the mirror to examine Nora's choice. It was an old outfit from the back of her wardrobe that Suzie had stopped wearing when she put on weight, but couldn't bear to give it away. The top was deep-wine in colour and the matching skirt dropped almost to her ankles, but clung to every curve.

"You look lovely." Nora gave her an affectionate smile. "And the heels really set it off."

Suzie nodded. Those shoes had been at the bottom of her wardrobe for years too because she'd bought them in a sale and never had anything to wear them with. They were suede and the colour of toffee and, though she didn't have a matching handbag, Nora pointed out that her casual, canvas shoulder bag held both colours of her outfit in its bright cheery pattern. She couldn't stop staring at her own image. Whereas Mandy's outfits made her look hip and sexy, this outfit made her look classy and elegant. She met Nora's eyes and smiled. "Thanks. I love it."

"And I bet Douglas will too."

CHAPTER
EIGHTEEN

Douglas stood on the doorstep, smiling. "You look smashing."

Suzie was glad that Nora had diplomatically left, as, when he opened his arms to her, she almost fell into them, tears in her eyes as he held her close. "I can't believe that it's really you. That all this time you've been Mandy's boss and I never knew."

"It's me, all right." He pulled back to smile down into her face. "Now, there *is* a photo exhibition but it will be open until ten. What do you say we go have a bite to eat first and catch up? I want to hear everything about you."

"Likewise." She grinned at him before throwing her arms around him again. "It's so bloody good to see you, Doug."

"And you, sweetheart."

"Tell me, when did Doug Hamilton become Douglas Thornton?" she asked.

He chuckled. "Thornton is my mother's maiden name and I thought it would look good on a book cover. When I returned to Ireland, I kept using it. I suppose I feel more like Douglas Thornton now. Doug Hamilton is dead and buried."

Suzie shivered. "Don't say that."

He smiled. "I don't mean it in a negative way. I'm just not that man anymore."

"Can I still call you Doug?"

"You'd better," he grinned.

They got into the cab he had waiting, and Douglas told the driver to take them into the city centre. His arm around her shoulders, he drew her down side streets and alleys, finally stopping outside a small, plain doorway. "It doesn't look like much but I promise you, the food is amazing."

"Ah, fuck the food, Doug. I doubt I can even eat. I never thought that I'd lay eyes on you again. I thought you'd gone for good."

"You don't get rid of me that easily and, trust me, you will eat," he said and led her inside.

"You see?" Doug gestured at her empty plate.

Suzie laughed and licked her fingers for good measure. "This reminds me of us eating beans on toast in my flat."

He smiled. "They were happy days. How long has it been?"

Suzie hesitated as she met his eyes. "Twenty-four years."

"Of course. Stupid of me." Pulling himself together, he gave her a rueful smile. "How on earth did you cope living over our garage?"

"Are you kidding me? That place was a palace compared to our house. I'd so much space and privacy and I felt safe."

184

He grimaced. "Is your dad still alive?"

"No, he died years ago but was a bastard to the end. Happily my mother survived him by six years, so she had some peace."

"She stuck with him?" His eyes widened in disbelief.

"Of course, even though I asked her to move in with us. Marie, remember my other sister?"

He nodded.

"She lives in Canada with her family and she wanted mam to go and live with her but she wouldn't. Still, Da didn't lay a finger on her in recent years. I warned him, if he did, I'd have him in prison even if I had to lie through my teeth to put him there."

"You were so tough and feisty. I always admired that."

Suzie threw back her head and laughed. "Feck off, Doug. When you first saw the state of me and heard I was pregnant you didn't want to hire me."

"Admittedly, I may have had my doubts."

"Not as much as your wife," Suzie muttered, and then clapped a hand over her mouth. "Aw, shit, sorry, Doug. I didn't mean that."

He chuckled. "You did and you're right. Pamela was a dreadful snob but you weren't exactly friendly either. At the start you were so prickly and it was bloody impossible to get a smile out of you. But once we saw how talented you were and that you weren't afraid of hard work, we realised that Gina had found a gem."

"Ah, Gina." Suzie smiled, remembering her first boss who soon became a great friend.

"Are you still in touch with her?"

"No," she admitted with a guilty sigh. "My husband, John, was from Limerick and his work and family were there, so I moved when we married and lost touch with all of the CML gang."

"Did you have more children?"

Suzie nodded, smiling. "Two, a girl, Sharon, and a boy, Noel."

"Were you happy?" he asked.

She wasn't sure how to answer that. Thanks to her brain injury there were some hazy bits about the problems in her marriage but she knew there were some. "Reasonably," she said finally. "When Sharon and Noel came along with their pale skin and freckles and looking nothing like Jess, there were whispers. And, though John stood by her to the end, he wasn't as close to her as he was to his own children. Still, I'm sure I'm the only one who noticed."

"She was such a sweet child," Doug said with a sad smile. "How could anyone not love her?"

Suzie shrugged. "In fairness, at the beginning he was wonderful and I think he believed that he'd be able to treat her as his own but, I suppose, human nature kicked in."

"Did Jess ever ask about her real dad?"

Suzie looked at him with guilty eyes. "Jess thinks John *is* her dad, that's the way he wanted it."

"But all your friends and family knew," he said, confused.

"Mine did, yes. I explained what we had decided and then we moved to Limerick to start afresh. Given John hadn't ever had another girlfriend and travelled a lot, it was easy to convince his friends and family that Jess was his. We concocted a story that we'd dated a few months and then broke up and, when he came back to ask me to marry him, he discovered he was a dad."

"And they swallowed that?" He looked astounded.

She chuckled. "I'm sure some had their doubts but they didn't dare say it to his face. Besides, as I said, he was great with Jess back then."

"That's quite a story. You never thought of telling her over the years?"

"I promised John I wouldn't."

"But since his death . . ."

"A promise is a promise, Doug." It struck her then that she didn't owe John such loyalty but she wasn't sure why not.

"What about your obligation to Jess?" Doug persisted.

Suzie bristled. "I've always done right by Jess," she snapped. "What would be the point in telling her now?"

"She would understand why John treated her differently." Just like in the old days, he wasn't remotely put out by her tone, fixing her with his calm gaze.

"Leave it, Doug."

He gave a resigned nod and topped up her glass. "How did John die?"

"He was in charge of purchasing for a food-processing plant and he was visiting the farm of one of his suppliers and got caught between two pieces of machinery. He was only thirty-eight, Noel was just nine."

"Dear God, that's horrific, I'm so sorry."

"You have no idea," she assured him with a sigh. "But I had to keep going for the kids' sake."

"Amanda told me that he was the love of your life and that you haven't dated since."

Susie smirked. "Did she, now?"

"It's not true?"

"No, it is. I loved John but, I'll be honest, marrying him meant not only security but a dad for Jess."

"That doesn't sound very romantic," he said, looking disappointed.

Suzie chuckled. "I don't suppose it does but, truly, we were happy and John was the perfect family man."

Doug looked at her with sad eyes. "I'm sorry you lost him so young and I'm even sorrier that you've found no partner since."

"And neither have you?" Suzie studied him.

He shook his head. "Pamela was irreplaceable."

"And yet you were still unfaithful." She sighed and put her hand over his. "I'm sorry. That was out of order."

He shrugged. "It's true."

"There were issues on both sides in your marriage and, in the end, Pamela was happy," she reminded him. "So very happy, Doug."

"I was, too, more than I'd ever been. Life is fucking cruel."

"Shite," Suzie agreed, remembering the dark days when they'd watched the cancer consume Pamela and how distraught Doug had been when she died. "When you disappeared like that we were worried sick about you."

188

"Sorry. I should have let you know my plans but I didn't really have any. I wasn't thinking straight. I just knew that I had to get away. Everything reminded me of Pam. Everywhere I looked, I saw her: at work, in a restaurant and at home. I'd wake up in the morning and smell her perfume and, for a moment, I'd think there'd been some mistake and she was still there. I'd have gone out of my mind if I'd stayed. And I knew that Mal was well able to take over."

"And he was. He ran that company as if it was his own. Such a good man, a lovely guy."

"Is he still married to that witch?" he asked.

Suzie laughed. "No idea. I exchange Christmas cards with Jack and Gina — they have three kids now — but I lost touch with Malcolm."

"I sent postcards to the office from whatever countries I travelled to, but, once CML closed, I lost touch with them."

"I was sad to hear CML had stopped trading."

He gave a wry smile. "When times are hard, the first thing to go are the luxuries and, let's face it, our clients knew how to throw the most lavish events."

Suzie nodded, remembering the premier-class travel to exotic locations, the limos and the five-star hotels. "They were mad times."

"But fun, and" — he touched his glass to hers, his eyes full of pride — "we were one hell of a team."

"Have you really been living like a hermit?" she asked.

He chuckled. "Is that what Amanda said? I suppose it's true but I have my writing."

Suzie smiled but felt sad, too. Doug had been such a vibrant, larger than life character in his day, confident and fun-loving, but that man was gone.

He studied her and shook his head. "I still don't understand why men haven't been beating down your door. You're gorgeous."

She laughed. "That's down to my accident. Over the years, thanks to lack of exercise, three pregnancies and my obsession with chocolate eclairs, I looked like a beached whale and I took to living in sloppy sweatshirts and stretch trousers."

"You're speaking in the past tense," he pointed out. "Has something changed? You know Amanda warned me not to get my hopes up about our 'date'. She said that you were rather unpredictable at the moment. I was flattered that she thought you might be attracted to an old man like me."

Suzie laughed. "I am!"

He pulled a face. "As a surrogate dad, yeah, I know."

She started to fold and unfold her napkin as she considered whether this was one of the times she should speak her mind or keep her mouth shut.

"What's on your mind, Suzie? When you start fidgeting, something's up."

"You know me too bloody well," she complained. "Tell me to mind my own business if you want but, do you have feelings for Mandy?"

His eyes widened and then he burst out laughing. "Of course not. Why on earth would you think that? I'll be seventy next year, for Christ's sake, and she's not even forty."

"Age difference never bothered you in the past," Susie retorted.

He looked taken aback by her candour. "You don't pull your punches, do you? That was different. I was a young man, I loved women, I had needs and I had marital problems. But why on earth would you think Mandy is interested in me?"

"She's dissatisfied with her life. I think she always has been." Suzie frowned. "You know I have no idea why I'm saying that, it's not as if I remember, thanks to the knock on the head."

He frowned. "I thought you'd made a complete recovery."

"Not complete," she admitted, and explained her symptoms and how her family were reacting.

"I'm sorry, Suzie. That can't be easy. The strange thing is, I haven't noticed any difference in you."

"You knew me BC."

"BC?" He frowned.

"Before children. I had to change my vocabulary once Jess started to talk."

"Ah, I see. But do you feel all right?"

"I feel fine," she assured him. "Now, to get back to Mandy."

"Must we?"

She ignored his frown. "All I'm saying is that time is marching on and I think she's getting nervous. She wants to see the world and she hasn't found a meal ticket yet."

He sank back in his chair and folded his arms, eyebrows raised. "And she has me in her sights?"

"I think so but I could be wrong. She's not a bad person but . . ." Susie struggled to find a nice way to say that her sister was a gold-digging tart. "I just don't want you falling for one of her lines. She'd spend every penny you have if you let her, and that's the embarrassing truth."

Doug gave a short laugh as he reached for the wine and poured the last of it into their glasses. "Don't worry, Suzie. I'm very definitely off the market."

"What is it with your sister?" he asked after they had finished their meal and were strolling aimlessly through the city. "It's not just about money. She has an odd attitude towards men. They're like buses, arriving one after the other, but she tires of them within weeks, sometimes less. Did someone break her heart in the past? Is that what's made her so cold and hard?"

"She's not *that* bad." Suzie felt obliged to defend Mandy. "I told you, she's just never satisfied. The grass is always greener, you know?"

"Mark my words, a man made her that way."

Suzie frowned. His words triggered something in the back of her mind but it slipped away again before she could identify it. Damn brain! "She's always said that she doesn't want to be tied down or have kids and I believe that part. She never showed any interest in mine until they became completely independent. But forty is looming and maybe my accident has made her consider her own mortality. I think she's afraid of growing old alone."

"And poor? And I'm the answer to her problems. It makes sense, I suppose. I'd be dead long before her. She'd be a rich widow."

Suzie snorted. "I don't know about marriage, but she definitely expects you to take her to Zagreb. So, mister" — she nudged him — "I wasn't being overprotective. I was just marking your card."

"Thanks, sweetheart." He squeezed her to him. "It's true that she's been in bad form since I asked for your number." He stopped and looked at his watch and then at her. "Are you tired?"

"Not at all."

He smiled. "Great. Then let's continue this back at my place. I'd love you to see it and we've still got so much to talk about."

"We have."

CHAPTER
NINETEEN

After giving Suzie a quick tour, Doug poured them two large brandies and showed her into his study.

"It's a lovely house."

"I should have bought something smaller but I couldn't resist that garden."

Susie sat down on the comfortable leather couch that faced the French windows. It wasn't quite dark and the scattering of garden lights illuminated wild, untamed plants and a pond in the distance. "It looks like a jungle out there."

He laughed. "Yes, it would drive Pamela nuts, wouldn't it? To be honest, I always hated how manicured our garden and home always was. I suppose this is my little rebellion."

"Thrill-seeker." She chuckled.

"I'll show you thrill-seeking." He leaned forward, his eyes mischievous. "Come to Croatia with me."

"I can't, Doug," she said, although she was tempted. "I've only just agreed to look after Bobby. I can't just feck off, no matter how much I'd like to."

"Then we'll go some time during the school holidays." He shrugged.

"But how can you do that? Haven't you been invited for a specific event?"

"Trust me. It's not the big bash Mandy seems to think. Once I write another promotional piece on their wonderful country, they'll work around my availability and I'll work round yours."

Suzie gave a wistful sigh. To travel somewhere she'd never been was exciting; to go with someone as much fun and as knowledgeable as Doug would be brilliant. Keith, Sharon and Bobby went away every year and, in her current condition, she knew Keith would pull out all the stops to spoil his wife. "Can you give me some time to think about it?"

"Sure. It's a beautiful country, Suzie. You would love it and I'd love to take you. Also, it would make it absolutely clear to Mandy that she and I have no future."

Suzie shook her head and sighed. "What?"

"She's gorgeous and you always had an eye for beautiful women —" Suzie stopped when he winced. "Sorry, but you know what I mean."

"I've told you, I'm not that man any more, Suzie. When Pamela and I finally sorted out our various issues, I was the happiest man on the planet. I knew with certainty, then, that I'd never want another woman and" — he shrugged — "I haven't."

"Aren't you lonely?" she asked.

"Aren't you?" he countered, his eyes curious. "Haven't you missed having a man around? Missed sex? You're so young." He shook his head, looking almost shocked that she'd been celibate for so long.

Suzie burst out laughing.

"What's so funny?"

"It's twenty years since we've seen each other and we're talking as honestly and openly now as if we were never apart."

"Why wouldn't we? We're old friends. As time goes by you realise there's no time for pussyfooting around issues — which, incidentally, is what you're doing right now," he added with a glare.

"Sex?" She thought about it for a moment. "I suppose I was never really around men other than the dads I'd meet at the school gates and I'd stopped bothering about my appearance. No man would have given me a second glance. God, that does sound sad, doesn't it?"

"It does, but you've turned it all around. You look great, sweetheart."

"I feel it most of the time and, now that I've been shocked into realising you only live once and the clock is ticking, I am going to make the most of it."

"Good for you. So, let's start with you accompanying me to Croatia."

She chuckled and sipped her brandy. "You don't give up, do you?"

"No. Like you said, we only have one life. If you truly cared about me you'd come. I haven't had a travelling companion since I lost Pamela."

"Don't try to guilt me into it. I said I'll think about it. But you do realise it would mean we'd have to come clean and tell my family, Mandy included, that we're very old friends."

196

He sighed. "I don't want to be Douglas Hamilton again. I don't want the dinner parties with fake friends who have an agenda. I'm done with all that."

"You don't have to do anything you don't want to do. But wouldn't you like to meet up with Mel, Jack and Gina again?" she wheedled. "I know I would."

"That would be nice," he admitted.

"And I'd love you to meet Sharon and Noel and see Jess again. I wonder, will she remember you?"

His expression softened. "Hardly. She can't have been more than three when I last saw her."

"I think she remembers the man who chased her round the garden and pushed her on the swing." Suzie's eyes filled up. "And she remembers the pretty lady who plaited her hair."

"It was a happy time. Pamela was nuts about Jess. She should have had children."

"Don't start." Suzie remembered how he'd tortured himself after the funeral about all he'd deprived his wife of, motherhood being the most important and heart-wrenching.

He cleared his throat and wiped his eyes. "Okay then. I'll 'come out' as Doug Hamilton in a small way, meet your family and get in touch with Mal if . . ."

"If . . .?"

"You come to Croatia if and when your commitments allow. We can let Mandy think we had a mad, passionate fling when you worked in CML and now we're taking up where we left off." He pulled a face. "Although that wouldn't be fair to your kids. They'd be horrified if you took up with a man twenty years older than you."

"Twenty-one," Suzie corrected him with a grin. "Do you really care what anyone thinks, Doug? I certainly don't. I've lived my life doing everything that was expected of me and putting up with crap, first from my da and then my husband. I'm not going to make excuses or apologise for anything I do any more."

"What crap did you put up with from John?" he asked, curiously.

She frowned. "Do you know, I'm not sure. But I've noticed that I keep saying things like that so I figure he must had done something to seriously piss me off."

He laughed. "Tell me about Jess. She's, what, twenty-seven now? Is she married?"

"I wish. I'm afraid she seems drawn to bastards. Ah, but, Doug, she's so clever and pretty. She's working as a freelance journalist." She named the various publications Jess was published in and Doug's eyes widened.

"That's pretty impressive."

"Isn't it? Pity she's shagging one of her editors, married of course and a sleazebag of the highest order."

He groaned. "I'm sorry, Suzie."

"Me too, but I tore into her and I think she might have dropped him. I hope so."

"Tell me about the other two," he prompted, and Suzie gave him a potted history of John's children.

"Losing their dad and then almost losing you too must have been devastating for your family," he said

198

when she was finished. "It's a miracle that they came through it unscathed."

"I'm not sure they have. They can't handle me being so different and I've forgotten so much. So many memories . . . gone."

"But you're alive, sweetheart. You can make new memories."

She knew that he was thinking, unlike Pamela. It was true. "I've been lucky," she agreed, "but I'm not so sure about my family."

"It's strange. We assume when someone wakes up from a coma that all is well and it's a cause for celebration. We never think of the many other possible outcomes. It can't be easy for you." His eyes were full of sympathy.

"It's harder on them, even I realise that. Yet I still want to shake them and tell them to deal with it." Suzie looked at him. "I'm an awful bitch, aren't I?"

"You can't control this, Suzie. You need to remember that. Your family will adjust, with time. It's only been, what, a couple of months?"

She nodded.

"Too soon to throw in the towel. Do you feel okay, other than that?"

"I get very tired, but I was back with the consultant and he says that's natural. He was quite pleased with my progress. He gave me a letter saying I was okay to travel but don't tell Mandy that. I don't want to make any plans just yet. I think Jess would throttle me if I told her I was heading off to New York."

The truth was that, having heard some of the stories at the TBI support group, she felt nervous about travelling too far from home. She thought about telling Doug about the meeting she'd gone along to but didn't want to bring down the mood of the evening.

"Are you tired now? Would you like to go home or can I interest you in another drink?"

Suzie didn't tell him that it was way past her bedtime. She felt more comfortable here with Doug than she had with anyone since she'd woken up, and she didn't feel at all tired. "I'd like to stay a little longer but I'll settle for a nice cup of tea, please."

"We forgot all about the exhibition," he said, standing up. "How are you going to explain where you were and what you were up to?"

"I don't intend to explain, remember?"

"Fair enough. We can catch it another day, if you like."

She fluttered her eyelashes and put her hand over her heart. "Are you asking me on a second date, Mr Thornton?"

"I suppose I am." He chuckled. "We don't have to tell anyone just yet about Doug Hamilton, do we? Only it would be fun to wind Amanda up."

Suzie thought about her manipulative sister and smiled slowly. "It would, wouldn't it?"

CHAPTER
TWENTY

"Mum was on a date?" Jess stared at her brother. She'd taken him out for brunch, to celebrate the end of his exams and to check him out.

"She was," Noel said before scooping up egg, bacon and sausage on a piece of toast and shoving it in his mouth.

"Details," Jess urged impatiently.

"She went to some art exhibition with Mandy's boss."

"Mandy's boss?"

"And then they went to dinner. She didn't come home until one."

Jess stared at him. "You're kidding, right?"

"Nope."

"But when did they meet? Is she seeing him again?"

"I don't know. I don't give her the third degree the way you and Shaz do," he retorted. "However, judging from the dopey grin on her face this morning I'd say, yes."

"Wow. I can't believe it. After all these years she's actually found someone. I hope she doesn't get hurt. She is quite vulnerable at the moment."

Noel rolled his eyes dramatically. "Will you stop worrying? I'd have thought you'd be happy. At least if she's preoccupied with someone else, she'll let up on you."

"She already has. We've called a truce of sorts, for Sharon's sake."

"Well done." He nodded his approval before reaching for more toast.

"Did Mum tell you the plan to get her through the pregnancy?"

"Yeah, I'm in. It should work out fine. The more time Mum spends with Bobby the better it'll be for both of them."

"You think? Sharon's terrified of leaving him alone with Mum."

"When she starts to lose her temper, I'll take the kid up to my room and let him play inappropriate games online."

She laughed. "He does seem more content when he's playing on your tablet."

"That's because it requires his total concentration, and when he's focused he's calm."

"Since when did you become such an expert on kids?" Jess raised her eyebrows.

"I was talking to Cal about it. He's studied all that sort of thing."

This was the opening that she needed to bring the conversation around to what was troubling Noel, although he seemed fine today. "Oh. How is Cal?"

"Great."

"You'll be able to chill out together a lot more now the exams are over. How did they go?" she added casually.

"No problem at all."

"So why were you climbing the walls for weeks before?"

He shrugged and looked away. "I'm a perfectionist, that's all. If you remember, you were just the same."

"I suppose I was. I'm a bit jumpy right now thinking of all the work I've got on this week."

Noel grinned and produced a blister pack of what looked like sedatives. "Take one of these, they work wonders."

Jess frowned, picking up the pack. "Aren't these Mum's?"

"Yeah."

"You can't go taking stuff prescribed for other people, Noel, that's dangerous. She'll murder you if she finds out."

"Who do you think gave them to me?" he retorted.

"I don't believe you." Jess eyed him suspiciously.

"Ask her." Noel snatched the tablets from her hand and pocketed them. "It's no big deal, Jess. I couldn't sleep and then I was too tired to study and then I panicked. These got me through the last couple of weeks."

"So now you don't need them anymore, do you?" She held out her hand.

"You're not my mother," he grumbled, looking like a sulky teenager.

Jess decided to change tack. "I'm glad they worked, Noel, but it was irresponsible of Mum to give them to you."

Noel gave an exaggerated sigh. "Chill, Jess. People do it all the time."

"Well, they shouldn't. If you need help, see a doctor and get something that's been prescribed for *you*. My God, what if she gave these to Bobby when he's hyper?"

"She wouldn't," Noel protested.

"Are you sure of that, given her unpredictability?" Jess rubbed distractedly at her temples. If Sharon knew about this, her blood pressure would go through the roof. "Maybe I should say something to Keith."

"Aw, for crying out loud, Jess, why spook the guy? Don't you think he has enough to worry about?"

He did. Of course he did. But Jess was terrified of keeping this information to herself. Who could she talk to? Nora, maybe? Yes, she would take it seriously and might even talk to Suzie about it. Jess was glad to see that their friendship seemed to have recovered a little and Mum was spending less time with her sister.

"Jess, don't open your mouth, promise me," Noel said, looking agitated.

"Okay, I won't. Keith doesn't need any more on his shoulders. I'll have a word with Nora and see what she thinks."

"Why do you have to tell anyone? I'll be there most of the time that Mum's looking after Bobby."

Jess stared at him and then nodded. "You're right. The only person we need to talk to is Mum. Not only should she not be passing on medications, she should have them under lock and key now a child's going to be in the house."

He gave a weary sigh. "That's not a good idea."

He was drumming his fingers on the table and no longer meeting her eye. "Noel? Whatever it is, tell me."

"Okay, okay, just don't have a canary, right?"

Jess crossed her arms and waited.

"Mum only gave me the sedative a couple of times. After that, I helped myself. I wasn't being underhand: I just didn't want her to know I was having such a rough time."

"Why didn't you talk to me, Noel?" Jess felt dreadful now. She had been completely blasé about her brother's exams and written off her mother's concerns, assuming that she was simply fussing over the blue-eyed boy the way she always had. Jess met Noel's gaze and held it. "Hand them over."

He hesitated, his hand going protectively to his pocket. The action upset her. "Noel, if it's no big deal, why won't you hand them over?"

"I suppose it's like a security blanket," he admitted.

"Fair enough, I understand that. But you've a long summer ahead of you to enjoy. You don't need them." He looked doubtful, his hand remaining over the pocket. "Okay, then, tell me why you would take one now."

He shrugged. "I don't know. I just feel happier and safer if I have them."

"They've become a habit, that's all, but it's a habit you need to kick. If you take them when you don't really need to, they'll become ineffective."

He frowned and she realised she'd got through to him. "Make an appointment to see the doctor and tell him what's been going on. I'm sure that he'll be able to give you something to help."

He looked at her, his eyes hopeful. "You think?"

"I'm positive."

He dug into his pocket and tossed the sedatives on the table. Jess slipped them into her handbag. He snorted. "I look like your dealer."

"Shut up, we'll get thrown out," Jess hissed, glancing round the busy café, though she couldn't help giggling. "Are there any more of these knocking around the house?"

"No. I just picked these up from the pharmacy."

Jess tried to hide her shock that he'd gone as far as taking her mother's prescription to the pharmacy and was grateful that he was being so open now. Whatever problems he'd had, she was pretty sure she'd caught him in time, or he wouldn't be this frank with her. "Where does she keep her medicine?"

"In her locker by the bed, in the bathroom cabinet and I think there's some in the kitchen drawer, too."

Jess rolled her eyes. "Unbelievable. Still, at least it gives us a reason to have a serious chat with her and put it all in one place and out of Bobby's reach."

Noel nodded, relieved. "That's definitely the way to go. We can handle this between us, Jess. There's no need to worry anyone else. Deal?"

206

"Deal." She stood up. "Let's go talk to her now and get it over with."

Sharon sat next to her son, rubbing his back as he rocked himself, moaning quietly and stroking his storybook with the velvety cover. Keith had tossed it in the bin a few weeks ago, saying it was scruffy and falling apart, but Bobby had gone in after it, screaming. That had provoked an argument between them but now, thanks to Baby, there were no more rows. Keith was gentle and caring, treating her like a piece of delicate china. The downside of that was that he worried even more Bobby would hit her during one of his tantrums. Sharon pulled the sleeve down over the scrape on her arm. Bobby hadn't consciously hurt her: he'd just been lashing out and she'd got in the way. She could sense his fear and anger, and the fact that she could do nothing to stop him hurting himself or anyone else fuelled her frustration.

When they had asked Suzie to mind Bobby, Sharon's concern hadn't been for Mum but her son. Now, she wondered if her mother would be up to the job and if it was fair to ask her. While she looked great and seemed healthy — physically, anyway — Suzie was slight and not that strong. Feeling her anxiety start to rise, Sharon put a hand on her stomach and forced herself to slow down her breathing. "Think of Baby" was her new mantra, and it was a good one. She may have failed Bobby but she would have another chance if they managed to make it through the pregnancy.

Sharon clutched her son tighter, feeling that her thoughts were a betrayal, as if she were trying to replace him. But she wasn't. She loved her son and would never stop fighting for him. She and Keith had never managed to have that discussion. Priorities had changed. Now they were simply firefighting and hoping for the best. At least Jess and Noel were onside.

She had been touched but not really surprised that Jess was being so supportive, but Noel's reaction had blown her away. He had come over all macho and protective and told her not to worry about Mum, that he and Jess would take care of her. Then he'd talked about all the things he'd do with Bobby and the great new movie out next month that Noel was sure he'd like. Immediately, she had opened her mouth to protest that Bobby hated noise and crowds and flashing lights, but stopped herself. Sharon wasn't going to be negative and she trusted her brother and sister. Besides, she'd put together an enormous folder of information that would help them through. She chuckled as she imagined their faces when they saw it.

Writing it had been a revelation. Over the years she had started doing things out of instinct to make Bobby's life easier, but on paper she could no longer pretend that this situation was "normal". The thought brought tears to her eyes. If she could do nothing else during this pregnancy, she would at least read up on her son's behaviour. It was time to face facts. Bobby needed help and she wasn't equipped to give it to him. Sharon thought of the last meeting with his teacher and shuddered. Keith would have been horrified if he'd

208

been there. Bobby stirred and looked up at her and she pressed her lips to his forehead.

"Drink?" she asked softly.

"Juice."

She stopped herself from telling him to "say please" and, patting his back, went into the kitchen to get the drink and some of the breadsticks he loved. She set them on the coffee table and he sat up and drank before lining up the sticks, humming to himself, and then munching them in order. It was the sort of behaviour that drove Keith mad, and now she understood why. Keith also knew, deep down, this wasn't "normal". Lord, how she'd come to hate that word, how she avoided using it at all costs. Sharon rubbed his back as he enjoyed his snack. "You're going to Granny's tomorrow after school, Bobby. Won't that be fun?"

He hung his head. "Granny doesn't like me."

"That's not true," she protested.

"But you said so to Daddy."

Sharon cursed herself. She needed to be more careful what she said around her son. "I was only saying Granny gets cross when she's tired. Not just with you, darling. Anyway, Aunty Jess might be there, and who else, do you think?"

"Percy!"

Sharon rolled her eyes. "Yes, Percy, but who else?" She was trying not to think about the dog. Who knew how the animal would react if Bobby lost it?

Her son said nothing for a moment and then straightened and smiled. "Uncle Noel?"

"Yes! You like Uncle Noel, don't you, Bobby?"

"He's funny." His smile grew broader. "We play games and paint!"

Sharon gave a dramatic groan. "Finger painting? That's so messy."

He giggled. "Messy!"

"I think you're going to have lots of fun and come home covered in paint."

His smile was replaced by a frown. "Granny doesn't like messy."

"That's okay, sweetheart. I've talked to Granny and she says that messy is fine. Once you're in the kitchen with Uncle Noel," she added, hurriedly.

To make life as easy as possible for her mother and to equip her with things Bobby was familiar with, Sharon had put together a crate full of art materials and also disposable plates and cups that Keith would drop over later.

"Guitar?" Bobby asked.

"Yes, I'm sure that Uncle Noel will play his guitar for you. What will you sing, Bobby?"

"Bob the Builder."

She laughed. "I thought so. Okay, sweetie, it's almost bedtime. Let's get the crayons and make a picture for Daddy."

As gentle as a lamb, Bobby did as he was bid and she put on some soft music. The meditation classes had taught her the soothing healing power of it and she sat back and closed her eyes, enjoying this peaceful moment. Realising how much more time Keith and Bobby would be spending together, Sharon had come up with this idea of Bobby drawing a picture for his dad every evening. She had explained to her husband that the quality of the picture didn't matter a damn.

"Just praise him, thank him and give him a hug but —"

"Don't kiss him, I know, I've got it," Keith had promised, and it was working. Slowly. Bobby was starting to relax with his dad and she was touched when Keith had picked up a crayon and drawn a picture for his son. He was a natural artist and it was an excellent replication of Bobby's favourite car. Bobby had laughed and laughed and insisted on taking it up to bed with him.

There was the sound of a key in the door and Sharon put a hand on her son's arm. "Daddy's home."

"But it's not ready yet," Bobby shouted, frowning and colouring furiously.

"Don't worry," she soothed. "I'll bring Daddy into the kitchen for his dinner and then you can surprise him."

Mollified, Bobby kept colouring while Sharon hurried into the hall to waylay Keith.

"Hi, sweetheart." He smiled and folded her in a warm hug. "How are you?"

"I'm fine." Sharon closed her eyes and luxuriated in the feel of his strong arms around her. She turned her mouth for his kiss and instantly pulled away wiping her mouth. "Ugh, you taste of coffee."

He chuckled. "Oops, sorry. I'll keep breath mints in the car in future. Still feeling nauseous?"

"Not as much."

"Good. How's Bobby?"

"Really good today and excited about spending time with Noel," she said, going into the kitchen. "He's just finishing off your picture so I promised to keep you out of the way."

"Didn't I tell you it would all work out?" He followed and washed his hands as she took the cottage pie out of the oven.

"Don't jinx it," she warned. "So, how were things in work?" Keith worked long hours as a freelance surveyor and she hated the thought of his being put under further pressure.

"Fine. I've offloaded some projects onto Stan and Margaret and, if I keep on top of my email and get some work done on the weekends, it'll be fine."

"They've only just graduated." Sharon frowned at the thought of him trusting the reputation of his business to his two new recruits. She set his plate in front of him and went to make a cup of camomile tea for herself. "Are you sure they're up to the job?"

"I'll vet their reports before they're sent out," he assured her. "Now, stop worrying. Remember the amount of time we spent at the hospital when your mum had her accident? We coped then, didn't we? And we'll cope now."

She nodded, comforted by his words and the confidence in his voice. It had been a long time since they'd been this close and that was keeping her blood pressure under control more than any medication. Thank you, Baby.

CHAPTER
TWENTY-ONE

Mandy heaved a sigh of relief as she finished the latest wad of pages Douglas had left on her desk. He seemed to be writing morning, noon and night and, when he wasn't writing, he was whistling and smiling. She wanted to punch him. She was being the perfect PA, attending to his needs, business and personal, but she knew that, even if she cartwheeled through the house buck naked, he wouldn't notice. He didn't join her for a cuppa any more or tease her about men. Mandy missed it, missed him. As she sat feeling sorry for herself, Douglas mooched in wearing a goofy smile.

"How's it going?"

"I finished that last chapter. I'm just printing it off now."

"Congratulations, well done."

She sat up to award him a glimpse of her cleavage and black lacy bra but, oblivious, he went to pour himself some coffee. "Want one?"

She sighed, slumping back in the chair. "I'm good, thanks."

"Amanda, I was thinking. I wanted to send Suzie some flowers. Roses seem a little obvious. Any ideas what she would like?"

Flowers? Really? After one date?

"Amanda?"

She looked up to see that Douglas was waiting for her answer. "Daisies. She likes daisies."

He smiled. "Wonderful. Thank you."

And her love struck boss disappeared back into his office. Mandy's dreams of a luxury break in Zagreb were going steadily down the toilet. He wouldn't put his new romance at risk by taking her with him — unless, of course, Suzie told him to get lost and, rejected, he needed a shoulder to cry on. Now, Mandy was an expert at consoling men whose wives didn't understand them. She just needed to put Suzie off getting involved with Douglas. She imagined her sister would be examining every aspect of the date right now and looking for reasons why he wouldn't call. Grinning, she stood up and went to the office door and knocked gently.

"Yeah?"

She adopted a concerned expression. "Douglas, I don't want to interfere —"

"Rubbish, you love interfering," he retorted.

She smiled and shrugged, acknowledging that. "True and, as you may have noticed, Suzie is nothing like me."

He nodded, his lips twitching, but whatever witty retort he'd been about to make died on his lips when he noticed her serious expression. Good, she finally had his attention. Mandy wrung her hands as if she were having trouble finding the words. "Suzie's quite the innocent, to be honest. As I told you, there hasn't been anyone in her life since her husband passed away. That devastated her. She adored John."

"She did?" Douglas's eyebrow shot up in disbelief.

Feck, so she'd told him all about John? Mandy pulled a face and nodded. "Yes. Not that he deserved it. The thing is, everything is happening so fast you may actually scare her off."

"Forget the daisies?" he asked.

She smiled. "I think so. A polite text would work better and then in a week or so you could ask her out again."

"A week or so?" His eyes narrowed and she couldn't quite read his expression.

"It's just a suggestion. I don't know if Suzie told you but she has a lot on her plate. Her eldest daughter's going through a high-risk pregnancy and Suzie will be looking after her grandson over the next few months. He's quite a handful and it's going to be very tiring, physically and mentally." Well, that bit was definitely true. Mandy thought her sister needed her head examined, taking on that kid. She adopted a concerned look, like the loving sister she wasn't. "I just hope it's not going to prove too much for her."

"So, are you saying that I should let Suzie set the pace?"

"It would probably be best. She likes to feel in control and, since the accident, she's quite easily overwhelmed."

"The last thing I want to do is upset her in any way."

215

He wore a deep frown and Mandy congratulated herself on a job well done. "That's what I thought, Douglas, and I'm sure it will all work out fine."

"Did she say if she enjoyed our evening together?" he asked.

Mandy was able to answer this honestly. "I haven't been talking to her. As I said, there's a lot going on in the Connors family at the moment. I'll probably drop by later. Would you like me to give her a message?" she offered.

"Tell her I had fun."

Suzie collapsed onto her bed, exhausted. Had it really been only three days? Thank God it was Friday and Keith would be taking over for the weekend, because she was ready to scream. In fact she *had* screamed at one stage, along with Bobby, when he'd sent a pot plant crashing in the hall and water, soil and ceramic shards had flown all over the place. Despite Jess and Noel's help, Suzie had never known time to pass so slowly as when she was solely responsible for her grandson. She'd tried everything to distract Bobby but it was impossible to hold his attention for more than a couple of minutes, and teatime was a complete nightmare. She had tossed Sharon's folder in a corner, snorting in disgust. She'd raised three children and her daughter thought she needed a manual in order to feckin' babysit for a few hours? But now all three of them were beginning to realise that, not only was Bobby a full-time job, he was an extremely complicated child. Desperate, Suzie swallowed her pride and took a look through Sharon's notes but, right now, all she wanted was dinner and a long, hot bath. There was a tap on the door. "Come in," she called, and Jess appeared with a cup of tea.

"I thought you might need this."

Suzie sat up and smiled. "I do. Thanks, love."

Jess sat on the end of the bed and yawned. "Noel's gone out to get curry."

"Good, because I haven't the energy to cook."

"It's been one hell of a long week."

"You can say that again. I don't know what I'd have done without you two. Noel has the patience of a saint, hasn't he?"

Jess grinned. "It's not much of a stretch for him to be Bobby's playmate."

"I suppose. I can cope with most of it but I wish I didn't have to feed him. It's a nightmare."

"Sharon said there's some recipes in the folder."

"Fuck the recipes." Suzie shook her head impatiently. "I made him a lovely spaghetti Bolognese yesterday and he literally spread it all over the table, picking out all the pieces of carrot, and, when I gave out to him, he started screaming blue murder. From now on it will be sausages, fish fingers or chicken nuggets, and, if he doesn't like it, he can starve for all I care."

"I know it's hard, Mum, but if we send him home upset then Sharon will be anxious that it's not working out and that's defeating the purpose."

Suzie groaned, knowing she was right. "We may keep her blood pressure under control but I'm not so sure about mine." She glared as she sipped her tea. "Get that damn folder, will you?"

"This is unbelievable," Jess said, leafing through the ring binder as her brother unpacked the cartons.

"I've only had a quick look but I thought it was mad." Suzie got a plate and set the naan bread in the centre of the table, before fetching water for herself and Jess and a beer for her son. "The sooner Sharon has this baby the better. Then she won't have so much time to obsess over her son."

"Give her a break, Mum," Noel said, turning the folder round so he could read it. "Bobby's no average kid."

Suzie snorted. "Huh. You can say that again."

"Why isn't he talking more?" Jess asked. "The teachers must have said something to Sharon about that."

Noel skimmed through the pages as he ate. "If they did, she didn't put it in the folder."

"She says that he doesn't make friends easily," Jess said. "I can understand him being quiet with us — kids are often shy around adults — but I noticed, when we were at the playground, he keeps away from the other children. Is he always like that?"

Suzie nodded. "He's a loner all right. He's more interested in Percy than people, although" — she grinned — "that's understandable."

"Has he any friends at school?" Jess asked.

"He's only in Junior Infants, love. I doubt any of them make real friends at that age. I've certainly never seen him with any one child. In fact, he usually comes out from school alone."

Jess frowned. "That's a bit sad."

Noel wiped his mouth and stretched back in the chair, the folder in his lap. "You know, she may not be admitting it to us or even herself, but Shaz knows damn well that Bobby's got a problem."

Suzie felt a pang of guilt. She should have known that without having it spelt out for her, but, even when she'd cast an eye over the folder earlier, all she'd seen was an obsessive and over-protective mother. "What do we do?" she asked her children, because she felt completely out of her depth.

Noel closed the folder and patted it. "Exactly what it says in the instruction manual. Sharon knows him better than anyone. Also, I was saying to Jess, we need to get Cal on board. This is more his area of expertise."

"I'll happily take his advice if he's got any," Suzie said wearily.

"The first few days were bound to be hard, Mum," Jess said.

"Of course they were," Noel agreed. "I'll nip into town tomorrow and pick up a few bits and pieces to keep him amused."

She smiled fondly at her youngest. "Thanks, love."

"Now, to much more exciting stuff." Jess leaned forward on the table, smiling. "Have you heard from your date?"

Suzie suppressed a grin. It was ridiculous how much fun she and Doug were getting from acting out the lovesick-couple routine — until he'd told her Mandy's comments, which had put a darker slant on things. Her sister was really doing her damnedest to come between them. So much for blood being thicker than water. "I thought we got on well, but all I've had is a one-line text thanking me for my company," she said, truthfully, not mentioning the hours they'd spent on the phone since. Susie's first day with Bobby had been a shock to the system and the first person she'd thought to call was Doug. Perhaps it was because he had been such a support when she was nineteen, pregnant and terrified. He had a great way of diverting her and making her laugh. They'd talked each night since and, as a result, she'd gone to sleep a calmer woman. But minding Bobby had still taken its toll.

"Perhaps he's away on business," Jess said.

"Or maybe he's just not that into you."

"Noel!" Jess glared at him.

"Sorry but I've always wanted to use that line." He grinned at his mother. "I'm sure that you'll hear from him. He's probably afraid of looking too eager."

Despite trying to keep up the charade, Suzie couldn't help smiling. "How long would you leave it if you were playing it cool?"

"Five days," Noel said.

"Three days," Jess said at the same time.

"You see? That's just desperate," her brother said, and Jess chucked a dishcloth at him.

"But we're not kids," Suzie said. "We're too old for silly games."

"Tell Mandy that." Jess laughed. "She seems to thrive on games."

220

★   ★   ★

When she was ready for bed, Suzie went out to refill Percy's water bowl and give him a last cuddle. "Goodnight, sweetheart," she said, closing the door and turning off the lights. Halfway up the stairs her phone beeped and she stopped to pull it out of the pocket in her jeans. It was a text from Doug.

Hi Suzie. Fancy a chat to let off some steam? D. x

Her tiredness forgotten, Suzie carried on up to her room, grinning and feeling ridiculously happy.

CHAPTER
TWENTY-TWO

Jess found a parking spot near to the flat and was walking up the path when she heard her name being called. She turned round to see Louis coming towards her, his face grim. "What are you doing here, Louis?" she hissed when he reached her.

"Hey, don't be like that," he said, looking upset. "You didn't reply to my texts or drop by the office."

"I emailed you my article — didn't you get it?"

"I did, and it was great, but" — he brushed his knuckles along her arm and smiled down at her — "I wanted to apologise."

She looked up at him, surprised to see remorse in his eyes. "Apologise?"

"Yeah, I came on a bit strong the last time. I was out of line. I'm sorry, Jess."

She gave a small smile, relieved that he was ready to be reasonable. "Apology accepted."

"Can I come in for a minute?"

She started to shake her head. "I don't think that's a good idea —"

"I won't stay long," he promised. "I just wanted to explain. I've really missed you, Jess."

She felt her resolve weaken. When he was nice, he was very nice and right now he was looking at her with such love and regret. "Five minutes, that's all, Louis."

His face broke into a wide smile. "Thank you."

Jess led the way upstairs, thinking Cal would murder her and she could only imagine her mother's reaction. But Jess wasn't going to fall back into old ways. He'd apologised and, hopefully, if they talked it would clear the air and make working together easier. She opened the door to the flat and immediately he slammed it closed and pressed her up against the wall.

"Louis!"

He covered her mouth with his in a hard, punishing kiss as his hands pushed up her skirt.

Jess put both of her hands on his chest and tried to push him away. "Louis, no, what are you doing? What's got into you?"

"I told you, I've missed you." He ran a finger along the line of her panties and licked his lips, his eyes dark with lust.

"This is some apology." Jess glared at him, her heart racing. "Stop it, stop it now!"

"You are so fucking sexy when you're angry." He slid a hand under her top and squeezed her breast, hurting her.

"Louis, no." She tried to push him off but he was too strong for her and seemed turned on by her resistance. Her skirt was around her waist now, and he was prising her legs apart with his knee, his upper body pinning her in place and he held her wrists above her head in one hand, rendering her helpless.

223

Jess squeezed her eyes closed. This couldn't be happening. And then she felt his breath on her neck and cried out when he bit it and then did the same to her breasts through her top. She'd never known him like this before and she felt real fear as his hand left her to fumble with his trousers. His hand roughly tugged her panties to one side and she opened her mouth to scream but immediately he covered it with his own, effectively silencing her.

Just do it, get it over with, she pleaded silently, tears rolling down her cheeks. If he noticed, it didn't bother him. He was beyond reason, pushing into her hard and fast like a crazed animal.

Within minutes it was all over and Louis had pulled out and gone into the bathroom to clean himself up. She stood there for a moment, shocked and trembling, before stumbling into the bedroom. Wrapping the duvet round her, Jess sat on the edge of the bed, her teeth chattering.

She heard the toilet flush and the sound of him going into the kitchen and opening the fridge.

"What's wrong with you?"

He stood in the doorway, clean and tidy and drinking a beer as if nothing had happened. Jess stared at him in shock. "You hurt me!"

"Oh, come on, you know that you enjoyed it. You are so hot." He glanced at his watch. "Pity I've got to go. Maeve's invited a gang over for a barbecue. I told her I was just nipping out to stock up on beer and wine." He winked. "I'll call you."

As the door closed behind him, Jess curled up in a ball waiting for the tears to come but she just felt empty and cold. Dragging her aching body into the bathroom she turned on the shower, praying that, for once, there was hot water and sighed as steam started to rise. Stepping in, she flinched at the scalding water on her skin but made no move to lower the temperature, just stood there. She winced as the pressured jets of water found the bruising on her neck, breasts and tail bone where it had been pounded against the wall. As Jess gently soaped the soft flesh of her inner thighs, which stung from the friction of his trousers rubbing against her, she suppressed the four-letter word that pulsated in her brain. This wasn't a stranger: it was Louis. They'd been seeing each other for months and he'd never behaved like that before. It must be like he said: he'd missed her and been rougher than he realised. So why did she feel dirty and used? She wound a towel tightly around her and went back into the bedroom. Sitting down in front of her dressing table, she stared at her reflection. There were marks on her neck and chest. She let the towel drop to her waist and saw the same on her breasts. Opening the top drawer, Jess pulled out underwear, jogging pants and a warm sweatshirt. Despite the hot shower, she was still shivering. Her phone beeped.

"Katie," she said, hoping her friend somehow sensed she needed her. Going back into the hall, Jess retrieved her phone from her jacket pocket, still lying on the floor along with her bag where she'd dropped it when he'd grabbed her. She looked at her messages and saw it was from Louis.

I can't wait to do that again. L. x

Jess didn't want to dwell on exactly what it was that he wanted to do again. He'd missed her. He couldn't wait to make love to her. She could almost see Katie's lip curl at her describing what had just happened as making love. But he'd wanted her, desperately. That's all it was. She shouldn't have fought him. That was why she had this bruising. He hadn't meant to hurt her.

Calmer, Jess went into the kitchen, put on a pot of coffee and settled at the kitchen table with her laptop and started researching the planned changes to the secondary school curriculum and the arguments for and against, noting her sources and following up links.

An hour into it, the phone rang.

She looked at the display before putting the phone to her ear. "Hey, Shaz."

"You were supposed to call me." Her sister was reproachful. "How did it go?"

Jess hadn't a clue what she was talking about and then remembered she'd promised to call Sharon and let her know how the first week had gone. "I do work for a living and have deadlines to meet," she snapped.

"Sorry. I was just anxious to hear if Mum behaved herself."

"Everything went fine, Sharon. Mum didn't whack Bobby and he was as good as gold," Jess lied as they had all agreed they would.

Sharon laughed. "I'm his mother, Jess, and I love him dearly, but even I wouldn't describe him as 'good as gold'."

Jess smiled. "The point is, we coped quite well. Mum managed to keep her temper under control, Noel played online games with him, he did lots of colouring and I taught him a few card games. He's going to be a shark if he ever takes up poker."

"He is quite a sharp little cookie, isn't he?" Sharon said, proudly.

"Yeah, so stop worrying."

"It's just that he's whiny when he gets home and Keith had trouble settling him this evening. I suppose it will take him a while to adjust to the new routine."

"Of course it will," Jess soothed. "And remember, he's used to being with you all the time. He's bound to have missed you."

"I hadn't thought of that," Sharon said, sounding relieved. "Thanks, Jess." There was a wail in the background and Sharon sighed. "And that's my cue to hang up. Bye."

"See ya." Jess fetched a bottle of water and was just settling back to work when the phone rang again, making her jump. She hesitated when she saw Cal's name. She wanted to talk to him but after what had just happened . . .

"Jess?"

"Hey, Cal. Sorry, I know I should have called."

"Don't worry about it. Noel told me that you all have your hands full. Are you working?"

"Trying to but not getting very far," she admitted.

"Fancy taking a break? I thought we could go for a walk along the seafront and catch up."

Jess peeked out of the window. It had been windy and overcast earlier, but the sky was clear now and the wind seemed to have died down. Maybe a walk was exactly what she needed to settle her, to make her feel normal again.

"You're on," she said. "I'll meet you outside The Sheds."

As she rounded the corner on to the seafront, Jess saw him leaning on the railing, his back to the beach as he looked left and right. Two girls jogged past him and gave him the once-over before carrying on, pulling faces and giggling. Jess smiled. He was a good-looking guy and she could understand him catching their eye. When he spotted her, Cal waved. She waved back and waited for a break in the traffic before crossing to join him.

"Hey." He bent to give her a quick hug, and she froze. Sensing it, he stepped back, his eyes searching her face. "Jess? Is everything okay?"

Swallowing back tears at the concern in his voice, Jess nodded. "It's been a tough week."

Cal took her hand and led her towards the promenade, and Jess fell into step beside him, conscious of his fingers laced through hers. She stared down at them, contrasting them with the fingers that had dragged at her clothes earlier. She shivered and forced herself to take a slow, deep breath of sea air.

228

"Are you sure you're all right?" Cal paused, glancing over at her.

Jess ached for him to hold her in his arms and make everything go away, but she forced a nod and a fake smile. "Yes, you were right, this was a great idea. I'll be good for another couple of hours after this."

"It's almost nine o'clock," Cal said. "Are you planning on pulling an all-nighter?"

"I might." Jess shrugged. "Tomorrow is the one day that I get to sleep in."

"You've had a tough few months and just when it looked like life was back to normal, you find yourself babysitting too. Don't push yourself too hard. Your work will suffer for it."

"Perhaps you're right," Jess conceded, although she figured if she did have an early night, she would just lie there dwelling on what Louis had done to her. She stopped in her tracks. Done *to* her? Not done *with* her? She couldn't gloss over this. Louis Healy hadn't made love to her: he'd assaulted her. He had — No. She would not use *that* word. She hated the way it kept popping into her head. This was the man who'd held her while she cried over her mum. But something about Cal's straightforward, honest and respectful manner made everything about Louis seem sordid and evil.

Jess had been so determined to keep him at bay but he'd taken her off-guard. Taken her — yes, he'd certainly done that. She thought of Cal's affectionate hug when they met. Had Louis ever held her like that? With affection and respect? Or was it all just about sex, as Mum said? He'd seemed crazy for her and had often told her how hot and sexy she was. Jess was usually naked within minutes of their meeting. Louis said he couldn't keep his hands off her. But he'd never behaved as he had today. What had happened? Had she done something to make him treat her like that?

"Jess? Jess, are you okay?"

She started as Cal turned her to face him and rested his arms on her shoulders. She looked up to find him staring down at her, looking seriously worried. "Sorry!" She shook her head as she tried to think of some way of explaining her silence. "I, eh, I just panicked. I thought I'd forgotten to email my latest piece to the Sunday newspaper," she said, knowing that sounded lame. "I'm all over the place at the moment, to be honest, Cal."

"Right." He studied her for a moment, his expression making it clear he didn't swallow her explanation for an instant.

Jess struggled to think of a way of distracting him and then remembered her conversation with Noel this morning. Dear God! Had it only been this morning? She gave Cal a bright smile.

"Now, do you want to hear some good news for a change?" She took his hand and tugged him along.

He allowed her to divert him and she told him of her chat with Noel. "Mystery solved," she said when she'd finished telling him of Noel's dabble with sedatives.

Cal kept walking but said nothing.

"Well?"

"I don't buy it."

Jess frowned. "Why not? He had the pills in his pocket, he used Mum's prescription for himself —"

230

"I get that. It's the reason why that doesn't make sense. Noel's been through plenty of exams and they never bothered him to that extent before."

That was true. "Maybe he's nervous about leaving the security of university life and going out into the big bad world. He hasn't turned twenty-one yet so he's the baby of the family and spoiled rotten."

Cal shrugged. "Sorry, I still don't buy it."

Fed up and tearful, Jess stopped and scowled up at him. "Has it ever occurred to you that perhaps you read a little too much into things, Cal?"

He gave her a sad, knowing smile and shook his head. "No, I can't say it has."

She looked away from the intensity of his gaze and started walking again, her hands dug deep into her pockets. "So, Doctor, what do you think is bothering him?"

Cal sighed, the expression on his face one of frustration mixed with concern. "Look, Jess, I'm not trying to be difficult. I'm just worried about a mate."

Feeling ashamed, Jess put a hand on his arm. "Sorry. That was out of order."

He shrugged off the apology. "I can understand you wanting to believe his act, but, believe me, that's all it is, an act."

Jess felt a shiver of fear run through her, her thoughts for the first time diverted from Louis. What if he was right? What if her brother was in trouble of some kind and she'd missed it? She couldn't take that chance. She'd spent all that time by her mother's bed wondering whether there was something she could have done to prevent her injury, which was completely irrational. But, if Cal's instincts told him something was wrong with Noel and she did nothing, she would never be able to forgive herself. This was the first time he had ever come to her for help, and he wasn't just a trained psychologist: he was Noel's best friend.

Jess drew him to a halt and stepped in front of him to look up into his eyes. "I believe you and I trust you. What do we do?"

He looked relieved and, draped his arms loosely over her shoulders again. It was such a casual, non-threatening gesture, yet a strangely intimate one. Again, Jess couldn't but draw comparisons between the rough way Louis had manhandled her and Cal's gentleness.

"Your nephew."

Jess frowned, distracted. "Bobby? What about him?"

"Noel's been asking my advice, so I thought that I'd suggest the three of us meet up for a chat. Maybe together we can get to the root of what's really bothering him."

"Sounds good," she said with a grateful smile. "You could come round to my flat. I'll talk to him and set it up."

Cal walked her home, refused coffee, telling her to go to bed and rest, and then turned as he was closing the gate. "By the way, I didn't buy your excuse either."

"What excuse?" she asked, confused.

"When you went as white as a sheet and didn't speak for about five minutes you said it was because you were afraid you'd forgotten to send an email. I don't buy it.

But don't worry, you can tell me what really sent you into such a panic when you're good and ready. Goodnight, Jess."

She watched his big but graceful figure amble back down the road, marvelling at the man's insight. And, if he was right about her, then maybe he was right about her brother.

CHAPTER
TWENTY-THREE

Nora studied Suzie as she waited in line for their coffee, and didn't like what she saw. It was only a couple of weeks since she'd started looking after her grandson but it was clearly too much for her. Apart from looking slightly dishevelled, Suzie was cross and making no effort to hide it. She'd nearly snapped Nora's head off for taking so long to decide whether she wanted a muffin or croissant. She let Suzie sit down and take a few gulps of her cappuccino before saying anything.

"Better?" she asked.

"A little. I thought I'd never get out of that house."

"Who's with Bobby?"

"Noel's there, and Jess will be in later. And Aileen, God bless her, said she'd drop sausage and chips in to them for their tea."

"So what are you going to do with your day off?"

Suzie smiled for the first time since they'd met. "I'm meeting Doug."

"He called? That's wonderful, Suzie. I'm delighted. Doug, eh?" she teased. "I knew that there was an instant connection between you two."

Susie's smile grew wider. "There was — is. We talk every night and, to be honest, I don't think that I'd

234

have gotten through the last couple of weeks without those calls. I'm so worked up by the time Bobby goes home, but after a chat with Douglas I'm ready to face the next day."

Nora couldn't believe her ears. They had become close so fast. "How many times have you seen him?"

"Only once. I'm far too tired by the time Bobby goes home to do anything. Noel basically threw me out of the house today."

"Good for him."

"Yes. He's been great, Jess too. Doug won't be free until one, so that's why I called you."

"Thanks a lot." Nora pretended to be offended.

Suzie laughed. "Oh, you know what I mean. I know you're usually in Dublin on Wednesdays and I thought we could have coffee and a natter."

It was good to know that Douglas was helping Suzie unwind, but Nora couldn't help wonder what effect looking after such a difficult child was having on her friend's damaged brain. She also worried how Suzie was behaving when she was alone with Bobby. "Do Keith and Sharon know that you're having a tough time?"

"Of course not. That would defeat the purpose, which is to keep Sharon calm."

"What happens at the end of term?" Nora queried. "Didn't you say that Noel will be working at the yacht club? And Jess must be writing for half a dozen publications at the moment."

"Don't be so bloody negative," Suzie said crossly. "Yes, it will be a longer day but I won't pick Bobby up until about eleven. As for Noel, he's going to arrange his hours so that he'll be here for some of the time and Jess says she'll still pop in and out. She takes that laptop with her wherever she goes. Still, I have to admit, there are days when I really envy you, Nora."

"Me, why?" Nora asked, startled.

"Because you've no kids to worry about, you're healthy, you have a job and you're footloose and fancy-free. Your life is fucking perfect."

"As if you'd be without your children," Nora teased. "Do you know, I'm beginning to see glimpses of the old 'you'? Not only did you agree to take on Bobby without hesitation, now you're protecting Sharon by not telling her how hard it is. A few weeks ago you would have laid into her and Keith every evening, giving them all the gory details of what Bobby had got up to. And I don't care how sick Sharon was or is, you would still have got in a few rubs about how she spoiled her son. Now you're holding your tongue and letting off steam afterwards. That's serious progress, Suzie."

Suzie stared at her. "I never realised."

"Why would you? It's been so gradual. I probably only notice it because I don't see you often."

"Oh, I hope you're right, Nora." Suzie's eyes filled up. "I so hope that you're right."

Nora slid across and put an arm around her. "Hey, don't cry. You should be happy. Go and have a nice day with Douglas."

Suzie wiped her eyes and nodded. "Yes. Yes, I will."

"What are you two going to do?"

Suzie looked surprised. "Do you know, I have no idea? I was so relieved to have a few hours off, I never asked."

"It doesn't matter, does it? You're happy simply spending time with Douglas." Nora smiled affectionately at her friend.

"I am. He's a lovely man and makes me feel good. He's better than any meditation session. Shit. That reminds me. We have a class tomorrow night. Do you think I'm changed enough to be trusted to spend time with Sharon without telling her that her son is driving me round the bend?"

Nora grimaced. "Probably not. It might be safer if you let her go alone. Anyway, if you spend the evening worrying about letting something slip, the class isn't going to be much use to you, is it?"

"True." Suzie yawned and rubbed her eyes.

Nora looked at her, worried. "I don't like you being this tired. The doctors said you had to get plenty of rest and avoid stress."

Suzie gave a wry smile. "Funny, that's exactly what they told us about Sharon. Don't fuss, Nora. I'll be right as rain after a nice break and a good night's sleep. Now, I'm off for a blow-dry. I was too bloody tired to do my hair myself this morning, so I decided to treat myself."

"Good for you." Nora stood to hug her. "Have a lovely time."

When she was alone, Nora picked up her phone and called Jess. She was sure the girl knew the stress her mother was under but she wanted to hear Jess's version of events.

"It is hard work," Jess confirmed with a sigh when Nora filled her in on what Suzie had said. "There is something wrong with that child: his behaviour is odd at best and exhausting and sometimes . . ."

Nora's ears pricked up when Jess hesitated. "Yes, sometimes?"

"He's violent, Nora. He gets into a rage and lashes out, and he may be small but, believe me, he's strong."

Nora was shocked. "But he must be the same with Sharon and Keith. How would they not have warned your mum what she was letting herself in for?"

"I think Mum knew all along," Jess said. "As for Keith, I'm not sure what he knows or doesn't know. Either Sharon's keeping him in the dark, he's in denial or he's an idiot." Jess went on to tell her all about the binder Sharon had prepared all about her son. "You wouldn't believe the detail. It's clear that she knows there's something wrong."

"Keith must know and is sticking his head in the sand."

"Maybe Bobby behaves better when his dad's around. Oh, I don't know, Nora," Jess said, sounding fed up. "I really don't."

Nora bit her lip, wishing she could help. She'd been worried about Suzie before the call, but now she felt even more anxious. "Has Bobby hurt your mum?" The moment of silence confirmed her worst fears. "Oh, no."

238

"Nothing serious, Nora. Just a few scratches and a couple of bruises."

Nora knew it wasn't her business but she couldn't keep silent. "Jess, your mum is still recovering. And, apart from tiring easily, she's so thin now that Bobby could easily knock her over. What if she had another fall? What if she hit her head again?"

"I hadn't thought of that," Jess admitted, sounding worried.

"Sorry, Jess. I don't mean to scare you. Maybe you and Noel should have a chat with Keith or Suzie's doctor. Oh, I don't know but someone must be able to help. And, if you want me to come and stay with your mum and help out, Jess, no problem. You only have to call and I'll hop in the car."

Jess thanked her and, after chatting for a few more minutes, rang off as one of her editors was on hold. Nora felt bad about burdening her but she was truly worried. She felt that Suzie's health was at risk and what kind of a friend would she be if she said nothing?

Jess put down the phone, feeling both scared and defensive. She chatted to Beth, who'd been on hold, making some notes as the editor told her what she wanted.

"I'll need it by Monday. Can you do that, Jess?"

She groaned inwardly but forced herself to give a sunny confident reply. "No problem, Beth. I know exactly the angle I'll take."

"I knew I could rely on you. Thanks, Jess. Talk soon."

Jess tossed the phone onto the sofa and stared at her screen, her mind on her mother. What was the solution to this problem? Jess knew why her mother was keeping the truth from Sharon. It was the same reason she and Noel were. They were all terrified how it would affect Sharon's health. At first Noel hadn't paid any attention when she and her mother complained about Bobby. Until he witnessed, first-hand, one of his nephew's meltdowns. Noel had tried to restrain Bobby and was shocked as he'd fought back, kicking and punching. Noel arrived another day to find Jess rubbing cream into Suzie's arm where Bobby had pinched and twisted the skin because she'd tried to make him eat his vegetables. Now, they'd reverted to bribing the child. By the time Keith arrived he was usually in front of the TV, eating ice cream.

But Nora was right. They had to do something. She thought of Cal's suggestion that they meet up and figure out a way of dealing with Bobby. That was an excuse to try to find out what was going on with Noel, but now she realised they really could do with Cal's advice. If he didn't have any answers, she wasn't sure who else to turn to.

Jess parked the car and ran down the street to the offices of *Femme*, stopping outside the door to catch her breath, smooth back her hair and straighten her clothes. Shoulders back, she walked in, smiling broadly at the receptionist.

"Hi, Rhona."

"Hey, Jess. Amelia sends her apologies, she's running a little behind. Can I get you a coffee while you wait?"

Relieved to have more time to compose herself, Jess thanked her, sat down and took out her phone. She sent a text to her brother asking him to call round later this evening and to bring Cal with him. They needed to talk about Mum and Bobby. She sent Cal a copy of the message. Within seconds she had two replies.

Okay.

And from Cal:

Well done. See you later.

That done, Jess tucked the phone into her pocket, switched on her laptop and gave her full concentration to her notes as she waited to go into the meeting.

CHAPTER
TWENTY-FOUR

Suzie walked out of the hair salon, crossed Dame Street and wound her way through the alleys of Temple Bar. Douglas had sent her a text to say that he was waiting in a pub on Fleet Street. She checked her reflection in a shop window — looking good — before going inside the busy pub to look for him.

"Suzie!"

She turned to see him beckoning her from a table by the window and wriggled her way through the crowd to join him. "Wow, it's packed, isn't it?" He smiled as she dropped into the chair next to him, and leaned over to hug her. He looked good, younger somehow.

"A coach party just arrived," Douglas explained. "You look lovely, Suzie."

"I look wrecked," she retorted, "but I got my hair done to make me look less so."

"It sounded like you've been having a really tough time with your grandson. I felt for you."

"It would have been worse if you hadn't been at the end of the phone," she assured him.

He grinned. "Talking to you has never been a hardship. Now, shall I get you a drink or would you prefer to go somewhere quieter?"

242

"Let's go for a walk," she suggested.

He stood up and held out his hand to her. "Let's."

They wandered along through the shoppers and street performers, chatting, and finally found themselves in the National Gallery where Suzie listened, fascinated, as Doug showed her his favourite paintings and talked about the use of light and standard of brushwork, throwing in some funny anecdotes about the artists themselves.

He looked down at her in amusement. "You're really getting into art, Suzie Clarke, aren't you?"

"I am," she admitted. "It must have something to do with the bang to the head. I always appreciated a nice view or a pretty picture but it would never have occurred to me to visit a gallery. That was the sort of thing for the likes of you and Pamela, not someone like me."

"Rubbish. Art belongs to everyone," Doug assured her.

Suzie shrugged. "Maybe, but if you'd told me a few years ago that I'd be content to spend my afternoon off in an art gallery, I'd have laughed my head off."

He squeezed her hand. "Hungry?"

"Famished," she said and realised how late in the afternoon it was. The time had flown.

"Chinese or Italian?"

Suzie wrinkled her nose as she thought about it. "Italian. I fancy something with lots of garlic, washed down with lots of wine."

"I thought you had a two-glass-only policy," Douglas teased.

"Fuck that," she said and clapped her hand over her mouth as her words echoed round the enormous room.

He threw back his head and laughed. "Aw, Suzie, don't ever change."

She looked at him, thinking her kids wouldn't agree. She banished the thought. She was on her day off. She clocked a security man glaring at them. "I think we should get out of here before that geezer throws us out."

"Come on, then."

"Bye now," Suzie called out and gave the man a cheery wave before following Douglas out into the sunshine.

"You've spent the last couple of weeks listening to my woes and I know so little about what you've been up to since . . . since you left. Travelling and writing, obviously, but what else?" They were sitting sharing a plate of antipasti and sipping a crisp white wine. She could get used to this. On a day like this with good food and great company, she could forget all about her cares and responsibilities.

"Travelling and writing is quite time-consuming," he pointed out, flashing his gorgeous smile.

"You know very well what I want to know, Doug Hamilton. There must have been women, especially now you're famous as well as rich."

He laughed. "Travel writers are rarely either."

"Stop avoiding the question," she retorted, glaring at him.

"I told you, Suzie. There have been no women." He kept his eyes on his wine. "I grew out of all that."

244

"I won't tell Mandy tales out of school, if that's what's worried you."

He shook his head, his smile sad. "There's nothing to tell. I'm a changed man, partly because of you. I have a lot to thank you for, Suzie."

"Thank me?" She frowned, confused. That wasn't the way she remembered it. If anything, it was the other way around. He had given her a job when she was pregnant, put a roof over her head when her dad threw her out and stood firm when his wife demanded he evict her. She could still remember Pamela's outrage when he'd moved her into the flat over his garage.

"When I stepped down as MD and had the bypass and you moved in" — Doug sighed — "that was one of the most difficult periods of our marriage. Escaping to see you kept me sane. Looking back, I think I'd have left Pam, only I knew if I did, she'd throw you out. So, I hung in there and, because we were forced to stay together, we stopped arguing and started talking, really talking, for the first time in years. If it wasn't for you, Susie, I wouldn't have had those last few precious years with my wife."

Suzie reached for his hand. "Life is so fucking unfair. Pam was far too young to die and so soon after you'd sorted out your differences." She shook her head as she remembered the way Pamela's eyes had lit up when she looked at her husband in those last couple of years. She'd transformed from a cold, hard woman into a warm and tender one. "She was so happy, happier than I'd ever seen her."

"I was, too." He put a hand to his mouth and Suzie's heart broke at the hopelessness in his eyes.

"Sorry, Doug, I didn't mean to bring you down."

He opened his eyes and smiled. "You didn't. It's nice to be able to talk to someone who knew her. I'm so glad you got to see what she was really like."

"She loved you, Doug, and I know that you adored her. But you were always such a flirt. Has there really been no one since?"

"Ah, Suzie, I'd forgotten how direct you could be." He chuckled.

She frowned. That was the second time he'd referred to her being the same as he remembered. "You don't think I've changed?"

Doug put his head on one side and looked at her as he considered the question. "You're more confident," he admitted, "but, then, you're older and have been a wife and mother, so that's to be expected. That apart, yeah" — his smile was full of warmth and affection — "you're still my Suzie."

She shook her head and reached for her wine. "Makes you wonder. Anyway, you were telling me what happened after you left CML."

"When I left Ireland, I took the first flight I could get a seat on," he told her. "I ended up in Chicago and, yes, I'll be honest, I drank too much and played the field for a while. There, satisfied? You wouldn't believe the number of women who are attracted to a sad, unshaven man with an Irish accent. But I soon got bored of hanging out in bars, feeling sorry for myself. I never was cut out to do nothing.

246

"So I went to Boston and got work as a tour guide. I found the route a little unimaginative so I came up with my own alternative, specifically aimed at Irish and British tourists. That did quite well, so I was given the task of setting up similar operations in New York and Washington DC. That's when I started to take notes about the different places I visited and anecdotes about locations or personalities that the other operators missed. One man asked what other countries I arranged tours of and so I decided to take the business to Europe."

"But not Ireland."

He shook his head. "No. I was asked to, many times, but I wasn't ready to come home. I started off with the obvious places — Paris, Berlin, Rome — but the Eastern bloc was the unknown and it attracted me. I suppose I was still running away. I was ahead of the game, though. There were hardly any English-speaking tourists interested in going there. But I went anyway and wrote about the places I visited and submitted them to their tourist departments. Soon I was being commissioned to write specific pieces to draw tourists to the lesser-known areas."

"Jess would be fascinated; you two have to meet. You could make money anywhere, couldn't you?" Suzie was lost in admiration. "You're a true entrepreneur."

He shrugged. "I don't know about that. It was all accidental. I was trying to escape the past, and stumbled upon opportunities to help finance my travels."

"But you didn't need to work, surely? You were loaded."

He laughed. "Not really. In Ireland I still had a lot of bills to pay, and the mortgage on the house and the lease on the CML office premises were enormous. That's the downside of good locations: no matter how tough times get, the cost of owning or leasing property doesn't change much. Then there was the banking crisis and by 2010 we had lost two-thirds of our clients and the ones that remained had tightened their belts considerably. I didn't want to close CML but I knew the sooner I did it the better the severance package I could put together for Gina, Jack and Mal, and poor old Noreen too, of course."

She frowned. "What about Greg?" she said, remembering Doug's younger, cocky brother whom Gina had drooled over for months before she saw sense and started dating Jack.

Doug's expression darkened at the mention of his younger brother. "I haven't set eyes on him since I left Ireland and I don't want to. He took advantage of my grief and got me to sign a few papers that I thought were invoices relating to the services and maintenance of our mother's house. It was a relief to hand over the responsibility to someone else but, it turns out, I basically signed over some bonds to him. He conned my poor mother, too. Then he fucked off to Melbourne."

"Bloody hell!" Suzie looked at him, stunned. "I have to be honest, I was never a fan, but I didn't think he'd sink that low. I take it your mum's passed on?" Suzie

248

remembered that the woman was quite old when she first met Doug.

"Would you believe that she only died three years ago at the tender age of ninety-three?" he said with a whimsical smile. "I felt bad for leaving her, letting her down, but I was with her when she died at least."

"You didn't let her down: Greg did."

"He wouldn't have been able to if I'd had my wits about me and stayed in Ireland."

She stared into space. "We all have regrets, Doug, but there's no point in beating yourself up about things you can't change."

"Wise words." Doug smiled at her as their main course was served. "Enough sad stories. Eat up, you'll need the energy. We're going to get some exercise today."

They were on a bus heading north of the city but Douglas still wouldn't tell her where they were going. Finally he jumped up and grabbed her by the hand. "Come on, this is our stop."

She got off the bus and blinked. "You've brought me to a graveyard? Seriously?"

"Glasnevin is not just a graveyard: it's where all the famous figures from Irish history are buried."

"Fascinating." She rolled her eyes as he led her across the road to the main entrance.

He grinned. "It will be, I promise."

And it was. Their tour guide was entertaining and made her country's history sound a lot more interesting than she remembered from her school days. But she was even more spellbound by his anecdotes about the various liaisons, particularly that of William Butler Yeats and Maud Gonne.

"The years come and go but people don't change much, do they?" she said as they sat over a coffee afterwards. "Do you think Maud loved him?"

"Who, Yeats? Who knows?"

"She packed a hell of a lot into her life. That's what I want to do, Doug."

"Have you made a bucket list?" he teased.

"I have." She saw his look of surprise. "No, it's more of a to-do list about things I need to put right before I die, family stuff."

"Your family are adults, Suzie. Let them get on with their lives and concentrate on your own."

"There speaks a man with no kids," she retorted. "They may be adults but they'll always be my babies."

"You'll turn into an interfering old bat that they'll only invite round once a year out of duty if you don't loosen those apron strings," he warned. "What about you, Suzie? You said you wanted to travel, try new things, meet new people, so where exactly is it you want to go, what do you want to do? And, more to the point, when are you going to start?"

Suzie shrugged. "I have Bobby to look after now, not to mention Percy, so I'm no longer free to take off whenever I choose."

"You won't be looking after Bobby for ever and you can put the dog in a kennel or take him with you. Turn your dreams into a reality while you're still young, Suzie."

"You told me that I should be careful with my money," she protested.

"You don't have to spend a fortune to see the world," he assured her. "Just be smart. If you are happy and fulfilled, you will be better able to cope with anything that life throws at you."

She raised her eyebrows. "Easy, Doug. You're beginning to sound like some kind of bible-basher."

He chuckled. "I suppose I am but I don't think I'd have got through that first year after Pam's death if I hadn't left the country. Going somewhere that no one knows you is liberating. In Dublin I was pitied for months because my wife was dying of cancer. Then I was the poor widower that people whispered about but were afraid to approach. In Chicago I was just a guy in a bar."

"I can see the attraction," Suzie admitted. Her own experiences when John was killed and since waking from the coma hadn't been that different. "I'm not like you, though, Doug. I love my home. And, while I'd like to take holidays in faraway places — some of the ones you've written about — I'd always want to come home."

"I'm happy for you," he said and she could see a wistfulness in his eyes.

"Set up a night with the gang, Doug," she said on impulse.

He looked taken aback. "We have a deal."

"We do, and I'll keep my end of it, but it will be at least a couple of months before I could go to Croatia with you. A night out with old friends would do us both some good right now."

"All right, then." He sighed, but he was smiling. "I suppose Doug Hamilton has to reappear at some stage."

CHAPTER
TWENTY-FIVE

Jess gave her little flat a whirlwind tidy and had just brushed her hair and slicked on some lip gloss when the doorbell rang. She hurried down to answer it and smiled at the sight of her brother bearing a massive pizza box.

"Oh, well done, bro. I'm just in the door and never got a chance to stop by the supermarket."

"Like you were going to cook for us," Noel jeered, climbing the stairs.

"Hi, Cal. Thanks for coming." She smiled up at him and he surprised her, yet again, by bending to press his cheek to hers. It was gentle and not in the least intimate, and yet it felt good. She inhaled his spicy aftershave and stepped back, blushing. He seemed to fill her small hallway. "Come on up," she said and led him up to the flat and into the tiny kitchen, where Noel had left the pizza on the table and was hunting in the fridge for beers.

"Plates?" she asked.

"No need," Noel said, pulling up a chair, opening the box and taking a slice.

"How are things, Jess?" Cal asked, folding himself into one of the chairs.

"Fine, busy. You?" Jess pushed the box towards him.
"Yeah, I'm good."

Jess poured herself a glass of wine and then helped herself to a slice of pizza. "Mmm, this is delish." She closed her eyes, nodding her appreciation.

"So, I've been telling Cal about our weird nephew," Noel said, washing down his pizza with a mouthful of beer. "He had some thoughts." He nodded to his friend before stuffing a huge chunk of pizza into his mouth.

"Noel, you have the manners of a pig." Jess looked at Cal. "I'd appreciate any advice you can give us, Cal. We're completely out of our depth. Nora added to my worries today. I'll fill you in on that later," she said when her brother looked up, eyebrows raised.

Cal sat back and twisted his body sideways in an effort to get more comfortable. "I'm no expert and I haven't met the child so I'm just throwing some things out there. Can you tell me more about him first?"

Jess tried to give Cal a balanced and fair description of her nephew and a few examples of his behaviour.

Cal listened carefully, asking the odd question. When she'd finished he leaned forward on the table and looked at her. "When did he start behaving like this?"

Jess frowned. "I think he's always been like this. When he was younger, it seemed cute. He's always been shy and clung to Sharon, though."

"He's never bothered playing with other kids," Noel said between mouthfuls.

Cal nodded. "What makes him happy? What relaxes him?"

254

"Playing video games, watching TV or playing with his toys," Noel said.

"And he likes to colour, although he's not very good at it."

"Does he do these things alone?" Cal asked.

"Pretty much," Jess said. "Once he's engrossed in something, he's oblivious of everyone."

"I never thought about that before, but you're right," Noel said. "If I try to discuss a movie or game with him, he doesn't have much to say."

Jess looked at Cal. "What do you think?"

"I think he should be assessed for ASD. From what you've told me, I'm surprised he hasn't been already. If you've noticed these things, his parents must have."

"ASD?" Jess frowned.

"Autism spectrum disorder," Cal explained. "In the old days it was just called autism, but now they know there are many different types and levels, some worse than others."

Jess shook her head. "Bobby isn't autistic."

"Note the word 'spectrum', Jess," Cal said gently. "From what you've said I'd say Bobby has a mild version. Doctors are wary of labelling any child until tests have been carried out, but the sooner they get started, the sooner Bobby can get the help he needs."

"I still don't think he has it."

Noel stared at Jess in disbelief. "Seriously? Are we talking about the same kid? The one who lines up his food, has no real friends and throws tantrums almost daily?"

"I know that he's difficult but he's smart. He's good at reading and writing and he's great at maths," Jess argued.

"Do you honestly think that he's a little devil everywhere except in school?"

"But they would have said something to Sharon."

"They probably have." Noel sounded weary.

Cal looked from one to the other. "She may be finding it hard to face."

Jess met his gaze. His eyes were warm and kind, nothing like — She shivered and forced herself to concentrate on the subject at hand.

"Does he hate loud noises or bright or flashing lights?" Cal asked.

Jess remembered Bobby, cowering in a corner, his hands over his ears last Hallowe'en, and how her mum refused to take him to the cinema anymore because he always threw a tantrum. She gave a reluctant nod.

"Does he only play with a couple of toys and seem almost obsessed with them?" Cal went on.

Noel groaned. "Mum's snow globe and a couple of his cars."

"Does he talk, or hum, or rock himself?"

Jess swallowed hard and looked at her brother. "How could we have been so blind?"

"Hey, don't beat yourself up." Cal touched her arm. "All little kids have habits, some stranger than others. When you're around someone all the time, you stop seeing them or think it's just that child's quirk. Do you know, many parents, mostly dads, only recognise that they also have ASD after their child is diagnosed? It's a relatively new condition. When we were kids, autistic children were either naughty or thought of as slow or simple. These days we know different and are better able to help those affected live full and happy lives.

"ASD kids aren't good at interacting with other people or understanding social cues, but those things can be learned. Many of them are quite smart. They may be poor at sport or interacting yet excel at maths, music or art. Can Bobby walk okay? Dress himself? Use the bathroom?"

Jess nodded. "He's only been fully toilet-trained a few months and he's a bit clumsy and awkward, but he's relatively independent."

"And he can talk?" Cal asked.

"He doesn't say much but, when he does, he speaks quite well," Jess told him.

"That's great." Cal gave her a reassuring smile. "It sounds, unless I'm completely off track, as if he might have quite a benign form of autism."

Noel looked at him. "Wouldn't his teachers have noticed?"

"He only started school last September, right?"

Jess nodded.

Cal shook his head. "Then it's much too early to make a judgement. I don't believe any teacher would say anything until they had a chance to observe him for longer. If his parents brought it up, though, that would be a different matter."

Noel met her eyes, his expression grim. "I'll bet some conversation has taken place, Jess. Think about

Sharon's folder. After what Cal's told us, don't you think that she knows more than she's letting on?"

Jess thought about the incredible amount of work Sharon had put into ensuring her family had all the information they needed to mind her son. She looked at Cal. "Whenever he's upset, she holds him really tight around his middle until he calms down. He hates his skin to be touched and only lets Sharon kiss him, and then only on his forehead or hand."

Cal nodded. "That would fit in with an ASD profile, but he needs to be assessed. Then he can start working with the special-needs team in his school."

Jess rested her chin on her hands and sighed. "I feel dreadful now. I've been so angry with him at times, and Mum's going to feel so guilty."

"I wouldn't bet on it," Noel muttered. "Even if Bobby's diagnosed she probably won't believe it."

"How is your mum?" Cal asked, watching Noel carefully. "I haven't seen her since she came home."

Noel gave a weary sigh. "She's made a full recovery, physically, but she's like a different person. She's completely insensitive, loses her temper at the drop of a hat and swears all the time."

"You never mentioned that before."

Noel bent his head and shrugged. "What's the point? It is what it is."

"She was always so kind to me," Cal mused.

"To everyone," Jess said. "Especially Bobby. But, since her recovery, he seems to drive her mad."

"Basically she doesn't give a crap about any of us now."

Despite Noel's flippant tone, Jess could hear the crack in his voice. She met Cal's eyes and slipped her arm round her little brother's shoulders. "She cares. She cares a lot. Especially about her darling son." Her teasing brought a smile and Noel leaned his forehead against hers. She fought back her tears and stood up to get the guys another beer and make some coffee.

"Interesting." Cal declined the can.

"What is?" Noel asked.

"In both cases it's as if the wires in the brain have got crossed or tangled, with unpredictable results. Your mum and Bobby probably have more in common now than ever before."

"Maybe but it sure as hell isn't bringing them closer," Noel assured him.

"I was telling you Nora called." Jess refilled her glass and, leaning against the worktop, told them about the conversation with her mother's best friend.

Noel groaned and put his head in his hands. "What do we do, Jess, or should we just stay out of it?"

"We can't possibly stay out of it now," Jess protested. "We have to do something. I just wish I knew what."

Thirty minutes of arguing, Cal acting as referee, and they were still no nearer a solution when the doorbell rang. Jess froze. Maybe she'd just ignore it.

"Jess, someone's at the door," Noel said.

"Oh, right." Thanks, Noel. Thanks a lot. She went downstairs and opened the door a crack and, as she'd feared, Louis was outside.

"Hello, darling." He pushed the door open and reached for her.

Frightened, Jess held him at arm's length, glancing nervously over her shoulder. She was afraid of Louis but she was even more afraid of what would happen if Noel and Cal witnessed him manhandling her. "You have to go. My brother's here."

Louis groaned. "Fuck. Call me when you get rid of him, Jess. I want you."

"Just go, Louis," she said, her stomach heaving at the lust in his eyes.

"Give me a kiss first," he said, lowering his mouth to hers.

Jess heard a noise and turned to see her brother glaring down at them. She stepped back. "Louis, this is my brother, Noel."

Louis tilted his head in acknowledgement, his eyes twinkling with amusement. He looked back at her. "Like I said, call me when you're free and we can discuss that . . . care-in-the-community piece."

"Will do," she said and shut the door after him.

"What the hell? I thought you'd dumped him."

"I have, Noel, but I still work with the man."

"You don't kiss a boss."

Jess tried for a careless laugh but it sounded unconvincing even to her. "Louis's like that with all women, it doesn't mean anything. I can handle him." Another lie, she realised, leading the way back upstairs. She pulled up short when she saw Cal standing in the doorway. He must have heard everything. She flushed and begged him with her eyes not to say anything.

"Everything okay?" he asked, his expression grim.

"Fine," Jess said brightly.

"It was her boss looking for a quick bonk," her brother told him.

"Noel, cut it out." She glared at her brother, mortified.

"Hey, don't be so touchy, I'm just kidding. But how you could ever have had anything to do with a guy like him —"

"Noel, grow up and stop embarrassing your sister," Cal said quietly, his eyes on her. She couldn't quite read his expression. She looked away, wishing the ground would open and swallow her up.

Noel flung himself down on Jess's sofa. "Where were we?"

"You had decided, I think, that your brother-in-law was the best person to approach," Cal reminded them.

"Yeah. You do it, Jess, he'll listen to you."

"Thanks," Jess muttered. The thought of confronting Keith was daunting. She looked to Cal. "I doubt he'll heed me."

"Don't be confrontational or judgemental," Cal counselled. "Tell him you're worried about Bobby and the behavioural problems you've observed. Say you and Noel are concerned for both him and your mum and suggest he has a chat with Bobby's teacher. They must know about these things, know the normal behavioural parameters for that age group."

Noel brightened. "He can't take offence at that, can he?"

Jess wasn't so sure but she nodded. "I'll do my best."

They stood up to leave and Noel excused himself to use the loo. Immediately, Cal came over to her. "Is that guy giving you trouble again?"

She studied his face and saw only concern. "He doesn't like being given the brush-off," she admitted.

His expression darkened. "Let me deal with him, Jess."

She shook her head and put a hand on his arm. "No. Thanks, Cal but I'll call you if I run into trouble."

His eyes held hers and then he smiled and touched her cheek. "Call me anyway," he said, and turned away as her brother came back into the room.

CHAPTER
TWENTY-SIX

Noel and Cal had gone and Jess was left wondering how she was going to broach the matter of Bobby with Keith. She had to get him alone if they were to have this conversation. The last thing she needed was either Sharon or her mother walking in on them. The safest option was to invite him to the flat. She could say she wanted to give him an update on how the arrangement was working out. That should be enough to put him on alert.

She just hoped that Keith would listen and not stick his head in the sand, as her sister seemed to have. From what Cal said, with the right support, Bobby's future could be a bright one. But getting such news would still be quite a shock. Keith must be stressed out already between worrying about Sharon and —

Jess's phone rang. She froze when she saw it was Louis, her hand going to her neck, where there were still some marks from his bites. She let the phone ring and then ring again. Then a text came through.

I know you're alone. Meet me.

He was watching the flat? Should she ignore him? He'd hardly come hammering on the door at this hour.

Her phone beeped again.

Maybe I'll just come over.

She stared at her phone, truly frightened now. Quickly she flicked through her contact list and found Cal's number. He didn't live that far away. She rang, praying he'd pick up.

"Jess?"

She closed her eyes at the concern in his voice. "Can you come over?"

"Is he there?"

"No, but I think he's on his way."

"Don't open the door to anyone. I'll be with you in five minutes and I'll phone you when I'm at the door."

"Thank you," she said, but he'd already hung up. She stood up and went to peer out of the window, and yelped when the doorbell rang. She looked at her phone and checked the signal. It was fine, so it wasn't Cal. It had to be Louis. The bell rang again a couple of times and then she heard the outer door open, and voices. What the hell was going on? What was Louis playing at? He was putting his job and marriage at risk, and for what? Sex? Sex with a reluctant partner. The four-letter word came to mind again and she shuddered. Again, the raised voices had her ear pressed against the door of her flat.

As quietly as she could, she opened her door and peered down the dark stairwell. It was deserted but a light was coming from under the door that led into the main house. She heard laughter and sighed. Obviously the landlady had company, who must have rung Jess's bell by mistake. She went back into her flat, closed the door, turned the key and put on the safety chain for good measure. Her hands were shaking and she began to open cupboards in search of wine, but all she could find was a dusty bottle of gin. She poured a measure into a tumbler and downed it in one. After refilling the glass, she went into her tiny lounge and perched on the arm of the sofa, where she could watch the road outside. Where was Cal?

There was a bang downstairs and she started, spilling half her drink down the front of her top. This man had turned her into a nervous wreck, but she knew that she'd only herself to blame. She'd let him walk all over her and, when she finally found some backbone and told him it was over, he'd been turned on. She thought of him pounding her into the wall in the narrow hallway and began to tremble. Louis Healy had raped her. He'd *raped* her. And, if he got her alone, he'd do it again.

Her phone rang and relief washed over her when she saw Cal's name on the display.

"Jess? I'm downstairs."

She didn't even answer but rushed downstairs to let him in. As Cal stepped into the hall she flung herself into his arms.

"Hey! Jess, what is it?" He pulled away to search her face but she was staring past him and let out a frightened whimper when an engine roared to life and Louis's car disappeared round the corner.

Up in the flat, Cal placed a mug in front of Jess, but she kept a firm grip on her glass of gin, mainly because, if she let go, she knew her hands wouldn't stop shaking.

"What happened?" Cal asked, stirring sugar into his coffee.

"Louis wanted to come over and I ignored his calls, but he knew I was here." She raised her eyes briefly to his. "He won't leave me alone. I think he likes me saying no."

Cal stopped stirring and she watched as he carefully set the spoon down. "Does he listen when you say no, Jess?" he asked, his voice quiet and controlled.

She dropped her gaze. "No."

Cal clenched his fist. "He hurt you?"

"I don't think it was intentional," she said, wondering why she was still defending the man.

He thumped the table with the heel of his hand, making her jump. "Jesus, why didn't you say something, Jess?"

Jess shook her head. "I feel so ashamed."

"Ashamed?" he almost shouted. "Sorry," Cal said when she shrunk back in the chair. He took her hand. "Jess, there is no reason for you to feel ashamed."

She couldn't look at him: it was too humiliating. "I brought it on myself."

"No one brings violence on themselves."

"I told him it was over and yet, when he came round, apologising, I let him in."

"And he hurt you?"

Jess could hear the anger in his voice but said, "Yes. I was such a fool. Why did I let him do it? And why did I let him leave, thinking that it was okay to treat me like that?"

266

"He forced himself on you?" Cal pressed, his expression grim.

She nodded. "I tried to push him off me but he was too strong," she said, keeping her eyes on the glass in front of her. "Then I just wanted it to be over."

"Listen to me, Jess." He put a gentle finger under her chin and tilted her head. His eyes were soft and kind and she felt tears in the back of her throat. "This is not your fault. He did this to you."

She looked at him through her tears.

"Tell me you know that, Jess. Tell me, sweetheart." He brushed her hair back from her face. "Tell me."

"I should have been stronger," she wept.

"Did you say no, Jess?" he asked.

"Yes, yes, I did."

"Then he should have stopped. This is not your fault," he repeated. "He raped you, Jess."

His words sent her over the edge and she rested her head on the table and sobbed her heart out. She was aware of Cal rubbing her back and murmuring something, she didn't know what, and she didn't care. It was soothing.

"Do you want to report him?" Cal asked, when she'd calmed down.

Jess straightened and shook her head. "No. It was a while ago and it would just be my word against his."

He studied her for a moment. "Don't try to deal with this alone, Jess. You don't have to."

"I'll be fine now," she assured him, hating that he knew this about her. "I just needed a good cry. Don't worry, I won't let him in again." She forced a smile. "We never figured out what's up with Noel."

Cal clearly wasn't happy to drop the subject but allowed her to sidetrack him. "No, but we can get together again after you've talked to Keith."

She nodded, although she wasn't sure she could face him again after tonight. Every time she looked at him she would be reminded of her confession. And, when he looked at her, he would see Louis.

"Something did occur to me," Cal was saying, unaware of the way her mind was working.

"Oh?"

"Noel hasn't applied for any jobs."

"So?" It wasn't unusual to take some time out after university before settling down, and Noel had a summer of sailing to look forward to.

Cal shrugged. "I thought it was odd."

"It's probably because he wants to support Mum through Sharon's pregnancy." Jess stood up. She really needed Cal to go now. She felt tired and if he kept looking at her like that, his knowing gaze full of pity, she'd end up in tears again.

He seemed to read her mind for, after a brief, awkward hug and instructions to lock up, Cal left.

She had just put the chain on the door when her phone beeped. After a few moments, she found the courage to look at it, relieved to see it was only a message from Noel.

Did you talk to Keith?

Keith. Of course. She sighed and checked her watch. It was almost eleven but, while her sister would be asleep, she knew her brother-in-law stayed up quite late. She fired off a text, asking him to drop in sometime. Moments later the phone rang. Oh, shit, he wasn't supposed to call! Taking a deep breath, Jess answered, trying to sound upbeat. "Hi, Keith."

"Hey, Jess. What's up?"

Get right to the point, why don't you? Caught on the hop, she struggled to switch her thoughts from Louis and Cal back to Bobby. She searched for the right words that wouldn't alienate him or freak him out. "I just wanted to fill you in on something I didn't want to bother Sharon with."

"About Bobby?"

"Yes." She gulped at the silence at the other end of the line.

"And you can't tell me over the phone?"

No, Jess thought. This really wasn't a conversation to have on the phone. "I think it would be better if we met," she said, her voice firm.

"Will you be home in the morning? I could be there about nine thirty."

Tomorrow? She sighed. Still, the sooner it was done, the better. "That's fine, Keith. See you then."

If Jess needed distraction from her encounter with Louis, she had it. She dreaded the chat she had to have with her brother-in-law. Why had she agreed to do this? She should have at least asked Noel to be there as moral support. Maybe she should text him and ask him to come round, but she knew that her mother would be suspicious if her lazy son was up that early in the morning. No, Jess would just have to do this alone.

She resigned herself to a restless night; the only thing sustaining her was that getting Bobby help was of far greater importance than dealing with her own problems. Nora's concerns about her nephew hurting his mother or the new baby had really upset her. That was what she needed to keep in mind as she tried to get through to her brother-in-law. Whatever his faults, she remembered his terror at the thought he could lose Sharon. She needed to use that love to make him face up to the fact that steps had to be taken, and soon.

Jess lay in bed but, instead of worrying about talking to Keith, she found herself thinking about Cal and the concern and tenderness in those beautiful eyes that seemed to see into the depths of her soul. Was that how he looked at his clients? Was he being kind because she was Noel's sister, or did he have feelings for her? She recalled his words earlier that evening: "Call me anyway." But that was before she'd told him what Louis had done. That was a stumbling block she wasn't sure they could overcome. Still, she could dream, and dreaming of Cal was infinitely preferable to lying awake worrying about the next confrontation with Louis. Because, if there was one thing Jess knew for certain, he'd be back.

CHAPTER
TWENTY-SEVEN

Keith lay awake, listening to his wife's steady breathing and wondering what Jess had to say. He'd been expecting a call, of course, but not quite so soon, although he'd noticed today how tired Suzie looked. She'd been unusually quiet, too, which probably meant that she was afraid to open her mouth as, once Suzie got started, there was no stopping her. Sharon seemed unaware of any problems but, then, Keith had gone to great lengths to ensure that he was the one who collected Bobby every day.

Much as Suzie was worried about Sharon, he still didn't trust her to keep her comments and criticism to herself. He couldn't keep them apart for ever, but he'd do his best until Bobby had settled into the new routine. It seemed to be working out pretty well, although he had a feeling that Jess was going to shatter his illusions on that score. He glanced at the clock, switched off the alarm and slipped out of bed to go and wake his son and make breakfast.

Bobby *would* pick today to act up. From the moment Keith had woken him, he had been sullen and unresponsive. Now he sat at the kitchen table, rocking, his breakfast untouched.

"Eat your Rice Krispies," Keith said quietly, and left his son to take tea and toast up to Sharon. She yawned, stretched and gave him a sleepy smile. "Thanks, sweetheart. You spoil me."

He helped her to sit up and kissed her. "You deserve to be spoiled. Did you sleep well?"

"Yeah, not bad at all. How's Bobby today?"

"All is quiet," he reported honestly. "You look better." It was true, he realised, caressing her small bump. She was more relaxed and her forehead was smooth. Noticing that made him realise how her brow had previously been almost permanently creased in a frown from the stress and anxiety of looking after their son. Now, though, there was a healthy glow to her skin and her eyes shone. If it weren't for his meeting with Jess, he'd be tempted to come home after he'd dropped his son to school and hop back into bed beside her.

"I was thinking that I might pick Bobby up from school today and spend the afternoon with him and Mum. I feel guilty that I've hardly seen her lately when she's being so good. And, although Bobby took a while to settle, he seems fine now."

Keith hesitated, thinking of his silent, brooding son downstairs. "Not today, sweetheart. It's going to get quite warm this afternoon. Too warm for you to walk to school and then another twenty minutes to your mum's." As Sharon opened her mouth to protest, he

272

played his ace. "Besides, Suzie might think you're checking up on her. Leave it for a couple of weeks."

Her eyes filled with doubt and she sighed. "Maybe you're right."

"Why don't you meet Lisa and Shelley for a coffee instead?"

"Lisa got herself a morning job and I couldn't listen to Shelley's twins for the morning. They're teething and a nightmare." Sharon patted her tummy and smiled. "Are you listening in there? You had better be a little angel."

Keith chuckled. "I know, why don't you go for a massage? You were saying your back ached."

Her face lit up. "Oh, yes, that would be nice. I'll give the spa a call and see if they can fit me in."

He pulled a few euros out of his back pocket and tossed them on the bedside table. "It's on me. Now, I must get our son to school." He kissed her. "See you later."

"Send him up to say goodbye," she called after him. "And, thanks, darling."

Keith hurried down to the kitchen and made an extra sandwich to put in his son's lunchbox: he'd be ravenous by break time.

It was after nine when they got to the school and Keith had to walk Bobby down to the classroom.

"Sorry. Mondays!" He rolled his eyes and laughed while the teacher just gave a polite smile and sent Bobby to his desk.

"Do you have a moment, Mr Mulvey?"

"Sure."

She led him back into the corridor, leaving the door ajar so that she could keep one eye on her class. "I won't delay you. I just wondered if you and your wife had thought about my suggestion."

Keith frowned. "Suggestion?"

She seemed flustered by his reaction. "She was worried about him and asked how he was in school. I suggested he might benefit from some one-on-one assistance?"

What the hell? Keith was about to ask her to explain but it was clear that she already had. Sharon just hadn't passed it on. He nodded. "Of course, I'm sorry. My wife has been ill and we haven't had an opportunity to discuss it."

"Oh, I'm sorry to hear that."

"Thank you. She's a lot better now, but needs to take it easy. I'll talk to her and get back to you about the, er, assistance."

"That's fine. Please don't worry about it. I'll keep a special eye on him."

"I'd appreciate that." He shook her hand and strode down the corridor, across the playground and out onto the road.

Once safely in the car, Keith thumped the steering wheel and gave a strangled roar. What was Sharon playing at? Why hadn't she told him that she'd talked to Bobby's teacher? He was sorely tempted to go straight home and confront his wife, but he needed to calm down first. In this frame of mind, he certainly wouldn't do her blood pressure much good. Anyway, he had a meeting to go to.

Jess opened the door, her eyes darting past him, before giving him a nervous smile. "Hi, Keith. Come on up."

He followed her, knowing that, whatever she had to say, he really didn't want to hear it. He thought of the teacher's words and how Sharon had kept it from him, and his gut instinct was to run and keep running.

"Coffee?"

"Please."

"How's Sharon?"

"Stronger and calmer." He smiled. "Thanks to you guys."

"That's good." She sat down opposite him, ignoring her coffee and pulling nervously on the sleeve of her jersey.

He sighed. The way she was beating about the bush, this must be bad. "So, you wanted to talk?" he prompted.

She bit her lip and then nodded. "It's about Bobby. He's been quite agitated since he's started coming to Mum."

"She said he was fine, so did Noel." Keith frowned at her. "So did you."

"Yes, well, we didn't want to worry you. We thought that he'd settle down."

"He will," Keith quickly assured her, willing her not to tell him to make other arrangements.

Jess nodded. "Yes, hopefully he will as he gets more used to us and the house. Mum's been great. She's even managing to control her temper and her swearing," she gave a weak smile, "but it's taking a lot out of her, Keith."

"I'm sorry to hear that." Keith was racking his brain for a solution that would keep everyone happy. "Sharon won't let him go to a childminder or an afterschool club. I suppose I could try to finish work a little earlier so Suzie doesn't have to mind him for as long."

"That's not why I called you," Jess interrupted, tugging more frantically on her sleeve. "Look, Keith, some of Bobby's behaviour worries Noel and me. Unlike Mum, we haven't ever spent this much time with him, so, well, it was a surprise. And when we studied Sharon's binder —"

He looked at her, bemused. "I don't understand. What binder?"

She frowned. "The folder of tips Sharon put together for us about Bobby. Didn't you know about it?"

He stared at her, then sighed and shook his head. "I suppose I shouldn't be surprised. She doesn't think anyone's capable of looking after him the way that she can."

"That's probably true. When you read it from cover to cover, it comes across that Sharon thinks there's something wrong with Bobby."

"What's wrong is that she's spoiled him and unless he gets his own way he throws a tantrum."

Jess looked at him and the concern and pity in her eyes unnerved him.

"I don't think it's that simple, Keith."

276

He sat back and crossed his arms. "Why don't you tell me what you *do* think, Jess? You've obviously got an opinion."

Jess didn't get annoyed at his sarcastic tone. Instead, she held his gaze and answered, her voice quiet but clear. "Have you noticed how he doesn't get jokes or realise when you're teasing him? The way he prefers to play alone, always with the same toys, deliberately isolating himself? How he eats his food in a specific order? The way he rarely responds with more than a couple of words when you try to engage him? Normally, at that age, you can't shut kids up."

"He's like me. I was quiet and had favourite toys and, yes, I could be a right little pain in the arse. So, he's a bit odd. What about it?"

"How does he get on at school?" she asked.

That stopped Keith in his tracks as he remembered the teacher's words earlier. Bobby needed help. She had discussed it with his wife, said Bobby needed one-on-one assistance. "Fine," he lied, dropping his gaze. "He's great at maths," he added for good measure.

Jess frowned. "We've been talking, Noel and I, with Cal —"

Keith's eyes widened. "Noel's mate?"

"He's a psychologist and knows more about kids than we do," she explained, "and he suggested that perhaps Bobby should be tested for ASD."

"What's that?"

"It's autism spectrum disorder."

He looked at her in horror. "My son is not autistic."

"That's what I said," Jess assured him, "but there's no harm in getting him tested. Cal said that, if he was diagnosed, then he could get the help he needed. Apparently it's quite common for it to go under the radar in mild cases. Family become so accustomed to their kids' quirks, they dismiss them. Often it's the teachers who spot something."

Keith shook his head, feeling angry and frightened. The more she said, the more sense it made, but he couldn't and wouldn't accept that there was something wrong with his son. "With all due respect, Jess, you're a journalist, not a doctor, and I'm not impressed with you discussing my son with friends."

"And I . . . we wouldn't, normally, but when Bobby hit Mum —"

"What?" Keith felt sick.

She sighed. "Don't worry, she's fine, but Noel was a bit freaked out and so he asked Cal's opinion."

"Is that the only time Bobby's hit her?" Keith asked, thinking of the times he'd had to restrain his son.

Jess sighed and shook her head. "No, I've seen him lash out before and I've been on the receiving end a couple of times. I've never felt that he did it to hurt me, though. It was always as if he was out of control and didn't even realise he was doing it. The truth is, Keith, we're feeling out of our depth. We don't know if we're doing something to cause Bobby's mood swings or how to deal with them."

Keith closed his eyes, wishing she'd stop. He didn't want to hear any of this. "For fuck's sake, Jess, all you

278

have to do is mind him for a few hours. You don't have to psychoanalyse the child to do that."

She lifted her chin and met his eyes, still calm. "We're worried about Mum getting another fall or a knock to her head."

Keith groaned. "You want me to find someone else to mind him."

"No." Jess shook her head, vehemently. "We wouldn't be having this conversation if we weren't concerned about Bobby too and, of course, we want to get Sharon safely through this pregnancy."

"Then what exactly are you suggesting I do, Jess?" he said, feeling angry and frustrated and, more than that, fearful.

"Talk to the school, to Bobby's teachers, and get their opinion. They see him every school day and, according to Cal, they'll probably have noticed the signs if he *is* on the spectrum."

Keith narrowed his eyes. "Or else?"

"It's not an ultimatum, Keith," Jess said, visibly upset now. "We just want what's best for everyone. If you ask Mum, she'll keep telling you that she's coping fine, but that's not true. The fact that she's lying should tell you how worried she is about Sharon. She'll do whatever it takes to keep her and the baby safe."

Keith stood up and went to stare out of the window. He didn't believe that Bobby was autistic but perhaps it would shut them all up if the child was assessed. After all, if Suzie didn't mind him, who would?

"Cal says that there are some great medications now and the schools have care assistants to help children with ASD. But first he must be officially assessed and diagnosed."

He took a deep breath and turned back to his sister-in-law. "I've got to go."

Jess put a hand on his arm as he went to walk past her. "I didn't tell you to upset you, Keith. We only want to help and we will, in any way that we can."

He forced himself to smile. "I know that."

CHAPTER
TWENTY-EIGHT

Sharon had come upstairs for a nap when she heard a noise downstairs. She sprang up on the bed, her heart thumping in her chest, as she realised there was someone in the house. She went to grab her phone and realised that she'd left it on the kitchen table downstairs. Shit! She looked around for something that she could use as a weapon but there wasn't time. The second stair creaked and Sharon froze. Someone was coming upstairs. Terrified, Sharon edged backwards until she was pressed against the headboard, her eyes on the door and her hands protectively across her stomach. The steps got closer and then paused outside her door. Sharon watched in horror as the door handle turned and let out a bloodcurdling scream.

"Sharon, will you stop? It's only me. *Sharon!*"

She opened her eyes and saw that the man who'd grabbed her and whose eyes she had been clawing at was her husband. "Keith? You scared the living daylights out of me. What on earth are you doing home?" She collapsed back on to the pillows, cradling her tiny bump and hoping that Baby's heart wasn't racing as fast as hers.

"Sorry, sweetheart, I didn't mean to scare you. I did call your name when I opened the hall door. Are you okay?" He plonked down next to her and kissed her, looking both guilty and worried.

"Yeah." Sharon smiled. For all of the terror associated with a diagnosis of hypertension, she was glad of it. She and Keith were closer now than they had been in years. He picked up the bottle of water from the bedside locker and held it out to her.

"Thanks." She took a drink. "Why are you home? Is it Mum?" Her eyes widened. "Bobby?"

"It's about Bobby. Don't worry, he's fine," he added quickly when she clutched the covers. She watched as he stood up and crossed the room before turning and resting against the windowsill.

"I was talking to his teacher this morning."

Sharon gulped but forced herself to stay calm. "Oh? Is everything okay?"

"Come on, Shaz, you know very well it isn't," Keith retorted, a flash of annoyance crossing his face. "Tell me exactly what she said to you about Bobby falling behind and why he needs help."

She gave a stiff shrug. "That's about it."

"No, it is not. There's the small matter of him not getting the help he needs unless you and I approve it. How could we possibly do that when you didn't even tell me?"

"Are you surprised?" she said, feeling defensive. "You know that I've been worried about him but you always insist that it's my fault for spoiling him. And you're always criticising him and putting him down. If I told

282

you what the teacher had said it would confirm that you were right and you would . . ." She stopped.

He came over and knelt before her, his eyes demanding an answer. "I would what, Sharon?"

She looked at him and then squeezed her eyes closed, gulping back her tears. "Reject him."

"Jesus, Sharon, is that what you think?"

She opened her eyes to see him staring at her in horror, and she cried harder.

"You think I'd turn my back on my own son?"

Anger bubbled up to replace the tears and Sharon wiped them away and glared at him. "You already have," she spat. "For the last year or so you've practically ignored him." Oh, God, the genie was out of the bottle. "You're spending more time with him now not because you want to but because of me and the baby. And, when this child is born, what hope will Bobby have of ever getting your attention again?" Distraught, she sank back onto the bed and waited for him to let loose. When he said nothing she looked up and was staggered when she saw tears in his eyes. "Keith? Look, I didn't mean it. I'm sorry. It's just hormones."

He slumped back onto the floor and buried his head in his hands. "No. No, it isn't."

"You have been great recently, drawing the pictures with him and —"

Keith shook his head and put a finger to her lips. "Let me talk, please."

She nodded silently, tears running down her cheeks.

"The truth is, Bobby embarrasses me. I'm ashamed of him. I hate his tics and his grunts. I hate that he doesn't look me in the eye and stiffens when I try to give him a hug." He stared at some point above her head, defeat in his eyes. "I knew there was something wrong and couldn't face up to it." Finally his bloodshot eyes found hers. "I talked to your sister this morning."

Sharon sat up. "Jess? Why?"

"They're having a tough time with Bobby but didn't want to say so because they don't want to worry you." He stopped and took a drink from her water bottle before continuing. "Noel told Cal about Bobby and the sort of things he did." Keith's eyes met hers. "Cal said it sounded like it might be ASD. I didn't even know what that was but I'm guessing you do, don't you, Sharon?"

She looked at him, scared, and nodded slowly. "Yes." Now that Keith was ready to listen she wasn't sure that she could talk. Vocalising the situation would make it real and they would not only have to face it, but do something about it, too.

"Tell me. Please?"

She looked down at her hands in his, resting on her bump. "When I told his teacher my concerns, she mentioned autism. I went through the roof, but she assured me that, if she was right, he was very low on the spectrum and they could help him."

Keith wiped his face on his sleeve and took a deep breath. "So what happens next?"

284

"I think we can organise an assessment through the school. Lana, his teacher, is lovely and very good with Bobby. She'll tell us what we need to do."

Keith squeezed her hand. "Then I'll call and see if we can set up an appointment for tomorrow."

"Have you any other questions?" The principal, Mr Quinn, looked from one to the other.

Sharon shook her head, overwhelmed. "I don't think so. There's just so much to take in."

Bobby's teacher gave her a sympathetic smile. "Don't worry. You can call any time, Sharon, and I'll do my best to answer your questions."

"How long will all this take?" Keith asked, running an agitated hand through his hair.

"A few months, perhaps more, I'm afraid," she replied. "I know it's frustrating but it involves two departments and sometimes it's hard to get them all on board at the same time."

"Are we talking bureaucracy and red tape?" Keith's lip curled in disgust.

"The departments are under resourced and short-staffed and, as ASD isn't a life-threatening illness, it's not at the top of their list of priorities," the principal explained. "I know it's frustrating, but please be assured that, pending a diagnosis, we will do our best for Bobby and, where and when possible, he will have access to our SEN and SNA teams."

"All these acronyms make my head spin," Sharon said with a nervous laugh.

He smiled. "Sorry, the school lingo is full of them." He rummaged in his drawer and produced some booklets. "These will help. That's the school's special-needs policy, and this is the department's booklet, and there's a leaflet on how you can help Bobby at home. You should have a chat with your GP and there are some good, local support groups in the area."

"There are a lot of things that Bobby can get involved in that will help," the teacher added. "Art and music are great ways of calming ASD kids, and helping them to concentrate. There is lots of help out there for him and for you. Don't be afraid to ask."

Sharon followed Keith outside, surprised she was able to walk given how shaky her legs were.

He pulled her tight to his side and she burst into tears. He wrapped his arms round her and held her as she cried, kissing the top of her head. "It will all be fine, sweetheart, I promise."

"It's a relief in a way," she said, balling the tissues in her hands as they drove home and trying to look on the bright side. "Bobby's not badly behaved at all. He's not responsible for his behaviour, and now we've set the wheels in motion to help him."

Keith patted her knee. "We have."

"We need to find out what triggers the tantrums or at least learn to spot the signs when he's about to throw one so that we can head him off at the pass," she continued.

286

"It would be great if we could," he agreed. "I had no idea that intolerance to noise and lights were symptoms of autism. So much makes sense now."

Sharon nodded. "I always thought it odd when he didn't laugh at jokes. I thought he had no sense of humour. Now I realise that he just didn't get the joke. Lord only knows what he makes of all the slagging in my family. No wonder he's wary of my mother. One of her favourite sayings when she's cross is 'I'll murder you!'"

Keith groaned. "And he'd think that she meant it. We're not the only ones who need to be educated."

"I know." Sharon had been worrying about how they were going to ensure that her mother didn't set Bobby off. "Hopefully, knowing that Bobby can't help being the way he is will make Mum more understanding."

"Do you want to go straight there and break the news?" Keith asked as they sat at the traffic lights.

"I suppose so," Sharon said, reluctantly. The lights changed and Keith turned right towards Suzie's house. "I hate the thought of him being labelled, Keith."

He nodded. "I know, but he'll be able to cope with life better once he gets the help he needs. And so what if he's not going to be a college professor?"

"I'm much more concerned about his social skills," Sharon said. "I don't want him to be Billy No Mates."

"But he's content in his own company. There's nothing wrong with that. You know, some of the world's most successful people are just like him."

Sharon knew that Keith was trying to cheer her up, but she couldn't help but catapult them fifteen, twenty, thirty years from now. Would Bobby be independent or still reliant on them and, if the latter, what would happen to him when they died? Shivering, Sharon dismissed the ridiculous thought. She had enough things to deal with now without worrying about the future. "Should we tell people?"

He scowled. "Other than the family, I don't see why. It's nobody's business."

"Then people will still think that he's just badly behaved and disobedient," Sharon said, wondering if the reality was that Keith was still ashamed of his son.

"Who cares what strangers think? We know the truth and hopefully, as we get to understand ASD better, we'll be able to help Bobby to control his behaviour." He sighed. "I can see us going to an awful lot of meetings and classes. Still, at least we can sort it out before Baby comes along."

"Are you kidding?" Sharon stared at him. Had he not heard a word that the teachers had said? There was no easy or speedy solution to Bobby's problems. "You do know there's no cure for ASD, don't you?"

"Of course I do," he snapped. "But he can change and learn to live a normal life within his own limitations. Whatever schools or doctors say or do, we'll be his main teachers, Shaz. We're the ones who'll make or break him."

That was a scary thought but he was right. Sharon prayed that she was carrying a daughter. If she had another son she knew that they would always be comparing the two. She slipped her hand over Keith's on the wheel. "I'm sorry."

"Me too." He shot her a guilty smile. "We're both upset. It's a lot to take on board."

"We'll do whatever it takes to help him and give him a good quality of life, right?"

"We will." Keith drew up outside Suzie's house. "Ready?"

Sharon shook her head, suddenly nervous. "Maybe we should wait."

He looked at her. "Why?"

"I don't know but —"

"Cooee! What are you two doing here?"

Sharon turned her head to see her mother on the doorstep, hands on her hips.

Keith shrugged. "That settles that, then. Come on."

"Hi, Mum." Sharon hugged her mother.

"You look better, love, but what are you both doing here at this hour?" Suzie frowned at Keith. "Is there something wrong? Is it Baby?"

"Baby is fine, and so is Sharon. "Is Noel in?"

"He's in the kitchen, why?"

Sharon glanced at Keith and then back at her mum. "We just wanted a word with you both."

"Autism." Sharon's voice was barely a croak. Tears threatened but she swallowed them back. "It's not Bobby's fault that he's disruptive and disobedient, Mum."

"Are you saying the boy is simple?" Suzie asked.

Sharon cringed and Noel glared at his mother.

Suzie glared back. "What? All I'm saying is, that's shite. I don't believe it for a minute. He may be odd and bloody hard work but that child is clever."

Laughing and crying, Sharon embraced her. "Oh, Mum, that's the nicest thing you've ever said about him."

"Well, I mean it. That's why I get so angry with the boy. I know he isn't stupid and he should know better."

"It's not really about his intelligence," she said. Tired, Sharon settled back and looked to her husband to explain.

"There's a whole spectrum of autistic behaviour from very mild to severe," Keith explained. "As I said, there's no diagnosis yet but Bobby ticks most of the boxes. For example the way he wants to take the exact same route to school every day. How he rarely looks at you when he's talking to you. How little he talks, for that matter. How he wants to wear the same pyjamas every night and prefers to draw pictures using just one colour."

"But he's so clever," Suzie insisted.

"No doubt about that," Noel agreed. "You wouldn't believe how quickly he picks things up on the Xbox."

"He remembers everything too," Sharon said, beginning to feel more hopeful. "It's like he absorbs anything he reads or watches on TV and, once it's in his head, it stays there."

"Like the name of every bloody train on *Thomas the effin' Tank Engine*." Suzie rolled her eyes.

"He'll sail through exams," Noel said, sounding almost envious.

Sharon had to laugh. She was feeling better now that everything was out in the open. Between his family and school, Bobby would get the support that he needed.

She knew that there were schools specifically for children with special needs and she intended to find out more about them, but she liked the idea of Bobby growing up with "normal" kids. One day he'd have to take his place in the world, and the sooner he adapted to it the better. She was terrified for him and what lay ahead but that wasn't going to help her, the new baby or Bobby. She needed to rest as much as possible so that she had the time and energy to cope with all of this, and, with that in mind, she looked over at her husband, eyebrows raised, and he immediately nodded.

"We should go, Shaz. You look done in."

"You do, love. Go home," Suzie said. "And don't worry, we'll look after Bobby."

Sharon sighed as Keith drove her home. Her back was aching and she felt exhausted and sad and relieved.

Keith shot her a worried look. "There's a long road ahead, love. It's not going to be easy."

"I know," she assured him. "At least we're not alone. The school and my family are behind us and, yes, I know my mother will still lose her temper and say things she shouldn't but, at least when she calms down, she'll realise what she's done and maybe give Bobby a cuddle. That's progress."

He patted her hand and smiled. "Yes, sweetheart. That's progress."

CHAPTER
TWENTY-NINE

"You won't believe what just happened," Noel said dramatically when Jess walked in. She dropped her backpack. "Benedict Cumberbatch dropped by?"

"Not that exciting," Suzie chuckled. "Keith and Sharon were here."

"After Keith left you yesterday, he went straight home to talk to Sharon," Noel told her. "And they met with Bobby's school this morning."

Jess sank down into a chair. "And what happened?"

"It seems Sharon had talked to the teacher who agrees with Cal but Shaz couldn't deal with it and was afraid to tell Keith."

"I knew it." Jess sighed. "It's no wonder that she fainted. She must have been a nervous wreck, bottling all that up."

Suzie looked grim as she made the third pot of tea that morning. "I hadn't thought of that. We really are going to have to keep a close eye on her."

"She'll be much better now, Mum," Noel said. "You could see how relieved she was that it was all out in the open."

"So, what now?" Jess asked.

"What happens is, we have to be patient with Bobby." Suzie set a mug in front of her daughter.

"Don't worry, Mum," Jess said, looking at her mother's worried expression. "No one expects you to turn into a saint overnight. When he's here he'll still annoy you as much as he did yesterday, so don't put yourself under too much pressure."

"Deep breaths." Noel grinned. "Isn't that how your meditation guru says you keep calm?"

Suzie cuffed him across the head but she was smiling. "If I managed to keep my cool raising you lot, I can manage little Bobby, smartarse. I'd better get my act together: he'll be out in twenty minutes."

"I'll collect him and take him to the playground," Noel offered. "He can terrorise the other kids and come home exhausted."

Suzie laughed. "I won't say no. Thanks, love."

"I'd better get going too," Jess said.

Suzie frowned. "But you just got here."

"Only to cadge a cuppa. I've a meeting in half an hour with Amelia. She wants me to do a piece on Irish female entrepreneurs." Jess hugged her. "Why don't you catch forty winks before Bobby gets here? You'll be able to control your temper better if you're rested."

Suzie nodded and stroked Jess's hair. "Good idea, I'll do that."

"I'll walk out with you, Jess," Noel said. "See ya later, Mum."

"Is it my imagination or has Mum softened a little?" Jess murmured once they were outside.

"I think it's the shock." Noel chuckled. "Thanks for talking to Keith, Jess. I knew he'd listen to you."

"I didn't think he would act on what I said, at least not this quickly. He seemed so negative."

"Timing," Noel told her. "The teacher had said something to him when he dropped off Bobby, so he was already reeling before you opened your mouth."

"Poor guy." Jess sighed. "I wonder why Sharon didn't tell him."

"Who knows? But I'm glad you did, sis, good on ya."

"It's Cal we have to thank. He armed me with the information that persuaded Keith to take action."

Noel grinned, his eyes mischievous. "Call and tell him, he'll be delighted. You know he fancies you."

"He does not," Jess retorted, but blushed.

"He does, trust me — although he's probably not your type. After all, he is single."

"You are so funny." She glared at him.

"Call him," Noel repeated, backing away, grinning. "I bet he asks you out."

"Don't be ridiculous." Jess slid into the driver's seat and let her hair fall over her face to hide her grin. This was ridiculous. She was acting like a damn teenager again.

"We'll see," her little brother called over his shoulder as he sauntered off with a wave.

She drove off, her mind on Cal. She knew that, if she made that call, Noel would be proven right, but Jess wasn't sure she could face him. She couldn't believe that she had told him about Louis attacking her. He'd been completely cool and calm — presumably, that was

294

down to his profession. But she had seen the anger in his expression and she knew that if he came face to face with Louis, there was a good chance he'd punch the man. She smiled at the thought. It was nice to think of a man defending her honour. It was especially nice that it was Cal. But had he been angry at Louis for hurting his best friend's sister, or because he cared about her?

Jess liked to think it was the latter, but she was afraid that confiding in him had changed the dynamic of their relationship. Was she now a victim, deserving of his sympathy, someone who had to unburden, accept and heal? The very idea made Jess shudder. She refused to allow Louis to reduce her to the status of victim but, then, why didn't she stand up to him? Threaten him with disclosure to his family and employer or simply give him a knee in the balls, as Katie would undoubtedly do? That wasn't her way, though. Jess sighed. She just wanted him to leave her alone.

She glanced at her phone on the passenger seat and frowned as she realised Louis had made no contact since driving off the other night. Was he backing off or simply biding his time? She hoped he wouldn't turn up on the doorstep again. Surely he wouldn't be *that* brazen — although, the way he'd behaved lately, Jess wouldn't put anything past him. Maybe she should ask Katie to stay with her tonight. Louis wouldn't dare to pester her if her friend was present. Maybe he would finally get the message that she wanted nothing to do with a married man. Any lingering attraction she'd felt to Louis died that awful night in her apartment.

Jess parked her car and, glancing at her watch, saw that she had ten minutes to spare before her meeting. On impulse, she called Cal before she lost her nerve.

"Hello? Jess?"

"Hi, Cal."

"How are things?"

She heard the concern in his voice and sighed. "Fine. More than fine, thanks to you. I talked to Keith and, not only did he listen, he and Sharon went straight down to see Bobby's teacher this morning. They've requested that he be assessed."

"That's fantastic news, well done."

"I just wanted to thank you. It wouldn't have gone so well if you hadn't advised me."

"You can thank me in person if you like."

She could hear a smile in his voice and imagined a mischievous twinkle in his eyes, and she felt a warm, fuzzy feeling, glad she hadn't imagined this thing between them. "What did you have in mind?" she asked casually.

"A drink tonight, in O'Neill's?"

Her heart sank. That was where Louis and the gang went after work and the last place that she wanted to go, but she didn't want to tell Cal that. She was determined not to mention the man again.

"Sounds good to me," she told Cal.

"Great. See you there at six?"

"I'll be there."

Jess stepped into the shower feeling pleased with herself. Fired up from her meeting with Amelia, she

296

had set up a few interviews with three prominent business women and then written the introduction to the piece and now she had an evening with Cal to look forward to. How chuffed her mother would be if she knew that they were going on a date. What should she wear? Something casual that didn't look as if she'd made too much of an effort. It was only a drink in a pub and there was always the possibility that this wasn't a real date. She was still dithering when the phone rang and Katie's name flashed up.

"Hi, Katie. How did it go?" She knew that her friend had finished her accountancy exams today.

"Who knows? I'm just glad they're finished. I think I may have just about scraped through. So, where are you taking me to celebrate?"

Jess felt a pang of guilt. "Sorry, I'm busy tonight. My brother's friend, Cal, asked me out."

"That gorgeous hunk with the come-to-bed eyes?"

Jess laughed. "That's the one. Am I forgiven?"

"Only if we go out tomorrow night instead — *and* you tell me all the gory details."

"Deal," Jess promised, smiling. "Now I have to go. I can't decide what to wear."

"Something totally indecent," her friend advised.

"Goodbye, Katie." Jess tossed the phone on the bed and went back to selecting a suitable outfit. She realised she was looking at all of her clothes with a critical eye. Were they provocative or too sexy? She tended to dress casually, but something about her had attracted Louis's unsolicited attention. If he saw her with Cal, would he think she was deliberately taunting him, parading a new boyfriend in front of him? Would he come over later to question her about it? Feeling sick, Jess picked up her phone and sent Cal a text suggesting a different venue. He replied seconds later.

Fine, see you there.

Instantly she relaxed and reached for a red summer dress that complemented her dark colouring and, for once, left her hair loose around her shoulders. She didn't bother with jewellery and wore flat sandals, her only makeup eyeliner and lip gloss.

When Jess walked into the pub, the expression in his eyes told her that she'd got it right. He was looking pretty damn gorgeous himself in black jeans and a short-sleeved, black polo shirt.

"Hi, Jess." He stood up, smiled and leaned over to touch his cheek to hers. "What will you have to drink?"

"I'm buying the drinks, remember?"

"Fair enough. A pint of lager, please."

She went to the bar and ordered the beer and a spritzer for herself. "Cheers, and thanks again," she said when she returned, raising her glass to him.

"I think that you're crediting me with more than I deserve. From listening to you and Noel it sounds like you had reached the same conclusion. Well done, you, for having the guts to say something. Most people pretend nothing's happening and hope it will go away."

Jess nodded as she remembered her brother-in-law's sad expression. "Keith was quite polite and civil but it

298

was obvious that he felt I was interfering, and he didn't like it."

"When he sees the benefits of acknowledging the problem he'll be fine. You all will, especially Bobby."

"True, although I'm not so sure about Mum. I doubt she'll ever be the same grandmother to Bobby again."

"Hey, don't write her off just yet," Cal told her.

"Let's change the subject. I am fed up with all things Connors." Jess didn't want to bring the mood down by dwelling on her mother. "Tell me about you and your work. Noel says you're part of a large practice in town."

"That's right, but I'm not planning on staying there. I'm more attracted to the research end of things."

"Good." Jess flashed him a grin. "Now I won't worry that you're analysing me all evening."

"I hate telling anyone what I do," he confided. "So many people profess that they would never go into therapy but, after a few jars, they latch onto me and start telling me all their problems."

"You're quite safe tonight," Jess assured him. The very last things she wanted to talk about were her problems. Tonight she wanted him to see that she was fun and carefree.

"You're different," he told her.

She held his gaze. "I am?"

"Yeah. You're not people, you're Jess. A very attractive woman and a talented journalist."

"Have you even read any of my articles?" she teased, used to people praising her without having read her work.

"I certainly have," he assured her. "I like your writing style. You don't force your opinion on the reader but provoke them to think and question."

"Thank you," she said, truly complimented by his praise. "What drew you to psychology?"

"The mind is the final frontier," he said, his face animated. "Helping someone work through and conquer their problems is very rewarding, especially if it can be done without medication. I'm interested in the research because there's still so much for us to learn."

"Sounds more exciting than treating people. It must be depressing, listening to problems."

"All medicine involves listening to problems," he reasoned. "Once you learn to keep a professional distance it's fine. Those who usually end up sitting in my office can't see a way out. My job is to help open their eyes to the fact that, no matter how bad things may seem, there are always options."

"Are there?" Jess said, thinking of the mess she'd got herself into with Louis.

"Always."

She looked up and saw the certainty in his eyes and smiled, realising he knew exactly what she was thinking. It was disconcerting and yet comforting. Jess could so easily open up to this man but she didn't want him as a therapist: she wanted more. Was she crazy? Her history with men was disastrous. She'd always gone for losers or attracted men who already had at least one woman on the go and, she knew from Noel, Cal had never been in a long-term relationship either. Perhaps he wasn't as perfect as he seemed.

"What's going on in that head of yours?" He watched her, eyes twinkling, his head on one side.

"Why now?" she blurted out.

He looked confused. "Sorry?"

"You've known me for years and never shown any interest in me. So, why now?"

Cal looked completely wrong-footed, embarrassed even.

Jess had no idea why she was being confrontational. The poor guy probably couldn't wait to escape. But she'd swallowed so many sweet, flattering words from lots of guys that she'd had enough. All she wanted and needed from Cal was some straight talking. "Well?" she pressed.

"When we were younger, I didn't have the guts to ask you out," he said, looking almost shy. "And, by the time I did work up the courage, you were seeing that guy, Jamie?"

"Jeremy," she said, staring at him.

"Yeah. What a twat."

"He was," she agreed, smiling, although at the time she'd thought he was wonderful and was devastated when he decided to take a year out to travel and didn't even ask her to go with him.

"And then I was studying and I'd moved into my own flat and didn't see as much of Noel and, I suppose, I figured I'd missed the boat."

Jess couldn't believe her ears and was touched by the anxious way he was watching her. A warm glow spread through her and she smiled at him. "The boat's back in port now."

★ ★ ★

A couple of drinks later, they were sitting a lot closer and talking about everything and anything, as if they hadn't seen each other in years. Which in a way was true. They may have been in the same city and met occasionally but they'd never really *talked*.

"You're kidding me." Jess burst out laughing when he admitted a love of country-and-western music. "You kept that quiet. Just as well: Noel would never let you live it down."

"He knows, and he doesn't," Cal confirmed, with a dramatic eye roll.

"I'm sure there must be a support group where you could get help," she teased.

He put a hand to his heart. "Wow, a double whammy! A pot shot at my profession *and* my musical taste."

"I think you'll survive." Jess beamed at him, wondering when was the last time that she'd laughed so much with a guy. Never?

"Come on, then, tell me, what sort of music are you into?"

"I like songs from all genres and all eras: blues, jazz, rock, pop and some heavy metal."

"No country-and-western?" he asked, looking crestfallen.

She shook her head, laughing. "Sorry, no country-and-western."

"Then it will be my mission in life to convert you and you'll be perfect — except for your lousy taste in men."

302

She started at his reference to Louis and was about to correct him, but she didn't want to go down that road and spoil this lovely evening. Besides, she was distracted by the way he was looking at her and the warmth of his arm against hers. "Lousy taste? I'm here with you, aren't I?"

"That's only because you wanted to show your gratitude and I'm your brother's mate," he said with a melodramatic sigh.

Jess sobered and put a hand out to touch his face. "That's not true."

His eyes locked on hers. "I'm glad to hear it." He turned his head and pressed a warm kiss into the palm of her hand. "You're beautiful." She shook her head, dumbfounded. "What?" he asked, catching her hand and holding it to his cheek when she tried to move away.

"I don't know how you can be interested in me after everything I've told you."

"Nothing you've told me has stopped me thinking that you're perfect."

She stared at him, searching his eyes and was overwhelmed by what she saw there. "Perfect?"

"Except for your lousy taste in men, but a slight imperfection makes you human."

"Hmm. So what's *your* slight imperfection?" she asked.

He grinned. "I like country music?"

"Ah, yes, good point," she smiled.

His eyes held hers. "Which, when you think about it, makes up a perfect match."

Jess agreed immediately when Cal later suggested they go home. Outside the pub, he hailed a cab and directed the driver to her flat. In the intimacy of the cab, they sat in silence, holding hands.

"Coffee?" she offered, hoping she didn't have to make any. She wanted a kiss from that mouth that had distracted her all evening. To her astonishment, Cal shook his head.

"No, thanks, but I'll see you to your door, just to make sure the coast is clear."

Jess was brought down to earth with a bump and glanced around nervously, checking for Louis's car.

Cal took her keys from her and, looking around him, went ahead to open the flat door and made her stand on the landing while he checked the flat. He smiled when he came out, holding out his arms to her. "All clear."

"Thanks," she said, cuddling into him and trying to recover the warmth and safety she'd felt in the cab.

"Hey, it's okay," he said, sensing her tension. He leaned his forehead against hers and massaged her shoulders. "I'm sorry, Jess. I didn't mean to frighten you."

"I'm fine."

Cal pulled back to look into her face. "No. You're not. I know writing for the *Gazette* is important to you, but is it worth all this stress and anxiety?"

"Probably not," she admitted.

304

"I like you, Jess Connors." He kissed her just beneath her ear lobe. It was a light but incredibly sexy thing to do and she shivered and gave him a shy smile.

"I like you too."

He sighed and looked at her with such desire. Jess was tempted to beg him to stay — and not for coffee. But, looking slightly tormented, Cal stepped back and smiled. "Jess?"

"Yes?" she said, sensing he was weakening.

"Humour me, lock up now so that I won't spend my night worrying about you."

"Will do." Disappointed, she followed him downstairs.

"Goodnight, Jess." He gave her a soft kiss and pulled the door closed.

"Goodnight, Cal." Jess locked it and, touching her lips, went back upstairs, smiling.

She made tea and took her mug into the bedroom, her mind moving between the wonder of Cal's declaration and horror of Louis's assault. Her hand went unconsciously to her throat. Had she fooled herself that his sexual attraction was something more because then she didn't feel so dirty? Had she let Louis grope her just to get the work she craved so much? Did she deserve the cool hostility of the other women in the office? Yes, yes to it all. Cal was right: she should walk away. Why was she hesitating?

As if sensing that he was in her thoughts, a text came through from Louis. She shrank from her phone and crept to the window, peering out through the curtains. Had he been waiting for her to come home or, worse, followed her? The road was quiet and there was no sign of his car. I'm getting paranoid, she thought, picking up the phone. She opened the message and read.

Drinks on Friday in local, lots of contacts. You should be there.

She'd heard that there had been a promotion in the *Gazette* and there was a reception to celebrate it but Jess hadn't intended to put in an appearance. She couldn't bear the thought of being in the same room as the man, never mind talk to him. And he wouldn't be content with her simply showing up: he'd waylay her at some stage, she was sure of it. The thought terrified her. She needed to talk to Katie. She hadn't said a word about what was going on as Katie had enough on her plate with her exams. But now Jess couldn't wait to unburden herself. Katie was smart. She'd figure out a way to put an end to this stalking and, well, everything. She had to, or Jess thought that she'd have to abandon her flat as well as her job.

CHAPTER
THIRTY

Mandy tucked the receiver between her chin and shoulder and poured herself another mug of coffee. She needed it. Suzie was in full flow and there was only so much family shite Mandy could handle. Her sister was sounding just like her old self, and that wasn't a good thing.

"How are things going with Douglas?" she broke in when Suzie stopped to draw breath.

Her sister hesitated before answering, a sure sign that she was practising her new control technique: don't open your mouth until you know what's going to come out. Another practice that pissed Mandy off. How long would it be before her sister was back to her old self and remembered everything?

"We've only been out twice," Suzie said.

Mandy's ears pricked up. That was it? That was all that she had to say? And how come Douglas had asked her out again after he'd agreed to give Suzie more time? She didn't like this, didn't like it at all. There was some rustling at the end of the phone, followed by a muttered curse.

"What's up?"

"I got a letter from Maurice. He wants to come visit."

"John's brother?"

"How many Maurices do you know?" Suzie asked, her voice loaded with sarcasm. "I need this like I need a hole in the head."

"He's a widower now, too, right? I always thought he fancied you."

Suzie snorted. "All Maurice ever fancied was free board and lodgings. There must be something on in Dublin or he wouldn't be coming."

"Tell him you won't be there," Amanda said.

"Then he'd expect me to leave him the keys. Anyway, he knows I never go anywhere."

Mandy frowned. "What about our trip to New York?"

Suzie's sigh was heavy. "How can I go away now that I'm looking after Bobby?"

"Aw, for feck's sake, Suzie. I was looking forward to a holiday," Mandy complained, although she brightened, realising that Suzie would have less time and energy to socialise and that Douglas wouldn't be able to whisk her sister off to Croatia. He hadn't mentioned doing so but, given his obvious infatuation, Mandy expected him to invite Suzie to accompany him.

Mandy heard the front door close and had an idea. "Well, Suzie, nice chatting but I'd better get some work done. You have a great time with Maurice."

"Huh, you're very funny. I don't suppose that you'd like to take him off my hands. He's loaded and childless, a very attractive prospect, I'd have thought."

"No, I wouldn't dream of playing gooseberry, Suzie," Mandy said loudly, "but tell him I said hi."

"What are you on about, Mandy? You're not making sense."

"Ha, do I ever? Listen, you two have fun. Must run. Bye, Suzie." She hung up, aware that Douglas was standing behind her and had heard every word. Good.

"I got more milk if you fancy a coffee."

Mandy gave a yelp and spun round. "Douglas! I wish you wouldn't creep around the place like that. You frightened the life out of me."

"I don't creep," he said. "You were just so engrossed in your *personal* phone call that you didn't hear the door."

"That personal call was during my break and made on my own phone." She smiled sweetly. "A coffee would be nice, if you're making one."

He raised an eyebrow. "Who exactly works for who round here?" he grumbled but took another mug down from the shelf above his head. "How's Suzie?" he asked.

Amanda suppressed a grin. Bingo! "All flustered getting ready for a visitor."

"Oh? Anyone important?"

"Maurice, her widowed brother-in-law. He's a nice man. It will be good for Suzie to have some company and it will take her mind off her grandson. I hope she doesn't overdo it. She spoils Maurice rotten, cooking all his favourite dishes, although I expect he'll take her out every night. It's good they're still so close. Suzie dropped a lot of friends after her accident because she couldn't really remember them, but not Maurice."

Amanda studied him from under her lashes, trying to gauge his reaction. He was playing it cool but she wasn't fooled. Douglas wouldn't be at all happy that Suzie was having a man to stay.

"She takes too much on herself."

"You're not wrong," she agreed, "but only for people she cares about. The rest of the world can go to hell, as she has no problem telling them."

"That's good," he said and went back into his office.

Mandy grinned. Mission accomplished.

Douglas closed the door on her, shaking his head. She really was a piece of work. Not for the first time he wondered how two such different people could spring from the same gene pool. He was thrilled now that Suzie had agreed to come to Zagreb. It would put Amanda in her place, once and for all. For the first time since Pam died, he found himself looking forward to a trip. Suzie deserved a break and he was looking forward to pampering her and showing her the city.

He'd been thrilled to discover that her interest in art and architecture was genuine. She really wanted to learn more about both, and he was happy to be the one to teach her. It reminded him of how eager she'd been to learn all about their systems in CML, staying late to bring herself up to speed, determined to prove herself.

Suzie hadn't changed quite as much as they all thought. He remembered the feisty girl in bargain-basement clothes and luminous nail varnish he'd interviewed all those years ago. She'd had a sharp tongue then, too, but behind those flashing eyes was a defensive, fragile young girl who didn't give her trust easily. Motherhood had mellowed her, though, and perhaps her experiences had taught her to hold her tongue.

There was a knock on the open door and he turned round to see Amanda standing there. He smiled at her. "Heading home?"

"Yeah. See you tomorrow."

"No." Suddenly, Doug couldn't bear the thought of having her around. He was finding it harder to hide what he truly thought of her. He forced himself to smile. "Take the day off, Amanda. In fact, take two. You've been putting in a lot of hours lately, and I have some business to take care of."

"What sort of business?" she asked, a suspicious frown marring her beautiful face. "There's nothing in the diary."

"That's because it's personal," he said, and took a cruel pleasure at her disappointment at being shut out.

"But you don't have a private life," she shot back, a malicious gleam in her eyes.

It was an effort, but he wouldn't give her the satisfaction of showing his annoyance at the remark. "That was the case," he agreed, "but it seems that there's hope even for losers like me." Her eyes widened and he hurried on as she opened her mouth to respond. "I must grab a shower. Enjoy your break, Amanda."

She stood, speechless, as he walked past her and went upstairs. He stood on the landing and listened as she gathered up her belongings and then let out a sigh of relief when the door finally closed behind her.

He decided to go ahead and have the shower and then take a wander down to the village and have a bite to eat. On a whim, Doug dressed in a pair of his new jeans and a blue cotton shirt that Amanda had chosen for him. He slipped on his new deck shoes, put his keys, phone and reading glasses into the pocket of his jacket and walked out into the summer evening, his heart light. The wine bar he liked wasn't open for another hour, so, stopping to pick up a newspaper, he went into the nearby pub, ordered a pint and settled down on a bar stool to do the crossword. He glanced up a couple of times at the group at the other end of the bar who looked and sounded as if they'd been here a few hours. He was pondering whether to have another pint or go and eat when a hand clapped him on the back and he looked up into the bloodshot and slightly unfocused eyes of Nigel Brennan, a prick of the highest order.

"Doug? Doug Hamilton? It is, isn't it?" The man gave a loud bark of a laugh.

Doug drew back from the fumes emanating from the other man and took his outstretched hand more to steady the other man than anything. "Hello, Nigel."

He winced as he suffered yet another thump.

"My God, I thought you were dead," the man bellowed. "The life you've led, you should be!"

I'm in better shape than you, Doug thought, looking at the man's broken veins and red nose. And Nigel must be fifteen or twenty years younger. Doug gave a brief smile and looked back at his newspaper, hoping the man would move on.

"You've been off the radar for some time, Doug. I haven't seen you since . . ." The man faltered.

"Pamela's funeral," Doug said. This was what he had been running from for years.

"Of course. Terrible. We lost her far too young."

Doug got up to leave. He couldn't listen to this bullshit. "Good to see you again, Nigel."

"Don't go. Come and join us."

"Another time, I'm meeting someone for dinner."

Nigel gave a knowing grin. "A lovely lady, I don't doubt. Still lead in the pencil, eh? If you don't get lucky, come back later." He winked and nodded towards his friends. "That redhead is gagging for a ride."

Doug looked at him in disgust and glanced at the redhead in question, who looked young and fresh and innocent. He wanted to tell her to get the hell out of here and go home, but why would she listen to an old man? "Have a good evening, Nigel," he said and left the pub.

He felt tainted for ever having associated with the likes of Nigel and countless other feckless bastards. He'd found out who his true friends were when his life fell apart, and they'd been his long-term employees, Malcolm and Jack. They'd sat with him as he'd spent his nights in the pub, drowning his sorrows. They'd cleaned up after him and put him to bed and, God help him, even held his hand as he cried himself to sleep. And, along with Gina, they'd kept his business afloat when he couldn't go on. Suzie was right: it was time to meet up with them again.

Douglas went into the restaurant and, after making sure that he didn't know any of the other customers, took a seat at a table at the back of the room. A smiling waitress handed him a menu and he quickly made his choices. Embarrassed by the number of expensive vintages on the wine list that had once lined his own cellar, Doug ordered a bottle of the house red. He pondered how Nigel had recognised him, despite his wrinkled face and greying hair. He grudgingly acknowledged that Amanda was right. He had let himself go and all it took was a haircut and nice clothes for him to be recognised again. It was the first time that had happened since he'd returned to Ireland three years ago. Pamela had been unimpressed when he'd hired Suzie, describing her as plain, plump, coarse and "common". His wife had been such a terrible snob but she'd also been loyal. After his heart attack and bypass, she'd taken over the running of CML and kept everything running smoothly until he'd fully recovered, tolerating his interventions and, acknowledging — grudgingly — he was right, Suzie was good.

Doug's thoughts were interrupted by his phone ringing, and he smiled when he saw who was calling. "Hi, Suzie. How are you?"

"I was lying on the bed, dozing and I started thinking about Jess and how frightened she is of dogs. Do you remember her being attacked, Doug?"

"Yes, now that you come to mention it, although I'm surprised that *she* does. She was so little."

"Can you tell me about it?"

"You don't remember?"

"No."

"It was the dog from next door. I can't recall what breed he was but he was big. He'd never given any trouble before but he got sick, a tumour, I think. Jess was in the garden playing and you had gone inside to get sunscreen. Pam was watching from the window and saw the dog appear. He'd burrowed a hole under the fence. It must have been the sound of Jess laughing that attracted him. Pam wasn't really concerned but she went outside in case Jess was frightened. But, before she reached Jess, the dog had pounced."

"Oh, God."

Doug heard the anguish in her voice. "Forget about it, sweetheart."

"No, Doug, tell me. Please? I want to know."

Doug sighed. "Pam whacked him with a chair and he ran away, but he'd already bitten Jess. The wound wasn't that bad but there was a lot of blood and, when you saw her, you were hysterical; Pam wasn't much better. Jess only needed a few stitches in the end but you were upset because it was on her face." Doug gave a sad smile. "Pam kept telling you that Jess would look even prettier with a fringe and eventually you calmed down. The neighbours were very upset. The dog was put down the same day and they bought Jess a big cuddly toy."

"Like that made up for what their bloody dog did to my daughter," Suzie said, sniffling.

"It wasn't their fault or the dog's, Suzie. No one could have foreseen how the tumour would affect him. They'd had him since he was a puppy and he had never given them any trouble before."

Suzie was silent for a moment. "I told Jess that Percy was trained to be gentle, that he was different and would never hurt anyone, but that's not true, is it? He could get some virus or disease and go mad and kill and —"

"No, Suzie, stop this. The chances of Percy ever doing anything remotely violent must be a million to one. Besides, if you knew that he was sick, given what happened to Jess, you'd be a lot more careful."

"If I remembered to be," Suzie retorted. "My mind isn't what it was. Who knows what I'll remember and what I'll forget?"

Doug could hear the hysteria in her voice. "I'm coming over."

Suzie was pale and still seemed upset when she opened the door to him. "Sorry for dragging you over here."

"You didn't. I invited myself." He presented her with wine and chocolates and held up a ball. "So, where's the mutt?"

She cracked a smile. "He's no mutt. I'll have you know Percy's a thoroughbred."

She led him into the kitchen, where Percy sat by the sofa. He wagged his tail when he saw Suzie and then turned his head and looked up at Doug from enormous, sad eyes. "Come and sit down and let him get to know you."

Doug sat down, held out his hand to the dog, talking to him in a low voice, and scratched his ear. The dog had a good sniff, licked his hand and then settled at his feet. "He's a lovely dog."

"I hope he goes to a good home."

Doug looked at her. "You're not getting rid of him."

"I have to."

"Did Jess ask you to?" he asked, knowing the answer.

"No, but —"

"Then stop being so dramatic. He's a good dog and he's found a new home and owner. Don't take that away from him on a whim."

Her face fell and she reached down to stroke the dog. "Stop trying to make me feel guilty."

"Why not? You should feel guilty. Percy lives here, Jess doesn't. She hasn't asked you to get rid of him, so, until she says otherwise, keep him locked up when she visits, yes?"

She looked from the dog to him and then back at Percy again and nodded.

"Good. Now that Percy's sorted, let's watch a horror movie and drink some wine."

She smiled. "It might scare the dog."

"Don't worry, I'll cover his eyes."

CHAPTER
THIRTY-ONE

As soon as Jess woke, she reached for her phone and sent Katie a text. It was after nine but Katie was probably still out cold, so Jess decided to go back to sleep for a couple of hours. After the last couple of weeks, she'd earned a duvet day. Her phone rang and she grabbed it, surprised and relieved that it was Katie. "Hey."

"Hi, Jess. I take it you're home alone in your own bed."

"Of course I am," Jess retorted, grinning. "How's your head?"

"Fine. The gang were going on a pub crawl and I was too tired for that malarkey, so I had a nice, quiet dinner with Mum and Dad."

"And I was home in bed with a mug of tea by ten. We are such hellraisers!"

"So, tell me, how did it go with the hunk?"

"It was nice."

"Nice?" Katie snorted. "That's it?"

"It was *very* nice," Jess amended.

"There was no chemistry?" Katie asked, sounding disappointed.

"Oh, trust me, there was plenty of chemistry." Jess smiled and closed her eyes, thinking of Cal's mesmerising eyes and the thrill that ran through her when he'd kissed the palm of her hand.

"Then, I don't understand. What's up?"

Jess hesitated. She wanted to tell Katie everything but, not on the phone. "Can we meet for a coffee?"

When Jess arrived at their favourite café, Katie was on the far side of the room, taking off her jacket. Jess waved and went to the counter.

"You look great," she said, joining her friend and dropping her bag on the floor. Katie was a beautiful girl, but today she was positively blooming.

"It's relief." Katie smiled. "I can't believe that the exams are finally over and I'm finished with classes and studying. I thought I'd sleep for a week but I actually feel energised."

"I'm glad for you. You've worked so hard."

"Speaking of working hard, you look tired. Are you overdoing it? Working for four publications can't be easy."

"I love it but I do have a problem."

Katie reached for her hand. "What is it? What's wrong, Jess?"

And, caving in the face of her friend's concerned expression, Jess told her all about her relationship with Louis.

"Why am I only hearing about this now?" Katie looked almost shell-shocked.

"I didn't want to distract you from your exams."

"You knew he was married?"

"I didn't at first but I figured it out."

"No wonder the women in the *Gazette* aren't your greatest fans."

Jess groaned. "Don't remind me. I'm not sure how much they know and how much is guesswork."

"Well, now that you've split up, you can mend some fences."

"It's not that simple." Jess gave her a lame smile.

Katie's eyes widened. "You *have* dumped him, Jess?"

"I've tried but he won't be dumped."

"Just tell him to feck off or get Noel and Cal to pay him a visit."

"That's not the answer."

Katie rolled her eyes and gave an exasperated sigh. "It's quite simple, Jess. There's no need to turn it into a major production."

"I'm not, honestly," Jess said and, haltingly, told Katie everything that had happened since she finished with Louis, including the details of "that night".

Katie had paled as she talked and, when there was silence after she'd finished, Jess sneaked a look at her friend. She was shocked to see tears in Katie's eyes.

"He raped you," Katie whispered.

Jess flinched. There it was again, the word that she tried so hard not to think about, never mind say.

"No."

"Yes."

Jess shook her head. "It got out of hand, he was excited and turned on by me fighting him off."

Katie stared at her in disbelief. "Were you excited?"

"No!" Jess suppressed a shudder. "I felt cheap and dirty and . . . used."

"He raped you," Katie repeated, her voice soft.

Jess didn't bother denying it again. "I'm going to deal with it. I'm going to talk to him."

"When?"

"There's a work thing on, Friday night. I'll tell him then."

"What makes you think that he'll listen to you? He obviously hasn't up to now."

"Because I feel stronger now that I've told you and Cal."

Katie still looked dubious. "I'm coming with you."

"On Friday?" Jess asked, and her friend nodded. She smiled, relieved. "Thank you. I was hoping you would. You're going to have to hide your feelings, though. All of the staff will be there. If you're rude to him everyone will know that something's been going on and that would be the final humiliation."

Katie stared at her, looking grim and gave a brief nod. "Fine. I'll behave. What does Cal have to say about all of this?"

Jess smiled. "Mostly he listens, but he thinks I should stop writing for the *Gazette*."

"I don't care how much you like the work, it's not worth it. Anyway, the readership must be quite small in comparison to the others."

Jess nodded. "I've decided to hand in my notice next week."

"Why not today?" Katie pressed, obviously thinking Jess would lose her nerve.

"I don't want him to be angry on Friday." She met Katie's eyes. "I'm afraid of him."

"Okay, that's it. You're staying with me until we know that you're safe."

"Are you sure?" Jess said, overcome with relief. She'd thought about moving home but was afraid that her mother would be suspicious.

"I'm not inviting you, Jess. I'm telling you. We need to sort this out — and soon." Katie shot her a guilty look. "I'm going away."

Jess raised her eyebrows. "On holiday? Cool. Where?"

"It's not a holiday, Jess. My uncle has offered me a position in his transport business. The pay will be pittance but it will be great work experience."

"Absolutely. That's fantastic, Katie. So where is this company?"

Katie met her eyes. "Jersey."

Jess stared at her in shock. "Jersey?"

Katie nodded. "I'm sure it won't be for long, and I'll still be applying for positions in Dublin."

"It's great, really. I'm happy for you. When you're not working you'll be able to soak up the sun and play the tourist." Jess tried to hide her disappointment. She really was happy for Katie but dreaded the thought of losing her friend, even if it was only for a couple of months.

"I am excited," Katie admitted, "but I hate leaving you with all this Louis business going on."

Jess forced a smile "Like you said, I'll have to sort it out quickly, won't I? When do you leave?"

"The end of next week," Katie murmured.

"Wow, that soon." Jess could hear the panic in her voice.

"Yeah, sorry."

"Don't be silly. Now we've even more reason to go out tonight and celebrate."

Katie looked relieved. "We do. Where shall we go?"

Jess enjoyed a few girly days with Katie and was reminded what it was like to be carefree. The long chats in the garden or over a glass of wine were great therapy and she realised how much she would miss her friend. But this would be great work experience for Katie and it would look good on her CV so she was determined to send her off, smiling.

They went shopping together and bought Katie a lovely suit, perfect for interviews. Katie was on a high, thinking of all of the opportunities ahead. Her excitement was contagious and Jess felt stronger about the prospect of meeting Louis on Friday. Well, perhaps not stronger exactly, but more confident. At least Katie would be there to support her.

Jess had switched off her phone, telling her family that it was in for repair and giving them Katie's number if they needed to contact her; and the relief she felt from not jumping every time a text came through was immense. She also, after a moment's hesitation, sent Cal Katie's number too. Just in case.

When Friday evening arrived, Jess dressed down in jeans, a faded blue shirt and flat boots. She examined her reflection in the mirror and was confident that she didn't look remotely sexy. Tying her hair back in a high ponytail, she went in search of Katie.

She found her friend in the bathroom, putting on her makeup. Katie eyed her. "You look as if you're going to the supermarket instead of a party."

"Good. That's the look I was going for."

"Are you nervous?" Katie asked, her eyes full of sympathy.

"Terrified," Jess admitted.

"I won't leave your side, I promise."

When they arrived at the pub, the party was in full swing. Jess immediately spotted Louis, holding court. He was too engrossed to have spotted her yet and she had time to check out the room. She looked around for a familiar face and spotted Eve and Maria, a couple of journalists she'd met a few times. They were on the far side of the room to Louis and Jess decided that would be a safe place to hide out.

"This way." She tugged Katie towards them and, after making the introductions, went to the bar to buy a round of drinks. Surreptitiously, she looked around. There weren't many people she knew and she felt out of her comfort zone. Jess had never had problems mixing before but Louis's presence in the room after all that had transpired between them had turned her into a nervous wallflower. But she had to look confident and above it all so, pasting on a wide smile, she carried the drinks back to the three women, nodding and saying hello as she went.

324

"Where is he?" Katie murmured, when the other two women were chatting.

"Over there, by the pillar, dark suit, red tie," Jess said, nodding in Louis's direction.

Katie looked over Jess's shoulder, wrinkling up her nose in disgust. "What did you see in *him*?"

"Does it matter?" Jess said, irritated and turned to compliment Eve on a piece she'd written during the week. It was about the current homeless crisis, something they all had an opinion on, and they were soon engaged in a lively debate. Jess watched Katie argue a point with Maria and marvelled, as always, at how comfortable her friend was in any situation. Enjoying the chat, Jess began to relax. Soon she would circulate and to hell with Louis. It was important to keep in touch with colleagues and make new contacts in the industry.

"Ladies, why are you depriving us of your lovely company?"

Jess froze at the voice next to her ear. Louis slipped one arm around her and the other around Eve. Her colleague immediately stepped out of his embrace with a roll of her eyes and Jess turned away to pick up her drink, moving out of his reach.

Maria eyeballed him. "Hi, Louis. We were just talking about the increasing prevalence of harassment in the workplace. I was saying to Jess that she should write a piece on it."

Looking slightly uneasy, Louis shoved his hands in his pockets. "Sounds like a plan. Know anyone that you could interview?" He looked straight at Jess.

325

Completely thrown by the question, she was at a loss for words.

"I know someone," Katie said, moving closer. In her heels, she towered over Louis and he looked up at her with narrowed eyes.

"And you are?" he asked, with a cool smile.

"Katie Coburn. I'm a friend of Jess's." She didn't offer her hand.

"Nice to meet you." His eyes went from her to Jess. "I'll look forward to reading the article. Paul!" Louis waved to a man across the room. "Excuse me."

"What an asshole," Katie murmured.

"A total scumbag," Maria assured her. "Don't look so worried, Jess. You don't have to write anything. I just thought that he could do with a shot across the bow. The man's been mauling you since you started writing for the *Gazette* and you're not the first."

Jess stared at her. Had everyone noticed? Her cheeks flushed with humiliation.

"Why doesn't anyone report him?" Katie asked as Jess stood, speechless.

"He's harmless, really. Once you make it quite clear that you're not willing to play along, he backs off." Maria looked Jess straight in the eye. "It's his wife I feel sorry for."

Mortified, Jess excused herself and pushed her way through the throng to the loos. Shaking, she locked herself into a cubicle, flipped down the seat and sat down. It was clear that not only did Maria and Eve know what Louis was up to, they knew that she hadn't

326

resisted. She stifled tears of shame as she heard someone come into the room.

"Jess?"

She sighed in relief at Katie's voice. "In here."

"Open up."

She reached up and lifted the latch and her friend came in, locking the door behind her.

"You okay?" Katie leaned against the door and looked down at Jess.

"No."

"Cheer up, this is good news."

Jess looked up at her. "Didn't you hear them?"

"Didn't you?" Katie retorted. "He's pathetic and, as soon as you show some balls, he'll back off. It's obvious from talking to Eve and Maria that he's just a perverted bully."

"But what about what he did to me?" Jess protested.

Katie sighed. "Sorry, Jess, but you let him into your life. You let him use you and, because you were so eager to please, he obviously thought he could get away with anything. Now you need to tell him that he can't."

"I've been such a fool, Katie."

"No." Katie sighed. "He took advantage of you after your mum's accident when you were vulnerable."

"You're right. I was so upset about Mum and he was kind and really seemed to care. When I wasn't at the hospital, I ran to Louis and took the comfort he gave me."

"You had me to run to." Katie looked hurt.

"I did, and you were great." Jess stood up. "But sometimes there's nothing quite like having a man's arms around you."

"I know. So, what now?"

What now? The time for dithering was over. She'd seen the challenge in Maria's eyes and knew what she had to do. "If I can get through the rest of this evening without dying of embarrassment and shame, I will try and find a moment to talk to Louis."

"Not somewhere isolated," her friend warned.

"No." Jess had no intention of going anywhere alone with Louis.

"And you need to be tough," Katie pressed.

Jess gave a grim laugh. "Don't worry. This time I won't leave him in any doubt that I'm serious. And, if he still won't listen, I'll report him to the *Gazette*'s board."

Katie grinned. "Good girl. Come on, let's get back out there. Hold your head up high, have a stiff drink."

"Lead the way," Jess said and, taking a deep breath, went out to rejoin the party.

The rest of the evening wasn't as bad as she'd expected. Louis kept his distance, probably because Katie never left her side, and there were no further incidents. Jess had had a little too much to drink but that was down to nerves. She was about to suggest to Katie that they head home when she heard a familiar voice behind her.

"Do you come here often?"

Jess swung round and laughed as Cal grinned down at her, hazel eyes twinkling. "Cal!" Thanks to the wine and a couple of shots of tequila, she threw her arms around him. "How great to see you."

He looked slightly startled but linked his hands loosely around her waist. "And you."

"Aren't you going to introduce me?" Katie asked, looking on, amused.

"This is my best friend, Katie Coburn. Katie, this is Cal McLoughlin."

She shook his hand, smiling. "Great to finally meet you, Cal."

"Likewise." Cal grinned and glanced back at Jess. "Can I get you two a drink, or am I interrupting something?"

"Just a boring work do that Jess dragged me along to for protection," Katie assured him. "A glass of wine would be lovely."

"It hasn't been boring," Jess protested.

"Not once you stay on the right side of the room," Katie agreed, her eyes going to where Louis was standing.

Jess looked at Cal and saw his eyes narrow as he followed Katie's gaze. His eyes came back to search hers.

"Is everything okay?"

She smiled and nodded. "All under control."

"Good. I'll get the drinks."

"He is seriously hot," Katie said, watching him walk away. "Want me to leave you two alone?"

Jess was sorely tempted but decided against it. "No, I've had far too much to drink to be trusted and so have you. I think we should stick together."

Katie put an arm round her shoulders. "You're right, hon. We don't need men to have fun, do we? Still" — her eyes glimmered mischievously as she watched Cal coming towards them — "I imagine you could have lots of fun with this guy."

"Hands off," Jess warned, giggling. "You can have Louis."

"I'd rather chew my own leg off," Katie assured her. "Must use the loo, 'scuse me!"

Cal handed Jess her wine and set Katie's on the ledge beside them. "Your friend seems like fun."

"She is. So, what brings you here? Are you with a group?"

"I was with a couple of mates. We were just leaving when I spotted you, so I came over to say hello."

Jess beamed at him, happily. "I'm glad you did."

CHAPTER
THIRTY-TWO

An hour later, Cal put the two of them into a taxi.

"He's lovely," Katie sighed, waving to him before leaning her head on Jess's shoulder.

"He is," Jess agreed, aware of her silly, dreamy, drunken smile. Next thing she knew, the driver was asking for directions. They arrived at Katie's little flat in Milltown and Jess nudged her. "Come on, sleepy head, we're home."

Jess helped Katie to bed and then walked unsteadily into the kitchen and drank a large glass of tap water before carrying another into the sitting room. She flopped on to the sofa-bed, smiling. It had turned out to be a much nicer evening than she'd expected. There hadn't been an opportunity to speak to Louis, which was a pity, given how fired up she'd been, but bumping into Cal had been a bonus. He'd obviously been happy to see her tonight and, when he'd kissed her goodnight, he'd held her close, his lips lingering on hers. Suddenly she had a yearning to hear his voice. Grinning, she pulled her overnight bag out from under the sofa-bed, took out her phone and switched it on. There were a number of texts, which she decided to ignore for now, but, when she was looking for Cal's number, another text came through. Smiling, she figured it had to be him, forgetting she'd told him that she was leaving her phone off. Her smile faded when she saw it was from Louis. Mindful of her wish to talk to him, she read the text.

I was going to drop in but it seems you went home with lover-boy. See you tomorrow.

Saturday? What did that mean? Still, it didn't seem angry or threatening but why did he want to see her? Despite her earlier bravado, Jess didn't relish the idea of taking Louis on, but, after the conversation with Maria and Eve, she knew she had to. It had dawned on Jess that Cal was keeping his distance until Louis was out of the picture. So, if she wanted to date him, she needed to bite the bullet. And there was one thing Jess was sure of: she definitely wanted to see Cal again. She didn't bother responding to Louis's text and decided against calling Cal. Once ready for bed, she drank all her water. Tomorrow was a big day and she needed a clear head. Turning off the light, Jess settled down on the lumpy bed, determined that tomorrow night she would be back in her own bed, safe and sound.

The next morning, Jess wrote a note to Katie and set it on the bedside locker along with a glass of water and two painkillers. Then, taking her carryall, she crept out of the flat.

On the bus she read Louis's messages. They started out mild and got progressively more menacing. She decided to forward copies of them to Katie's phone, just in case she needed proof at a future date. Gazing out of the window, she hoped that Louis would be reasonable and not force her hand. She'd decided to meet him at her local coffee shop. It was quiet but small, and she'd feel safe there.

Jess waited until she got to her flat to send him a text. After a moment's hesitation, she was about to send Cal a text, too, to let him know her plan and then remembered him saying he was working this morning. She decided to leave it and call him later to fill him in.

Seconds later, Louis replied, saying that he'd see her there in an hour. She stared at the text, suddenly nervous, and took a few deep, settling breaths. She paced the flat and left fifteen minutes early but, as she went to leave the house, Jess gasped to find Louis on the doorstep.

"What the hell are you doing here?" Jess said, hearing the tremor in her voice and hoping he didn't. Louis was looking smug, almost triumphant. She wondered whether she should scream or shout, but Louis was already gripping her arm and marching her towards the stairs. She thought about the last time this had happened and felt sick and helpless. "Stop it, you're hurting me," she said, but it came out as a whisper. Where was the strong woman who was going to stand up to him?

Louis took her keys and opened the door to the flat, pushing her inside. Jess felt herself falling and put her hands out to save herself, but her elbow collided painfully with the wall. She lay on the floor, winded, staring up at him, and suddenly her fear turned to anger. Fine, she might end up raped, dead or both, but she'd had enough. "What the fuck do you think you're doing?"

"I saw you with your boyfriend and I thought you needed reminding of what it's like to be with a real man," he said, his hands fumbling with his belt.

All her fears disappeared at that. Cal was ten times the man Louis was. She scrambled to her feet. "Real man?" She laughed in his face. "Real men don't need to screw around to prove themselves. Real men don't need to force themselves on women."

Louis raised his eyebrows, a sly grin on his face. "Oh, please, you love it rough, you love it all. You're a randy little slut, Jess, and don't pretend otherwise."

Jess raised her hand to slap him and then let it drop to her side. He'd probably enjoy it. She pulled herself up to her full height, came to stand in front of him and looked him in the eye. "Get out, Louis, and don't come back."

He folded his arms. "Or what?"

Despite everything, she could see this was exciting him, and she decided it was time to douse that flame, once and for all. "If you don't go now, I'll make a complaint to the board."

He laughed. "Saying what? This has nothing to do with the office, although I have dreamed of bending you over my desk."

334

"You're right," she conceded. "The affair has nothing to do with work. But intimidation, harassment and violence afterwards, that's a different thing."

"You exaggerate your own importance," he sneered. "You're a freelancer. They don't care about you."

"If I was the only one I'd probably agree," she said, her confidence growing, "but I'm not, Louis, am I? You've put yourself out there quite a bit." She shook her head and assumed a disappointed expression. "Silly. Careless. Haven't you heard that you should never shit on your own doorstep? I wouldn't be the only one complaining, and you know what? From what I heard last night, I'm the least of your worries." She saw a flicker of fear in his eyes. Maria and Eve were right. Louis was, like all bullies, weak and spineless behind all the bluster. Jess went to the door and opened it. "Now get out and don't bother me again or I promise your days at the *Gazette* are numbered."

"Bitch," he spat, and strode out of the flat and down the stairs, banging the front door behind him. Jess sank into the nearest chair, trembling, all her bravado gone.

But she'd done it. She'd confronted him. It was over. On Monday, Jess would send Louis a formal email, copying it to Personnel, saying that, due to her growing workload she would no longer be able to write for the *Gazette*. No doubt there would be a lot of speculation as to the real reason she'd left but, while that was humiliating, she hoped it would save another girl from the same fate.

The doorbell rang, echoing through the hall and making her jerk up in the chair. He wouldn't have come back, would he? She went to the window and peeked out, sighing in relief when she saw Cal's car. She hurried down to let him in. He stood, unsmiling, on the doorstep, her jacket in his hand.

"You left this behind last night." He shoved it at her and turned to leave.

"Hey, stay for a coffee," she said, alarmed at his abruptness.

"I think it's best if I go."

And then she realised that he'd obviously seen Louis leave. She shook her head. "Cal, I want to talk to you."

"Sorry. I have to be somewhere. Bye, Jess." He turned away and walked down the path without a backward glance.

"Cal!" she called but he didn't even turn around. She stared after him in disbelief. That was it? How could he possibly misinterpret the situation, knowing how afraid she was of Louis?

"He must have seen something," Katie insisted, swallowing a couple of painkillers with a mouthful of coffee and putting on her sunglasses.

"We're inside and it's not even sunny outside," Jess pointed out of the café window at the grey sky. Despite her misery she couldn't help smirking at her friend's sorry state. She was glad she'd had the foresight to drink so much water last night.

"It's bright," Katie complained, "and my head hurts. Did Louis kiss you in the doorway? Cal must have seen you together."

336

"All Cal could have seen was Louis leaving after I threw him out."

"Oh, well done you! I was going to give out to you for seeing him alone."

"Believe me, that wasn't the plan. I told him to meet me here but he came to the flat instead and attacked me."

"Again?" Katie paused, her mug halfway to her mouth.

Jess shook her head. "He dragged me upstairs and pushed me into the flat and I fell. I was sure that he was going to rape me."

"Fuck's sake! How has he been getting away with this? What did you do?"

"I stood up to him, Katie, just like Maria said," Jess told her, feeling really proud of herself. "I told him if he came near me again, I'd report him and I'd be the first in a long line of women doing the same."

Katie pushed her glasses up onto her forehead and looked at her in surprised admiration. "Good for you. What did he say?"

Jess shrugged. "What I expected. No one would heed me, blah, blah, blah. But, I scared him, Katie. It was obvious. He won't be bothering me again."

Katie frowned, taking off the glasses and resting her chin in her hands. "How do you know that he won't try to shut you up?"

Jess had to laugh. "He's the editor of a small newspaper, not the head of the Mafia."

Katie shook her head. "I don't know, Jess. He could stalk you or lie in wait and rape or beat you up."

Jess looked at her, bewildered. "Last night you were the one encouraging me to stand up to him."

"Yeah, I know." Katie sighed. "But in the cold light of day, without wine, it doesn't seem that easy."

"It really is," Jess said, feeling more confident since hearing what Eve and the very sharp and impressive Maria had to say. These women had worked in the company for years. Eve was a respected journalist, having previously worked for a tabloid that had gone out of business. Maria, a political commentator, gave up her job to raise her young family and, now that her children were at school, had accepted the less demanding position with the small local paper. The two women were respected by all their colleagues and, with them behind her, Jess felt sure that Louis would leave her alone; he'd be stupid not to. And, whatever else he was, Louis wasn't stupid. She looked over at her friend, who, hangover forgotten, was looking concerned. Jess squeezed her hand. "I can't begin to tell you how great it felt standing up to him."

"Good for you." Katie took refuge again behind her glasses. "Now, what about Cal?"

"What about him? If he could be put off that easily, he's obviously not that interested in me." Jess had looked forward to telling Cal of her confrontation with Louis, but he'd got the wrong end of the stick and, without even talking to her, decided she was guilty. Of exactly what, she wasn't sure. It took the good out of her victory and made her wistful about what might have been.

"Not interested?" Katie snorted. Are you kidding me? He couldn't take his eyes off you last night."

"Maybe, but this morning he seemed to have a change of heart."

"It's a misunderstanding. Phone him or send him a text, explaining."

Jess thought of the look of disgust on Cal's handsome face and shook her head. "I tried to explain and he walked away. I'm not going to crawl, Katie. I've just rid myself of one man who treated me like dirt. I'm not going on to another."

Katie groaned. "Oh, come on, Cal is nothing like Louis. He's a lovely guy."

"He is." Jess relented. "But he made his mind up without giving me a chance to explain. I deserve better than that." Katie grinned, making Jess frown. "What?"

"It's just nice to hear you valuing yourself."

"Was I that pathetic?" Jess sighed, fed up of this weak image she seemed to have. Why hadn't she inherited some of Mum's spirit?

Katie took off the glasses and gave her a stern look. "Listen to me. You are not and never have been pathetic and, if Cal doesn't realise what a great person you are, then it's his loss."

"Thanks, Katie." Jess smiled.

"You're welcome. Now, as I feel worse than death, I think food is in order."

"Curry?" Jess smiled.

"Perfect."

"Then, let's go." Jess put her arm through Katie's and led her out onto the street.

CHAPTER
THIRTY-THREE

Suzie walked into the kitchen and gasped in horror at the sight of lines and shapes in black marker all over the floor. Her head started to throb and she didn't know whether she wanted to scream or cry. She'd had a lousy night, then trekked off to the supermarket this morning and staggered back with her bags, in the rain. And now, this.

Steeling herself not to go into the lounge and ask Bobby what the hell he thought he was doing, Suzie fetched the scrubbing brush and a basin of soapy water and set about cleaning her tiles. Once it was done, she would have a cup of tea, calm down, then make the child his snack and explain, calmly, that he wasn't allowed to draw on anything other than paper.

A low whimper made her close her eyes. Fuck it. With all the fuss, she'd forgotten to let the dog out, something she always did just before Bobby arrived. Mindful of the child's temper, she still kept Percy penned in while he was there. The poor animal didn't seem to mind. This was the first time he'd made a sound. She abandoned her cleaning, and went in to the dog, smiling when he wagged his tail in delight and rubbed against her legs.

340

"Ah, you're gorgeous, Percy. Come on, boy, let's go outside." The rain clouds had dispersed and the sun was out. Suzie sat on the step and held her face up to the warmth. The light breeze was refreshing and she took a minute to ground herself and enjoy this rare moment of peace. "What am I going to do with this little fella?" she asked Percy. He looked up at her with sympathetic eyes and licked her hand, making her smile. "You don't have the answers either, huh?" A bloodcurdling scream came from the house and, jumping to her feet, Suzie charged inside, the dog hot on her heels. Bobby was on his knees on the kitchen floor, wailing.

"What is it, darling? Did you hurt yourself?"

"You broke my house!"

Suzie shook her head in confusion. "What house?" He hadn't brought any new toys with him, and there certainly wasn't a house here.

He flung a hand out at his marks on the floor. "My house."

Ah, so that was it, although how the lines and shapes on the floor were meant to be a house she had no clue. "I've told you before, Bobby, we only write and draw on paper. Now go back inside while I clean this up."

"No, my house!" he yelled.

Percy came to stand in front of her. "It's okay, Percy." But she was relieved to hear the front door. "In here, Noel," she called, although she knew he'd follow the noise.

His head came round the door and he took in the state of the floor and his nephew crying. He took one look at her face and crouched down beside Bobby. "Let's go and play a game upstairs, mate."

"She broke my house," Bobby told him.

"I'm sure she didn't mean to."

"She did!"

"Well, you can build another one later —"

"At home with his daddy," Suzie cut in. Honestly. There was only so much she could take.

As Suzie went to sit down with a mug of tea, her mobile rang. "Ah, for feck's sake, can't I have any peace?" she muttered irritably, scanning the room for the phone. She spotted it on top of the fridge and cheered up when she saw her caller was Doug. "Hello? Connors madhouse?"

Doug gave a rich chuckle. "Having a good day?"

"No, having a shite day. Oh, sorry but it has been really —"

"Shite? Does that mean you don't fancy dinner this evening?"

"I'd love it, Doug, but I'm too tired to doll myself up and go out."

"Then why don't I pick up some food and come over?"

Suzie thought about that. Noel was going out and it would be nice to have some company, especially his. She and Doug were such an unlikely pair, yet their shared memories and experiences had created an unexpectedly tight bond. She found it laughable that her family believed he would date someone like her, and yet Doug had changed, just as she had. While she still saw the dapper, immaculate charmer with a twinkle in his eye, she could understand Mandy seeing a sad old man. But a rich one, damn it, and she wouldn't let her sister anywhere near him.

"Have you nodded off?"

"Sorry, I'm distracted. Sounds like a great idea, Doug. Is about seven okay?"

"Perfect," he agreed, sounding really pleased.

"Grand, see you then."

By the time Keith arrived to collect Bobby, the kitchen was sparkling clean again, but Noel still told him what had happened as soon as his brother-in-law walked through the door.

"What?" Noel said when his mother glared at him. "Didn't we agree we'd be open from now on?"

She looked at Keith. "Honestly, love, I didn't give out to the lad and he's fine again now."

Keith sank into a kitchen chair, looking despondent. "I wonder why he did it."

"I called Cal," Noel said, "and he has a theory. Bobby had been restless and Mam told him to draw a picture."

"That's right. And he was grumpy and said he didn't know what to draw —"

"And you told him to make a house, right?" Noel finished for her.

"Yeah, a house."

Noel smiled. "And he did."

Suzie looked from one to the other and pointed at the blank sheets of paper. "No, he didn't."

"Cal told me that autistic children tend to take things literally."

Keith's eyes widened as understanding dawned. "He didn't draw one, he *made* one."

"Yes and it was brilliant," Noel told him. "It was like the floor plan an architect would come up with."

Suzie thought back to the lines and shapes covering her floor and gasped as she looked from one man to the other. "Holy shit, you're right. It was fucking amazing." Keith shot a nervous look at the door and she clapped a hand over her mouth and grinned. "Oops, sorry."

"He's a smart little guy." Keith's eyes were full of pride. "Where is he?"

"He got bored playing games and came down to watch Thomas."

Suzie looked at her son in surprise. "I haven't seen him, and the television hasn't been on since he got here." She felt sick. Where the hell was Bobby? Had he gone outside? Had he run away because she was cross with him?

"I'm sure he's sitting in a corner with a book," Keith said calmly and started going from room to room, calling for his son.

Noel shot her a guilty look. "I'll check upstairs."

Seconds later they both returned, without Bobby. "Maybe he made his own way home," Suzie said, trying not to think of the three main roads between their two houses.

Keith prowled between the kitchen and lounge and returned with a small, dog-eared cushion in his hand.

"He wouldn't have left this behind. He never goes anywhere without it."

Suzie thought about how Bobby often sat out on the front step. Could someone have taken him?

"The back garden," Noel said, going into the utility room to open the back door.

"The dog's gone," Suzie said, surprised as she followed them outside and collided with Noel as he pulled up short. "What? What is it?"

"Shush," he whispered, and stepped aside to let her see.

Bobby was hunkered in against the shed, wrapped around Percy and fast asleep. It was hard to know where the boy ended and the dog began. Percy looked up at her with an expression that seemed to say, "I've got this." Keith moved towards them but Suzie put her hand out to stop him. "Leave him. That tantrum must have taken a lot out of him. He's quite safe," she assured Keith when he hesitated. "Let's go inside and have a coffee. You can watch him from the window."

"I've never known him to nod off like that before." Keith said, looking out at his sleeping son.

"Me neither." Suzie sat down, tired. "Make the coffee, Noel, will you? I'm done in."

As her son got to work, Suzie looked through the window but neither dog nor boy had moved. She looked up at her son-in-law's nervous expression. "Really, Keith, Percy is an assistance dog. He'll look after Bobby. It's strange, though. I've kept the dog in his bed while Bobby was here, just until they got used to each other. And yet today, when he was upset, Bobby went to him."

"Or Percy went to Bobby," Noel said, setting down three steaming mugs. "Aren't dogs supposed to be intuitive? He always goes to sit beside you when you're fed up, Mum."

"That's true."

"I just can't understand it. Bobby's never been around dogs. You'd think he'd be terrified, especially given Percy's size."

"Perhaps Percy understands Bobby more than we do," Suzie murmured. "Bobby looks more comfortable with him than he is with me."

"That's because you're a pain in the arse, who's always screaming and shouting," Noel teased.

She took a swipe at him. "Have more respect for your mother. Keith, sit down, for feck's sake."

Reluctantly, her son-in-law took the seat nearest the window and Suzie told him all about the dog's history and how, in the short time he'd been with her, he'd already become protective and seemed to know what she needed, often before she did.

"He's awake!" Keith hopped up again and Suzie and Noel joined him. They stared in wonder as the little boy put his arms around the dog and buried his face in his coat, giggling. Then Percy stood up and turned towards the door, looking back at Bobby and waiting patiently for the little boy to stand up and follow him.

"Bloody hell," Keith muttered at the happy grin on his son's face. "We're buying a dog."

"You've had quite a day," Doug said, pouring the wine as Suzie opened the cartons of aromatic Thai food.

"You could say that. Aw, chicken in green curry, my favourite. You remembered."

"Extra spicy, although I wasn't sure if that was just something you were into when you were pregnant." He grinned.

She laughed. "I did have some cravings, right enough, but I love this dish any time."

He wandered round the room as she set out the plates and cutlery looking at the family photos. "This is Jess?" He held up the photo.

Suzie looked over and smiled. "Yes. That was taken at Sharon's wedding."

"She's stunning. So is your other daughter," he added hurriedly. "There's just something special about Jess — it's hard to pinpoint."

"Whatever it is, she must get it from her dad," Suzie said with a wry smile. "She looks nothing like Sharon or Noel."

Doug leaned closer to study it. "But she has your nose and the same dimple in her chin."

Suzie smiled. "Yeah, that's all Clarke."

He moved on to another photo of Suzie with her husband. "John?" he asked.

She nodded.

"You looked happy."

"We were. Well, most of the time."

Doug crossed to the mantelpiece crammed with family photos. "There aren't any photos of Jess with her dad."

"Aren't there?" Suzie pretended surprise.

Doug glanced at her, his eyebrows raised. "You know there aren't."

"Come and eat before the food goes cold."

He joined her on the sofa. "Hasn't she ever asked questions? She must have noticed that she looks nothing like John or her brother and sister."

"If she has suspicions she's never mentioned them to me," Suzie said, curtly.

"But don't you think it would help to tell her? Then she would understand John's feelings towards her."

"We've been through this, Doug," Suzie said, rapidly losing patience with him.

"Maybe she'd like to track down her real dad," Doug continued, not at all deterred by her clipped reply.

"And how in hell could she do that? Put an ad in the Spanish newspapers saying, 'If you fucked a drunken, blonde punk in Dublin, June 1988, you could be my dad'?"

Doug smiled. "I'm sure it could be worded a little better than that. What was his name?"

"No idea," Suzie admitted. "He was gorgeous and, yeah, apart from the colour of her eyes, Jess is the spitting image of him. But trying to find him would be like looking for a needle in a haystack. Anyway, I'm sure he's married with his own kids. The last thing he'd want is a skeleton like this coming out of the cupboard."

"If that was the case he wouldn't come forward, would he? I'd be chuffed if I found out I was a dad,

348

especially of someone as wonderful as Jess," he said, sounding wistful.

Suzie sighed. It was hard to stay mad at the man. "You haven't met her since she was three."

"So? She was a great kid then and I've no doubt she's turned into a wonderful young woman. Smart, too."

"Not always." Susie scowled as thoughts of Louis Healy came to mind. "She hasn't dated a decent guy yet, and as for her latest . . ." Suzie shook her head in disgust.

Doug stopped eating and took a sip of his drink. "An unfaithful lying bastard like me, eh?"

Suzie looked at him, curious now. There had been so much speculation about her boss and what he got up to. She'd always wondered how much was truth and how much was fiction. "Why did you do it, Doug?"

"What?"

"Why did you cheat on Pamela?" She wondered, had Pamela suspected him of being unfaithful and, if so, had it bothered her? Back in her early days at CML, Suzie had thought that Pamela was a frigid woman, interested only in material things. But, after Jess was born, she discovered that Pam was as vulnerable as the rest of them.

Doug sighed and pushed away his food. "Pamela wasn't demonstrative because she never learned how to be. She had a rather strange upbringing. Her parents were decent people but detached. The first real love Pamela experienced was mine and she didn't know what to do with it. Any public display of affection embarrassed her and made her uncomfortable. I thought I'd break that down in time but the more that I tried, the further she retreated. Finally I stopped and played around a little, just flirting. I thought if I made her jealous it would provoke a reaction."

"But it didn't?"

He shrugged. "Pamela just ignored it and carried on as normal. I assumed that meant she didn't care, and I got harder and" — he sighed — "crueller."

"You didn't know that she wanted children, Doug," she consoled him.

He looked at her, his eyes full of guilt. "I did, Suzie, but I kept saying no. The last time she brought it up, she was in her mid-thirties. It was almost a throwaway remark, something like, 'Are you sure you don't want a family, because the clock is ticking?' And I said no and . . ." She saw him struggle with his feelings. "She was sterilised."

Suzie stared at him, shocked. "What?"

"Apparently, she had some gynaecological problems and her doctor advised that, if she didn't want children, she'd be better off without her womb."

"I didn't know."

"Neither did I, but it all came out the day Jess was born. I remember thinking it odd when she told me she was going on holiday with a couple of girlfriends. She'd never done that before and she wasn't close to any of the women she knew. It turns out she was in a private clinic in Dublin. She was torn apart with remorse afterwards. That's when her problems really started."

"The bulimia?" Suzie said, remembering noticing Pamela's strange eating habits.

He met her eyes and nodded. "All my fault."

Suzie pressed her lips together. She felt angry with him and pitied Pamela. The poor woman must have been devastated and she'd suffered through it all alone. Suzie was beginning to regret pushing him to talk. She felt like tearing into him, but what good would that do now? Anyway, in the end, the couple had resolved their differences and he'd been the perfect husband.

"Why didn't you want kids?" she asked instead.

"Honestly? I never fancied the hassle and, selfishly, I hated the thought of Pamela's body being taken over like that. When I got to know you and lived through the pregnancy with you, and then Jess came along, it changed everything. But it was too late." He gave a wistful smile. "So Pam and I concentrated on Jess instead."

Suzie swallowed the lump in her throat and her anger disappeared, leaving her feeling sad. Poor Pam. Suzie vowed to be nicer to her kids and to Bobby. Her family meant the world to her and she couldn't imagine a life without them.

"You know, you could still tell Jess," Doug said. "I got a lot wrong and I've much to be ashamed of. But you, Suzie? What did you do except get carried away one night when you were happy, carefree and a little drunk? Do you honestly think anyone would condemn you for that, least of all your daughter?"

Suzie shook her head.

"Like I said," he said with a kind smile, "it's never too late. If I hadn't come to my senses that day and confronted Pamela, I'd never have had those last wonderful years with her."

Suzie looked at him, shaking her head. Was he for real? Just when he and Pam had sorted out their differences, the poor woman had been diagnosed with liver cancer. Those last "wonderful" years had been peppered with visits to doctors and consultants, time in hospital and the pain of watching a beautiful woman turn into a frail skeleton.

"What?" He raised his eyebrows.

"You could hardly call it a wonderful time, Doug."

He thought for a moment and sighed. "Perhaps not, but at least we were finally close and able to truly support each other. And, believe me, she supported me just as much as I supported her."

Suzie absorbed this. Had she ever had that with John? She'd thought so to begin with but, when she looked back, she remembered the guilt she'd felt at almost apologising for her daughter's existence.

It wasn't that she was ashamed of Jess. Suzie had just been embarrassed about being an unmarried mother. Still, she didn't think Jess had ever been aware of John's indifference or felt left out. Suzie had more than made up for it, almost neglecting the other two when they were babies in her efforts to make sure that Jess didn't feel threatened by the new additions to their family.

"I think it would bring you and Jess closer if you told her the truth. Think about it."

Suzie shook her head. "Shut up and eat."

CHAPTER
THIRTY-FOUR

Realising it was probably a little early for visiting, Jess let herself into her mother's house as quietly as possible and crept into the kitchen. Noel had called an hour ago to say that he'd crashed at Cal's last night and had to go straight into work. Mum, it seemed, had had a long and stressful day yesterday and he asked her to stop by and let Percy out so that Mum could sleep in and get some rest before picking up Bobby.

Considering how Jess felt about dogs, she wasn't impressed but, having heard about the previous day's scare, she figured her mum could probably do with the rest. Noel assured her that Percy was a pussycat and rang off, laughing at his own amazing wit. Halfwit more like, she thought, with a reluctant smile.

Jess stood at the door into the utility area, trying to work up the courage to go in. The dog gave a soft whine as if encouraging her, but she still couldn't bring herself to open the door. She had never so much as touched a dog since being attacked but it was hard to ignore Percy's whimpers. She could just fling open the back door and retreat into the safety of the kitchen, couldn't she? For her mother?

Her heart thumping in her chest, Jess pushed open the door. The large, golden dog lifted his head and wagged his tail at the sight of her but made no move to get up. She looked over at the back door, wondering if she could stretch far enough to open it without actually going into the room, but chances were she'd fall in on top of the animal. Taking a few deep breaths, she sidled along the wall, never taking her eyes off him, and, having flung the door open, ran back into the kitchen. Seconds later she heard him pad outside and watched from the kitchen window as he did his business. She hurried in to refill his water bowl before he got back. He'd just have to wait to eat until her mother surfaced. She returned to her post by the window and watched the dog amble round the garden before returning inside. Jess stood in the kitchen doorway as he lay back down in his bed and looked up at her, wagging his tail again. "Okay, so maybe you're not so bad," she muttered.

Jess wandered into the lounge and did a double-take at the mess. The remains of last night's dinner and an empty wine bottle and two glasses stood on the coffee table. Lover-boy must have dropped by, she mused as she started to gather up the dirty dishes. This thing between Mum and Douglas seemed to be getting serious. She looked forward to meeting the man who'd put a smile on her mother's face and a pep in her step. Jess froze as a floorboard creaked overhead. She looked up, wondering if he'd stayed over. That would be seriously embarrassing. She needed to get out of here.

"Noel?"

Jess sighed as she heard her mother's voice call down. She went into the hallway. "It's Jess, Mum."

"Oh, hello, love." Suzie came to the top of the stairs, yawning. "I had a late night."

"I was just looking at the aftermath." Jess grinned and nodded towards the lounge.

"Oh, feck off, it's not that bad." Her mother clamped her hand to her mouth. "Oh, my goodness, Percy!"

"I just let him out and gave him water."

Suzie's eyes widened. "You did?"

"Yeah. Noel stayed over at Cal's and was going straight into work, so he asked me to drop by. He figured you might sleep in after your day with Bobby. Bad, eh?"

Suzie sighed. "Not really, but it was tiring. Thanks for coming over. I know it can't have been easy. But isn't he a darling?"

"I wouldn't go that far, but he didn't attack me, so that's a plus."

Her mum chuckled. "Wait until you get to know him. You'll soon be under his spell like the rest of us. Bobby seems to adore him."

"Really?" That was good news, Jess had to admit.

"Yes, honestly. He fell asleep wrapped round him yesterday and the dog never moved a muscle." Suzie yawned again. "Listen, let me grab a shower and then I'll make us a cuppa."

"Are you sure you don't want to get more sleep?"

"No, I'll have some breakfast and then take the dog for a walk. I didn't get a chance to yesterday."

Jess went back into the lounge, threw open a window and, bending to plump the cushions, found a small photo album under one. She didn't remember seeing it before and, curious, she sat down and started to leaf through it. The first few photos were of strangers, young people fooling around, and, from the look of the clothes, they were snapped in the eighties. She studied each of the faces and gasped when she recognised her mother, looking so young and — Jess giggled — like a punk! She continued to turn the pages and, while they were all of the same people, occasionally there was an older, attractive man present too. She pulled up short at a photo of her mother, heavily pregnant. She touched her fingers to the bump. "That's me."

"What's that?" her mother said, coming down the stairs, towelling her damp hair.

Jess held up the album. "This photo of you pregnant — it's with me, isn't it?" She laughed. "It has to be, you're so young."

Suzie stood in the doorway and gave an embarrassed grin. "Wasn't I enormous?"

"You look a little cross."

"Of course I was. Who wants to be photographed when they look like an elephant?"

Jess chuckled. "Did Dad take the photo?"

Her mother appeared flummoxed. "I don't remember who took it. I'll put on the kettle."

Jess followed her, taking the album with her, wondering why her mum seemed so uncomfortable. "Who are these people?"

"They're the guys at CML, the company I worked for until a year after you were born."

"And then you moved to Limerick with Dad?"

"That's right."

Jess turned to the last photo in the album. It was a shot of all the gang surrounding the hospital bed. Her mother was flushed and beaming, cradling her baby, and the older man from the previous shots had his arm around her.

"Who's this guy?" she asked, skirting around the dog to show her mother the photo.

"That's Doug. He was the MD of CML."

"He seems very friendly."

"He was a nice man."

Jess frowned, trying to process that, when her phone rang. It was Katie.

"Hey, where are you? I thought we were going shopping."

Jess glanced at her watch. "Shit, sorry, Katie. I'm on my way."

"What's up with you?"

Jess looked blankly from the dress she held in her hand to her friend's exasperated expression. "Sorry?"

"You've barely opened your mouth all morning. If you wanted to cry off you should have said so. It's not like you're any company."

Jess put the dress back on the rail. "Sorry."

"What's happened?" Katie's eyes narrowed. "Don't tell me that asshole has been bothering you again? If he has, I'm going to go and sort him out, once and for all. I can't go to Jersey and leave you like this."

"It's not Louis." Jess sighed. "I was at Mum's when you called. I found an old photo album with shots of her pregnant with me and some taken in the hospital, just after I was born."

Katie's face broke into a smile. "Aw, that's nice. Isn't it?" she added when Jess didn't respond.

Katie took her by the arm and steered her out of the shop. "Let's grab a coffee."

When they were seated at a table in a crowded café across the road, Katie rested her chin in her hand. "Okay, out with it. What has you so preoccupied?"

"Dad's not in any of the photos. In fact, Dad's not in the album."

"So? Maybe it was his album and he was the photographer." Katie shrugged.

Jess shook her head. "Dad was never into any of that."

"Ah, but first-time daddies are a sentimental lot and want to capture everything their first-born does. It's the novelty factor. There are zillions of photos of Philip around the house and hardly any of the rest of us," she complained. Jess frowned at that. Their house had always been full of baby photos of Sharon and a good few of Noel, but there weren't any of Jess. "Fuck," she murmured.

"What?"

Jess looked at her. "I don't think my dad's my dad."

Katie burst out laughing. "You figure that on the basis that there aren't more photos of you?"

358

"No. I figure it on the basis that: one, the album just has photos of Mam with the people she used to work with before she got married; two, there are pictures of her pregnant with me, and of us in the hospital, and I've never seen them before; three, Dad was never as close to me as he was to Sharon and Noel; and lastly" — she ticked her fourth finger — "I look nothing like him, or Sharon and Noel, for that matter."

Katie looked dubious. "I think that you're blowing this out of proportion."

"I don't think so." Jess knew, in her gut, she was right. "Mum acted all weird when I found the album."

Katie's eyes lit up. "I know! She must have got pregnant before they got married, and she's embarrassed by that."

Jess shot her a look of disbelief. "My mother isn't easily embarrassed, especially now. And why would that matter to me? Why would I care? No, there's more to it than that. And there's a man that appears in lots of the photos with her."

"Oh!" Katie's eyes widened. "And do you look like him?"

"Not at all," Jess sighed. She couldn't figure out the puzzle but she was sure that there was one.

"Your imagination is running away with you," Katie said. "You'll be telling me next that your da owns a worldwide newspaper chain and you're his sole heir."

Jess burst out laughing. "Smartarse. With my luck, it's more likely that he's broke and would only come out of the woodwork looking for a loan."

Laughing, Katie excused herself to use the loo and Jess went back to brooding. Was John her dad? If not, why hadn't her mother told her? Suzie had always been open with her children about her own upbringing and how Granddad had treated her and Granny. Why would she lie about Jess's father? Katie must be right. It was her imagination. She was looking for mysteries where there were none.

Jess hadn't had much of a relationship with her dad, but that wasn't uncommon. And it wasn't as if they fought all the time. On the contrary, John had always been perfectly civil and she'd lacked for nothing. He just seemed absent from her life in a way that he hadn't with Sharon and Noel. She'd never given that much thought before and she didn't remember being conscious of it growing up. A typical teenage girl, she was more absorbed in her own life than in the family dynamic but that album raised questions she'd never considered before.

Jess knew little of her mother's life before she moved to Limerick. The people in those photos had obviously been a lot more than workmates: they looked like good friends. Why had Mam never talked about them? And what had prompted her to unearth this album now? Had she been showing it to her boyfriend? Why show him photos of so long ago? Especially the one of her pregnant that she hated? Wouldn't it be more usual to show him ones of Dad and her kids? Damn it, Jess was just going to ask her about it, and she wouldn't stop until she had some answers. Mam might tell her to feck off and mind her own business, but Jess wouldn't back down. And, if Dad wasn't really her dad, then Jess wanted to know who was.

CHAPTER
THIRTY-FIVE

Sharon glanced across the table at her son and then looked, wide-eyed, at her husband. Keith just shrugged and smiled. Since Bobby had come home from his granny's yesterday, he'd been quiet, but not in a bad way. He seemed content, and there was a slight smile playing around his mouth.

"So you like Granny's dog, Bobby?"

"His name's Percy. He's my friend."

"Aw, that's nice. Dogs are great. They always love you no matter what."

"I love him too," Bobby said with an emphatic nod.

This morning her son had hopped out of bed and got ready for school without either of them having to hurry him along.

"I'm lost for words," Sharon said when Bobby went upstairs to brush his teeth.

"I know. Do you think your mother would let us adopt Percy?"

Sharon laughed. "I think we're going to have a tough enough time coping with a new baby and Bobby without throwing a dog into the mix."

"True." He sighed.

"He'll see Percy all the time," Sharon said.

"Soon he'll be asking to move in with his granny."

"Huh, he can dream on." Bobby had a long way to go before her mother truly accepted him, and Sharon worried about the challenges ahead when there was a new grandchild. "I hope Mum won't fuss over the new baby too much and make Bobby jealous."

"Stop worrying." Keith pulled her in close against him. "Bobby doesn't notice things like that or take offence."

Sharon didn't agree, but she wasn't going to spoil the moment by saying so. Bobby might seem insulated in his own little world, but some of the comments he came out with had made her realise how clued in he actually was. She still wasn't sure if it upset him. He'd seemed so pragmatic when he'd said his granny didn't like him, it had made Sharon feel quite sad.

She'd had numerous chats with Bobby's principal and teacher and they'd introduced her to other mothers in similar circumstances. It was a comfort to hear their stories and she soon realised that Bobby truly was on the lower end of the scale. She'd taken to counting her blessings. Bobby might be clumsy, detached and prone to violent mood swings, but there was no doubt in her mind that he was smart.

"Any word on his assessment?" Keith asked.

"Nothing. Apparently it could take months or more."

"Bloody crazy," Keith fumed. "Maybe we should go private. And, you know, there are schools for children with special needs. If we have to pay, we'll pay. I'll take out a loan if necessary."

Sharon was touched by his determination, but not every problem could be solved by throwing money at it. "I think we should wait," she cautioned. "I like Bobby's school and the staff. There are a few autistic children there and, talking to their mums, they seem to be doing well. The teachers are already giving Bobby help, even though they haven't been allotted the extra resources to cater for him, and Bobby likes them. Besides, I think our children should be in the same school. He shouldn't ever be made to feel different."

Keith dropped a kiss on her hair. "You're a great mum, Shaz, you know that?"

She thought back on the time she'd wasted knowing her son was different, but saying nothing because she didn't want her fears confirmed. That hadn't been good mothering. She caressed her bump, making a silent promise to do better, regardless of what life presented her with.

Mandy groaned as her phone pinged. She rolled over in bed and opened one eye, sitting up when she saw that it was a text from Douglas.

Taking the morning off, meeting with friends. Latest chapters on your desk. D.

She frowned. Friends? What friends? Douglas didn't socialise. Douglas didn't do anything. What had got into him? She'd reckoned that, with Suzie fully occupied with Bobby, things might return to normal but she hardly saw him these days. Still, she thought as she wrapped the soft duvet around her, perhaps Douglas had developed a taste for living and, who knew, maybe Zagreb was back on the cards. She just needed to keep him away from Suzie and find some interesting things to do in Croatia that might surprise and entertain him.

That was it! She had been so fixated on her own pleasures, she hadn't thought about him. Mandy was weary of parading herself in bars and clubs in the hope of finding a rich man who would give her a good and secure life. Why do it when there was one right under her nose? She didn't care about the age difference: it meant he'd make few or no demands.

Mandy decided it was time to turn on the charm. She needed to show an interest in his work and be kind and pleasant. Perhaps she'd even cook him lunch. Maybe not, she thought with a wry grin. Her cooking abilities were limited and there was no sense in highlighting the fact. But she could pick up the pâté and chowder he loved from his favourite deli when she was in the village. Her thoughtfulness would surprise him but, might also make him suspicious — Douglas wasn't stupid. She needed to be subtle about this. As it turned out, she didn't have long to wait for an opportunity to show him her caring side.

Mandy arrived into work the following morning to find her boss crumpled at the bottom of the stairs, a sickly shade of grey. "Douglas, what is it?"

"I've a sick stomach and I'm feeling dizzy," he mumbled.

"Did you fall down the stairs?"

"Just the last couple, but only because I was groggy. I've spent most of the night in the bathroom."

"I'll call the doctor." She expected an argument but Douglas directed her to his address book, where she'd find the number of his GP.

"Gastroenteritis," the doctor pronounced, cheerfully, after spending less than five minutes in the bedroom. "Give him plenty of fluids, no solids for a couple of days, and he should stay in bed as he'll feel quite weak."

"He fell down the stairs," Mandy told him.

"As a result of the weakness." He smiled. "Nothing to be concerned about. There's a lot of this about. I suggest, though, that it would be best to sleep in separate rooms for the duration. It's very contagious."

"Excuse me? I'm not his partner. He's my boss," she exclaimed, disgusted that he thought she looked old enough to be Douglas's wife.

"Sorry, I'm new at the surgery. I suggest you contact a relative. Someone should stay with him for a few days, just to keep an eye on him."

"Thank you, Doctor." Mandy nodded and showed him out, smiling as she closed the door. It looked like she'd have to play Florence Nightingale.

After running back upstairs to check on him, Mandy took Douglas's prescription to the pharmacy and then stopped off at the deli, delighted to discover that they had clear, homemade chicken soup. She bought a couple of portions and brought them back to the house. When she looked in on him, he was sleeping, so she decided to leave him until he came looking for her. She took his mobile phone from the bedside table and pocketed it. After all, the man needed his rest. It had nothing to do with the fact that this was a perfect opportunity to come between the happy couple.

Rather than wait for Suzie to call him or be discovered reading his texts, Mandy called her sister. She let her drone on about the kids and the dog for a little and then cut in on her.

"Oops, sorry, Suze, I'd better go. Douglas isn't well so I'm playing nurse as well as PA at the moment."

"What's wrong with him?" Suzie asked, her voice full of concern.

"A bad dose of gastroenteritis. He's confined to bed, fluids only, with strict instructions not to infect anyone. Apparently it's dangerous for old folks, babies and pregnant women. I suppose he'll be housebound for a while. Not that he's the energy to leave the bedroom at the moment."

She sat back with a smug grin as she imagined how torn her sister would be. Did she run to her new beloved's bedside or put her daughter's and grandchild's safety first? No contest.

"Oh, that's terrible."

"He should be okay in a week or ten days, according to the doctor."

"But who'll look after him?" Suzie fretted.

"Don't worry. I'm taking good care of him."

"You?" Mandy bristled at her incredulous snort. "Oh, sorry, Mandy, there's someone at the door. Be sure and give Doug my best."

"Will do." Amanda lied. Doug? Doug? No one called him that. How could they have got this cosy so quickly? Despite the fact she'd known him for much longer, Mandy felt like the stranger.

She'd never experienced an easy camaraderie with any man. It was always sex-charged, hot and intense at first, and then it burned out faster than a firecracker. She had never remained friends with any of her ex-lovers. Once the desire was gone, she was too. There was only one man she'd ever been interested in hanging on to and, well, he'd got away in every sense of the word.

Hearing a noise upstairs, Mandy quickly dissolved a rehydration sachet in a large glass of water and carried it up to Douglas.

"Feeling any better?" she asked.

"No."

She put the glass down and helped him into a sitting position. "Take this, and then get some more sleep."

"I need to check my email."

"I'll take care of all that."

He glanced at the clock. "What are you doing here at this hour?"

"The doctor said it was a bad idea to leave you alone, so I'm staying over."

"You don't have to do that," he protested, but his voice was weak.

"It's fine. I don't mind."

Douglas sat up, groaning. "I need the bathroom."

Mandy helped him across the hall and groaned in disgust while she waited. When he came out, she forced a sympathetic smile. "Let's get you back into bed."

"I owe you," he muttered as he slumped weakly back on the pillow.

"Don't worry, I'll collect." She smiled. "Call if you need anything," she added, but he was already drifting back to sleep.

CHAPTER
THIRTY-SIX

Once the house was tidy and the washing on the line, Suzie put on Percy's lead and, looking out at the threatening clouds, grabbed a light raincoat, just in case. She wasn't really a morning person but, if she didn't walk the dog before Bobby arrived, she was usually too tired to do it afterwards. Maybe she should take Aileen up on her kind offer and let her take Percy out occasionally.

Suzie was just about to let herself out into the side passage when she heard the doorbell. She sighed. "Hang on, Percy, I'll go and get rid of whoever it is."

"Hello, Suzie."

She blinked twice as she looked at the skinny, hunched figure of her brother-in-law on the doorstep. Fuck it! She'd completely forgotten he was arriving today. She opened the door wide and gave him a weak smile. "Good to see you, Maurice. How are you?"

"Not looking forward to seeing this specialist but, I suppose, he wouldn't have dragged me up here if he didn't think he could do something to help."

"Specialist?" Suzie led the way into the kitchen, shrugging out of her coat and taking the lead off Percy, who, after cocking his head on one side, went to sniff the newcomer. What specialist? She couldn't for the life of her remember Maurice telling her he had health problems.

"Didn't Noel mention it? Bowel trouble. Enough said." Maurice waved away the implications. "Lovely animal." He scratched the dog's ear.

"I hope it's nothing serious." Suzie looked at him. He really didn't look well.

"It is what it is," Maurice said with a shrug of defeat. "That's why I'm delighted Noel is coming home."

Suzie shook her head in bewilderment as she filled the small teapot, absently adding four teabags. "What do you mean, Maurice?"

"Noel coming to work on the farm."

Suzie hooted with laughter. "Ah, Maurice, what are you talking about? Noel's going to be an engineer, not a farmhand."

"But sure he gave up the engineering course. He'll be starting a part-time agricultural-science course in October." Maurice looked at her, pity in his eyes. "Ah, that knock to the head caused more damage than I realised. Sorry for your trouble."

"There's nothing wrong with my bloody head," she snapped. "I'm telling you, you've got it wrong. Noel's been studying like mad for weeks. He just finished his exams."

His eyes widened and then slid away from hers. "Maybe I have," he mumbled.

Suzie watched Maurice tug at his collar, looking flushed and uncomfortable, and knew, in that moment, her son had been lying to her. She abandoned the tea and dropped into a chair. Percy slumped down next to her, resting his head on her feet. Of course Noel had lied. He knew that she'd hate the idea of his going back to Limerick, let alone this mad notion of taking up farming.

Suddenly, she was angry. "When did all of this come about, Maurice? When did you and my son get so bloody cosy?"

He looked taken aback at the bitterness in her voice. "We always got on well, Suzie, you know that. And we grew closer after John passed."

"I thought you were being a caring uncle, not looking for cheap labour."

Maurice looked as if she'd slapped him. "How can you say such a thing? The lad has always had a love of the land. We chatted at Christmas and he told me that he hated his course and couldn't see a future in it. All he's ever really wanted is to farm. He only took the engineering course for your sake. But the closer he got to qualifying, the more he realised he couldn't hack it. He'd made his mind up to tell you but then you had the accident. The poor lad was devastated. And then, thank God, you woke up fine and it seemed everything was back on track. Until Sharon got pregnant and you had to look after her little fella."

"Bobby." Suzie fondled Percy's ear and the dog licked her arm.

"Yes, well, Noel told me that he'd have to hang around for a while and give you a hand, and that's fine, I'll manage . . . somehow."

Suzie trembled with anger. Her son was a fool. She could imagine Noel working his arse off for bed and board and a few lousy quid because Maurice was a tight-fisted bastard. She glared at him, forgetting the sympathy she'd felt for him just minutes earlier. "You stupid old fool. Noel loved his dad, which is why he feels some stupid sense of obligation to go back to Limerick. He's no farmer. You'll have to find someone else, Maurice. I didn't put him through university so that he could throw his life away slaving on the Connors' farm, seven days a week in all weathers."

Maurice sat up, ramrod straight and glared back at her, his watery blue eyes cold as ice. "He would be no farm labourer. He's my brother's son. Peggy couldn't have children, God rest her, and Noel is the nearest I have to a son. He would be learning from me as well as from college and I'd leave the lot to him and die happy, knowing it was in good hands. Noel's a fine young man with a good heart."

"He's a fool and this is a romantic notion, nothing more. Come the winter months he'll be on the first bus back to Dublin and looking for a nice cosy office job, mark my words."

"It's not a notion, Mum."

Suzie spun round to see her son standing in the doorway, his eyes sad and his face ashen. "It's what I want, more than anything."

She stood up and ran at him, her blood boiling. "How could you?" Suzie slapped his face.

Unprepared, Noel staggered sideways and stared at her in shock.

Maurice was on his feet and had her by the arm. "Holy Mother of God, Suzie, what are you doing?"

Suzie stared at her son, horrified, as his cheek turned an angry red. She opened her mouth to apologise, to beg him to reconsider, to persuade him to stay, but nothing came out. He was watching her, his eyes begging her to understand, but she couldn't say the words he wanted to hear. Blinded by tears, Suzie turned on her heel and picked up the lead. "Percy," she called, and walked out of the door.

Jess hesitated when the phone rang and she saw it was Cal. She was torn between curiosity and anger. Curiosity won out.

"Yes?"

"Jess, I know what's wrong with Noel."

Immediately she forgot her plan to be cool. "What is it?"

"Nothing serious. I'll fill you in later. But he and your mum had words and she's walked out. That was a couple of hours ago. Noel can't find her in any of her usual haunts and now he has to go and pick up Bobby."

So Cal was calling her only because Noel had asked him to, Jess thought, but shook off her disappointment. It was more important to find Mum. She was so unpredictable at the moment and she might be wandering round upset too. Jess sighed as she remembered she'd no car and would have to walk to her mother's.

"What is it?" Cal asked.

"My car's in for a service."

374

"I'll pick you up."

As she waited for Cal, Jess tried to phone her brother but he wasn't answering his mobile and the house phone was ringing out. What the hell was going on?

She was watching for Cal and was out of the door before he'd even pulled up. It had started to rain quite heavily and she quickly jumped in beside him. "Why did Noel call you and not me?" she asked, not bothering to say hello.

He raised an eyebrow at her curt tone. "*I* called *him*. He was in a rush, so I offered to call you and fill you in."

"Thanks," she mumbled, chastened. "What did Noel say to send Mum off the deep end?"

"From what I can gather, it was your uncle Maurice who spilled the beans."

"What beans?" Jess asked. "And what has Maurice got to do with it?"

Cal glanced over at her. "Noel didn't sit his exams."

"What?" Jess gaped at him.

"Yup. Apparently he wants to be a farmer and work with your uncle."

"He's going back to Limerick? For good?"

"It looks that way."

Jess sighed. "No wonder Mum's upset. That's a double whammy that'll have knocked her for six."

Cal glanced over at her, eyebrows raised. "He was bound to fly the nest sooner or later."

"That's not what bothers her. It's the fact that he's chosen Limerick and Dad's family over her. Also, Dad died on a farm," she reminded Cal.

"She's in shock. She'll get used to the idea. To be honest, I'm relieved that there was such an innocent reason for your brother's strange behaviour."

"Me too. I wonder where the hell he's been spending his time. All that moaning about studying for his exams." Jess shook her head. "He should go into acting. He's probably been sitting in Internet cafés all day, playing games."

"Actually, he's been taking some part-time courses and working in the bar at the yacht club to finance them."

"He's a dark horse," she mumbled, but was glad that there was nothing more sinister going on. Poor Noel. He must have been a nervous wreck wondering how to break this to their mother. Jess was hurt that he didn't feel he could confide in her. Had he talked to Sharon? she wondered.

Cal pulled up outside her mum's house. "Let's check the house in case she's come back." Does she have the dog with her?" Jess asked him.

"Yes, I think so."

Well, that was something. If these assistance dogs were all they were cracked up to be, Percy should keep Mum safe. Jess let herself in and called out, but the place was deserted. There was a note on the kitchen table from Noel saying that he'd gone to collect Bobby and would come home via the park, in the hope of finding Suzie there. Maurice had gone to his appointment at the hospital and wasn't sure what time he'd be back. Jess tossed it back on the table. "I wouldn't expect dinner on the table if I were you, Maurice," she muttered.

She went back outside, shaking her head at Cal's questioning look.

"What do you want to do?" Cal asked.

Jess scrambled back in beside him, shaking the rain from her hair and looking worriedly at the sky as there was a flash of lightning. "She can't be out in this weather, but where would she be able to go with a dog?"

"Is there a friend that she'd turn to?"

"Maybe she's gone over to Sharon's," she said and taking out her phone, called her sister. After establishing that her mum wasn't there, Jess filled Sharon in on this morning's events and hung up.

"No joy?" Cal asked as she finished the call.

Jess shook her head. Sharon hadn't seemed interested in Noel's change of career and didn't understand why their mum was so upset. She was more concerned about who would be looking after Bobby if Suzie didn't show up.

"What now?" Cal asked.

"I'll check next door. She might be hiding there."

Jess knocked on Aileen's front door. The woman gave a surprised smile. "Hello, Jess. Come in out of that rain."

"Hi, Aileen. You haven't seen Mum, have you?"

"No." The woman frowned. "Is there something wrong?"

"She had a row with Noel and stormed off with the dog a few hours ago."

Aileen nodded in understanding. "She's been using walking a lot to keep her calm, although this isn't really the weather for it. I wouldn't worry, love. She's probably taken shelter in a coffee shop."

"Any idea which ones wouldn't object to the dog?" Jess asked.

"There's one on the far side of the park." the woman nodded. "Yes. That's where she'll be."

"Brilliant. Thanks, Aileen."

Jess went back to join Cal and filled him in on what Aileen had said.

"Let's go, then."

They were just about to drive off when Jess spotted a hunched figure and sodden dog making their way slowly up the road. Her heart went out to her mother, hating to see her like this. "Cal." Jess nodded towards her mother.

"Great. Maybe I should go and let you two talk."

Jess was tempted to ask him to wait but knew that it would be best if she talked to Mum alone. "Yeah, probably. Thanks for everything." He looked at her for a moment and she thought that he might be on the point of saying something, but in the end he just nodded and said goodbye.

Jess shook her head in frustration and walked towards her mother, the rain still bucketing down. "Mum, you're soaked through. Come on, let's get you into some dry clothes and have a cuppa."

Her mother said nothing but led the way down the passage, letting herself in the back door. Jess followed and went to put on the kettle. She heard her mum murmuring to the dog as she dried him and settled him in his bed. Then she came into the kitchen and flopped down at the table.

"You should change," Jess said, gently.

Her mum ignored that. "Did you know that Noel hasn't been attending university? That he didn't sit his exams?"

"No." Jess looked at her mother's angry expression as she accepted the mug of tea and wrapped her hands round it. "I know it's not what you want for him, Mum, but I'll be honest: I'm relieved. I was afraid that he was on drugs."

Suzie looked up at her, eyebrows raised. "Why would you think that?"

Jess shrugged. "He seemed to become dependent on your sedatives very quickly."

Suzie didn't appear to be listening. "I can't believe he'd go into farming after what happened to his dad. How could he do that to me?"

Jess looked at her in disbelief. "He's not doing anything to *you*, Mum. He's doing it because it's the future that he wants. He could end up in a more dangerous job as an engineer. We can't live our lives worrying about what *might* happen."

"He's going to Limerick." Suzie said it as if Noel had announced he was moving to Afghanistan.

"I think that's great, to be honest. He's going to live and work with his father's family. Don't you think Dad would be proud of him?"

"John's dead. What about me? Don't I count?" Suzie said bitterly. "I've had a hard enough life raising the three of you alone, and now I'll be spending my days worrying about Noel on a bloody farm. I blame your father for this."

Jess raised an eyebrow. "He didn't get his love of the land from Dad. If I remember rightly, he spent more time on the road and staying in fancy hotels than he did on farms." She saw her mother frown and ploughed on. "Dad had a freak accident, Mum. I know that it must have been heartbreaking to lose him at such a young age, and I can understand why you wanted to come back to Dublin. But maybe Limerick and farming is in Noel's blood. Just the way that Dublin is in yours and mine."

It took a moment for her words to sink in, but, when Suzie raised guilty eyes to meet hers, Jess knew that her gut instinct had been right. "John Connors isn't my dad, is he?"

CHAPTER
THIRTY-SEVEN

Suzie's head pounded, past and present colliding, at the memories Noel's bombshell had triggered. She stared at her daughter, at a loss as to what to say. Doug had asked if Jess had suspicions about her father and she'd been so smug, so confident that her daughter was blissfully ignorant. Why today, Jess? Suzie wasn't sure that she could cope with much more.

She was saved from answering by the arrival of Noel and Bobby and immediately took refuge behind her grandson, bringing him out to Percy and letting him help her groom the dog. As her hand covered his small one, combing Percy's golden coat with long, slow strokes, she tuned out the sound of her son and daughter discussing her and talked softly to Bobby and Percy. Her eyes felt heavy. The long walk and trauma of the day was making her sleepy. Maybe she should take a leaf out of Bobby's book and curl up with the dog.

"Why are you crying?" Bobby asked, sounding more curious than concerned.

Suzie touched her cheeks. "I honestly don't know, Bobby." She wiped the tears away.

"You're all wet."

"I am. Percy and I got caught in the rain — drowned, we were."

"Drowned?" Bobby frowned. "You're not dead."

Suzie smiled. "It's an expression. I just mean that we were soaked to the skin."

"Percy's all dry now. Will we make you dry too?"

"I think I can manage that on my own, love." Suzie listened, but couldn't hear any talking from the other room. Moments later, the door opened and Noel looked in.

"Why don't you go and have a rest, Mum? Bobby and I have a date with *Mario Kart*, and I'm going to win." He winked at the child.

Bobby was on his feet in an instant. "No, *I* will!"

"Then let's go." Noel gave her a long sorrowful look before following his nephew up to his room.

Suzie hugged the dog. "Aw, fuck it, Percy. What am I going to do?"

Suzie shut herself in her bedroom for the rest of the day. Let Noel manage without her, she was beyond caring, although she felt slightly guilty about deserting her grandson. He had been so good, seeming to sense her sadness and, not unlike Percy, had shown his support by staying close by. It was nice to know someone cared.

But Suzie had been distracted from Maurice's revelation by Jess. Not her realisation that John wasn't her dad but her comment about him staying in fancy hotels. Her expression had been shrewd, knowing and brought to the surface memories that Suzie now wondered if she'd deliberately repressed. John had been unfaithful and Jess had known it. For how long? Suzie wondered. Of course, she'd known too, she remembered now, the sudden awareness bringing back the hurt and anger again. But she hadn't made a fuss. It was easier to ignore it. Could she really blame him? She'd "let herself go" and was probably an embarrassment to him. So, the more time he spent "travelling", the more she ate, secure in the knowledge that, whatever he got up to when he was away, he would be discreet and he would never consider leaving her or his family in a million years.

She thought of Jess, just turned sixteen when John died and what a great help she'd been, comforting Sharon and Noel and supporting Suzie. What had she made of her mother's marriage? No doubt she would hear soon enough. Jess was in fighting form these days and Suzie knew that they would have to sit down and have a frank conversation very soon.

She heard the hall door close and looked at the clock. It was after six and Keith had collected Bobby over an hour ago, so it must be Noel heading off to work. She got out of bed and crept to the door, opening it softly. The last thing she wanted was to have to face him, not tonight. There was a note on the landing.

Gone to work, home late and heading out with Maurice in the morning — he's staying in a

*guesthouse. Keith's off work tomorrow so you
have the day to yourself.*

Noel x

Maurice, fuck, she'd forgotten all about him. So, he
hadn't had the guts to come back and face her. Suzie
climbed back into bed, relieved. Devious old bastard,
good riddance to him. Suzie would never forgive him
for encouraging her son into farming and taking him
away from her.

Her phone rang and she reached for it, hoping it
wasn't one of the kids, because she really didn't want to
talk to any of them.

"Hey, stranger."

"Doug! Are you feeling any better?" Delighted to
hear his voice strong and well, Suzie snuggled down.
She'd missed him.

"I've been fine for a week," he retorted.

Suzie's eyes flew open. "Mandy told me that, when
you weren't on the loo, you were asleep."

Doug groaned. "And you believed her? She told me
that you were having a rough time with Bobby and busy
preparing for your brother-in-law's arrival."

"And you believed her?" Suzie countered, smiling.

"We both should know better by now. So what have
you really been up to?"

Suzie's good humour disappeared as she thought
back on her day. "Trying to deal with a lot of shit and
drowning in it."

"What is it? Bobby?" he asked, concern in his voice.

384

"No, surprisingly. He's been pretty good lately. It's Noel. I slapped him. I'm sure the 'old' Suzie would never have done that or, if she had, would be full of remorse now. But I'm not. I'm mad as hell. I can barely look at him."

"You slapped Noel?"

"Yes." Suzie did feel ashamed of herself but it had been such a shock. "He's been lying to me," she said, defending herself. "He opted out of engineering in December and he's going to work on his uncle's farm in Limerick."

"And you're not happy?"

"Of course I'm not happy! Oh, and Jess knows."

"Knows what?" Doug sounded completely confused now.

"That John isn't her dad."

"You told her? Good for you."

"I didn't," Suzie admitted. "She worked it out for herself. I'm not sure how or when. Noel and Bobby arrived in before I could say anything. I stayed in my room after that. It seemed safest. Jess couldn't ask me any more awkward questions and I couldn't throttle Noel." She sighed, feeling lonely and cross, and a little peckish. "I don't suppose you fancy another takeaway?"

Suzie showered and changed, opened a bottle of wine and, closing the curtains on the miserable evening, lit a fire. She set the small coffee table and allowed Percy in. After having a good sniff around, he settled next to the fireplace. She was lighting some candles when Doug arrived.

"Let's start with Noel," he said after he'd hugged her and they were setting out the food.

"He's been lying to me," Suzie repeated. "After a nice cosy chat with his uncle Maurice, he gave up engineering and, all of a sudden, he wants to be a bloody farmer, in Limerick."

Doug frowned. "He's not going to get a qualification?"

"He's switching to agricultural science."

"Oh, well, that's good." He held up his hands when Suzie glared at him. "I know you'll miss him but most kids are leaving the *country* these days, not just the county."

"It's not that," Suzie said, annoyed that he didn't understand. "He's going back *there*. I haven't been back since the funeral and he needn't think that I'll visit him. I'll never set foot in that place again. As for the farming, that bloody business made me a widow and left me with three devastated young kids, with only Nora to turn to."

"I thought he was in purchasing."

She rolled her eyes. "Purchasing meat. Going to farms, vetting farmers and their stock."

"Hardly the same as being a farmer. Okay, sorry," he said when she glowered at him. "Didn't John's family support you?"

She shook her head. "His parents were quite old and had never shown much interest in him, let alone me or their grandchildren. I don't think they forgave him for not staying to work the farm with his brother. Maurice and his wife had no children and were a dry pair. When

386

he was widowed, Maurice kept to himself unless he was after something." When Doug said nothing, Suzie looked up from her food and met his solemn gaze. "What?"

He looked over at her. "The truth?"

"Of course," she said irritably.

"Your concern about Noel's safety is, frankly, ridiculous and I think masks what's really bothering you. You can't hold him back just because you weren't happy in Limerick."

Suzie felt hurt. He was supposed to be on her side. "Thanks for your support."

He shrugged. "You're the one who always says you prefer straight talking."

"But he's not doing this for the right reasons, Doug. Noel adored his dad and was so young when John died. Noel's doing this on a whim, because he thinks his dad would approve."

Doug shrugged. "Then he'll soon tire of it. It's a hard life and, if you're right, he should be longing to get back to the city by Christmas. He's young, Suzie. He's meant to make mistakes. We all did."

His words made Suzie's reaction seem melodramatic. And, if she was honest, she wasn't really worried that Noel would suffer the same fate as his dad. She was mad that he was leaving her for Maurice and Limerick. He was her baby and, after John died, she'd given him so much love and attention that this felt like a betrayal.

"So, tell me about Jess. How do you think she guessed?"

She sighed as her thoughts turned to the look on her daughter's face this morning. "The last night you were here, I had a little too much to drink."

He chuckled. "We both did. I had the hangover from hell the next day."

Suzie didn't laugh. "I slept in the following morning, and when I came downstairs Jess was here. She'd found the photo album and started questioning me about it and how come John wasn't in any of the photos."

"And she put two and two together."

Suzie sighed. "She must have. I don't know. We haven't talked about it yet. I don't know what I'm going to say to her."

Doug poured the wine. "I know that you wanted to keep it under wraps, Suzie, but this seems like a perfect opportunity to tell Jess the truth."

Suzie's food suddenly lost its flavour and she reached for her glass. "She'll hate me. Mind you, she probably does anyway."

"Why would she hate you? If you're honest with her I'm sure it will bring you closer than ever," Doug said with conviction.

Suzie was sceptical but, before she could comment, Percy was on his feet and barking at the door. "Hey, Percy, what's up?"

"Wow, he's loud."

"There must be someone outside. It better not be Maurice or I'll let him have it." Suzie was about to go to the window to check but froze when she heard the key in the hall door. "Feck. It's Noel."

"Stay calm, Suzie," Doug warned her.

388

She took another sip of wine, her eyes on the door. "I'm not making any promises."

"Mum? Where are you?"

"Jess." She shot Doug a horrified look and he squeezed her hand.

"It will be fine."

"In here," she called, her voice unnaturally high pitched.

Jess pushed open the door and pulled up short when she saw Doug. "Oh, sorry. I didn't know that you had company."

Doug stood and Suzie watched his face break into a happy smile. "Jess!"

Her daughter blinked a couple of times and then looked at her mother, a question in her eyes. "This is my good friend Doug, Jess."

Jess came closer, not taking her eyes off him. "Doug." Her eyes widened. "You're the man in that photo album." She shook her head. "I don't understand."

"You're right, this is Doug Hamilton, the man in the album and the MD of CML. By total coincidence, he is also the travel writer who Mandy works for."

"We're having a bit of fun at her expense," Doug confided. "She doesn't know we're old friends. I go by the name Douglas Thornton now."

Jess continued to stare at him and Suzie wondered if she remembered him. "Doug knew you when you were little."

"You probably don't remember." Doug's smile was affectionate.

"Are you my dad?" Jess blurted out.

His eyes widened and then he sighed, looking pensive and shook his head. "Unfortunately not."

Jess looked from him to her mother. "So, who is? Please, Mum, just tell me."

Suzie avoided Doug's gaze, which was pleading with her to be honest.

"You can't look me in the eye and tell me that John was my father."

Suzie gave a weary sigh. "He was your father in all the ways that counted."

Doug went to stand up. "I should go."

Suzie reached for his hand. "Please don't." She couldn't handle the thought of doing this alone and Doug might be able to fill in any gaps because there were still parts of her past that evaded her. She looked into her daughter's eyes. "I was single and pregnant when I went to an interview in CML. Doug was the MD, although his wife, Pamela, was running things when I joined."

"I just dropped in and meddled," Doug added, obviously trying to lighten the mood.

Suzie squeezed his hand and he returned the pressure. "My dad threw me out when he found out about you, and Doug took me in. We lost touch after his wife died and I never realised that Mandy's Douglas Thornton was also CML's owner, Doug Hamilton."

Jess's eyes slid to Doug's and she gave a small smile of acknowledgement before looking back at Suzie. "You still haven't answered the question. Who's my dad?"

"I'm afraid there's not much I can tell you other than he was gorgeous. You have his colouring, his hair and the same wonderful smile."

"What was his name?"

Suzie felt herself flush under her daughter's steely gaze. "I don't remember," she mumbled.

Jess flopped into a chair. "So I was the product of a one-night-stand?"

Suzie gave a guilty nod. "I'm afraid so."

"Didn't you consider abortion?" Jess asked.

Suzie looked up at her and smiled. "Not for a moment. But I did plan to give you up for adoption. I wanted you to go to a good home and have all the opportunities I never had. But then Doug gave me the job and a home" — Suzie smiled at him — "despite his better judgement. So, you see I owe him a lot, we both do."

"One of my better decisions. CML was a small company," he explained to Jess, "and we worked as a team, so it was important your mum fit in. And, despite the huge chip on her shoulder, she did."

Jess absorbed this for a moment. "So when did you meet Dad? I mean John?"

"When you were about six months old, I started working again part-time from the flat. I met John at one of the conferences we organised and he invited me out for a drink, and," Suzie smiled, "we hit it off straight away and he didn't care that I was an unmarried mother."

"So you loved him?" Jess looked a little disappointed.

"I did. He was lovely to me and, more importantly, he was great with you, Jess. Marrying John was a chance of a new start where no one knew me or would judge me. John adopted you as soon as we were married and raised you as his own. No one in Limerick ever knew that you weren't his."

"He loved me?" Jess looked at her in disbelief. "I think you mean he tolerated me. So much makes sense now."

"He did his best, Jess."

"It didn't feel that way. You know that you've turned him into some kind of saint since he died?"

"That's not true."

"Yes, it is. Have you forgotten all his business trips? Because *I* haven't. He missed my fifteenth birthday and never even phoned."

"I had forgotten the trips until you mentioned them today," Suzie admitted. "And it brought it all back. When did you know he was —" Suzie stopped, not sure how to word it. Not sure how much her daughter knew.

"Carrying on?" Jess supplied. "I'd suspected it for a couple of years. He'd hang up the phone when I walked into the room or take the dog for a walk and not let any of us go with him. Then one day, he called telling you that he had to stay on in Longford for a meeting first thing the next morning and when I was coming out of Eileen Doody's house that evening I saw him sitting in his car, kissing a woman."

Suzie was aghast at how much her daughter had kept to herself all these years. "Oh, Jess, I'm sorry. That must have upset you."

392

"I was more angry than upset," Jess said. "It wasn't just one woman either, was it?" Jess leaned forward in her chair. "The night before he died —"

Suzie shook her head and put up her hand to stop her daughter, feeling sick.

"Where was he, Mum? Was he with a woman?"

"I don't know." Suzie massaged her temples with trembling fingers. "I don't feel well."

"Jess . . ." Doug started, but she ignored him.

"You must know."

Suzie shook her head as the images flashed through her mind but, the more that she tried to focus, the more confused and upset she felt.

"Jess, I think that's quite enough," Douglas interjected, casting worried glances in her direction. "I think you should go. This is clearly distressing your mum and it's not her fault that she can't remember."

Jess shot him a guilty look and then glanced back at her mother. "No, it's not. I'm sorry, Mum. Thanks for telling me the truth."

"Are you okay?" Doug asked after the hall door had closed.

Suzie shook her head, trying to unravel the various memories and grasp at the snippets of truth in Jess's words, and then she gasped as the fog cleared momentarily.

"It's true. John was unfaithful. Something Jess said earlier triggered the memory. I don't know how many women there were but certainly more than one."

"I'm sorry."

But Suzie continued to stare into space, caught up in a memory struggling to surface. "Jess is right. He was with a woman the night before he died. She was waiting in his hotel room for him to come back to her. A young policeman let it slip but I wasn't that surprised." She shook her head, frustrated. "There's something else, just on the edge of my memory but I can't reach it."

"You've had a long and traumatic day, Suzie. You need sleep."

She nodded silently and stood up, feeling as if she was in some sort of trance. "Yes. Let yourself out, would you, Doug?" she said and walked out of the room. Percy followed her upstairs and lay down by the side of the bed and, putting out an absent hand to pat his head, Suzie drifted into a troubled sleep.

CHAPTER
THIRTY-EIGHT

Jess was shivering as she let herself into the flat, despite the fact that the rain had stopped and the evening sun had broken through the clouds. She lifted the phone to call Katie, desperate to talk about what had just happened, but her phone was switched off. Jess's eyes filled up as she remembered that Katie was on a plane, on her way to Jersey. She called Noel but his phone was off too. Probably just as well. He had enough problems of his own. Still feeling the need to talk, she left a message.

Jess tried to analyse her feelings. It was a relief to have it confirmed that John Connors wasn't her dad, that there was a reason he was distant and didn't show her the love that he'd showered on Sharon and Noel. She'd thought for many years that she must have done something to justify her father's lack of interest, and now she knew that it wasn't her fault at all. She would probably feel grateful to him for taking her in if it weren't for how he'd treated her mother.

How long had he cheated on her? Jess had become aware of it only in his last couple of years but it had made it hard for her to truly mourn him when he died.

Jess had felt angry that Suzie hadn't told her the truth about her father. Twenty-seven years and not a word. But, putting herself in her mother's position, she knew that she may well have done the same. Nice, kind and reliable, John must have been a very attractive option to a girl from such an unstable background. And, when she thought about the earlier years of her childhood, it had been a happy house.

Life had dealt her mother a tough hand and yet she'd achieved so much and been a pillar of strength for her three children, always loving and forever optimistic. At least she had been before the accident.

Although, now that she thought about it, Jess realised her mother was definitely improving. She was showing more self-restraint and it was clear that her memory was coming back. It was going to be a painful process. It was obvious that tonight she'd suddenly remembered more details of John's affairs than she let on. Jess felt bad for pushing her and reminding her of his infidelity. She was glad Doug had been there to intervene. In future, Jess promised herself to let her mum remember things in her own time.

Tomorrow, she would apologise for badgering her and she'd ask her out so that they could talk in private about her dad. Surely her mum must know something about him? She hadn't even thought to ask where he was from or how they met. And how in hell Suzie had managed to keep her parentage a secret for so long?

Her birth certificate must either have her real dad's name or say "father unknown". How had she not noticed that? When had she last seen it, for that matter? And then Jess thought of Mum's filing cabinet, where all the family papers were kept under lock and key. She'd insisted on handling all their school and university applications as they were so careless, and replacing birth certificates cost money. Jess smiled at her mother's innovative way of handling a tricky problem. She treated them all the same, so there had been no reason to question the way she did things.

Jess wandered around the flat, restless. If she stayed cooped up here alone she'd probably drink the full bottle of wine in the cupboard, so she decided to walk instead. Pocketing her keys and phone, Jess locked up and went outside, pausing on the step to take a deep breath of fresh air.

"Out to greet me? I knew you still cared."

Her eyes flew open to see Louis standing in front of her, swaying slightly. "What are you doing here?" she asked, wearily. "I told you the consequences if you bothered me again."

Louis moved closer, and slipped an arm round her. "I know you didn't mean it, Jess. You want me just as much as I want you."

She shoved him away and he stumbled. "No, Louis, I really don't. Now leave or I'm going to scream 'rape' and you'll end up in a cell for the night." She held his gaze to make sure that he knew she wasn't kidding.

"You heard her. Get lost."

Jess looked up to see her brother standing behind Louis. Her boss turned slowly, sighing. "You know, you've a lousy sense of timing?"

"Just go, Louis," Jess said.

"Fine. You're a lousy lay, anyway." He pushed past Noel, only to come up against the brick wall of Cal's chest.

"I think you owe the lady an apology," Cal said.

Her drunken boss raised his head to try to focus on the man blocking his way. "What's it got to do with you? Are you fucking her now?"

In the blink of an eye, Cal had slammed him against the pillar. "I think you should apologise and go home, don't you?"

Louis's eyes bulged as he tried to push Cal off him. "Hey, I was just kidding! Sorry, Jess. If you call off this animal I'll be on my way."

Jess nodded to Cal, who dropped him reluctantly, and Louis stumbled down the path, muttering to himself. "And don't come back or your arrest will be front-page news," she called after him.

"What an asshole. What did you ever see in him?"

Jess glared at her brother. "Don't start with me, Noel. I've had enough for one day."

"Mine hasn't exactly been a picnic. You left me a message and I came straight round to check on you, and now you're giving me grief?"

Jess looked at his sad eyes and haggard appearance and hugged him. "Sorry. Come on up." She turned to face Cal. "Thanks."

He shook his head, his hazel eyes sad. "Don't thank me. I've behaved like an idiot. He told me that you were together again and I believed him."

She stared at him. "That morning?"

He nodded, shamefaced. "He stopped me at the gate and said I shouldn't bother you, that you were going to need your sleep. He winked at me and I saw red. I'm sorry, Jess."

Jess thought of all that had gone on in the last few weeks — hell, in the last few hours — and Cal's misreading of a situation didn't seem that big a deal any more. She gave a weak smile. "I can hardly blame you for falling for one of his lines. I've been doing it for months."

He swept her up in a hug and she rested her head on his chest, revelling in the feel of his strong arms around her.

"Can you two put that on hold until I've gone?" Noel complained from the top of the stairs.

Jess reluctantly pulled back and smiled. Cal took her hand in his and they went up to join her brother.

While Jess made coffee, Noel sat drumming his fingers on the table, complaining about how unreasonable their mother was being.

"It's not easy for her, Noel," she said when he stopped to draw breath. "Her memory seems to be coming back in bits and pieces and I think she's confused and scared. I'm sure the circumstances surrounding Dad's death are in there. Think about it. It's like she's reliving it all. That has to be so painful."

"I suppose," he said, looking shamefaced. "Anyway, why did you call me? You sounded upset."

Jess handed him and Cal mugs before taking her own between her hands. Should she tell him her mum's secret? She didn't see any real harm in it. It might be a shock but it didn't really affect him or Sharon. Jess took a deep breath. "Not upset. In shock, I suppose. I've had some suspicions for a while and Mum just confirmed them. John Connors wasn't my father."

Noel grinned and then stared at her, his eyes widening as he saw that she was serious. "What?"

"Mum was a single mother when she met your dad."

"But why didn't they tell you, tell us?" Noel asked, still looking dumbfounded.

"I don't know. She got upset when I started asking questions and Doug suggested I leave it."

Noel frowned. "Doug?"

"Ah, yes, that's another thing. Douglas, her so-called boyfriend, Mandy's boss?" She smiled, remembering the man's astonished expression when she asked if he was her dad. "It turns out he was Mum's boss too before she was married. He gave her a job, despite her being pregnant. Granddad threw her out when he found out she was pregnant and Doug took her in. That's why they're so close."

Noel looked immediately suspicious. "What did he get in return?"

Jess looked at him in disgust. "It was nothing like that and, no, he's not my dad. I thought it might be him because I found a photo album with my baby pictures and he was in most of them."

400

"So who *is* your father?" Cal asked. It was the first time he'd spoken, but he'd been watching her intently as she talked.

She sighed. "No idea. All Mum's told me so far is that I look like him but she doesn't even remember his name. It was a one-night stand."

"So you're only my half-sister?" Noel looked a little forlorn.

She put an arm round his shoulders. "What difference does it make? Mum is still our mum and I'm your big sister and will continue to kick your butt when you do stupid stuff. Why on earth didn't you tell me that you wanted to be a farmer?"

Noel shook his head and sighed. "At first I wanted time to think about it, to make sure I was making the right decision. Then I needed to talk to the college to see what my options were. The plan was to finish the engineering course and then take a postgraduate in agricultural science. I was just about ready to tell Mum when she had the accident."

He raised sad eyes to meet hers. "That knocked me for six and I couldn't concentrate on anything, let alone engineering so I dropped out. When Mum came home, I couldn't leave her. I told Maurice that we'd have to delay our plans until she was back on her feet." He sighed. "Then Sharon got sick and we had to take care of Bobby and I certainly couldn't leave then.

"Meanwhile, I'm feeling seriously guilty about letting Maurice down. It looks as if he needs an operation but he won't agree to it because there's no one to look after the farm."

"Oh, Noel." Jess looked at him, distraught at all he'd shouldered alone. "Why didn't you talk to me?"

"Or me," Cal said, looking disgusted. "I thought we were mates."

"There was too much going on and, be honest, you and Sharon would have been furious with me if I'd told Mum my plans."

Jess was silent. She couldn't argue with that.

"You still could have talked to me," Cal insisted.

"It doesn't matter now, does it? She knows and she's furious, just as I knew she would be. She even slapped me."

"She didn't!" Jess said, astounded.

Noel sighed. "When she was gone for so long I was really afraid I'd sent her over the edge."

"Well you didn't. You know how Mum overreacts these days, but she's tougher than she looks." If only he knew how much their mother had already been through. Jess thought of John's philandering ways. But she wasn't going to tell him about that and she doubted her mother would, either. She put a comforting hand on Noel's arm. "She'll get used to the idea," she said with more conviction than she felt. Mum's memory returning was bound to throw up more details that they were all blissfully unaware of.

Jess thought of the various accounts she'd read of other brain-injury sufferers regaining their memory, and knew that there could be a bumpy ride ahead of them. But they'd come this far, they'd get through the rest.

402

She glanced at her brother who still looked miserable. "Cheer up, bro. If you want to be a farmer, then that's what you're going to be." She met Cal's eyes and mouthed, "Help."

"Jess is right, Noel," Cal agreed. "You may have to postpone it, but that's all."

"Surely Maurice could get a farm manager in the meantime," Jess said.

"He could, but he doesn't trust anyone who isn't family."

"He's a grown man, Noel," Cal told him. "It's up to him to make some sort of arrangement until you're free to take over."

"Does Mum know Maurice is sick?"

"She doesn't know how serious it is but, let's face it, she wouldn't care anyway. She can't stand the man."

"I still think you should fill her in," Jess said.

"Should I go home and talk to Mum now?" Noel asked, uncertainly.

Jess thought of how bemused and anxious her mum had been when she left. "Leave it for tonight. She's upset enough after our chat, and Doug's there, looking after her."

"Pick a moment when she's relaxed," Cal advised, "or wait until she raises the subject."

Jess groaned. "Er, don't you think there's something else we're forgetting?"

"What?" Noel looked at Jess.

"Shouldn't we bring Sharon up to speed on everything?"

"That might be an idea," Cal agreed.

Noel gave a grim smile. "No time like the present."

"This is like something out of a soap" was Sharon's incredulous reaction after a long three-way call. "Are you okay, Jess?"

"I'm absolutely fine," Jess assured her, warmed by the concern in her voice.

"Good. Don't worry about Mum, Noel. This hasn't been an easy time for her, either, and we have to remember that she's still in recovery. I'm sure, once she's had time to think about it, she'll give you her blessing. Jess has probably taken the spotlight off you for now."

Jess exchanged a surprised look with her brother. "You sound remarkably chilled, Shaz."

"All thanks to Percy," Sharon chuckled. "Bobby's been so much more relaxed these last couple of days and he and Mum are closer too."

When they finished the call, Noel stood up. "I'll head off. I have to see a man about a cow," he joked with a sad smile.

"Maurice?" Jess asked.

"Yup."

"It will work out, bro. Hang in there."

Noel hugged her. "Thanks, Jess. I'll talk to you tomorrow. Goodnight, Cal."

There was an awkward silence after he'd gone and Jess watched nervously as Cal moved over to sit on the sofa next to her. He took her hand, massaging her wrist with his thumb.

"You've had quite a day. It must have been a shock finding out that your dad isn't your dad, so to speak."

Jess thought about how comforted she felt now that she knew the truth. "It may sound cold but I'm glad John isn't my father. He never treated me the same as Sharon and Noel. He was always slightly awkward around me, as if going through the motions."

"And you turned yourself inside out trying to impress him and win his love," Cal guessed.

"That's the psychologist talking," she teased, "but, yes, you're right. I worked harder at school and took up basketball because he loved it, all in an effort to win some praise. I'd watch him help Sharon with her reading and fooling round, wrestling with Noel, and wonder what I'd done wrong. Still" — she smiled, although there was a lump in her throat — "I had Mum."

"Oh, Jess. I'm sorry. It was wrong of him. He'd taken you on and adopted you. He should have treated you the same. No wonder you've never had a successful relationship," he mused.

She groaned, pushing him away. "Oh, please. Don't tell me that I was searching for a father figure."

He shrugged. "Maybe not a father figure but someone who would approve of you." Cal drew her closer again and tipped up her chin so he could look into her eyes. "You're incredibly beautiful and clever, and yet you seem surprised and almost grateful when a man shows any interest in you."

"That's not true," Jess argued, flushing.

"Isn't it? I've watched you date some right berks over the years. I could never understand what you saw in them, but now it makes sense. You've never believed you deserved better, have you?"

His eyes held hers and Jess swallowed the lump in her throat. "That's ridiculous," she whispered, although when she thought about it . . .

"Not really. You wanted to be loved and, it didn't matter what lowlife offered it, you took it."

"Enough. This isn't a consultation." She tried to push him away again, but Cal held on tight.

"No, I'd never talk to a patient like this. But I'm not talking to a patient. I'm talking to the girl I've been dreaming of holding for years."

Jess searched his face, usually so guarded, and saw tenderness there and nervousness too. "Years?" she asked, gulping.

"Years. Occasionally there were minor distractions but I always came back to you."

"But why didn't you say something?" she asked, thinking of how she'd longed for him to notice her.

"I suppose, I didn't want to be one of your many boyfriends," he admitted.

She looked at him and saw the vulnerability in his eyes. Jess raised her hand unconsciously and caressed his cheek. "What *did* you want?"

He turned his mouth into her hand and kissed her palm. "I wanted to be the only one. I still want to be the only one, Jess."

She stared at him, afraid to hear him, to believe what he was saying. Yet, despite the fact that they'd

406

exchanged only a handful of kisses, there was no doubting the chemistry between them and the shiver that ran down her spine simply at the feel of his lips on her hand. Had she ever lost herself in a man's eyes the way she lost herself in his? When Cal looked at her, she felt he could see right into her soul and there was no place to hide. Was he truly different from the others? Could she trust these feelings? In his favour, Cal was her only boyfriend to earn Katie's approval, which was no mean feat. He wanted her to be "the one". Jess looked up at him. "Then what are you waiting for? Kiss me," she said.

Cal smiled, triumphant. "Gladly." He lowered his lips to touch hers in a soft, slow, sweet kiss and then started to trace tiny kisses all along the edge of her mouth until finally returning to mould his mouth to hers. Okay, so, on top of being handsome and kind and sensitive, he was a great kisser. Surely this man was too good to be true. Stop overthinking, Jess told herself and, winding her arms round his neck, she did exactly that and gave herself up to the moment.

CHAPTER
THIRTY-NINE

Suzie sat on the kitchen step, exhausted, absently fondling Percy's head. She was supposed to be going to the support group today but she couldn't be bothered. It depressed her rather than helped her, but, then, she'd never been into publicly sharing her feelings. She'd been raised to put up and shut up.

Doug called to check on her and tell her about the CML get-together he was planning. Suzie said yes and no in the right places but she wasn't really paying attention. When he asked if she'd talked to either Noel or Jess, Suzie found an excuse to hang up.

Jess had apologised for upsetting her and wanted to take her out to dinner, and Noel was always lurking around, obviously wanting to talk, but Suzie wasn't ready to talk to anyone yet, even Doug.

There was so much going on in her head that she didn't have the time or energy for conversation. The memories that had evaded her for so long were coming back, fast and furious. She went from being angry to upset to confused and sad and then back around again. Her days were spent staring into space and avoiding people, bar Bobby. For the first time, she welcomed and appreciated his quiet presence, finally recognising that his silence wasn't a sign of attitude or insolence but simply a part of his character. Not a bad trait. Too many people spoke when they had little to say.

Bobby certainly seemed to be more comfortable with her silence than the mindless, childish chatter she'd felt obliged to make. Sometimes the only noise in the house was Radio Two, playing quietly in the background while Bobby's pencil scratched on paper and Percy padded between them.

Suzie had taken to waiting until she was collecting her grandson from school to walk the dog. It was worth it just to see the child's face light up when he saw Percy waiting for him at the school gate. Once inside the park, Suzie would allow Bobby to take the lead and she'd carry his schoolbag while he walked Percy, his face screwed up in concentration. Then the dog would sit patiently while Bobby played on the swings before they made their way home. It meant a shorter and less stressful time pent up in the house.

If Noel was home, Suzie went to the supermarket or had a cuppa with Aileen, anything to avoid talking to him. She'd confided in her neighbour about her son's plans but said nothing about all the other stuff going on. She couldn't talk about any of it until she'd figured it all out herself.

"Cooee! Only me."

Speak of the devil. Suzie sighed as she remembered what day it was. She and Aileen always had a cuppa and a natter on Mondays.

"Hello, love." Aileen went to fill the teapot and found the kettle empty. "You haven't even filled it. What's up?" She carried it to the sink and then set it on to boil before sitting down at the table.

"Nothing." Suzie put her hand up to flatten her hair and tightened the belt on her dressing gown.

Aileen's eyes narrowed. "You look like death warmed up and it's eleven o'clock and you're not even dressed. Are you sick?"

"I've felt better," Suzie said, truthfully.

"Will a cuppa and a nice warm scone help?"

"Of course." Suzie said, managing a smile. The phone rang and she groaned irritably. There weren't many people she wanted to talk to but she relaxed when she saw the display. "It's Nora," she said, answering it as Aileen nodded and made the tea.

"Hi, Suzie. Is everything okay? I only just got your messages. I was away for the weekend and forgot my phone."

Suzie plunged straight in, her eyes on Aileen. "I've started remembering things."

Immediately she had both women's attention.

"Oh, that's great, Suzie," Nora said, all enthusiastic and, when Suzie said nothing, added. "Isn't it?" Suzie heard Nora's uneasy tone and glanced up at Aileen, seeing a similar look in her eyes. This wasn't a conversation to be had over the phone.

"Can we get together someday next week? You, me and Aileen? I need to talk to you both and clear up a few things."

"Sure. Wednesday?"

"Does Wednesday suit?" Suzie asked Aileen, who gave a solemn nod. "Yes, that's fine, Nora. Thanks, I appreciate it. I'll text you later with the arrangements."

"Sounds serious," Aileen remarked, buttering a scone.

"I suppose it is. There's just so much to tell you and so many questions I want to ask. I need to figure out what's fact and what's fiction, and I'm hoping that you and Nora will be able to help."

Aileen frowned. "I don't like seeing you so troubled. That's not going to help your recovery."

"I'm fine. It's just exhausting trying to make sense of everything going on in here." Suzie tapped the side of her head.

Aileen patted her hand. "I'll do whatever I can to help, Suzie."

Suzie and Percy were at the school gate when the bell rang. She smiled when she saw Bobby hurtling towards them. He dumped his schoolbag on the ground and crouched down to hug the dog. Percy accepted the adoration and licked the boy's cheek. Suzie could just imagine what Sharon would say if she saw that.

"Don't let Percy lick your face," she told him, picking up his bag.

"Why not?" He fell into step beside her.

"Dogs lick everything, even disgusting things, and you really don't want him to lick you with a poo-tongue, do you?"

"Yuck!" Bobby wiped his face in disgust. "Can I hold the lead?"

"No. Remember? Not until we're inside the park," she said.

"Okay." He smiled and trotted along beside her.

"Did you have a good time at school?"

"No."

"Oh. Why not?"

"We were telling jokes but no one laughed at mine."

"Did you laugh at any of theirs?" Suzie asked him, knowing he rarely understood humour.

"No."

"There you go, then. We all laugh at different things." She pointed at a man walking towards them with a huge German shepherd and a tiny Pekingese. "Look, twins!"

Bobby frowned. "They're not twins."

"You see? And I thought that was a good joke."

"It wasn't."

"See? We're all different." With that, the man stopped to let the larger dog relieve himself and then walked on, leaving the mess behind him. "Hey!" she called after him. "You need to pick that up." The man ignored her and kept walking. "What an arsehole," she said, angrily.

Bobby nodded. "He had a big arse too."

Suzie burst out laughing. "Now that was funny."

They were just home and Bobby was eating his snack when Sharon arrived. "Surprise!"

She came into the kitchen and hugged her son. "Hello, darling."

Suzie watched warily. "What are you doing here?"

"Keith said he might be delayed so I said I'd pick up Bobby. Have you done your homework?" she asked him.

"We're not in long. He's going to start straight after his snack, aren't you, Bobby?"

The child nodded.

"Don't forget your reading," Sharon said as he climbed down and went into the hall to get his school bag.

Bobby grunted and went into the other room. She smiled at Suzie. "A few weeks ago it would have taken an hour and lots of tears to achieve that."

"I know, isn't it great?" Suzie sat down, shooting nervous looks at her daughter. "Have you been talking to Jess or Noel?" she asked.

"I have."

"Is that all you have to say?" Suzie said, exasperated by Sharon's nonchalance.

"What do you want me to say? You got pregnant when you were single, so did I. The only difference was, Keith stuck around. Jess seems cool about it. That's all that matters, right?"

"But how will you feel if she wants to tell people?" Suzie asked.

Sharon shrugged. "It doesn't really affect me."

"It's bound to get back to Maurice," Suzie continued. "It will be a huge scandal."

"That doesn't worry me and I doubt it will bother Noel or Jess either." Sharon glanced up at her. "How about you?"

Suzie snorted. "That lot always gossiped about me anyway. What do I care?"

"There you go, then." Sharon helped herself to a pear from the fruit bowl in the centre of the table.

"It will be a lot harder on Noel if he goes to live there," Suzie pointed out.

Sharon wiped her mouth with a piece of kitchen towel and looked Suzie in the eye. "Mum, if you're trying to get me to talk Noel out of going to Limerick, you're wasting your time. He really wants to do this and I'm completely behind him."

Suzie's eyes widened as she looked at her younger daughter. "You knew he was going all along, didn't you?"

"He told me at Christmas that he was considering it, but then you had the accident and he never mentioned it again, and I didn't think to ask. Why are you so against it?"

Suzie frowned. "Farming is a hard life and it's dangerous."

"It's what he wants to do. I just want him to be happy. I'd have thought you would, too."

"I'll miss him." There. Suzie had said it. She had expected Noel to move out but hadn't thought he'd leave Dublin, and certainly not to go *there*.

"Oh, Mum." Sharon leaned over to hug her, and Suzie felt the firmness of her bump.

"Would you want Bobby to go away?" Suzie said into her daughter's shoulder.

Sharon stroked her hair. "Of course not. I'm sorry. But it's not far, not with the motorway. I know that you

414

have sad memories, Mum, but there were so many happy ones, too."

Suzie sighed and rested her head on Sharon's shoulder. "I suppose there were."

CHAPTER
FORTY

Mandy frowned at the note on her desk, reading it while she tugged off her jacket. Douglas was out but there was no mention as to where, just that he was having some friends over on Saturday night and asking her to book a caterer. In typical Thornton form, he hadn't given exact details as to whether he wanted, hors d'oeuvres or a five-course dinner. She sent him a text asking him to clarify. His response came back surprisingly quickly.

Casual supper for approx. 10. I'll pick up the booze.

She scowled at his mysteriousness. He was probably enjoying keeping her in the dark, knowing how curious she'd be — and she was. Her life must be seriously dull at the moment. She'd have to get out more. This Croatian trip had become a ridiculous obsession.

Douglas finally made an appearance as she was sitting eating a sandwich and reading a magazine. "Hi. Food is organised but I need to let them know what time you want it delivered, if you need crockery, glasses and cutlery, and if you want them to stay to serve."

"Oh, God, no, that's far too formal. All I need is the food."

"Who are you inviting?" Mandy asked, giving in to her curiosity.

"People who used to work for me a lifetime ago."

"Oh." Sounded like a boring pensioners' evening. Still, she was curious. "Am I invited?"

"Yeah, you can keep an eye on the caterers."

"Thanks a lot," Mandy said. She was unable to gauge his mood lately. Something was definitely going on but her probing had got her nowhere. Maybe Saturday would reveal something about her enigmatic boss.

Suzie phoned Nora to let her know she was running late.

"Take your time, sweetheart. Aileen and I are having a nice chat."

Slipping her phone back into her pocket, Suzie continued to walk along the beach, going over everything in her head again before talking to her friends. What she needed to know most of all was what she'd told them about John's infidelity. She knew that she'd confided in Nora but she wasn't sure exactly how much detail she'd gone into. It would be news to Aileen, she was sure. She'd put all that behind her when she left Limerick. Her overriding wish was to keep it from Noel and Sharon. Whatever he'd done to her and Jess, John had loved his children and they him, and she wouldn't take that from Sharon and Noel. Of course, she needed Jess to go along with that. Would she?

Stopping, Suzie stared out to sea, took a few deep breaths and turned to head back up the strand and across the road to the restaurant.

The two women were deep in conversation and halfway through a bottle of wine when Suzie arrived.

"I won't get much sense out of you pair, will I?" she joked, joining them at the round table in the busy restaurant.

"Not true." Aileen held up the basket with one slice of bread in it. "Soakage."

"Have you had enough time to think?" Nora asked gently after they'd ordered.

Suzie nodded, looking at each of them in turn. "I told you, my memory seems to be returning but I'm not sure that I can trust it. I'd like to run some things past you and see what's true and what's imagined. And, if you know something that I don't, please tell me. I need to know that my memories are as real as I believe them to be.

"Also, I've known you both a long time and regard you as my closest friends, but I've kept something from you because, well, I had to." She pulled a face. "At least, I *think* I've kept it to myself, but you may tell me different."

"This sounds serious." Aileen sat forward in her chair, looking concerned.

"It's not bad news and nothing to do with my health, or anything like that," Suzie reassured her.

418

"Thank goodness for that," Nora said, reaching for her glass. "Go on, then."

The two women listened intently, while Suzie told them about Jess, about John and his affairs, about Noel's decision to go into farming with his uncle, about Douglas Thornton's true identity and then there was the small matter of her sister.

"I was stunned that Jess knew what John was up to but, I suppose, she was a smart teenager and protective of me," she said, finally. "The other two don't know anything at all about their dad's affairs and that's the way I'd like to keep it. Their memories of their dad are untainted and, as that's all they have left, I don't want to take it away from them."

"It won't go any further," Nora promised, and looked at Aileen, who immediately nodded.

"Everything you've told us is in confidence, Suzie. I won't tell a soul."

"Thank you." Suzie shrugged and gave them a nervous smile. "I think that's everything."

"That's quite a lot to take in," Nora said. "Firstly, how's Jess?"

"Fine. It turns out that Doug was right and she had noticed John treated her differently. Now she finally understands why and that she wasn't to blame."

Nora frowned. "Well, of course she wasn't, the poor child."

Suzie said nothing. She wasn't going to start criticising her husband. The facts spoke for themselves. "You honestly never looked at her colouring and wondered?" Suzie smiled.

"Never gave it a thought," Aileen said with a shrug.

"Me neither," Nora said. "The other two are the image of John, and Jess is like you. And your memory is correct. You never even hinted at this before," she reassured Suzie. "You did exactly as John asked, even after his death. Not that he deserved such loyalty."

"Doug kept at me to tell Jess. He said she had a right to know. But I was so sure that she hadn't suspected anything, I didn't see the point."

Nora nodded. "You told me that you were sure he was cheating on you and I wanted you to confront him and threaten to leave and take the children away, but you wouldn't hear of it."

"I wouldn't have gone through with it. And it didn't seem fair to expose the kids to his behaviour. And" — Suzie sighed — "I suppose part of me still felt grateful to him for giving me and Jess his name and a home."

"Fuck that!" Aileen said, looking outraged. "You gave up everything to follow him to the middle of nowhere, gave him two wonderful children, and you were a good and faithful wife."

Nora was nodding her agreement. "You were a great wife, Suzie. It didn't matter how much he was out wining and dining in the name of work, you put up with it all without complaint and reared three kids almost single-handed."

"Did I tell you about Mandy coming on to him?" Suzie asked Nora.

Nora shook her head. "No but, to be honest, it doesn't surprise me. She'd flirt with any man with a pulse and certainly wouldn't let the small fact that he was your husband get in the way. You were crazy to let her come and stay."

"You never liked her." Suzie said with a wry smile.

"No, I didn't. I always felt she used you, and, no matter what you did for her, she never appreciated or even acknowledged it. When she moved in with you that time, I just didn't trust her. I always got the feeling she was envious of you."

"Hardly. The last thing Mandy wanted was a family or a boring life in the country."

"No, but I think she craved security. When you moved back to Dublin I expected you to see a lot more of each other, but it was quite the reverse. Now I know why."

"I still don't know if Jess knows about her. She walked in on John and I rowing one night but I don't remember what it was about or what she overheard. But she's certainly not close to her aunt."

"She might know. Jess was old enough to realise what Mandy was really like. Your sister isn't exactly a nice person. And, if there was no love lost before, it got worse after your accident. The kids blame her. Apparently she practically bullied you into going along that night."

Aileen nodded. "That's right. You were sick with some virus and on antibiotics, but Mandy had been given two tickets to the opening of the hotel's new leisure centre and begged you to go along. The bubbly was flowing and you know, Suzie, it always goes straight to your head."

Suzie didn't remember any of that but, then, the time immediately preceding the accident was all still a blank.

"The kids were stunned when you and Mandy became so pally after you came out of the coma," Nora said. "I know that I was flabbergasted. I knew you couldn't possibly remember how she'd behaved and it made me mad as hell. It was like she was laughing at you. And then those clothes she persuaded you to buy . . ." Nora practically growled, her eyes dark with fury.

"I didn't know any of the history between you," Aileen said, nodding, "but I never liked or trusted your sister, to be honest. When did you remember what she'd done?"

"It just came back to me when Jess walked in on me and Doug the other night, wanting to know if he was her dad." Suzie couldn't help smiling. "I thought he was going to have another heart attack."

She sobered again as she thought of the flashbacks she'd had since then. "It's odd. I've been so angry with Mandy, as if it had all just happened. And, the more I thought about it, the angrier I got at the way she's pushed her way back into my life."

"She's a bad sort," Aileen said darkly.

"I agree, although . . ." Nora hesitated.

"Go on." Suzie saw the mixed emotions cross her friend's face. "Please?"

"I was just remembering John's funeral. Don't be angry with me," Nora begged.

"Of course not." Suzie searched her face and gave her a small smile of reassurance. "Tell me."

"Mandy was distraught that day, and not in an attention-seeking way. I think it may have been the only time I saw her without makeup, and her face was a mess from crying."

"Crocodile tears," Aileen scoffed. "Probably mourning the fact that there was one less married man in the world for her to try it on with!"

Startled by her neighbour's vehemence, Suzie burst out laughing. Her two friends stared at her in shocked surprise, which only made Suzie laugh harder.

"What's funny?" Nora asked, starting to chuckle herself.

Aileen's lips twitched. "That injury knocked all the feckin' sense out of your head, woman!" she said, and then she was laughing too.

Nora shook her head, wiping tears from her eyes. "I've no idea why we're laughing. This isn't remotely funny."

Suzie finally managed to pull herself together. "I know but, I suppose, if we don't laugh we cry."

Nora nodded. "Don't waste tears on John or Mandy, for that matter. It's all in the past. You've seemed so happy these last few months and now you've a new grandchild on the way too."

"Yes, onwards and upwards," Aileen agreed, "but get that poisonous bitch out of your life."

"And make your peace with Noel," Nora added. "He's heartbroken."

"Yeah. Why are you so angry with him anyway?" Aileen looked at her in confusion.

"He never sat his exams and now, completely out of the blue, he's decided he wants to be a farmer." Suzie tossed her head in disgust. "And not somewhere local but on his uncle's farm in Limerick. Feckin' Maurice. I could murder him. I thought I was finished with that bloody family and place."

"Why do you hate it so much?" Aileen asked.

Suzie stared at her. "You have to ask? That's where my husband cheated on me and that's where he died. But not straightaway." Tears threatened again as Suzie remembered her shock when she saw John in the hospital that day.

"His injuries were horrific and yet he was conscious. He kept saying how sorry he was, over and over." She shook her head. "He was nine hours in surgery but died on the operating table. I wanted to die too at that moment. For all his faults, John was my rock. But I had to go home and tell the children their daddy was dead. I think that's reason enough to hate Limerick."

They were silent for a moment and then Nora handed her a tissue. "You asked us to fill in the gaps?"

Suzie wiped her eyes and nodded.

"I remember John's accident too, Suzie. But I remember it very differently. The children were at school when I got word what had happened. I picked them up from school, and took them back to my house. I'd rented a video, *Robots*, I think it was. We bought ice cream and popcorn and stuffed our faces and laughed until we cried. We had a lovely time. Ask Noel. Even now, he'll tell you he remembers that day. But not because of what was happening at the hospital.

"It was a dreadful day for you, but not for him. Sure, he cried when he found out his daddy was dead, but he didn't know the details. He didn't see John in hospital. He doesn't have the ghastly images in his head that you do. What he remembers are the happy times in Limerick, looking after the chickens, helping feed new lambs and sitting up on the tractor between his dad and uncle, as proud as punch."

Suzie smiled reluctantly. "I have a photo of that. It was probably the first time John had sat on a moving tractor in ten years. He was more used to the new shiny ones at the Ploughing Championships. If Noel really is into farming, it's not because of his dad. John was never interested in running the farm. He preferred the business side and wearing a smart suit, not getting up at six and mucking out. The only time he came close to getting his hands dirty was when he shook a farmer's hand," Suzie chuckled good-naturedly. John had never been cut out for the farming life and thanked God every day that he had a brother who was.

"Noel got his love of the land from Maurice," Nora said. "Remember how much time he spent over there?"

Suzie looked at her in surprise and shook her head. "Really?"

"Yes. You would be yelling at him to do his homework and as soon as it was done he'd be out the door, on his bike and off down the lane to help Maurice. We never saw him during the summer months. He'd be over there from the crack of dawn."

"I don't remember any of that." Suzie said, but, now that Nora mentioned it, she recalled a scruffy little boy with freckles who was always smiling.

Suzie sighed as guilt set in for the way she'd treated Noel these last few weeks. And she'd slapped him! She closed her eyes to stem the tears that threatened again.

"He was very withdrawn when he first came to Dublin," Aileen chipped in.

"Thanks for that, Aileen," she muttered and heard Nora sigh at her neighbour's tactlessness.

"Until Cal took him under his wing, of course," she hurried on. "Then he was grand."

Suzie smiled. That she knew was true. "Anything else I need to know?" she asked.

The other two women looked at each other and shook their heads.

"Have you talked to Mandy?" Nora asked.

"Have you told her you remember her making a pass at your husband?" Aileen added.

Suzie shook her head, dabbing her eyes with a tissue. Thank goodness she'd had the foresight not to wear mascara. "No, I've been avoiding her. I wanted to wait until I remembered everything before I talked to her. Doug's hosting a CML reunion at the weekend and she'll probably be at that."

"Why would he have invited her?" Aileen asked, frowning.

"Devilment! He wants her to know that we've been making a fool of her, pretending to be dating. He's really annoyed at the way she tried to come between us. I think he may be planning a confrontation of his own."

426

"Good for him," Nora said. "He's a sweetheart. I'm a little sad that you're just good friends."

"I thought he was too old for me," Suzie retorted.

"Technically, yes." Nora smiled. "But he doesn't look his age and you've been having such a good time with him."

Suzie smiled. "I have."

"Are you okay, Suzie?" Aileen asked. "This has been a very stressful few weeks."

"It has but, thanks to the meditation classes and Percy, I'm coping. I still get angry and upset, but then I remind myself that this is all history now and, as I said, I dealt with it a long time ago. I wish I knew for sure if I ever confronted Mandy, though. I can't believe she had the nerve to come back into my life the way she has. She seems to have no conscience."

"None," Nora agreed.

"And I still hate the idea of losing Noel. I'll miss him so much; Bobby will too."

"He'll visit," Aileen said, patting her hand.

"Farmers don't get much free time," Suzie assured her.

"You can come and stay with me," Nora offered, "and he can visit you there. No need to go near the farm or see Maurice."

"Thanks, Nora." Suzie smiled at her dear friend. "I'll think about it."

When they got home, Nora ran up to the loo and Suzie went into the kitchen to make them some tea and check on Percy.

"I've taken him out and settled him," Noel said from the chair in the corner.

Suzie started. "Thanks. Why are you sitting here in the dark?" She switched on the lamp and looked at him.

"I was waiting for you. I can't sleep until I know you're home safe. Role reversal, eh?"

"You won't know whether I'm home or not when you're back in Limerick," Suzie retorted, before she could stop herself.

"If you don't want me to go, I won't," he said, sounding weary and resigned.

Suzie settled on the arm of his chair and sighed too. "I want you to go. No, that's not true, I don't, but I understand you need to, and I want you to be happy. So go."

Noel looked startled. "Why the change of heart?"

"Thank Nora. She reminded me of how much you loved helping your uncle Maurice when you were a kid. I'd forgotten all that."

"I did try to tell you —"

"I know," she snapped. "Sheesh! I've said I'm okay with it. Do you want blood?"

"Just a little more grovelling." Noel grinned and enveloped her in a hug. "Thanks, Mum. You don't know how much this means to me. I promise I won't desert you until after Sharon's baby's born."

"I'd really appreciate that."

He kissed the top of her head and stood up. "Goodnight, Mum."

"Night, love."

She was still sitting there when Nora came in, smiling, and applauded her silently. "Well done."

Suzie nodded, sniffing back her tears. "Make me a cuppa, Nora, would you?"

CHAPTER
FORTY-ONE

The following evening, Suzie was sitting in the same small bistro, this time waiting for Jess. There was a child chuckling at a table nearby and Suzie smiled, thinking of her grandson. Bobby was easier to deal with now that they understood him better, and watching him make progress made her problems seem inconsequential. She felt hopeful. Sharon's pregnancy was going well, and she herself had survived a traumatic brain injury. She knew that she wasn't out of the woods yet, that she would still lose her temper from time to time and there were probably more memories waiting to shake her confidence; but she felt calmer and reminded herself every day of how lucky she was.

She also knew that, second time around, she would not be taken for a fool, and she certainly wouldn't waste time on people who were two-faced, unkind or had a hidden agenda.

Suzie had given up completely on the support group, feeling she didn't belong there. She just couldn't bring herself to open up to a group of strangers. The meditation, however, was wonderful and she put it to good use whenever she started to get anxious or annoyed. She was beginning to feel in control again and, now that she'd found most of the pieces of the puzzle that was her past, Suzie felt she'd be able to put it behind her and move on. She tried not to think about Noel and his impending defection to Limerick. That might take a little longer to adjust to.

Suzie's frown disappeared when she saw her daughter in the doorway. Dressed in a pretty blue summer dress that skimmed her slim figure, ending just below the knee, her hair loose around her shoulders, Jess looked beautiful. She was scanning the room looking for her, and Suzie waved to attract her attention. Jess made her way over, weaving in and out of the other tables and turning a few heads as she did so. Suzie could see Jess was apprehensive and, standing up, she held out her arms and smiled. "Hello, love. You look wonderful."

"Thanks. Am I forgiven?" Jess asked, looking relieved.

"Of course. We've been through all of that," Suzie assured her, squeezed her hand. "I know you probably have lots of questions, so shall we just order some wine and then we can order food later?"

"Sure." Jess looked relieved.

After they'd been served, Suzie took the initiative and got straight to the point. "I feel embarrassed and ashamed that I can't tell you more about your dad. What can I say? I had just finished all my computer courses — top of the class — and Chrissie, my tutor, said that I had a very bright future. So I went out and celebrated. One of the girls suggested cocktails and we all agreed. I hadn't really drank before that night. We were too skint at home and every spare bit of cash went into helping my mother meet the bills and put food on the table. The cocktails tasted like lemonade to me and I was so happy, I threw them back and danced all night long."

Jess smiled. "Do you even remember if you fancied him?"

"Well, of course I did. What kind of a trollop do you take me for?" Suzie retorted and then smiled. "He was gorgeous and a great dancer and he kept telling me how beautiful I was. I was so drunk but also stupid. He asked me to go back to his flat and I agreed. It was a crazy thing to do, leaving a club without at least telling my friends where I was going. I'm lucky that I only came out of it pregnant, he could have been a bloody murderer! I gave him my number but, of course, he never called. I was a gullible little idiot."

"So I do take after you," Jess said with a wry grin.

"Excuse me, I was a teenager. You're twenty-seven and old enough to know better," Suzie retorted, immediately regretting lashing out when she saw the look of shame on Jess's flushed face. She'd already said more than enough about Louis. It was wrong of her to keep punishing her daughter over him. "I suppose I was so annoyed about your affair with Louis because it was equally stupid. You were risking your career and good name and you've worked so hard to win the respect of your colleagues and readers."

"I know." Jess looked up at Suzie. "My dad, was he your first lover?"

"Yes, and John was the second, and that is the sum total of your mother's experience."

"You must have been devastated when you realised you were pregnant."

"I'll be honest, love — I cried when I took that test. Sorry."

Jess shook her head. "I'm sure that I'd be the same."

"You see, I'd worked so hard and getting a job was my ticket out of that house and away from Da. It also meant I'd be able to slip my poor mother a few quid. I went to lots of interviews but I was most excited about CML. Though I could put together spreadsheets and I knew all the basics of desktop publishing, I loved creating presentations and that was the job CML were looking to fill. They wanted someone with artistic flair and, if I do say so myself, I had flair." Suzie grinned at her daughter.

"What did CML do exactly?"

"They organised conferences for companies in Ireland and the UK. They were huge and yet it was a small outfit. Me, Gina and Jack — now her husband — were the design team. Then there was Malcolm, the accountant, a receptionist who was a pain in the arse and Doug and his wife, Pamela. Once we'd drafted up a few ideas, Gina and Pamela would pitch them to the customer and then we apportioned out the work and were left to our own devices to design the presentation."

"That sounds cool."

Suzie smiled. "It really was. Pamela, Doug's wife, wasn't happy about hiring a pregnant girl from the wrong side of the tracks but Doug overruled her."

Jess frowned. "But I thought that she was the one who looked after me and tried to rescue me from the dog."

"Yes, that's right but she was very different by then. That's a story for another night," Suzie said, giving her a sad smile.

"Granny must have been proud of you."

"She was but shocked when I told her I was pregnant. And Da, true to form, told me not to darken his door again."

"He didn't, did he?" Jess looked aghast.

Suzie nodded. She'd told her kids that her da was a violent man, but obviously they hadn't heard about this part of the story. "Ma wanted to fight him on it but she'd taken enough punches from him over the years. I wasn't going to be the reason she got a few more. She wanted me to go and stay with her sister up in Donegal until the baby was born, but there was no way I was going to pass up on the CML job."

"So what did you do?"

Suzie grinned. "I slept in CML's reception area. It was lovely and warm and the sofa was quite comfortable. I only planned to stay there until I got my first paycheque. Then I figured I'd be able to rent a room."

"But what about your clothes? What about showering?" Jess asked.

"Ma would call me when Da was out and I'd nip home to have a bath and change. All my stuff was stashed in the attic. I just carried the bare necessities in my rucksack."

434

"And you got away with it?"

Suzie smiled. "I did until Doug forgot his wallet one evening and came back to the office to find me snoring on his couch. He was suspicious of what I was up to and I had to explain the whole situation. Thankfully, he believed me but he said that I couldn't stay there. He told me to get in the car and I was scared he was going to drop me off at a homeless shelter. But, instead, he brought me home with him." Suzie chuckled as she remembered her reaction when the electric gates had silently opened. "You would want to see the feckin' mansion he lived in. Huge, it was, and in its own grounds. There was a flat over the garage and he said I could stay there for as long as I wanted."

"Wow. Your own pad. That was generous."

Suzie smiled. "He's a pretty amazing guy, but his wife nearly divorced him over it."

"Did she think he was sleeping with you and it was his baby?"

Suzie threw back her head and laughed at the idea. "Not at all. I was a kid in trouble and Doug was old enough to be my dad. Anyway, they were in a different league. I doubt it would have even occurred to Pamela that Doug would look twice at me. She just didn't want me lowering the tone of the neighbourhood. But Doug put his foot down and told Pam I was staying and that was that. I kept out of her way as much as possible. Not that it was easy. She was running CML at the time because Doug was recovering from a triple bypass. He wasn't one for hanging around doing nothing and hated being out of the office so when he wasn't nipping in to check up on us, he was dropping round to the flat for a chat. That's how we became such good friends."

Jess was silent for a moment and then looked at her. "Why didn't you give me up for adoption?"

Suzie smiled. "That was the plan but once I held you in my arms, I knew that I couldn't let you go. Besides, now I had some security, I figured I could give you a reasonable life. And I used to have nightmares about you being adopted by someone like Da, who would mistreat you." She shuddered, remembering nights when she'd woken up in a cold sweat. "So I decided that you were better off with me."

"Thank you." Jess squeezed her hand. "That seems like such an inadequate thing to say, but thank you." She said nothing for a moment and then looked up at Suzie. "Can I ask you a personal question?"

"You can ask me anything you like," Suzie assured her. It was incredible how good it felt to tell Jess the truth. She hadn't even realised that keeping it secret had eaten at her all these years.

"Did you love John?"

Suzie sighed. That was a question she'd asked herself a number of times over the years but now, when she was calm, she was able to look at John and their marriage a little more objectively.

"Yes, I loved him. We were very happy, especially in the early days when it was just the three of us. He was great with you then." She ignored Jess's raised eyebrow. "He was gentle, thoughtful and kind and, well, no guy had ever treated me with the respect he did. He was quite single-minded and hugely ambitious, though. He

436

was determined that we would live in Limerick which I was apprehensive about. But by then, Pamela had died of cancer and Doug had left the country and, without them, the flat didn't feel like a home anymore.

"But John gave me that. It was only in the last three years or so that he started messing about with other women. And, who could blame him? I wasn't interested in his job, couldn't relate to any of his colleagues or their wives, and made no effort at all to shift the baby weight after Noel was born so, in a way, I pushed him away."

Jess frowned. "Don't take the blame for his bad behaviour, Mum. You treated him like a king. To be honest, it used to annoy me, given the way that he was carrying on."

Suzie shook her head. "He was still a good father and he loved you, Jess."

Her daughter shook her head. "No, Mum. At least not the way he loved Sharon and Noel."

Suzie sighed, wishing Jess hadn't been so attuned to John's behaviour.

"Honestly, Jess, he really did care. But he was there for the births of Sharon and Noel and I think that had a huge impact on him. Also, Sharon looked so much like his mother. A true Connors girl. I know that it was wrong of him to treat you differently, Jess, but I don't think it was intentional, just instinct." Suzie sighed. "I never thought you'd noticed."

"I noticed." Jess frowned. "Never mind. You must have been devastated when you found out that he was unfaithful."

"It came as quite a shock," Suzie admitted. "It never occurred to me that he would do anything like that. He had such a strong sense of values. It's true," she said when Jess gave a snort of disbelief. "That's why I feel I have to take some of the blame. If I had been by his side at all those company dinners, the way he constantly asked me to, maybe he wouldn't have strayed."

Jess seemed to accept that but Suzie could see that she still looked troubled. "Go on, love. I told you that you can ask me anything."

"That night that I walked in on you, rowing. You were screaming at him and calling him names. I'd never even heard you raise your voice to him before that. What had he done?"

Suzie shook her head, happy that she could answer honestly. "I don't remember the details. I know it was about a woman because the one thing I do remember was seeing you at the door and feeling terrified that you'd heard. I didn't want any of you to know about his affairs. It would have broken up the family, forcing you into taking sides and Noel was only, what, seven?"

"Eight," Jess said. "But, yes, I suppose I can understand that."

"You never said anything to them, did you, Jess?"

Jess looked incredulous. "Of course not."

"Thank you."

"I didn't hear anything about other women that night, Mum. I assumed that you were arguing about me. I was always trying to figure out what I'd done wrong to make him stop loving me."

"You did nothing, Jess," Suzie cried, filled with impotent fury that John's careless indifference had had such an impact on her daughter. "We never once argued about you. John was proud of you, honestly, and I'm so sorry you thought otherwise."

Jess sighed. "It's okay, Mum. Thanks for telling me the truth, though. I feel better now that I know I didn't come between you."

"Never," Suzie promised, looking her daughter straight in the eye. "Now, can I ask you something? Would you mind if we continued to keep John's adultery from Sharon and Noel? Not for his sake but for theirs, Noel's especially. Losing him was traumatic enough without hearing that."

"Of course. I won't say anything, Mum. I've never told them anything, either about what I knew or how I felt." Jess frowned. "Noel was so much younger and Sharon was John's little princess. She'd just think I was jealous," — she gave a sad smile, "— which I suppose, was true."

"I'm sorry, love," Suzie said, thinking how empty and inadequate the words were.

"Don't be. It's fine. Lots of kids don't get on with one or both of their parents. At least in my case I know that there was a reason." She reached for a menu. "Now, let's eat, I'm hungry."

Suzie wasn't fooled by Jess's bright smile but knew that, hard as this conversation had been, it had brought her daughter some peace of mind. Unfortunately that was a feeling she didn't share. There was a piece still missing and Suzie wouldn't rest easy until she knew exactly what it was.

CHAPTER
FORTY-TWO

There were three texts from Doug when Suzie woke late on Saturday morning. The first asked how her night out with Aileen and Nora, and then Jess, had gone. The second reminded her of the party later — now it was a party? And the third suggested she bring Jess. There was a thought! Suzie knew that Gina, at least, would love to meet her daughter and Suzie would be proud to show her off. She wondered if Jess would be interested. She called her.

"I'd love to, Mum," Jess enthused, "although I'm not sure I'd want to stay long. You'll be talking about old times and I'd probably nod off."

Suzie chuckled. "True. Well, then, come along and say a quick hello, yeah?"

"Sure. I'll drive," Jess promised.

"Thanks, sweetheart." Suzie hung up, smiling, and went downstairs. "It's a lovely day, Percy. Will we go to the park and make the most of it?"

He stood up and wagged his tail, and she laughed. "Okay, then. I'll tidy up and we'll be off."

Once Suzie had grabbed a sandwich and taken care of the housework, she called the dog and put on his lead. As she wandered through the park, throwing sticks for Percy, her thoughts turned to her sister, as they had most days since she'd remembered Mandy's efforts to lead her husband astray. How could any woman do that to a friend, let alone her own sister? Was it about John at all or did Mandy simply want him because he was Suzie's? Or was it even more personal? Sometimes Suzie wondered if Mandy hated her. John was gone now and yet Mandy had inveigled her way back into Suzie's life and tried to keep her and Doug apart. There was something decidedly sinister about her behaviour. She racked her brains, trying to figure out what she'd done that made Mandy want to hurt her, but she honestly couldn't think of a reason. Mandy had been only a child when Suzie left home and she'd been a good big sister, trying to protect her from their da's moods.

They'd lost touch when Mandy had moved to London but Suzie had welcomed her into her Limerick home when her sister decided to move back and needed a place to stay while she looked for a permanent home. And what thanks did she get? Her sister had tried to screw her husband.

Anger flared and Suzie forced herself to practise her deep breathing, reminding herself this was ancient history and she'd cried all her tears a long time ago. She wouldn't allow herself to get upset today, not with a lovely evening ahead with her old friends. Suzie checked her watch.

"Time to get back and make myself beautiful, Percy," she said, turning for home. She was really excited at the thought of meeting her workmates again

442

and was convinced it would do Doug the world of good. He needed male friends and you couldn't get better than Mal and Jack. She hoped Mandy wouldn't be there but she'd decided against asking Doug not to invite her. He'd know something was up and he was riled enough without her telling him this latest little titbit from her past. Anyway, what could her sister say or do in a room full of strangers and her boss? Suzie figured that this was one situation where Mandy could be trusted to behave.

Suzie stood in front of her wardrobe and flicked through her clothes, remembering Nora's advice. Finally, she settled on her sleeveless, knee-length, black dress and a pretty red bolero-style jacket. She'd wear her chunky necklace to cover her cleavage, as Nora had suggested. When she was ready, Suzie stood in front of the full-length mirror and smiled. The silk tights and high black shoes made her look slim, elegant even. If you could see me now, Pamela, she thought with a wry grin. What would her old colleagues make of her? Would they even recognise her? It had been almost twenty-four years since they'd seen each other.

She heard the front door open and Jess's voice. "Mum, are you ready?" Her daughter ran upstairs and stopped in the doorway. "Wow. You look great!"

"It's not too much, is it?" Suzie frowned. What if the others turned up in jeans?

"No. It's perfect. What about me? Will I do? I don't want to let you down in front of your mates."

Suzie rolled her eyes. "You'd look terrific in a sack, but I do like that colour on you." It was a simple sundress in burnt orange and complemented Jess's tanned arms and legs. "It's good of you to dress up for me."

"It's not just for you," Jess admitted, shyly.

Suzie raised her eyebrows, noting the excited flush in her daughter's cheeks. "Oh?"

"I'm going to dinner with Cal later. He's downstairs. He's going to drop us to Doug's and pick me up when I'm done."

"You and Cal?" Suzie exclaimed, astonished at this turn of events.

Jess gave a bashful nod. "I know. Crazy, right?"

Suzie threw her arms round her and gave her daughter a tight hug. "It's wonderful. I always knew that he was fond of you, but you never seemed interested in him."

Jess blinked. "It was actually the other way round! I always fancied him but he treated me like a little sister."

"Well, you're together now and that's all that matters." Suzie sniffed back her tears and, grabbing a tissue, dabbed her eyes so that her makeup wouldn't be ruined.

"Hey, don't get too excited," Jess cautioned. "This is only our second date. It might not work out."

"You don't believe that for a moment."

Jess smiled broadly, her eyes shining happily "No, you're right. I don't."

"I'm so happy for you." Suzie took her arm. "Now, let's go. I can't wait to show you off."

Doug threw open the door and beamed at them. "Welcome. You both look gorgeous. Thanks for coming, Jess. I know the others will be thrilled to see you again."

"Thanks for inviting me. After all Mum's told me, I'm looking forward to meeting them, too."

Jess turned to wave at Cal before stepping inside.

"We only have her for a short time. She's got a date." Suzie hugged Douglas. "Are we the first to arrive?"

"Yes. Come in and I'll get you both a drink."

They followed him through to the kitchen and he produced a bottle of champagne.

"You *are* pushing the boat out," Suzie teased. "What are we celebrating?"

Doug poured it and handed them their glasses before raising his own. "Life?"

"A few short months ago we thought we'd lost you." Jess looked at her. "So I'll definitely drink to that."

"Aw, thanks, love." Suzie clinked her glass against theirs. "But don't let me have more than two glasses. Remember what happened the last time I drank champagne."

Jess's eyes widened and she turned to Doug. "Can you add some water to that, please?"

Suzie laughed but nodded when Doug held the jug up. "Yes, please."

"I hope you won't be bored, Jess," Doug said, "but at least you can have a laugh looking at our old photos."

"Are they that bad?" Jess grinned at him.

"No idea, but Gina tells me she has tons. You can have a good laugh at your mother's fashion disasters."

Suzie pulled a face. "Don't remind me. Is Noreen coming?"

"No. I asked Gina if she could track her down but, for some reason, she didn't seem too interested in finding her."

Suzie laughed and explained to her daughter. "She was CML's receptionist and a right pain."

"She was good at her job," Doug protested, "just a little old-school." The doorbell rang and he put down his glass. "This might be Amanda." He shot Suzie a worried look.

She clenched her glass but forced herself to smile. "Well, you had better let her in, then."

"Are you and Mandy fighting?" Jess murmured, when he'd left them.

"No. I haven't talked to her in a while but I remembered some things that made me realise why I didn't see her that often."

"What?"

"Oh, nothing specific. It just made a mockery of her friendliness since I woke up."

"I won't argue with you there." Jess squeezed her hand in a gesture of solidarity and Suzie gave her a grateful smile.

"Look who's here!" Doug walked back into the room followed by Jack and Gina.

"Suzie? Oh, my God, it's so great to see you. You look fabulous, love the hair!"

Suzie found herself caught up in a warm hug. "Hello, Gina." She smiled at the bright-eyed, bubbly woman. "You haven't changed a bit."

"Rubbish!" Gina patted her tummy. "But I do have three children to show for it."

She was slightly heavier, Suzie noticed, but it suited her. She turned to Jack, who bent to kiss her cheek. "And look at you." She grinned at his goatee. "Very George Clooney."

"You see?" Jack said to his wife. "It *is* sexy."

"It's bumfluff," Gina said, dismissively.

Suzie laughed. "Ha! This is just like old times." She looked around for her daughter, who had stepped back and was watching them with an amused smile. Suzie beckoned her over and slid an arm around her waist. "Remember my baby?"

Gina's eyes widened. "Jess?"

"Yes. Hi."

Gina kissed Jess's cheek. "I can't believe it. You're all grown up and so beautiful. Jack, isn't she lovely?"

"She certainly is." He smiled and shook Jess's hand. "I think our eldest would love to meet you."

"He's only twenty," Gina laughed, "but he's already gone through I don't know how many girlfriends."

"She's taken," Suzie confided, grinning broadly.

"Mum," Jess hissed, blushing.

"Am I wrong?" Suzie looked her in the eye and her smile broadened when Jess shook her head, looking like an embarrassed, lovesick teenager.

"We have so much catching up to do," Gina said, accepting a glass from Doug and smiling affectionately at her ex-boss. "I want to hear all about you both and what you've been up to. It's so good to see you again, Doug. How's the health?"

"Fine. Creaking along."

"You were flitting from country to country and then, bam, you disappeared off the radar. What happened?" Jack asked, his expression suddenly serious.

Doug was telling them about his new name and his writing when the doorbell rang again. "I'll get it," Suzie said and went into the hall. She grinned maliciously, imagining Mandy's face when she was greeted by her sister. She flung it open and blinked at the man on the doorstep. "Hello?"

"Suzie!"

She frowned. Did she know this handsome man? Then he gave her a lop-sided grin and she gasped, putting a hand to her mouth. "Malcolm?" He nodded and she threw her arms around him. "Oh, Malcolm. I'm sorry, I didn't recognise you. You look so different."

"I've lost about three stone since we last met," he told her.

"Well, it suits you. How's the family?" she asked, drawing him inside. Thank goodness he hadn't brought Caroline. Malcolm's wife had always managed to pour cold water on any party.

"All grown up now and Caroline and I are divorced."

Suzie grimaced. "Should I commiserate?"

Mal smiled. "No, not at all. We're both happier."

"In that case I'm glad. Where are you working these days?"

"I have my own accountancy firm in the city centre and I live over the shop."

"Good for you," she said, delighted that his life had obviously worked out so well.

448

"It's so good to see you again, Suzie. How's Limerick?"

"Oh, I left there eleven years ago when my husband was killed in an accident."

"Oh, I'm so sorry."

She nodded but didn't go into further details. This was a day for celebrating. "I live in Kilbarrack now and I'm always in and out of the city. I'm surprised we haven't bumped into each other over the years."

"We're here now so let's make the most of it."

"You're right." She hugged him again. "Come on. Everyone's in the kitchen and there's someone I want you to meet."

Suzie introduced Malcolm to Jess and left them chatting with Jack while Doug and Gina sat at the breakfast bar catching up. She was content to let the conversation flow around her, glad she hadn't been looking back on her time in CML through rose-tinted glasses. They were good people and she hoped that this time they would stay in touch. Her eyes strayed to Malcolm. She'd seen Gina's expression when he walked in. She was just as gobsmacked with the transformation. He must be in his mid-fifties, Suzie guessed, but he looked younger than she did. She wondered how much of that was down to losing weight and how much was due to being free of Caroline.

"Where are Amanda and the damn caterers?" Doug looked at his watch.

"Caterers?" Gina winked at Suzie. "Sure we can send out for pizza."

"It's all organised, or it's supposed to be," he grumbled.

Suzie knew his irritation was less about the food and more about his annoyance with her sister's meddling in their relationship but that was her battle and one for another day. Suzie's eyes were drawn to Malcolm again and she smiled when she caught his eye. He didn't look away, but returned the smile.

"What was that song you were always singing when you were pregnant?" Jack called over to her. "You nearly drove us all mad."

"'Bad Medicine'," Gina interjected with a groan.

"Bon Jovi." Suzie grinned. "I adored him."

"I hope you haven't inherited your mother's taste in music," Jack said to Jess.

She laughed. "Some, but not Bon Jovi."

"You can't talk, Jack," Suzie retorted. "You were big into Madonna."

"I think that was more about her sexy costumes than her songs." Gina laughed.

Jack smirked at his wife. "Someone who had a Jason Donovan poster over her bed is in no position to sneer."

Suzie raised an eyebrow. "How did you know what was over her bed?"

"I looked up at it a lot." Jack winked at her and his wife swatted his backside.

Doug laughed. "You two haven't changed a bit. How have you managed to raise three normal children?"

"Who said anything about normal?" Gina quipped, making everyone laugh.

"The party's in full swing I see."

Suzie spun round to see Mandy standing in the doorway. Fuck. She'd been hoping her sister had decided not to come.

"It would be going a lot better if the caterers had shown up," Doug retorted.

"They're here now. You were supposed to call them thirty minutes before you wanted the food served."

Doug opened his mouth to reply but Suzie put a hand on his arm. "We've been so busy catching up we never noticed. Let's move into the other room and leave them to sort out dinner."

Doug glared at Mandy but allowed himself to be led away.

"Aren't you going to introduce me?" Mandy called after him and Suzie could see the rage in her eyes.

Suzie answered as Doug fumed beside her. "Everyone, this is Mandy, my sister, and Doug's secretary."

"Assistant," Mandy corrected her.

"Assistant," Suzie repeated, rolling her eyes dramatically.

Everyone laughed and said hello as they passed her to go into the lounge. Mandy frowned when she saw Jess. "What are you doing here?"

Looking like a rabbit caught in headlights, Jess turned to Suzie but Doug answered.

"Jess is an honorary member of CML and the daughter of one of my best employees." Doug put a protective arm round Suzie.

"What?" Mandy looked totally confused.

Realising that Doug was in a dangerous mood, Suzie answered for him. She noticed that, while they were all drinking champagne and beer, he was holding a glass of Jameson. "Sorry, Mandy, we've been having a bit of fun at your expense. I had no idea until the day in the restaurant that Douglas Thornton was also Doug Hamilton, proprietor of CML, the company I worked for before I got married."

"You've been stringing me along?" Mandy looked directly at Doug. "You pretended not to know each other."

"We all pretend from time to time, don't we, Amanda? I pretended I didn't know Suzie. You pretended to be a good sister . . ."

"Doug." Suzie gave him a warning glance.

"No," Mandy said. "I want to know what he meant by that."

Doug looked at Suzie and nodded. "I have guests to entertain. Come on, Jess, Suzie."

"You go on. I'll be there in a minute." When he was gone Suzie turned back to her stony-faced sister. "He's on the whiskey — don't mind him."

"But I want to know —"

"Later, Mandy. Tonight isn't about you. It's a reunion of very old friends."

Mandy eyeballed her. "And Jess."

"And Jess. Now, can you please get a move on with dinner?" she said, and swept from the room, taking enormous pleasure from the furious look on her sister's face.

452

Suzie tried to get back into party mood, but Mandy's silent, brooding presence and steady consumption of wine was hard to ignore. She looked around and caught Malcolm's eye.

"Okay?" he mouthed, looking concerned.

She nodded and gave him a grateful smile, covering her glass with her hand as Jack went to refill it. Someone needed to keep a level head and, although Doug had returned to his earlier good form, he was still knocking back the whiskey.

The conversation turned to the evening that Suzie went into labour and Jess laughed until she cried as Gina told the story in her own dramatic fashion. Malcolm was the hero of the hour, she finished off, and he took a humble bow.

"My hero," Suzie laughed.

"And where was John?" Mandy's voice rang out, silencing them.

CHAPTER
FORTY-THREE

Suzie felt the tension in the room and was determined to dispel it. Mandy had caused her enough trouble already and, if she didn't put a sock in it, Doug would strangle her.

"I hadn't met John." She gave her daughter a reassuring smile. "He's not Jess's dad."

"What? Why am I only hearing this now? Do Sharon and Noel know?"

"They do now. It was a secret because that was the way John wanted it, and I respected his wishes. It would still be a secret if Jess hadn't stumbled on some baby pictures."

"And thought I was her father." Doug chuckled.

"You were like a dad to her," Suzie insisted, taking the opportunity to turn the focus away from her sister. "You adored him, Jess. He would read to you and you would sit in the window, watching for his car every evening. Pamela, Doug's wife, was the one who rescued you from that dog."

Jess's face lit up as she looked at Doug. "Was there a swing in your garden?"

His eyes widened in surprise. "There was! My back was broke from pushing you."

"So who's the father?" Mandy's harsh question cut across Jess's laughter.

Gina glared at her harsh tone and moved closer to Suzie, who shot an affectionate and grateful smile at her old friend.

"A lovely handsome young man, Jess is the image of him," Suzie said while Jess scowled at her aunt.

"But she has your lovely eyes." Gina smiled.

"He didn't want to be a dad, then?" Mandy continued her interrogation.

Jess moved forward and stood eyeball to eyeball with her aunt. "He never knew Mum was pregnant, not that it's any of your business. Mum has answered all of my questions, Sharon and Noel's too, and we're happy. That's all you need to know . . . Aunty."

There was an uncomfortable silence that Gina jumped in to fill. "Time to show you Doug's appalling taste in ties, Jess."

"What was wrong with my ties?" Doug protested, turning his back on Mandy, effectively shutting her out.

"They were enormous," Jack said, grinning as they crowded around Gina.

"That was the fashion of the time."

Jess looked over Gina's shoulder, trying to get a better look and then gasped. "I do remember you," she said excitedly, and then pointed to another woman in the photo. "And that's Pamela, isn't it?"

Suzie watched Doug swallow hard and nod.

"I remember her . . ." — Jess looked to her mum for confirmation — "gardening?"

Suzie nodded. "Yes, Pamela loved her garden. To give me a break, she'd sit you on a rug with your toys next to her while she was weeding. But all you wanted to do was mess in the dirt."

"And she'd sit me up on the draining board and wash my hands. I remember when she was lifting me down, she'd kiss my head and say, 'All done.'"

Suzie swallowed back tears and nodded.

"Excuse me." Doug got up and strode from the room.

"I'm sorry. I didn't mean to upset him," Jess said, crestfallen.

"You didn't," Gina assured her. "You're bringing back wonderful memories. But he loved her so much it's bound to be emotional for him."

Jess gave her a grateful nod and looked at Suzie. "I should really get going, Mum."

"You should indeed."

"It was wonderful to see you again." Gina stood and hugged her.

"You too. And thank you for looking after Mum so well when she was having me."

"How touching. I think I'm going to be sick," Mandy drawled and, picking up her glass, left the room.

Suzie scowled. "Ignore her, Jess. Go and enjoy your evening."

"Will you say goodbye to Doug for me?"

"Of course."

When she was alone with her friends, Suzie sighed. "Sorry about the dramatics."

456

Malcolm caught her hand. "You have nothing to apologise for."

"She's jealous of you," Gina observed.

Suzie rolled her eyes. "That's ridiculous. She's beautiful, single and years younger."

"Let's not talk about age." Jack pulled a face and put a hand to his receding hairline. "Now that your daughter is gone, you're the youngest person in the room."

"And you look it too," Mal said, gallantly. "Jess is a lovely young woman, Suzie. You did a good job there."

"Thank you," she said, and smiled at them all. "Now, I think there's been quite enough talk about me and my family. Tell me all about yours."

They were chatting happily when Suzie became conscious of raised voices in the hallway. "Excuse me." She grimaced and went out into the hall and was stunned to see her sister in tears, Doug standing over her, ranting.

"Doug!"

He whirled round and she could see that all the emotion of the evening coupled with the alcohol had sent him over the top. She put a hand on his arm. "Please, Doug. Go back inside."

"But Suzie —"

"You're the host and I want a word with my sister."

"I've got a word for your sister. Leave." Doug glared at Mandy and went back into the lounge.

"Don't start," Mandy warned Suzie, wiping her eyes.

"I've no intention of starting anything. I came out to see what all the racket was about."

"Of course you did. Saint Suzie, surrounded by her adoring disciples. But you weren't always a saint, were you? I should have realised that Jess wasn't John's child. He never talked about her the way he did about Sharon and Noel."

Suzie froze. Was she really going "there"?

"He talked to me a lot," Mandy continued, unaware of the flames she was fanning. Or perhaps she was. It seemed her entire purpose these days was to provoke. "But then you know that, don't you, Suzie?" she continued. "You've remembered everything. That's why you haven't been returning my calls."

Suzie didn't correct her. She realised she didn't know everything, but she had a feeling that very soon she might, if she let Mandy keep talking. "I know that you came on to him in Limerick, in my home."

Mandy's eyes widened and then she burst out laughing. "Is that what you think? I didn't have to *come on* to your husband, Suzie, I assure you. He was a more than willing participant. He couldn't get enough of me."

Suzie recoiled at her words, recognising the truth in them, another missing piece. This was the information her mind had refused to remember and acknowledge. She stared, mesmerised by Mandy's unashamed and triumphant expression. Struggling to hide her feelings, Suzie shook her head, pretending to be amused. "Believe me, you were one of many."

"No, I was the last!" Mandy's eyes flashed. "And you know why, Saint Suzie? Because, I was *the one*. He loved me."

458

Suzie stared at her. Was that true? She searched her scrambled brain. The fact that she wasn't shocked or upset suggested she'd heard this before. And she knew, in that moment, she'd confronted John and, though he'd admitted his weakness, he'd regretted it and begged her forgiveness. The realisation gave her strength. She looked at Mandy, her own sister, incredulous at the malicious pleasure she was taking in delivering this blow. There wasn't a shred of regret, shame or pity in Mandy's expression. In fact her face was twisted and ugly, her true personality exposed.

"You're kidding yourself, Mandy. John didn't love you. John loved sex and, I assume, got some perverse pleasure in screwing my sister."

"Is that what you told Doug? Your knight in shining armour?" she spat.

"Doug and I have more interesting things to talk about. John is dead and gone and I don't talk about his bad habits. His children don't need to know that he had a thing for cheap tarts."

Mandy bristled at that.

"They're not children any more. Maybe I'll tell them," she taunted.

"Don't even think about it," Suzie warned her, losing all tolerance with this nasty, vindictive woman. "Why are you doing this? Aren't you even remotely sorry for what you've done? For the way you've treated me?"

"No, not in the least! He loved me and I loved him. John was going to leave you and marry me."

"You're delusional." Suzie laughed, shaking her head in disbelief. "Even if he did love you, John loved his children, his good name and his status in the community a lot more. Why do you think he pretended Jess was his child? He loved me and wanted me to be his wife, but he couldn't bear the stigma of having a cuckoo in his nest."

"He'd have left everything and everyone for me," Mandy insisted. "If it wasn't for his accident, we'd be together now. I loved him more than you ever did but I had to stand by, the sister-in-law, at his funeral while you got all the sympathy and support."

Suzie remembered Nora saying how devastated Mandy had been at the funeral. Maybe in her own weird way Mandy really had loved John. She stared helplessly at her deranged sister, her anger subsiding. "He's dead, Mandy. There's no point in resurrecting any of this now. Do what I do. Remember the good times."

"That's easy for you. You have his name, his children and the status of being his widow. What do I have?"

Tears rolled down Mandy's face unchecked. Suzie had never seen her so upset. She was almost hysterical.

"You have your memories. You got the best of him, after all."

Mandy frowned. "How do you make that out?"

"I did his laundry, fed him when he bothered to come home and entertained his boring colleagues. I put up with his moods, his habits and looked after him when he was ill. But you? You got John the charmer, the romantic. You got to spend time with him in fancy hotels, eating lovely food and indulging in illicit sex.

460

And, be honest, the fact that he was my husband added spice to the relationship, didn't it?"

Mandy smirked but it soon turned back into a scowl. "Weren't you jealous?"

"Why, is that what you wanted? Is that what it was really about?" Suzie countered and she realised that Gina was right. Mandy envied her, envied her life. "Did you really love John or did you just want to take him away from me?"

Suzie gasped as another memory surfaced making her grasp the bannister to steady herself. It was how she had found out about John and Mandy. She'd received an anonymous note telling her the hotel, and even the room number, where she could find her cheating husband. Suzie had gone along and sat in a corner of reception, hidden by a plant. Although she was used to his women, Suzie had felt utterly shocked and betrayed when she saw that her sister was his latest conquest.

"*You* sent me that note." Suzie marvelled at the lengths Mandy had gone to in order to hurt her.

Mandy's face lit up. "Of course I did! John wanted to be with me but he didn't have the guts to tell you. So I decided to help things along. You were supposed to throw him out, but no" — Mandy gave a bitter laugh — "Saint Suzie did nothing. Such a good little wife, turning the other cheek and carrying on with your sham of a marriage. Now he's gone, and look at you." Suzie shrank from the venom in Mandy's eyes. "Look at you! The life and soul of the party, flirting with everyone and carrying on as if he never existed."

461

"Oh my God," Suzie whispered, as it dawned on her what all of this was about. Why Mandy was so bitter and why she'd come back into her life to torment her.

"What?" Mandy was eyeing her warily.

"Nora was remarking how upset you were at the funeral."

"Of course I was: I loved him."

"No." Suzie shook her head. "You saw all his family and friends and heard people stand up and talk about him as a husband, a father and a member of the community and you knew that he'd lied. You knew then that he'd taken you for a ride, literally. That he would never have left me."

"That's bullshit, all bullshit," Mandy practically screamed and, standing up, went in search of her coat. "I wish you'd never woken up," she spat as she pulled it on, a wild look in her eyes. "You deserve nothing! You were in the way, always in the way. You didn't even have the decency to die when you should have."

Suzie was still trying to process the last comment as Mandy headed for the door. "Where are you going?"

"What the hell do you care?" her sister said, and left, slamming the door behind her.

Feeling stunned and drained by the confrontation, Suzie went in search of the others and found them sipping brandy and liqueurs in Doug's study. Gina had taken off her shoes and was curled up on the small sofa and, when she saw Suzie, she shifted up and patted the space beside her.

462

"Is everything okay?"

Suzie nodded, but in truth, felt dazed and shell-shocked, her mind still struggling to make sense of everything.

Doug met her eyes. "Sorry, but that's been building for a while."

It took her a moment to react but then she nodded, vaguely, and reached out to squeeze his hand. "I know."

Mal looked at her. "What is it, Suzie? You look like you've seen a ghost."

"In a way I have." Suzie thought of the memory that had bubbled to the surface as her sister ran from the house. A gym and lots of giggling, her sister encouraging her to try out the equipment. And then a hand on her shoulder pushing her . . .

"Where is she?" Gina whispered, looking nervously at the door.

"Gone."

Doug's eyes narrowed. "Where?"

"I've no idea," Suzie said, "but I don't think she'll be back."

"Going on her behaviour tonight, I'd say you're well shot of her." Gina patted her knee.

Suzie nodded slowly. "Yes. I think I am."

For years she had turned a blind eye to John's womanising, and then came the ultimate humiliation: his eighteen-month affair with her sister. Eighteen months! And now she knew that Mandy had staged Suzie's discovery of their affair, in the hotel where she and John had held their wedding reception. What kind of sicko would do something so cruel? Again it struck

Suzie that this wasn't about John or love but Mandy simply wanting her life. The woman needed help. Her behaviour was bordering on psychotic.

"We were deciding on a venue for our next get-together," Jack said gently, bringing her back to the present. "Would you come out to our place? We live in Enniskerry but we have plenty of room if you wanted to spend the night."

"Yes, sure, that would be fine," Suzie said, still distracted.

"And if you want to bring along a friend," Gina said with a wink, "that would be fine too. You too, gentlemen."

Suzie chuckled. "There's only Percy, my dog."

"Likewise," Malcolm smiled at her, "except, no dog."

"Old and free and single," Doug confirmed.

Gina laughed. "Well, I'll be in touch after I've checked the family calendar and we'll set it up."

"Lovely. I'll look forward to that, Gina." She sighed, feeling suddenly exhausted. "I'm afraid I need to go home, but it's been great to see you all."

"We're going in the same direction. We can share a taxi," Mal said immediately.

"You're not annoyed with me for having a go at Mandy, are you?" Doug asked when they were out in the hall and he was helping Suzie into her coat.

"No." She hugged him. "It needed to come out in the open. But I think that there's something seriously wrong with Mandy, Doug."

"I'll give you a call tomorrow and we can discuss it then. Go home and get some rest. You've had quite an evening."

"I've had lots of them recently," she said with a shaky laugh.

Doug turned to shake Malcolm's hand. "Look after her."

"I will, Doug."

The sound of a horn woke Suzie and she realised she'd fallen asleep on Malcolm's shoulder. "Oh, I'm so sorry, Mal."

"It's fine, Suzie," he said with a warm smile. "After hearing about all you've been through this year and, on top of that, the carry-on tonight, I'm not surprised you're tired."

Suzie was distracted as the taxi turned onto the coast road. "You should have got out about five minutes ago," she pointed out, but was glad he hadn't.

"I wouldn't let a lady go home in a taxi alone, especially a sleeping one." Mal grinned.

"Thank you. Isn't it strange?" Suzie marvelled. "We haven't seen each other in almost twenty-five years, yet I felt as close to you all as if it was yesterday."

"Not so strange. We were always close. Can I be honest, Suzie?"

"Of course."

He looked into her eyes. "I don't want to wait until the next get-together to see you again. Would you like to go for a drink with me? Just the two of us?"

Suzie smiled at him. "I'd like that, Mal. I'd like that very much indeed."

CHAPTER
FORTY-FOUR

Jess closed the door on the cold and frosty night and hurried up the stairs to her flat, hoping that the heating was working. Sighing contentedly when the warmth hit her as soon as she opened the door, Jess kicked off her boots and padded into the kitchen. She put on the kettle and then went to check her email, smiling when she saw there was one from Katie. It was disappointingly brief but, when Jess read it, she let out a whoop of delight. Katie was coming home tomorrow and wanted to meet up. Jess immediately replied, inviting her to her flat with the promise of pizza and beer and lots of gossip.

It would be great to see her friend again. She had ended up staying in Jersey far longer than expected and Jess had missed her. She made a mug of tea and carried it and her laptop into the bedroom, quickly changing into pyjamas and huddling under her duvet. Rereading the email, Jess smiled. She had talked to Katie on the phone and they'd exchanged texts, but there was nothing like sitting over a coffee or glass of wine for a good gossip. Jess couldn't wait to see her and catch up on all the news.

Jess had confided only in Cal about her meeting on Friday with a major Sunday newspaper, too nervous of jinxing it by telling anyone else. She could barely sleep for thinking about it. Cal, however, was completely confident that she'd get it, pointing out her excellent experience and the hard-hitting articles she'd written during the summer on important political issues, sending them off to publications that she admired and would like to write for. And now one of them wanted her to come in and discuss a weekly spot. She was beyond excited. Her phone buzzed and she groped round for it and read the message from her sister.

Don't forget the party on Saturday nite! x

As if she could, Jess smiled. Sharon had been buzzing round like a demented bluebottle, determined to have one last big bash before the baby came along. Keith was worried that she was overdoing it, but the hospital had been really pleased with Sharon's and the baby's health on her last couple of visits.

"Leave her be," her mother had advised. "She needs something to focus all that energy on."

Jess responded to the text.

I'll be there.

She set her phone on the bedside table and plugged in the charger before going into the bathroom to brush her teeth. As she wiped her mouth on a towel, her eyes caught the framed cutting from the *Gazette* that she'd

468

hung over the loo to remind her of the moment she'd stood up to Louis. Smiling happily, Jess turned out the light and went to bed.

Katie arrived straight from the airport in a cab, breathless and red-cheeked. Jess, who had been watching out for her, ran down the stairs and opened the door.

"Hey, you!" She dropped her bags and embraced Jess.

"You look amazing!" Jess stepped back to admire Katie's black business suit, which was softened by a powder-blue blouse. Her blond hair was caught up in a knot, soft tendrils framing her face, and she looked every inch the businesswoman.

"I'm not dressed for this weather," Katie laughed. "It's bloody arctic out."

"Why didn't you tell me you needed a lift?"

"Mum was supposed to collect me but she's terrified of driving on icy roads, and apparently it's much worse in Meath, so I just hopped in a taxi."

"Well, you're here now. Come in and get warm. I'll make you a cuppa."

"Coffee, please." Katie followed her upstairs and made a beeline for the radiator. "So how's Cal?"

Jess turned and smiled. "He's wonderful."

"I'm glad it's working out for you two. I knew from the moment I set eyes on him that he was one of the good guys."

Jess made the coffee and handed one mug to Katie. "So, home to relax for a while before re-joining the workforce?"

Katie's eyes twinkled. "No rest. I start my new job next Monday."

Jess stared at her. "What? No way! When did all this happen?"

"I applied for a position in this huge accountancy firm and they called me for a second interview in their head office in London last week and rang the next day to offer me the job!"

"It's in London?" Jess said, disappointed but impressed at the same time when Katie told her the name of the company.

Katie shook her head. "No, of course not. I told you I wanted to stay in Dublin. I'll be working in their offices here, smack bang in the city centre."

Jess hugged her. "That's brilliant news, well done."

"How about you? How's life as a freelance journalist? Getting any meatier pieces to sink your teeth into?"

"Now that you mention it . . ." Jess grinned and filled Katie in. "I may borrow that suit for the interview."

"No problem. That is so exciting, Jess, and in the area you love, too. I'm delighted for you."

"I don't have the job yet." Jess crossed her fingers.

"You'll ace it. It's clear that not only are you smart but that you love what you do. Your mum must be so proud."

"She doesn't know. I haven't told anyone except you and Cal."

Katie nodded. "You're probably right. Much better to arrive with a bottle of bubbly when you get it."

470

"Katie, stop!" Jess looked around for some wood to touch.

"Fine, I won't say another word. Anyway, I'm more interested in hearing about your family saga."

"It's like something out of a movie, isn't it? Mum's been really open with me, and about John too."

Katie shook her head. "She must have been upset when she remembered what he'd done. As if going through it once wasn't bad enough."

"I know, but she's determined to keep Dad's infidelities from Sharon and Noel."

"That's admirable. Is she completely recovered now, then?" Katie asked. "Not embarrassing you anymore?

Jess laughed. "She's fine and, yes, she's much better behaved but I think that's a conscious effort for Bobby's sake."

"That must be such a relief. Now tell me about your mad aunt."

"Mad may be the word." Jess frowned. "After the party that night in Doug's, no one saw or heard from her. After a couple of weeks Mum was getting worried in case she'd done something stupid and went round to her flat, but the landlord said that she'd moved out. He got the impression that she was going abroad."

"I'm sure she's fine. You don't pack if you're planning on topping yourself."

"She's fine all right. Doug knew that Mum was worried about her and called a few friends in the travel business. He finally got a lead the other day. Mandy's in Ibiza, shacked up with some rich bloke."

Katie's eyes widened. "You're kidding?"

"Nope. It's typical for Mandy to land on her feet."

"What does your mother make of it?"

"She's glad that Mandy's safe and maintains that she'll be back in a couple of months when she gets tired of him or the money runs out."

"It's a bit sad, really, isn't it?"

Jess shrugged, thinking of Mandy's vicious behaviour at Doug's party. She had no sympathy for her aunt anymore. "On the plus side, Mum has taken over her job."

Katie's eyes widened. "No way!"

"Way!"

"So she's not looking after Bobby anymore?"

"She is. She works from home and Doug drops over if there's anything they need to work on together."

"That's brilliant. It will stop her missing Noel so much. And she's finally dating too?" Katie went on.

"Yeah, she's seeing Malcolm, a guy she once worked with in CML, Doug's company. He seems nice. I think Mum is quite smitten but she's playing it cool."

"It just goes to show that you're never too old to fall in love."

"Speaking of love, what's happening with Sam?"

Katie dismissed the guy with a wave of her hand. "That was just a bit of fun."

Jess wasn't fooled. From the little Katie had told her, it ran a lot deeper than that. "Jersey isn't that far away," she pointed out. "How did he feel about you coming home?"

"He said he'd miss me," Katie said with a sad smile, "and that he's never been to Ireland."

"So, invite him over."

"Maybe."

Jess decided to leave it at that. Katie didn't like to be pushed and, right now, she was probably focused on her new job. "So, food. We can stay in and order a pizza or go to the café on the seafront."

Katie shivered. "It's too cold to go out."

"In that case, why not change into something more comfortable and stay the night? I'll phone in the order."

"You talked me into it." Katie grinned.

When they were tucked up on the sofa, replete and sipping beer, Katie returned to the Connors drama that she'd missed out on. "How is the farmer doing?"

"Top form." Jess smiled. "Seeing the way he is now made me realise how miserable he was these last few months, and yet none of us noticed."

"I think you can be forgiven for that. You've had quite a lot going on," Katie pointed out.

"True." Between Mum's accident, Louis, and then Sharon and Bobby, Jess hadn't known whether she was coming or going.

"Is he in Limerick full-time now?"

"Pretty much, although he's come up to join us for Sunday lunch a couple of times."

"And how's little Bobby?"

Jess smiled. "He's much the same but we've learned a lot and so we're better able to handle him. Mum can even talk him down from a tantrum now."

"Good on her." Katie looked impressed. "That must be quite a relief for Sharon."

"It is."

"How's she doing?"

Jess laughed. "Totally stir-crazy but happy. Incidentally, she's throwing a party on Saturday and you're invited."

"Great. What's the party for?"

"No idea," Jess said with a grin.

Katie sighed happily. "When I think of the year you've had I never would have thought that things could turn out so well."

Jess nodded in agreement. "I know. I keep expecting to wake up."

Katie smiled at her. "So, have you and Cal any plans?"

"What kind of plans?" Jess said, playing dumb.

Katie rolled her eyes. "Should I buy a hat?"

Jess almost choked on her beer. "It's only been five months," she protested.

"Oh. My. God." Katie sat up, her eyes widening.

"What?" Jess felt her cheeks redden.

"You didn't say no. Come on. Out with it."

"Really we haven't talked about marriage . . ."

"But?" Katie prompted.

Jess sighed. "He wants me to move in with him."

"Yay!" Katie hugged her.

Jess pushed her off, laughing. "I've said no. It's much too soon. I've made enough mistakes, Katie. I want to get things right this time."

Katie beamed. "You are totally besotted with the guy, aren't you?"

"I am," Jess admitted, laughing.

"No more contact from Lecherous Louis?"

"No, thankfully."

"Is he still harassing the women in the *Gazette*?"

Jess lips twitched. "You're useless."

Katie frowned. "Why?"

"You changed in the bathroom and you've been to the loo twice and you didn't notice."

"Notice what?" Her friend looked completely baffled.

"Go and have a look, a proper one this time," Jess pushed her, smirking.

Frowning, Katie stood up and went into the bathroom. Seconds later there was a shriek and she came back, holding the framed press-cutting in her hands. "Oh. My. God. When did this happen?"

"Eve sent it to me a few weeks ago." Jess smiled. "I keep it there to remind me to stand up for myself in future."

"'We regret to announce,'" Katie read out, "'the resignation of Louis Healy, editor of the *Gazette*, with immediate effect, due to personal reasons.'" She paused to look at Jess with raised eyebrows. "Personal reasons?"

"Perhaps he's sick."

"Ha! Sick in the head." Katie continued to read the statement. "Yada-yada-yada," she said, skimming through the brief biography of Louis's time with the paper. "'On behalf of the management and staff of the *Gazette*, we would like to wish Louis well in his future endeavours.'" She looked up at Jess, smiling. "Oh, yeah, he's definitely been rumbled. No notice and no job to go to?"

"It does look suspicious, doesn't it?"

"Did you not ask Eve what the word was in the office?"

Jess shook her head. "I thought about it but I didn't think it was worth the risk. I managed to leave the *Gazette* on my own terms. I don't want to remind her of my relationship with Louis."

"She's one sharp lady. I doubt she needs reminding," Katie said.

"But she hasn't broadcast the fact and I appreciate that. I've moved on and I don't want it resurrected. Especially with this interview coming up."

"It'll be interesting to see where Louis pops up next."

"As long as it's not in a certain Sunday newspaper," Jess said, pulling a face.

"After this?" Katie held up the frame. "I think it's more likely he'll be reporting on births, deaths and marriages in some freebie rag, if he's lucky. The man's finished, Jess." Katie raised her bottle of beer. "What goes around comes around!"

"Indeed." Jess agreed, happy to be able to put that chapter of her life behind her.

CHAPTER
FORTY-FIVE

"What's the party actually for?" Cal asked as they stood in the hall, divesting themselves of coats and hats and handing them over to a very serious and self-important Bobby. He dusted snow from his hair.

Keith shrugged. "Early Christmas party? Celebration of Suzie getting the all-clear from the hospital? Take your pick. I went along with it because it was either that or she'd be redecorating the living room."

"Mum says that a burst of energy just before the baby's due is quite common," Jess said.

"We're going to dance this baby out," Sharon said, joining them and hugging her sister.

"You look b —"

"Don't say blooming," Sharon warned Cal.

He laughed. "I was going to say beautiful."

"I look like a whale," Sharon retorted, resting her hands on her bump. "I haven't seen my feet in weeks. That's a killer dress, Jess. You're looking pretty sharp too, Cal." She nudged Keith. "Take note."

Dressed in a nice shirt and jeans, Keith scowled at Cal. "Thanks mate," he said before hugging his sister-in-law. "You look very festive."

"Well, it is almost Christmas." She did a twirl and the skirt of her red dress flared out around her slim legs. "And, when I saw James Bond here," she nodded with some pride at her boyfriend, "I thought I'd better make an effort."

Cal, who looked as if he'd stepped out of a fashion shoot in his black suit and grey shirt, gave an embarrassed grin. "I'm trying to impress the relatives."

"You're doing a good job," Sharon assured him and then looked longingly at her sister's three-inch heels. "I can't wait to wear real shoes again."

"It won't be long now," Jess consoled her. "Is Noel here yet?"

"He is, and he's not alone," Keith said, waggling his eyebrows. "Don't mention the war."

"What war, Daddy?" Bobby asked, his eyes round.

Keith mouthed "sorry" to his wife and hugged his son. "Daddy was just being silly," he said.

"As usual," Sharon chimed in. "Percy has more sense, doesn't he, Bobby?"

"Percy's smart," Bobby agreed. "But Daddy's clever too."

"So what's that about?" Jess murmured to Sharon.

"Mum's in shock that her darling son has a steady girlfriend, and she's from Limerick."

"Ah, I see." Jess nodded in understanding. Suzie was gradually coming to terms with her son's departure but still harboured dreams of his moving back to Dublin once he got the whole farming business out of his system. As if *that* was going to happen, her daughters had laughed. "Is she nice? What's her name?"

"Finola — and, yes, she's lovely."

"Oh, good. Where is Mum?"

"The last time I saw her she was chatting to her old work pals in the conservatory. Is Katie coming?"

"She'll be along later," Jess said, and then looked up at Cal. "Ready to face my world?"

He dropped a kiss on her temple. "I've been ready for years."

She smiled into his eyes, still incredulous that this man loved her. "Come on, I'll introduce you to the guy who almost delivered me."

"Lead on, Macduff." Cal laced his fingers through hers and she tugged him towards the conservatory, waving across the room at Nora and Aileen, who were chatting with some other women. Suzie was falling around the place laughing at something Jack was saying, Mal by her side, a proprietorial hand on her back.

"Jess!" She smiled when she spotted her. "You look lovely, sweetheart. Hi, Cal. You look very smart too. Let me introduce you to my friends."

Cal shook hands with Doug, Gina and Jack and, lastly, Mal. "I believe I have you to thank for the safe delivery of my girlfriend," he said gravely, hugging Jess to his side.

"My part in that has been greatly exaggerated," Mal assured him. "Suzie was determined to give birth, and Jess was equally determined to make a grand entrance. All I did was try to keep Suzie calm as this lot were worse than useless."

"Your services may be required again," Suzie laughed. "Have you seen the size of my other daughter?"

"She looks great, though, doesn't she?" Jess said to her mum. "All that rest seems to have paid off."

"It certainly has. We have so much to be grateful for, Jess." Suzie looked at her and Cal with excited eyes. "Did Sharon tell you? Bobby's going for an assessment at the end of January."

Jess gave a happy sigh. "That's great news."

"He's going to be fine," Cal said. "You've all been great with him — especially you and Percy," he told Suzie.

"I won't disagree about Percy, but that child has done more for me than I have for him. Now I have a good think before I open my mouth and say anything."

"And I was quite enjoying the swearing phase," Doug chipped in.

"You wouldn't want me swearing at your publishers, would you?" Suzie retorted.

"It would make a change from me swearing at them," Doug laughed.

"So you're not ready to sack her yet?" Mal asked. "Pity. I wouldn't mind having her as my assistant."

"You'd get no work done then," Jack quipped.

Suzie swatted him with the back of her hand. "No idea what you mean by that, Jack."

Gina drew her and Jess to one side. "No word on your sister?"

Suzie nodded. "She's alive and well and living in Ibiza."

"But why did she leave?" Gina asked, obviously sensing a story.

Suzie seemed lost for words and Jess came to her rescue. "Mandy's always been a bit of a gossip, so we tended to leave her out of the loop. That night in Doug's was the first she'd heard that Mum had me before she got married and that John wasn't the father and she was furious we hadn't told her."

Gina rolled her eyes. "Talk about oversensitive. I mean, things like that weren't talked about in those days."

"I know," Suzie said, "and Mandy was only a child herself at the time."

"Families, eh?" Gina nodded towards her husband.

"What was that?" Jack cupped his ear.

"Nothing, darling," Gina said, with an innocent smile.

"I read your piece on housing the other day, Jess," Doug said, butting in. "It was excellent, couldn't agree more. I wish all the newspapers would give you more work like that instead of these asinine articles they ask you to do."

Suzie gave him a grateful smile for stepping in and diverting the conversation. She still wasn't comfortable talking about her sister and he understood that better than most. Jess exchanged a grin with Cal before looking from Doug to her mum. "Thanks, Doug. I hope to be doing a lot more articles on current affairs, every week, in fact." Jess went on to tell them about her new column with one of the most prestigious Sunday newspapers.

Suzie hugged her. "I'm delighted for you, sweetheart."

"That's fantastic news," Doug said with an affectionate smile.

"Congratulations, Jess, that's amazing." Gina looked at her in admiration.

"Well done, Jess." Mal smiled. "That is quite an achievement."

"Thanks, Mal. I'm really excited about it."

"Excited about what?"

Jess looked around and saw her brother standing behind her. "Hey!" She hugged him. "I've got a new gig."

"Cool," Noel said when she'd filled him in on the details.

"So, how's life as a farmer?"

"Spending all your time with your hand up a cow's butt?" Cal added.

Noel punched his arm. "You're thinking of vets, dork. I'm up earlier than I've ever been in my life and it's a seven-day week, but, yeah, I'm loving it."

"Aren't you going to introduce me to your girlfriend?" Jess asked.

"Sure." He looked around. "She's around somewhere."

"How did you manage to snare a girlfriend if you're working those hours?" Cal raised his eyebrows.

Noel grinned. "She's my vet."

"Ugh, so *she's* the one with her hand up cows' butts." Jess shuddered.

"Do you get a special rate, being the boyfriend?" Cal asked.

"I do. I'm trying to convince her to move in, then she'd be on call 24/7."

Jess rolled her eyes and nudged him when she saw Mum's ears prick up.

"You're moving in together? Isn't that a bit hasty? You haven't known each other that long."

"I've known her long enough, Mum," he said, his mouth settling in to a stubborn line.

A girl with lovely green eyes and a mane of curly, auburn hair appeared beside Noel. "Don't worry, Mrs Connors, I haven't said yes."

"Sensible girl. Wait until you know all his habits first," Suzie said.

"Jeez, thanks, Mum."

Finola laughed and stuck out her hand, smiling. "You must be Jess."

"That's me," Jess said, liking her on the spot, "and this is Cal."

"Cal, nice to meet you. Noel's told me all about you."

He smiled. "Only believe the good stuff."

She frowned. "Good stuff?" And everyone laughed.

"She's lovely," Jess whispered to her mum.

Suzie gave a resigned sigh. "I know. Come on, love, let's give Sharon a hand. She shouldn't be doing so much in her condition."

Jess allowed herself to be pulled away from the group towards the kitchen, stopping for a few minutes to chat with Aileen and Nora and to say hi to Suzie's new friends from the book club and meditation class.

Sharon was stirring a pot of chilli when they walked in. She looked up and smiled. "And about time, too."

"Sorry, Mum wanted to introduce me to the world," Jess said. "What do you want me to do?"

"You're on the cold salads and dressings. Mum, will you check on the rice and slice up the baguettes?"

"Only if you sit down," her mother retorted. "You've taken on far too much."

"It is a bit like feeding the five thousand," Jess agreed, putting an apron on to protect her dress. "Who are all these people?"

"Apart from Mum's guests, there's some of our neighbours and friends, a couple of mums of autistic kids at the school and a few of Keith's mates too." Sharon went to lift a heavy saucepan off the stove.

"Don't even think about it," Jess warned her. "So, Mum, now that we can talk, have you heard any more from Mandy?"

Suzie groaned. "Well, I told you she called me last month —"

"No," her daughters said in unison.

"Sorry, I've been busy and you know what my memory's like. But yes, she called, sounding a little drunk, to be honest. She was bragging about her rich boyfriend, the amazing house, his yacht and all the famous people she's met." Suzie rolled her eyes. "I couldn't get a word in edgeways."

"So she's done well for herself?" Sharon looked at Jess. "Typical, isn't it?"

"I wouldn't go that far," their mother said. "She's living with a guy that could be Doug's older, uglier brother and, word is, he's not a very nice man."

484

"How do you know all this?" Jess asked.

"Ah, it's a small world we live in. Nora was out there for a few days' holidays, she just got back. And she was strolling around the marina, admiring all these enormous yachts and heard shouting and a woman screaming. It was Mandy and her new man, on a huge boat, hurling abuse at each other, both rolling drunk. Nora said he was quite vicious."

"Just like Onassis and Maria Callas," Jess murmured.

"Jackie Kennedy," Sharon corrected her.

"No, he was with Maria for years before he dumped her for Jackie," Jess told her. "They fought all the time."

"Poor Mandy. She seems destined to be alone," Sharon said.

"She deserves everything she gets," Jess said, and received a warning look from her mother. "Sorry," she mouthed.

"Where's Bobby gone?" Suzie changed the subject and looked around.

"Watching a video upstairs, away from all the noise. I'm taking him up a picnic."

"I'll do it, if you like. He's turning into a grand little fella," Suzie said, pride in her voice, and Jess saw Sharon tear up.

"So have you met Finola yet?" her sister asked, dabbing at her eyes.

Jess nodded. "Yeah, she seems really nice."

"And fun, too, exactly what Noel needs."

"A pity she's not from Dublin," their mother lamented. "She might tempt him back."

"Mum, there's no chance of that," Sharon said firmly. "He loves it there and you know that Maurice is failing."

Suzie looked up, her eyes widening. "No. No, I didn't. I think Noel's afraid to mention his name to me. I'm sorry to hear that."

"Really?" Sharon raised an eyebrow.

"I may not be his greatest fan, Shaz, but I'm not made of stone. How long has he got?"

"Not long."

"And then Noel will have the farm." Suzie sighed.

"Don't be sad, Mum." Jess put an arm round her. "You want him to be happy, don't you?"

"Of course I do." Suzie glanced up at them. "Nora wants me to go back with her for a few days."

Jess stopped making the salad dressing to exchange a surprised look with her sister. "And?"

Suzie shrugged. "I suppose I should go. Apart from anything I should make my peace with Maurice."

"Good on you, Mum. Noel will be chuffed. Oh!" Sharon clutched her bump and bent over, her face screwed up in pain.

Suzie went to her side and put an arm round her. "Are you okay?"

"Yes, just Baby doing its nightly aerobics," Sharon gasped.

"Right. You're not lifting a finger for the rest of the evening," Jess said, unnerved. "Just sit there and tell us what to do."

She turned back to help her mother lift the pot of chilli onto the table, sneaking a taste. "Mmm, this is spicy. You should have a large portion, Shaz. It might bring on labour."

There was a splash and Sharon sighed. "I don't think that will be necessary."

Jess stared. "What the hell?"

"Her waters broke," Suzie said calmly.

"What?" Jess looked from her mother to her sister in horror.

"Relax," Sharon said with a pained smile. "It'll be hours before anything happens. We'll get everyone fed and watered, and then Keith and I can head off to the hospital."

"I'll get your bag ready and stay here tonight with Bobby. Everything will be grand. Oh, isn't this exciting?"

Sharon let out a piercing scream. "Oh. My. Good. God." She clenched her eyes shut and clutched the chair as yet another contraction ripped through her.

"You'll be fine, sweetheart," Suzie said, putting some cushions behind Sharon's back. "Jess, don't just stand there. Get something to mop up this mess."

Sharon let out another shriek, making Jess jump, and then opened her eyes wide and stared at her mother. "That was quite close to the last one, wasn't it?"

"It was. I'm afraid you're going to miss your own party. Deep breaths, love." Suzie glanced over at Jess, her eyes full of excitement. "Get Keith, Jess. Oh, and Mal, too. Just in case."

"Meet Grace Anabel Mulvey," Suzie carried her granddaughter out to the hall, where Noel and Jess waited with their partners and Malcolm and Doug. Keith was behind her, his eyes glued to his new daughter.

"Oh, she's beautiful," Jess breathed as her mum placed the tiny little bundle into her arms. "Is Sharon all right?"

"The paramedics are just making her comfortable and then they'll be off to hospital but they seem confident that she's in good shape," Keith said.

"She looks just like you," Mal said, smiling at Suzie.

"Ah, don't say that to the poor child," Noel joked.

Suzie cuffed her son. "Cheeky."

"Smile," Cal said, taking a photo with his phone.

"Congratulations," Doug said, his eyes suspiciously bright as he stared down at the tiny baby.

"Suzie, would you bring Bobby in to meet his little sister? And are you staying here with him tonight?" Keith asked.

"Yes and yes." Suzie hurried over to her grandson's room where he was now cuddled up in bed with his cushion, his eyes closing. "Hi, sleepy."

He opened his eyes. "It's very noisy."

"It's a bit busy out there, Bobby. The thing is, your mummy just had her baby. Would you like to see your little sister?"

He nodded and slid out of bed, running ahead of Suzie. Keith swung him up in his arms and smiled.

488

"You're a big brother, Bobby!" he said and took the child in to see Sharon and meet the new baby.

Within the hour, the ambulance had taken Sharon and her baby away, Keith following in his car and while the others went back down to join the stragglers from the party, Suzie sat by Bobby's bed and sang to him, smiling as his eyes started to close. They had all been nervous of how the child would react when faced with a sibling but he'd seemed to take it in his stride. Time would tell. Thinking of how her grandson hated noise, Suzie prayed her granddaughter was a quiet baby. That would make the transition a lot easier for her big brother.

As she sat there she thought back on this turbulent year and counted her blessings, the main one being that she was still around. She felt so proud of her children. Sharon for her strength and single-mindedness in doing her best for Bobby. Jess for her professional success, she was really carving out a career for herself, and Suzie was so happy to finally see her in a stable relationship with a lovely man. And Noel, her baby. Not yet twenty-one and proving to be a huge support to his uncle. She'd got more of an insight into his new life over a cup of tea earlier with Finola than she had from her son. The young vet had told her how Noel had been welcomed by both the locals and the wider farming community whose respect he'd won by returning to support his uncle at this difficult time. His open disposition and eagerness to learn were standing him in good stead and people were rallying around to advise and assist him. Suzie was proud of him and, she knew, it was time she told him so.

It wasn't surprising that Mandy envied her. She thought of her sister's betrayal and the things she'd said about Suzie's accident in those last few minutes at Doug's. That was the final piece of the puzzle and she'd decided to keep it to herself. For all Mandy's manipulations, the one she seemed to end up hurting the most was herself and Suzie wasn't going to add to that.

Realising that Bobby was asleep, she tucked him in and went downstairs, helped herself to a glass of wine and, noticing Doug sitting alone, nursing a Jameson and staring into the fire, made her way over to him.

"Penny for your thoughts," she said, sitting down beside him.

He looked over and smiled. "I was just thinking about the day that Jess was born."

"That was quite a day," she agreed.

"Congratulations, Suzie. You were a fighter when we met and you're still a fighter today. Everything you have, you've earned and you deserve."

"Thanks, Doug."

"Can I say something?" he asked, leaning forward.

Suzie sobered at his grim expression. "Of course."

"Don't let Mandy back into your life. No matter what she says or does, don't take her back."

Suzie stared back at him. "You know."

He inclined his head. "I didn't want to leave you alone with her so I just stepped outside and I heard everything."

490

"Ah. She was a bit over the top, Doug, but she'd had a lot to drink."

"Don't make excuses for her," Doug protested. "She slept with your husband and as for the accident . . ."

Suzie held up her hand. "You don't have to warn me about Mandy. I understand exactly what she is and what she's capable of."

"But you're not going to do anything about it." It was a statement not a question and Doug sank back in his chair, looking resigned.

"She's still my sister and she's got so little in her life, Doug. You know that."

"Which is why I'm worried that you'll fall for it the next time she comes running to you. She'll be after Malcolm next," he warned.

Suzie smiled. "And if he were the type of man to go along with that, Doug, then he's not the man for me. Trust me. Second time around I won't be so easily fooled."

Doug sighed. "It's rather depressing, really. Having to watch your back all the time."

"What we need is a break," Suzie told him. "You know that Croatia are still after you?"

He perked up. "I did tell you that they would work around me. Are you up for it, Ms Connors?"

Suzie gave a casual shrug. "Well, I'm going to be at a loose end. Keith is taking a month off and has an au pair lined up so I don't have to mind Bobby. And Aileen, my neighbour, will be ecstatic to take Percy."

"What about Malcolm?" he asked, his eyes hopeful.

"I told you months ago, Doug, I'm my own woman and I don't ask for permission from anyone anymore. But, don't worry, Malcolm trusts me and, he trusts you too. And travelling is on my 'to do' list so . . ."

He smiled at her, looking truly happy. "So, I'd better get cracking and organise the flights."

"I'm your personal assistant now. Isn't that my job?"

He considered that. "Normally, yes, but I'll take care of it this time before you change your mind and decide you want to stay home and drool over your granddaughter."

Suzie had thought that through very carefully and, believing that Bobby was a lot smarter than he was given credit for, had decided that this was a perfect time for her to disappear instead of fussing over his little sister. She sat back with her glass of wine and smiled. "That's fine by me, boss. Zagreb, here we come."

Acknowledgements

My thanks to the mothers who told me their stories about their sons with ASD (it is very rare in females). Some were more serious than others. Some had yet to be assessed while others were grown men with families of their own and living full and independent lives. The one thing that they all had in common were parents who pushed and fought until their children received the assistance they needed. This book is dedicated to them.